Robbie Taggart

Books by Michael Phillips

Fiction

THE RUSSIANS*
The Crown and the Crucible
A House Divided
Travail and Triumph

THE STONEWYCKE TRILOGY*
The Heather Hills of Stone-
wycke
Flight from Stonewycke
Lady of Stonewycke

THE STONEWYCKE LEGACY*
Stranger at Stonewycke
Shadows over Stonewycke
Treasure of Stonewycke

THE SECRETS
OF HEATHERSLEIGH HALL
Wild Grows the Heather
in Devon
Wayward Winds
Heathersleigh Homecoming
A New Dawn Over Devon

SHENANDOAH SISTERS
Angels Watching Over Me
A Day to Pick Your Own Cotton

The Color of Your Skin Ain't
the Color of Your Heart
Together Is All We Need

CAROLINA COUSINS
A Perilous Proposal
The Soldier's Lady
Never Too Late
Miss Katie's Rosewood

CALEDONIA
Legend of the Celtic Stone
An Ancient Strife

THE HIGHLAND COLLECTION*
Jamie MacLeod: Highland Lass
Robbie Taggart: Highland Sailor

THE JOURNALS
OF CORRIE BELLE HOLLISTER
My Father's World*
Daughter of Grace*
On the Trail of the Truth
A Place in the Sun
Sea to Shining Sea
Into the Long Dark Night
Land of the Brave and the Free
A Home for the Heart

Nonfiction

*with Judith Pella   **with Chris Schneider

Books by Judith Pella

Texas Angel
Heaven's Road
Beloved Stranger
Mark of the Cross

THE RUSSIANS
*The Crown and the Crucible**
*A House Divided**
*Travail and Triumph**
Heirs of the Motherland
Dawning of Deliverance
White Nights, Red Morning
Passage Into Light

THE STONEWYCKE TRILOGY**
The Heather Hills
of Stonewycke
Flight from Stonewycke
Lady of Stonewycke

THE STONEWYCKE LEGACY**
Stranger at Stonewycke
Shadows Over Stonewycke
Treasure of Stonewycke

DAUGHTERS OF FORTUNE
Written on the Wind
Somewhere a Song
Toward the Sunrise
Homeward My Heart

LONE STAR LEGACY
Frontier Lady
Stoner's Crossing
Warrior's Song

PATCHWORK CIRCLE
Bachelor's Puzzle
Sister's Choice

RIBBONS OF STEEL***
Distant Dreams
A Hope Beyond
A Promise for Tomorrow

RIBBONS WEST***
Westward the Dream
Separate Roads
Ties That Bind

*with Michael Phillips   **with Tracie Peterson

THE HIGHLAND COLLECTION • BOOK 2

Robbie Taggart

Highland Sailor

Michael Phillips
and Judith Pella

BETHANYHOUSE

a division of Baker Publishing Group
Minneapolis, Minnesota

© 1987 by Michael Phillips and Judith Pella

Published by Bethany House Publishers
11400 Hampshire Avenue South
Bloomington, Minnesota 55438
www.bethanyhouse.com

Bethany House Publishers is a division of
Baker Publishing Group, Grand Rapids, Michigan

Printed in the United States of America

Library of Congress Control Number: 2016901557

ISBN 978-0-7642-1861-3

The songs "The Bonny Sailor" and "Ratcliffe Highway" are from *Real Sailor Songs*, John Ashton, ed. 1891. Reissued by Benjamin Blom, Inc., 1972.

The song "Adieu, Sweet Lovely Nancy" is taken from the collection of songs, *The Valiant Sailor*, ed. by Roy Palmer, Cambridge University Press, 1973.

The song in the last chapter is *Shanty Hymn* by Bob Cull and is from his album "Last Horizon."

Scripture quotations are from the King James Version of the Bible.

This is a work of fiction. Names, characters, incidents, and dialogues are products of the author's imagination and are not to be construed as real. Any resemblance to actual events or persons, living or dead, is entirely coincidental.

Cover design by Eric Walljasper

Judith Pella is represented by The Steve Laube Agency

Dedication

To every man who is open enough and courageous enough to search for his manhood on the non-conforming path of God's course for his life. And to the women—mothers, sisters, wives, and daughters—who are such an integral part of that journey.

Contents

Introduction

When Robbie Taggart stepped out of a snowstorm onto the pages of Jamie MacLeod's story, we knew very little about him. Yet immediately we were intrigued by the fellow. As bits and pieces of his personality and roots gradually were revealed, the better we came to know him. We really could not help liking him! It was not long before we realized—this man's story has to be told.

Of course, at that point we knew only fragments of how that story might develop. Through Jamie's eyes we learned a great deal. She helped us see Robbie from new perspectives and gave us a broader picture of what made him tick. Yet we sensed there was more to it even than Jamie realized. Robbie Taggart soon became so real and compelling that we *had* to find out what became of him after he and Jamie parted! Thus we donned our boots and caps, struggled to firm up our sea legs under us, and set out to accompany this most fascinating Scottish sailor.

Robbie had often confessed to Jamie his itch for new adventures, and in the story of this part of his life, he winds up in the mysterious China of the 1880's. The future awaiting Robbie surprised even us a bit as the pages unfolded. After he had left Jamie at Aviemere, the train took him south and away from the Highlands, leaving Jamie behind to marry Lord Edward Graystone. Robbie pondered his future during those first days. Yet even in the midst of his uncertainty and soul-searching so uncharacteristic of his previous attitudes about life, it seemed inevitable that sooner or later Robbie's wanderlust would lead him again to the sea.

How glad we are that we didn't turn into landlubbers and abandon ship for more familiar territory!

From his first appearance at Sadie Malone's pub in Aberdeen, we must say we would never have guessed the sort of man Robbie turned out to be. We are thankful that the same Providence leading Jamie to Aviemere and guiding Robbie's footsteps led us on our travels in the writing of these pages. For the experience has been life-changing for both of us.

No doubt Robbie is such a captivating personality because he is in so many ways typical of all men. His quest to discover just what it means to be a man is a journey all men must make sooner or later. Like Christian of *Pilgrim's Progress*, Robbie's pilgrimage ultimately leads inside himself, to that Source of manhood, whose Voice is so near yet so difficult to hear until the ultimate tests of personhood are required.

Robbie's open and courageous stand to take the path perhaps less footworn, more difficult to discern in today's world, has been for us an illuminating adventure far beyond the mere penning of a tale. It is our hope and prayer that as you participate in Robbie's personal voyage, you will feel the roll of the waves under your legs, the spray of the sea on your face, and, perhaps, the call of the same Voice in your heart.

Michael Phillips
Judith Pella

Part I

Royal Navy

1

"Doon Frae the Highlands"

Summer had come to the Scottish Highlands, proving it to be the loveliest spot on any of the seven continents. Robbie Taggart knew this better than most men, for he had seen them all. Yet as he stared absently out the window of the speeding train at his final glimpse of the grand countryside of the north, he could not help wondering why he found it so difficult to stay put and settle down in this bonny land of his birth.

But the wide world was always calling—compelling him to move, to wander, to discover distant horizons. And so he followed the divergent paths of the earth, and the seas of the earth—if not searching for adventure, at least with a confidence that adventure would always come to him.

It was a fine June day. There had been snow just one week earlier, and in the distance he could see reminders of it on the receding Grampian Mountains. He thought he could just barely make out Ben Tirran to the northwest. And of course farther west, near the Glen Ey Forest, the peaks would no doubt still have remnants of snow upon them in early July, despite the warmth that had so suddenly followed the last of the spring storms.

Ah, it was indeed a fine land! He could smell the grassy hillsides as the train sped by. Yet the fragrant aroma only reminded him of the nostalgic smell of peat, a smell by which all true Highlanders are bound together in common love, and struggle against the harsh elements that make up the essential character of their homeland.

And was that, after all, why he found himself forever leaving the Highlands, yet forever longing to return? Was it because the land at once

15

drew him by its openness, its vastness, its solitude, its quiet, but at the same time repelled him with its harshness, its unforgiveness, its barrenness? The memory of the peat fire sending out its warmth and aroma through his aunt's little cottage where he and his family had often stayed during his roving childhood, was a pleasant one. Yet it took the advance of years for him to recall the difficulty with which his aunt had to trudge through snow and bitter cold to bring those peats into the house so that her guests might be warm.

It was indeed a hard land. Living a lifetime on it was not easy. Perhaps that is why he had chosen not to stay.

Yet still he had hesitated when the man he'd spoken with after climbing aboard several hours earlier had asked him, "An' why are ye come doon frae the Highlands, laddie?"

An answer had not come quickly to his lips. Because perhaps for the first time Robbie Taggart had experienced a sensation which was up till recently utterly foreign to him—that of being unsure of himself.

"Glamis, Cargill, Perth!" called the conductor as he strode through the car, trying to walk with a more important gait than his trim gray uniform occasioned. Pausing beside Robbie, he bent his iron-straight frame slightly and cocked his head with an air of official confidence. "We'll be in Cargill a good two hours, sir, an' ye'll fin' it worth yer while t' wait for yer lunch till then—'tis a pub in the toon I highly recommend."

"Thank you kindly, sir," replied Robbie with a grin. "I'll anticipate it with relish."

Having himself served on the Black Sea during the Crimean War, and partial toward navy men, the conductor made it his special duty to see to it that this young naval officer enjoyed a pleasant journey. In return Robbie had listened attentively to the man's tales of the "guid auld days," and the *real* war, as the man seemed now to so fondly remember the bloody time in the Crimea. Robbie liked the old blue jacket, and found himself amused at how seriously he took his present charge of conducting the Queen's train, very much, no doubt, in the same manner he must have carried himself aboard Her Majesty's frigate some twenty-five years earlier.

But Mr. Murdock had been a mere deckhand at the time, and no doubt greatly embellished the facts of his exploits in the Ukraine and Turkey. The sailors and "swabbies" did all the dirty work in the navy, and the only glory they obtained from the experience was what they managed to bring home through the eyes of their imagination. *But even Murdock's dirty work probably far surpassed anything I have done as an officer in the Royal Navy,* Robbie thought to himself. His commission certainly hadn't been what he'd expected.

When Murdock had passed on down the aisle, Robbie leaned back in his seat. What stories would he have to tell years from now of his own tenure in Her Majesty's Navy? He had certainly regaled Jamie with enough of them to bore anyone but that dear soul to distraction. And he, too, had embellished a good many of the facts, though he was not certain if it had been to hide some dissatisfaction within himself, or merely to impress Jamie.

Well, if it had been the latter, he had not been altogether successful. He had put up a stoic front, and in fact had probably never really realized that he'd loved her until it was too late and she'd made her choice. By then, what could he do? She had preferred the stern, roughly hewn Edward Graystone over himself.

Robbie cherished no exalted opinion of his own good looks. He was not much aware of his thick black, wavy hair and vivid sea-blue eyes set in high-boned masculine features, nor of his six-foot, muscular frame. He had been told often enough that he was handsome, but he had never put much importance in such things.

And the situation with Edward Graystone perhaps proved his perceptions well founded. Dashing good looks had certainly not won Robbie the fair maiden in *that* case. Graystone had possessed something else that had attracted Jamie.

Yes, Robbie envied the laird of Aviemere—not for his wealth, nor his title, nor for the vast estate, but rather because he held within his heart's possession the gentle, delicate Jamie MacLeod.

Dear Jamie . . . thought Robbie.

The weeks that had passed since their parting had brought a measure of healing. Yet he now knew that Jamie had been that pearl of great price for which a man would sell all he had to possess. He had not known it soon enough, for she had indeed worn a rough outer shell for many years. But he knew it now. And with the reminder came a sigh.

Robbie knew little about scriptural lessons, probably picking up this tidbit from a sea captain delivering his Sunday seaboard service. The higher implications of the passage were lost to him. But he knew a prize when he saw one, and the moment his eyes had been opened to Jamie's inner beauty, he knew she was the kind of woman a man would give up everything for. Everything, for Robbie, meant the sea, the carefree life, *his freedom.* He had not even paused to consider what such a sacrifice might mean to a man like himself, for whom freedom as a man was intrinsically linked to manhood itself. And he had tried to make light of the conflict in his heart when he realized she was in love with another man.

Yet as crushed as he had temporarily been to lose her, another part of him almost sighed with relief. Now he would be free to roam again. What was the matter with him? Did he not truly love her after all?

He remembered that day not long after he had first met Jamie when the tables had been turned. She was but a grubby shepherd lass, and as in love as she knew how to be with the more experienced, worldly wise sailor Robbie Taggart. He had said to *her*, when he had been the one to reject *her* offer of love:

"You know I care for you, and always will. I'll never stop being a big brother to you . . . that's not so bad, is it? Brothers and sisters love each other, Jamie. 'Tis just a different kind of love. . . ."

So, had he fallen into the same deception as the young and innocent shepherdess? Had he—the sophisticated man of great worldly experience—made a fool of himself? He would have thought the thing inconceivable a year earlier! Yet down inside that's exactly how he felt— a fool.

But in truth, Robbie knew little of love. Yes, he was well-versed in occasional *words* of shallow affection. And he knew the best pubs the world over. He knew how to deport himself in a brawl, and how to keep his money in his pockets.

But love . . . that was another matter.

Even Robbie knew that love entailed commitment, a trait his character was largely lacking. And though many young women from the four corners of the earth had fallen in love with the dashing and handsome Scottish sailor, he had remained aloof beyond a merry jig or a shared pint of ale. And those who knew Robbie best did not much mind, for his was the free kind of spirit that few felt equal to conquer. Yet neither man nor woman could say that Robbie was not a grand fellow, a true friend, loyal and forthright, who also knew how to have a good time.

All this had somehow changed with Jamie—changed . . . but he could not say how. And nothing that had happened helped him to understand that phenomenon called love, nor to fully grasp the conflicting emotions within his heart. He had lost Jamie to another, but he still possessed his freedom. He would not be tied to home and hearth, flower gardens and banker's hours. Yet suddenly, staring out the window with the lovely landscape racing past, he wondered at the price he had paid for his freedom. Were hearths and flower gardens such a bad thing for a man to live for?

Did a piece of him, after all was said about the footloose-and-fancy-free life, actually long for what Edward Graystone had? How foreign such thoughts would have seemed only a short time ago! But now, he wondered if he would ever have a secure foothold in life, a stopping place where he would feel completely at ease. Was he meant always to roam, to watch the hills of home fade from sight, to say *goodbye* rather than *hello*? Or did he, in reality, want it that way?

Another part of him loved his life, even though there were more farewells than he could remember. Only this most recent farewell had been harder than any previous one to dislodge from his mind. Never before had he pined for his home or for any lost love, save for a moment or two aboard ship when a mate would draw out a harmonica and softly play Robbie Burn's melancholy tune:

> My heart's in the Highlands, my heart is not here,
> My heart's in the Highlands a-chasing the deer,
> A-chasing the wild deer and following the roe—
> My heart's in the Highlands, wherever I go!

But Robbie was not a lover of the roving, independent, sea-faring life because he was a hard or insensitive man. Indeed, there were complexities within his character that seemed to contradict altogether the stereotype of the hard-bitten and crusty sailor. Even as he thought about Jamie, a tear tried to break the manly surface of his eyes, though he quickly brushed it away. And he knew now, as perhaps never before, that a part of him would always remain in the Highlands, not only because of the special love he felt for Jamie, but also in the deep affection she had opened within him for this rugged, matchless land.

"Cargill!" called Murdock.

"What . . . already?" exclaimed Robbie.

"Ye dozed right through Glamis, sir."

In truth Robbie had not dozed at all, but he had no idea his thoughts had been so deep as to cause him to miss an entire station.

"Next'll be Perth," the conductor continued. "An' afore ye know it ye'll be in Glasgow an' able t' meet up wi' yer ship."

"Yes, it won't be long," Robbie replied, with less enthusiasm than he knew he should be feeling.

"I'm truly envyin' ye."

"I'll be sure to think of you, Murdock, when I'm out on the high seas sucking in a deep draught of the salt air from the warm breeze."

"Ye're a lucky man indeed." Murdock sighed, then ambled on down the aisle, his shoulders drooping a bit, and his gray uniform appearing not so trim on his aging frame as it had before.

Robbie watched him go, wishing he had the heart to cheer him. But he could hardly lift another man's spirits when his own were so heavy they could sink all the way to Davy Jones's Locker. He might have been able to nurse his wounded heart with the consolation of his preserved freedom if only he could be certain it was freedom that would actually meet him at his destination.

But he was not as sure as Murdock that the Queen's Navy could provide adventure enough to restore the heart of one Lieutenant Robbie Taggart.

2

Out of Kilter

Robbie turned down the lamp and rubbed his weary eyes.

He could not stand to look at one more chart. He had been at it some six hours already, plotting imaginary courses for imaginary ships in imaginary battles. Unfortunately, his orders were not imaginary in the least.

Frustrated, forgetting the precariously perched open bottle of ink, he slammed his hand down on the oversized pages before him.

The next instant he lunged at the bottle, but not before a large black smear had spread over his day's labor. Almost the same moment came a brisk rap at the door. Ignoring the unknown caller, Robbie grabbed for a cloth in a frantic attempt to salvage his work.

"Just a minute!" he snapped, more distracted than angry.

The door opened, but Robbie did not immediately glance up.

"Is this how you greet a superior officer, *Mister* Taggart?" barked out a voice behind him. It was the last voice Robbie wanted to hear.

He quickly dropped the cloth and jerked around, the color fading

from his face. Not one to be easily intimidated, Robbie nevertheless had
but to hear that voice to know that trouble had come calling on him. In
a neutral environment nothing about the man would have caused him
the least anxiety. But on this particular assignment, the man behind that
dreaded voice held all the cards. He was the power, and he knew how to
exercise it to dominate others. In addition, he seemed to enjoy making
his subordinates squirm.

Commander Anton Barclay was not a large man. But a soldier or sailor
knows that a man's power does not always lie solely in his size. What he
lacked in stature—he was known behind his back as "wee Bonaparte"—he
more than made up for with his irascible ill-temper. Had a war been on,
Barclay would have been the kind of leader whose crew would unquestioningly follow him to certain death. Their actions, however, would not
arise out of loyalty or love toward the man, but rather from raw fear.
Civilians wondered at this unlikely man's effect on those under him. And
every time Robbie himself cringed under the commander's icy stare, he
could not help marveling at the weakness of his own knees.

Through the years Barclay had wielded his power with exacting skill,
using the privileges of his rank to his best advantage. He was highly
thought of at the Admiralty offices, had risen steadily, had built around
him a loyal and sometimes ruthless band of attendant henchmen, and was
thus in a position to rule the little world of his command with an iron
fist. Though flogging had been suspended a few years earlier, Barclay was
among a few who continued the practice with successful, albeit brutal,
results. Corporal discipline, however, was but the least of his methods
used to insure that his will was carried out.

Robbie had already fallen foul of the "wee Bonaparte" more times than
he wished to remember, and with an inward sigh of impending doom,
he snapped his frame to a taut attention, thrusting his ink-smeared hand
to his forehead in salute.

"I had no idea it was you, sir—"

"It is not your concern to have *ideas*, Mr. Taggart!" bellowed the
commander. "Your only concern is to deport yourself as an officer and
a gentleman at all times, and no matter with whom—even your lowborn
associates. And especially to show to me the respect of my position! Is
that clear? You are a representative of the Queen, God bless her! But
perhaps you are not equal to the task."

"I will try to be, sir. I think I am equal to it."

"Ha!" barked Barclay. "Then you are an egotistical buffoon, for there
are few indeed who will ever be equal to such a task!"

Robbie stood erectly at attention. Sometimes he wondered if Barclay purposefully baited him, hoping he would lose control. Being assaulted would no doubt be a small price for him to pay in exchange for being able to bring charges of mutiny against Robbie. Deliberately he tried to relax the tension building up in him; he would not give him the satisfaction!

"Now," continued the commander, unperturbed, "perhaps you can explain to me why this is the second night in a row you have burned the Queen's oil late into the night."

"I was working on these charts, sir." Robbie gestured toward the table.

"You are given sufficient time during *daylight* hours to complete this work," replied Barclay. "But then I forgot—you have been tramping all over the countryside lately."

"That was some time ago, sir." Even as he said the words, Robbie thought to himself that in a sense the accusation was valid. He had been back from his visit to Aviemere for over a month and had still not managed to catch up on his workload.

"Yes, before you came under *my* command," said Barclay in a tone laden with meaning. "You were with Simonson before, were you not?"

"Yes, sir."

"A fine officer . . ." added Barclay, allowing his sentence to remain intentionally unfinished. He was baiting Robbie again, but Robbie did not see his purpose in time.

"Yes, sir," Robbie agreed, this time with more enthusiasm in his voice. He had not known a fairer or more honorable man than his previous commander.

"A weak-kneed, dottering old man!" Barclay retorted. "And he spoiled you, Taggart! Made you think you were *somebody*. Gave you a promotion you didn't deserve. Do you really think you're cut out of officer's cloth? He gave you too much, Taggart—too much latitude. And now I have to work doubly hard to undo that fool's work!"

"He was a man I respected," said Robbie, trying to remain calm, but the defiance in his tone unmistakable. For perhaps the first time he was beyond caring what Barclay did to him; he couldn't listen to Captain Simonson being degraded without speaking up.

Apparently choosing to ignore Robbie's tone, Barclay continued in a different vein. "Well, he's dead now. Not around to hold your hand any longer, as is the brother of Dunsleve—that fool of a duke who purchased your commission."

"I believe I have succeeded on my own merit, sir."

"No doubt, no doubt!" replied Barclay with something like a smile.

"Of course you would think so! By burning lamps into the night, I presume."

"By performing my assigned duties well, and with honor," returned Robbie.

"You enjoy your work, then . . ."

Barclay drew out the words, then flicked a hand at the charts. "And you obviously must prefer the late hours. And I would be the last one to stand in the way of such diligence. Therefore, I want you to re-copy these charts and then make similar diagrams outlining each of the major naval battles of the eighteenth century, concluding with Nelson's victory at Trafalgar. Have them in my office by 7:00 a.m."

"But, sir, it's past 10:00 now."

"Is it?"

"I have duty at 7:00, sir."

"I am well aware of that, Mr. Taggart. I have my own duties as well, one of which is to make men of my officers."

With the words, Barclay made an abrupt about-face and moved briskly to the door, where he paused and turned once more toward Robbie. "I hope you are not under the misconception, Taggart, that you are going to succeed further in Her Majesty's Navy as easily as you have risen to your present *rank*—though I can hardly make myself say the word, such a mockery is your commission of things once held in such regard in this empire. Nevertheless, you are now under *my* command, and you will not find me as you found Simonson. You are going to get *nowhere*, Taggart. Do you understand me? But you are going to work harder than any mother's son ever did to get there!"

Barclay's final expression emphasized the triumph in his voice. When the door slammed shut behind him, it was some moments before Robbie was able to relax his tense frame.

For several minutes longer he just stood, staring at the door, seething with mingled anger and frustration. In his many years of roving he had always been able to get along with anyone. But in his last four years, which represented the eternity of his navy life, he had run headlong into a system which discouraged Robbie's kind of carefree good nature. He would have been better off not to have accepted the stupid commission. But it was too late for that now! He had endured the snubbing of the majority of his gentry comrades ever since. He had been able to take most of it, even laugh it off. But this Commander Anton Barclay was too much!

Perhaps it was true that he had been spoiled by the fair-minded

Simonson. He had taken a liking to Robbie, had seen his potential, and decided to encourage him. And it was a well-known fact—one he could not live down—that he had received his commission as a gift from the Duke of Dunsleve after saving the lord's life. One might have thought that a man respected by his commander and of a bent toward heroism might be well thought of. But such was not the case among the higher ranks of the Queen's Service. That was a realm of the gentry, and promotion was difficult enough in a peacetime navy top-heavy with aging brass and with few ships to go around. Robbie had quickly learned that if you were a lowly commoner who by some wild fluke chanced to cross the impenetrable barrier between seamen and midshipmen, further promotion was next to impossible. His advancement from midshipman to lieutenant had come quickly, barely after his first year. Simonson had been instrumental in that. But after three years he had not risen once, even within the grades of lieutenancy. He had heard that Simonson had taken a good deal of abuse for pushing through the promotion, and might have even hurt his own career in doing so.

That was the Navy, thought Robbie bitterly; *the gentry must protect their dominion at all costs.* About the only good thing to come out of those years was meeting Jamie. It was no doubt best for her to marry Graystone; what would he have had to offer her anyway?

Robbie sighed, then turned his attention back to the charts, suddenly feeling very tired.

As he picked up a pen, he realized that, despite the fact that he wanted nothing more than to command his own ship, the tardiness of a promotion was something he could deal with, if only that lack was compensated with some action. But he had seen actual sea duty only twice in the last four years. He might as well be working for some accounting firm. Though as he reflected on those two stints at sea, he wondered all over again if perhaps having to wait even ten years before being assigned permanently to a ship might be worth it. For life at sea, wearing the proud blue of the Royal Navy, could be rich!

Once he had been sent to Latin America with a detail of financiers to protect them while they attempted to collect debts from some local bankers and plantation owners. The excursion had proved routine in every way and totally uneventful, for the Latins had been at the time unwilling to cause any trouble before the might of the British Empire.

The second assignment, however, had been more like what Robbie had expected from the navy. He had been consigned to eight months duty on the Persian Gulf on slave patrol. Even forty-six years after slavery had been officially abolished throughout the British dominions in 1833, it still flourished in many parts of the world, principally Arabia and Asia. Robbie had never felt more vital and useful in his life, especially on that day when he had been in temporary command of the gunboat on patrol near Ras Tanura.

He spotted the trawler just before dawn. The look of it was innocent enough—a fisher out for his morning catch. But when the little boat made an abrupt turn to starboard, an action obviously triggered by the untimely sight of the gunboat, Robbie knew something was up. He instantly made chase. At that moment, with his engines ordered full steam ahead, he realized how far from innocent the trawler actually was. For it not only proved to be equipped with powerful steam engines hidden beneath the guise of a poor old scow, but it also had aboard two 13 cm. bore cannons, one astern and one port. They clearly intended to protect their "cargo" at all costs.

But Robbie had other ideas. British gunboats had, since the Crimean War, been feared throughout the world. The term "gunboat diplomacy" had been coined for just the kind of skirmish in which Robbie was about to engage the British crown, and *his* intention was to live up to the image.

The sea spray in his face had been exhilarating; now he tingled just with the memory of it. The speed of the gunboat could only be rivaled by the grandeur of a clipper under full sail in a strong nor'easter. But a clipper could not make such a pace in a dead calm.

When he began to close the gap between the two boats, the slaver first showed its guns. The first blast from the stern cannon went wide and Robbie wasted no time in returning fire. He shattered its jib-boom but caused no fatal damage. A volly of shots ensued lasting five minutes, until Robbie, having maneuvered his vessel to the starboard side of the slaver to avoid the port cannon, inflicted the final crippling shot. With a hole the diameter of a small birch in its starboard hull, the trawler was quick to raise the white flag.

Robbie overtook the slaver and boarded her with half his crew. The four wretched slave traders were unceremoniously hauled aboard the gunboat. It fell to Robbie to yank open the fore hatch where he discovered the most miserable sight he had ever seen. There in the hulls, huddled in a single mass, up to their waists in water from the sinking vessel, were eight human forms, all of tender age. The foul stench nearly sent Robbie reeling off his feet, and he had to step down into the filth to lift the creatures out, for they had not the strength to do so on their own. But when he held the youngest, a child of no more than five, in his arms, it was then he realized that he was performing a service that truly counted in this life. At that moment he felt proud of who he was, of his gallant blue uniform, and of the Crown that had enabled him to free these poor, half-starved creatures.

But since that time he had been landlocked, a subtle punishment he felt more and more every day, for the crime of his own low birth. He had freed those children who would have been slaves, and yet was he not himself locked into an even more insidious form of slavery in the name of the class system that had held down for centuries those in Britain not fortunate enough to be born into the aristocracy?

All of that was changing, though too slowly to do Robbie much good. Cardwell had tried, but the House of Lords had kept his military reforms at bay. And the Queen's *Royal Warrant* had helped considerably. Yet class distinctions still permeated everything, whether spoken of directly or not. And rather than causing him to despise his low birth, Robbie had come instead to despise the system that held a man's breeding against him. It was hypocritical, he thought, to make such an effort to free enslaved peoples throughout the world, when at home a slavery of class existed under everyone's noses, perpetuated by the rich and powerful.

Robbie had always judged men by different standards, and inside he knew he could hold his own against any lord, or son of a lord, in the Royal Service—even Barclay. He could take his stand alongside any man, either in the power of his fists or the strength of his mind. That's what mattered. That's what made a man a man, not money or breeding or fancy title. A man *was* a man for all that; yet it seemed as if the poet's powerful words were never so ignored as in his own homeland. Maybe that's why Scotland still resented England even after more than a century and a half of being politically united—because the southern giant looked down on her northern neighbor just as those in power looked down on men like Robbie.

After so many years of battling such attitudes, Robbie had to admit that a certain bitterness had begun to encase his heart. That day on the slaver, holding that young boy in his arms, had been a long time ago. Since then the grand uniform had faded, if not in reality, then certainly in spirit. The Crown had also tarnished a bit. And Robbie, too, was becoming a different man.

3

Final Insult

The days and weeks passed into months, and winter gradually descended upon the London barracks where Robbie was housed with his unit. While the passage of time is said to heal all wounds, and Robbie's heart had indeed managed to close over the scar that had resulted from his loss of Jamie, his dissatisfaction with his present life only deepened as winter drew on.

Barclay's innate ill-temper seemed particularly bent on Robbie. It was hard to tell why, and Robbie tried not to analyze it too deeply; thinking about it only made him angry. And in the Navy, to harbor anger toward a superior officer was a sure road to trouble. But Barclay had given him every low and dirty duty that could possibly be found, most of which even seamen were above doing. No other officer under Barclay's command had to endure what Robbie did. What was it about him that so annoyed the commander? No doubt the man would say he had an independent spirit that had to be broken.

Why he put up with it all, he didn't know! Up till now his optimistic nature had maintained its supremacy. But if things kept up this way much longer . . .

He paused to look at himself. There he stood in the middle of the barracks' common room, mop in hand, facing the entire place to clean. How could he possibly dredge up any optimism for that? And why had he been thus dispatched to such demeaning labor? Because the brass buttons of his uniform had not been shined to Barclay's satisfaction!

Robbie plunged the mop into the bucket of water, then slammed it down on the innocent floor with a *splat*. With each forceful stroke all he could think of was pummelling Barclay in similar fashion.

How could he, Robbie thought to himself, capitulate to the man's warped demands! *Why* should he! He was an officer in the Royal Navy! No one could take that from him, nor the inherent rights that accompanied the honor—though Barclay had often threatened to do so. Whether he could back up such threats, Robbie didn't know, but maybe that was why, after all, he choked down his ire and forced himself to comply with assignments none but a lowly enlisted man—from whom such things were expected!—ought to be made to do. One thoughtless action on Robbie's part, like stuffing this mop down Barclay's throat as he would love to do, would be the end of a less than brilliant naval career for Robbie. And he had no doubt the commander was watching and waiting for just such an indiscretion.

"I'll quit this blasted Navy," Robbie burst out to himself angrily. "Then I'll force that blaggard to stand up to me like a real man, without his rank to hide behind!"

Ah, the idea was a sweet one!

And no matter that Barclay was a good five inches shorter than Robbie, and probably a stone or two lighter—the tyrant would deserve what he got!

But Robbie continued to shove the mop in front of him with increasingly vigorous strokes, taking out his frustrations on the compliant floor. There was always the possibility, he mused, that eventually Barclay would be assigned a ship. He was an ambitious man and would be transferred into a position where his merit would at last be recognized and rewarded. No need to throw away these last four years, even if to a man of action like Robbie they had seemed an eternity. He had the beginnings of a good career here. If he could just wait it out, some day *he'd* have command of his own vessel. Then all this cowering servilitude would be worth it.

Twenty minutes later, the floor gleamed, and Robbie picked up the mop and bucket to start in on the remaining rooms. As he paused to give one final glance back at his labors, he heard a loud clamor at the outer door. Suddenly into the common room burst a dozen of his comrades. Taking no notice of Robbie or the newly shining floor, they quickly began to strip off their overcoats, soaked with the rain that had been falling briskly outside for more that an hour, shaking the garments out as they did so.

"Hey, ye blaggarts!" yelled Robbie, gesturing dangerously toward them with the mop.

But paying him no heed, talking and laughing among themselves, the men carelessly walked across to the fireplace, scraping their wet, mud-encrusted boots the entire length of the surface Robbie had so spotlessly cleaned.

With an angry oath, Robbie threw down the mop and turned to leave. He'd done his job! Let *them* be responsible for this new mess!

As he stepped out into the hall, as if on cue, there stood Barclay. Robbie nearly collided with him.

"Fetching fresh water, Taggart?" asked the commander, with a sneer that seemed to indicate to Robbie that the entrance of the party of men had been no accident.

"I've finished," Robbie replied, purposely omitting the customary *sir*.

"You call that finished?" returned Barclay, poking his head into the room. "Perhaps in the hovels where *you* were raised in the north. But not so in a gentleman's quarters."

"They messed it—they can clean it up! I completed the assignment you gave me!"

"*Your* orders are to clean this floor."

Robbie took a menacing step toward the commander.

"Are you refusing to obey a direct *order*, Taggart?" asked Barclay. It was not a question, however—but an invitation.

One blow was all it would take. Robbie could almost feel the immense satisfaction it would bring.

But when he noted that ugly smirk on Barclay's face, he knew he couldn't give in and provide him the satisfaction of having judged Robbie correctly as a hothead who had no business in the Queen's Navy. He wouldn't stoop to Barclay's level. He'd find some other way to get even.

But this was it! He'd clean the bloody floor again. But no more! They weren't going to push him around anymore. No man had to take such treatment. Somehow he'd find a way to get the lot of them off his back!

Later that night Robbie lay on his bed, exhausted. Mopping the common room floor had been but one of his duties that day. Yet worse even than the weariness he felt was the sense of loneliness. For a man who had long boasted many friends even in the remotest reaches of the world, his tenure in the Navy had proved a vast desert of isolation. As an officer he could not fraternize with the seamen with whom he would have found a welcome and common companionship. To do so would only have further prejudiced men like Barclay against him. Yet his common social station separated him from those of his own rank. There were some who were friendly enough, but always a gulf stretched between them. And the unspoken pressure from the more haughty seemed rather to be the norm.

Tonight he felt the loneliness more than usual. Perhaps what he felt was not loneliness at all but only the frustration of being so constantly under Barclay's thumb. He had to find a way to let off some steam or he was going to go crazy! He had not had a break from the commander's incessant duty for weeks, it seemed, and when he had finished that evening after supper, even Barclay, whose heart was colder than stone, could not lay another task upon him.

Tired as he was, he would give anything for a bit of fun!

Robbie thought dreamily of the *Golden Doubloon* in Aberdeen. So many happy times had he spent there in the old days, laughing and talking with his friends and dancing with good old Sadie Malone. He could not remember the last time he had kicked up his heels. Yes, he would have been able to shake off all his fatigue for just one merry jig.

He did have a few friends in London, and was well-acquainted with the pubs along the docks. Yet he hadn't frequented these places since his last attempt, shortly after he had been assigned to duty in London. What a shock it had been to realize immediately upon stepping across the threshold that he no longer fit in. He was still the same Robbie, but now he wore a uniform and an insignia that demanded respect. No longer did the blokes feel the freedom to slap him on the back and bend his ear with their questionable tales of adventure and excitement. Now he was an officer! And in their eyes it seemed to make him a different and unapproachable person. And at the same time, something seemed to rise unconsciously within him too, a sense that he had a certain dignity to maintain on account of his uniform. Therefore, involuntarily, he found himself hanging back too.

But if he couldn't fit in with the kind of men who had always been his friends, and he didn't fit in with the officers, and if his own commander seemed bent on destroying whatever his commission meant, then what *was* his place in the Navy? Where *did* he fit in? Was this what a man was supposed to endure in order to raise himself up? What good was it if you had to sacrifice your manhood in the process?

Robbie lay on his cot and sighed. Would the days of fun and excitement and adventure ever come again? He thought of Robbie Burns' famous line, *A man's a man for a' that*. Well, for *a' that* he'd been through lately, he didn't feel much like a man.

Gradually the voices in the hall grew louder and piqued Robbie's interest and curiosity. He was just desperate enough for something to do to cast off his pride and see what they were up to, even if it meant forcing himself into the other men's company. He'd begun to wonder if he'd ever be able to regain the abandon and laughter of his past.

He jumped from the bed and flung the door wide open.

"Looks as if you fellows are off for a night on the town," said Robbie with a friendly grin.

Before him stood three of his fellow officers, and Robbie's assumptions seemed to be well-founded; each was decked out in his dress blues, shined and polished and veritably gleaming.

"That we are, Taggart," replied one. "How about yourself?"

"Winnie," said another, "one look will tell you the man's beat. He'll be for his bed tonight."

"So I thought myself," added Robbie, "but sometimes a man wants more than rest. Where are you blokes off to?"

"The Savoy. We have tickets to the new Gilbert and Sullivan play."

"Would you be minding another companion?" asked Robbie.

"You might not find the theater to *your* liking, Taggart," one of the men replied.

"Have you even heard of *HMS Pinafore?*"

Yearning for something—anything!—to do, Robbie chose to ignore the intended insults of Winnie's two companions. "Actually, I like the theater very much," he said.

"Then why not join us?" said Winnie. "We do have an extra ticket since Gates pulled night duty. We were going to turn it in at the door, but—"

"Don't mind if I do!" interrupted Robbie.

"You'll have to change—it's nothing but the best tonight."

"I'll just be a minute or two," said Robbie. "You fellows want to come in and wait?"

"Oh, we'll wait out here. We don't want our presence to slow you down."

Robbie ducked back into his room, tore off the clothes he had been working in all day, and threw on his dress uniform. In his fumbling haste he took even longer with the buttons, and it took an extra minute to raise a proper shine on his shoes. But in less than eight minutes he deemed himself fit for presentation to the public. In his excitement just to be going out on the town—even if it was to a play, which would not have been his first choice as a way to spend the evening—he almost felt like a boy rather than a sophisticated twenty-eight-year-old navy man. But he didn't care! He needed to get away from these barracks!

He turned back toward the door, opened it, and stepped out into the hall.

The corridor was empty, and quiet as a graveyard. His so-called friends were nowhere to be seen. The whole thing had probably been some sick joke! They were no doubt at that very moment having a good laugh at his low-bred naivete.

Robbie slammed the door shut, then kicked his wall.

He looked toward his bed, then back at the door. Well, who said he had to stay here and spend the evening alone! He was all dressed now. Might as well make use of it! He didn't need them to find a good time.

Since when did Robbie Taggart need anyone to show him how to enjoy himself? He'd have a good time tonight—a rousing good one!

As he stepped outside, the cold air felt good on his skin, still hot with anger. The light drizzle did not faze him; he merely pulled his overcoat more tightly up around his shoulders and began searching for a coach. But before he had been successful, a figure stepped out of the shadows and greeted him with a salute.

"Evenin', Lt. Taggart."

Robbie peered through the darkness, and it took his eyes a moment to recognize the seaman as his old acquaintance, Willie Kerr. The two had served together on the same ship in their civilian days and now chanced to have been assigned to the same command after joining the Navy, though in far different capacities.

"Good evening, Kerr," replied Robbie tightly, his capacity for friendliness at the moment stretched to the limit.

"Wot brings ye oot on a miser'ble night like this 'ere one, sir?" asked Kerr.

"I'm off duty, and plan on having myself a good time."

"I can see yer change in fortune hain't changed ye none, Robbie—ah, that is, Lt. Taggart."

"Not a bit," replied Robbie, with not a little force in his tone, his defiance not directed toward Kerr so much as it reflected an anger at himself for the feeling that perhaps he had changed after all. Well, tonight was a night for the *old* Robbie Taggart. Tonight the *lieutenant* would stay behind.

"'Course ye're prob'bly bound fer one o' them fancy clubs wot the officers frequent, now as ye're a gent'man an' all."

"I wouldn't be caught dead in such company!" replied Robbie, with the hint of a smile.

Kerr laughed. "Ye wouldn't be 'eadin' fer some sleazy grogshop like the *Rum Runner*, now would ye?"

"That's exactly where I'm bound, Willie!" declared Robbie, though in truth the idea had only at that moment occurred to him.

"Wot a coincidence, fer that's where I'm goin' mysel'."

"Then do me the honor of joining me, Kerr."

"Ye hain't afeared o' bein' seen fraternizin' with an *inferior*—?"

"Hang it all!" Robbie shouted. "You are no more inferior than they've been telling me I am. And besides, I'm my own man, and I'll go where I please with whom I please. And what about yourself?"

"I'm game, sir."

"Then let's be off, man! I'll take care of the coach."

Robbie flung his arm around his new companion's shoulder and marched down the street, defying Barclay to discover him with company "unbefitting an officer." If he made an issue of it tonight, Barclay would morc likely than not find himself sprawled out on the floor trying to stop the bleeding from his nose!

4

Benjamin Pike

The *Rum Runner* had to be among the lowest of the low public houses along London's docks. The filth in the corners of the floor and the stench of cheap ale would have made the place unfit for human beings had the lighting not been poor and most of those who frequented it already half gone with inebriation by the time they stooped to enter its doors.

Robbie chose to ignore the seamier side of his surroundings, trying to imagine himself at Sadie's in Aberdeen, while valiantly attempting to reach that numbed state of consciousness that would help him forget what brought him here. He would do whatever it took to force upon himself the false impression that he was enjoying himself. Thus, after hoisting several glasses of dark ale to his lips, he stood and took off the jacket of his dress blues, tossing it aside with a flourish. If he thought he could do so without somehow the word getting back to Barclay and his winding up in the brig for a week, he would then and there have thrown away the whole uniform!

Yet notwithstanding his frustrations, Robbie was not one to sulk, or cling long to his anger. Before long the spirited atmosphere of the place played on his sour mood and began to lift it, though it was not the sort of lifting that would last. Robbie realized, even in the midst of it, that he'd have to return to Barclay and the others. But for the moment what he needed was a good laugh. To forget, even if temporarily, would enable him to face his duties again, until the next time they became unbearable.

He found little trouble gaining acceptance among the group of merrymakers, despite being an officer. Kerr vouched vehemently for Robbie, slapping him on the back and declaring that his old friend was buying drinks all round as a display of his good faith. Robbie remembered neither making such an offer, nor being such a "good friend" with Willie Kerr. But tonight was not a night to analyze and think deeply about such things. This was a night for fun—for the *old* Robbie.

Thus, warming quickly to the part, Robbie struck up the first tune of the evening:

> "'Here's adiue, sweet lovely Nancy,
> Ten thousand times adieu.
> I'm going round the ocean,
> To seek for something new.
> Come, change your ring with me, dear girl,
> Come change your ring with me,
> For it might be a token—of true love
> While I am on the sea.'"

When Robbie paused to take a breath, the whole group broke in with a raucous cheer and round of applause, then joined in on the next verses:

> "'There are tinkers, tailors, shoemakers,
> Lie a-snoring asleep,
> Whilst we poor souls on the ocean wide
> Are all ploughing through the deep.
> There's nothing to defend us, love,
> Nor to keep us from the cold,
> On the ocean wide where we must bide,
> Like jolly seamen bold.

> "'And when the wars they are all o'er,
> There'll be peace on every shore,
> We will drink to our wives and children,
> And the girls that we adore.
> We'll call for liquor merrily,
> And we'll spend our money free,
> And when our money is all gone,
> We'll boldly go back to sea!'"

The laughter and camaraderie, however superficial, acted like a balm to Robbie. He took the arm of a pretty barmaid and danced a jig to the lively tune of "Nancy Dawson," imagining himself back among his old friends in Scotland where he was accepted for who he was—where he belonged.

When several choruses of the tune had been played, they fell apart, laughing and breathless. Robbie called for another song, looking around for another partner. He had just spied a likely candidate when a heavy thud on his back stopped him in mid-step. Disoriented with drink and dance, his first thought was that one of the girl's beaus was perhaps readying to challenge him. With the gleam that hinted of battle in his eye, Robbie spun around.

"I knew me auld eyes was still faithful t' me!" said a raspy voice as gritty as salt.

Stopping short, and then staring blankly for the briefest of moments, Robbie's look of defiance gradually faded as a grin slowly spread over his face.

"Benjamin Pike!" he exclaimed, his hazy mind still unsure whether his eyes were telling him the truth.

"Aye it is, mate! In the flesh, I is. In the flesh!"

"Well, come over to a table, you old Scot's blowhard, and let me buy you a drink!"

They ordered two tall pints; then Robbie led the way through the crowded pub to a vacant table, while Pike hobbled after him with his one wooden leg and a crutch tucked under one arm. They were joined by Kerr, who had found Robbie's company that evening quite to his own advantage, though his presence went largely unnoticed.

"You haven't changed a hair, Ben!" said Robbie when they had settled themselves and clinked glasses in their first toast. "What's it been, five years?"

"More like eight!" replied Pike, who did indeed look exactly the same as he did when Robbie had last laid eyes on him eight years earlier, though whether the statement would be considered a compliment or not might be open to question. Pike's face was as marred and creased as a sunken vessel's timbers, though he had only passed his fiftieth year in the time since they had met.

"Though I can hardly say the same for you!" Pike fingered the linen of Robbie's dress shirt, then cast his small gray eyes down at the fancy naval trousers. A curious light passed over his face, but Robbie did not notice, and just as quickly it passed.

"He's a right good officer in the Queen's Navy," offered Kerr in a tone that might have been taken for pride.

"If I hadn't seen it wi' me own twa eyes . . ." said Pike. "Ne'er took ye for the type, Robbie."

"It's not a bad life," said Robbie, almost apologetically; the words struck a strangely dissonant chord with his recent thoughts.

"I tried to look ye up after ye left the *Macao*," continued Pike. His left eye began to twitch imperceptibly as he went on. "I asked all o'er Aberdeen. O' course, bein' in an' oot o' port mysel' I couldna look ye up proper."

"Why all the trouble to find me?"

"What wouldna a man do for the son o' an auld—a frien'—who—"

Pike stopped suddenly. Then as if to cover having said more than he intended, he quickly resumed. "What wouldna a man do for a true ship-mate? I thought ye had disappeared on me. Wouldna hae ne'er thought to look for ye in the *Navy*! An' an officer for a' that besides!"

"That's right faithful of you, Ben," said Robbie, noticeably taken aback by the old man's efforts to locate him.

"I should hae known that it would be futile to try to track down a rover like yersel'. But I might hae been more successful had I stopped to think that maybe ye'd stopped yer rovin'!"

"What makes you say that?" asked Robbie.

"Weel, anyone knows—"

Again Pike stopped short, this time punctuating his unfinished sentence with a wide grin, revealing two rows of yellowed and rotting teeth. "Aw, laddie," he went on, "I dinna want to be startin' oor reunion off wi' me castin' dispursions on yer chosen callin'. So I'll say no more aboot it. Besides, I'd lay me a five-bob that ye're still the same ol' Robbie under yer fancy uniform, anyways. 'Tis not so soon I'd be forgettin' that green lad that came aboard the *Macao* in '69."

"Nor will I," said Robbie with a great laugh. "Hardly seems possible that ten years has passed. I was only seventeen, and didn't know port from starboard."

"I'm surprised yer father ne'er taught ye."

"He never talked much of the sea."

"When I knew Hank," said Pike, his eye twitching again, "nothin' would hae kept him frae a good sea story. Somethin' must hae happened to change his notions o' the seafarin' life." As he spoke the same curious light passed through his eyes, which one might take at once for a longing after a past friendship, or an unexplained gleam of cunning.

"Didn't take too well to it, I suppose," said Robbie; "though he never tried to stop me from following his footsteps."

"An' 'tis a good thing too, for if he had ye would hae missed altogether the gran' days on the sea, makin' that run for the East an' back, tryin' to be first to arrive wi' the new crop o' tea." Pike took a long slow swallow of ale, then closed his eyes. Whether his thoughts were on the pleasing taste of the doubtful brew, visions of the glorious past, or a more immediate personal mission, it would be hard to tell.

"I saw the last of them," said Robbie softly, almost reverently.

"Ye should hae been there in '66!" sighed Pike. "Now that was a race! I was aboard the *Taeping*. We left Foochow bar with *Ariel* and *Serica* on the same tide. Didna sight one another again till the approaches to the Channel! Osborn was the Master o' the *Taeping* an' he drove us like animals. We caught a gale oot o' St. Helena durin' the watch. Osborn was below, sleepin' like a bairn—a sound sleeper him, that's one thing I can say o' him. Weel, the blag'ard had padlocked the sails! We all stood there lookin' in each other's faces, but every man o' us was more afraid to wake the captain an' admit that he had more nerve than us what was all afeared o' crackin' up. That gale drove us twenty knots an hour!"

"Impossible!" chimed in Kerr, incredulous.

"'Tis mighty fast," agreed Robbie, along with several others who had cocked their ears in Pike's direction, not wanting to miss a good yarn, even if it might be nine-tenth's fabrication.

"Twenty knots!" exclaimed Pike, slamming his fist on the table as if to seal with his fist the truth of his declaration. "Twenty knots an' up'ards. For three days it drove us. I swear ol' Osborn had ice in his veins—ne'er winked an eye!"

"And see what his foolhardiness got him!" offered one of the new listeners. "The way I hear it, he cracked up two years back."

"He wasn't in the *Taeping*, though," continued Pike, anxious to get on with his story. "Only the *Taeping* could hae made a run like that. When we reached the Channel, we knew we had outstripped everyone. Then I was lookin' off the starboard bow, an' I couldna believe me own eyes—there was *Ariel*! She couldna been more'n a few miles off."

"You couldn't stop the *Ariel*!" said one of the seamen with fervor.

"Bah! She wasna the craft o' the *Taeping*!" replied Pike.

"I was on her in '66," insisted the seaman. "We rode that gale too, and when I saw the *Taeping* up ahead, I said to myself, 'Jack, this one's going to go down in history!'"

"The *Taeping* won her, though!" emphasized Pike, unimpressed with the discovery of a fellow sailor who had shared the great moment fourteen years earlier, concerned only with pressing his point.

"After a run o' ninety-nine days," said the one called Jack, warming up to his side of the tale, and drawing his share of interest from the crowd, "she only grazed ahead o' us by ten minutes! All three ships came in on the same tide. *Serica* was only an hour behind!"

"I gotta tell ye," admitted Pike at last, "*Ariel* gave us a run for oor hard-earned pay."

"She was a grand one," said Jack. "I were proud t' be on her crew. When she went down in '72, I wept—an' I got no shame to say it, knowin' I'm among salty dogs I can count as friends. Loveliest lady I ever knew!"

"Sailors!" said one of the barmaids in a tone of mock disgust. "You're a blubbering lot—ain't fit for *real* women!"

"An' wot makes ye think ye know so much aboot sailors, Lucy?" asked Jack with a playful tone in his sodden voice.

"Why, I was married to one—that is afore he made a widow o' me. And at my tender age!"

Those within hearing all laughed merrily, for Lucy was well into her latter thirties, and every hard year had etched itself indelibly into her face.

Unperturbed, she turned to the other maid, who was considerably younger, and with a smirk and a snort at the seamen, said, "Don't never marry a sailor, Barbara. They'll bring ye grief every time."

"I'll never bring you grief, Lucy," said a young seaman with a wink.

"Ha!" Lucy bawled, whisking up her tray in animated scorn of the fellow's words. She paused alongside Robbie, glancing deep into his face with a touch of sorrow, and added, "But sometimes 'tis such a waste of a good man."

Robbie merely laughed, took up her hand and bid her to dance once more. What other response could there be to her insightful words than to laugh them off? Every man present knew that he was wasting his days away on a life that could never give him back even a tiny fraction of the love he put into it. But not a one among them could change his lot, nor would he if he were given the chance.

"Come on, Ben! Give one of the girls a dance with a crusty old salt!" enjoined Robbie to his companion.

Pike merely shook his head.

"Aw, Pike! For old time's sake!"

"Didn't you hear me, you young blag'ard! I said no!" yelled Pike sharply, casting a sinister glare toward Robbie and pounding his crutch on the floor next to him.

For an instant Robbie hardly recognized the look on his friend's face, not even noticing the change in Pike's feigned accent. If he had, he would no doubt have graciously attributed it to too much drink.

But the hostile glance disappeared as quickly as it had come. A smile quickly replaced it on Pike's face, followed by a laugh. "Ah! dinna ye be mindin' me, lad!" he exclaimed, patting Robbie on the back. "Ye go an' hae yersel' a good time o' it, an' leave me t' my ain' thochts."

An hour later Robbie returned to the table where Benjamin Pike had remained the entire time, neither singing nor dancing nor even smiling. Pike had never been much inclined to join into the shipboard music, Robbie recalled, even though the haunting melodies and nostalgic lyrics of home played such a vital part of making the lonely life at sea endurable for most sailors. He had never been the jovial sort in the least, always keeping his own counsel, the sort of man who always seemed to have a hidden history that none would ever know but which gnawed away at his innermost thoughts. Oh, Pike could be known to enjoy a good laugh on occasion, but his deep-throated gravelly chortle was never merry.

Yet Robbie would be the last to fault Pike, for the caustic old man of the sea had indeed taken the young novice under his coarse wing and taught him a great deal about sailing the high seas. Despite the fact that they had been friendly enough and Pike had often gone as far as calling Robbie "the son he would never have," Robbie had never been able to warm to the man. Perhaps that was why he had been so remiss in attempting to seek him out after their last parting. But the accident on the ship had kept Robbie off his feet for nearly a month. And when he could finally get around, Pike had already shipped out. In the eight years that followed he had to admit that he had given the strange old man hardly more than a passing thought now and then. It was a sad impasse, considering all the efforts the poor man had apparently made on his behalf. Well, he'd show the fellow a good welcome now, if nothing else.

"So, Pike," said Robbie, "it's plain to see what I've been up to, whether you favor the Navy life or not. But what about yourself?"

"The usual—tramping around, mostly to China and Australia," replied Pike, the Scots fading again from his tongue with the effect of the alcohol on his brain. "Even did a stint on a steamer; they're getting all the valuable cargoes these days, what with the canal. But I don't care if I gots to haul coal and chickens—'tis a sail for me any day!"

Pike paused, took a breath, then hitched up his small, wiry frame and added in what was meant to be a knowing tone, "But like yersel', my fortunes hae been changin'."

"How's that?" To all appearances the man sitting opposite Robbie did not look like one whose life had brought him good fortune at all. His coarse blue breeches and loose-fitting beige shirt, that might have at one time been white, showed liberal splotches of dirt and grease, were worn and even torn in spots, and in general gave the impression of a street derelict. His rimless red cloth hat, the same Robbie had grown accustomed to seeing him wear years earlier, sat atop greasy, thinning, gray-brown hair that hung, uncombed almost to his brown-edged collar. He could easily not have had a bath since the last time he partook of a dip in the deep blue sea, though in his present surroundings the odors hanging in the air of the *Rum Runner* sufficiently disguised any olfactory confirmation to his bathing habits. The overall effect of his look was to cause Robbie an inevitable curiosity concerning his statement.

Benjamin Pike leaned back in his chair and rubbed the stubble of his unkempt beard as if he were modestly reluctant to answer Robbie's question. When he finally spoke it was slowly, and with noticeable understatement, though he clearly expected his words to carry impact. "Well, laddie," he said, "I've got me own ship—an' that's the solemn trowth!"

"That's terrific news, Ben!" replied Robbie, not a little stunned, and also not quite sure he could believe the words. Benjamin Pike looked more like a washed-out drunk than a ship's captain. Although if it was true, he was genuinely glad for his friend.

"I know what you're thinking, lad," said Pike, closely watching Robbie's expression to verify his words. "What's an old blighter like me doing running a ship?"

That was exactly what he was thinking, Robbie thought to himself. But he said nothing further, waiting for Pike to continue. Certainly the man knew the sea as well as any Queen's admiral alive, and could steer a ship with skill to match anyone's. But just as he had himself never struck Pike as the Naval officer type, Pike would never have struck him as a ship's captain. He just didn't fit the part. But a lot could happen to a man in eight years, as Robbie well knew. Perhaps the years had been better to Pike than his appearance would have indicated.

"Well, I'll tell ye," Pike resumed after a drink of ale, "I gots respectable o'er the years, I have. Buckled down, as t'were. Decided I was goin' places, an' so why not go right to the top, eh?"

Here he made a deep chortling sound, which, out of any other throat would have been a menacing noise indeed, but Robbie had long since learned to take it as his form of laughter. He slapped Robbie on the shoulder. "Right to the top, do ye hear me, lad!" he repeated.

"I'm truly glad for you, Pike," said Robbie, masking his uncertainty with genuine enthusiasm.

"Ye were always nice to auld Benjy, lad. An' that's why I ne'er forgot ye."

"Tell me about your ship."

"Ah, a real bonny vessel she is, man! *Sea Tiger*'s her name, an' she's the sleekest clipper ye ever hope t' lay eyes on! She recorded makin' 354 miles in one day last season! An' you should see her main yard—78 feet across. Why, 'tis a dream, lad. A dream the likes o' you an' me dream of all our lives! An' that's jist what it is for an old salt like me to be her master. 'Tis only too bad ye can't hitch up wi' me—jist like in the auld days!"

"Ah, Ben, don't tempt me," said Robbie thoughtfully. "But I have too many other responsibilities now."

"Ye'll never find a ship like her in yer Royal Navy! She makes the *Macao* look like a lugger. An' there's good money t' be had, if ye know what t' haul."

"And you don't think you're a wee bit prejudiced in her favor?" laughed Robbie.

"I'll vouch fer 'is word!" put in Kerr, who had till now remained silently engrossed in his drink.

Pike shot him a dark glance, but Robbie had already begun to speak again.

"I didn't realize the two of you were acquainted," he said.

"You know how it is," said Pike, grinning largely again—too largely, it seemed—" 'tis a regular brotherhood on the sea. Everyone knows everyone else. Why, who'd have thought that old Jack there"—with the words he gestured toward the other side of the room—"would have been on the *Ariel* in '66? We shipped together—when was it, four, five years ago, wasn't it, Kerr?"

"Aye. Just afore I made the mistake o' joining up wi' the Jack Tars."

"Ye know, Robbie, lad," said Pike quickly, adroitly steering the subject back in another direction. "I jist keep comin' back to what I said before—my ship just ain't gonna be complete wi'oot ye, man! There's riches t' be had!"

"I'm afraid it'll have to be. I've put in several years to get where I am. A lieutenant's commission doesn't come to a man like me but once in a lifetime, and I'd be a fool to give it up now."

"An' jist what would ye be givin' up, Robbie, I ask ye?"

"I told you—I'm a lieutenant, that's what!" Robbie replied fiercely, his old frustration momentarily surfacing.

"So, now ye're a big man, is that it?" Pike goaded. "Ye give the orders now, eh? No one can push ye aroun' no more, that it? Ye're master o' yer own fate!"

"Well, it's hardly quite like that," admitted Robbie. He shifted his weight in the chair, squirming with just how well Pike's words had pinpointed his annoyance with his situation.

"I can see it in yer eyes, lad!" exclaimed Pike. "Why the moment I laid me auld eyes on ye, I said t' mysel', *Robbie ain't a happy man these days! He ain't free no more—an' he ain't but half a man so long as he ain't his boss!* Ain't I right? Ye're not feelin' like ye're all a man's supposed t' be, havin' t' bend at the knee t' do their biddin'?"

"The Navy's not a bad life," replied Robbie. But the lack of enthusiasm in his voice revealed the lie in his heart.

"Hoots, man! Who ye tryin' t' fool? 'Tis me, yer auld frien'! I ken ye better 'n that! Why, when's the last time ye saw some water?"

"The Thames is right out my window."

"Ha, ha!" laughed Kerr drunkenly. "He gots ye there!"

"Shut up, you fool!" growled Pike. "I'm serious. An' ye ought to see that, Robbie. The Thames? Bah! Ye call that water! I'm just trying to look out for ye like I always did. I can see through all the sham o' the bright uniform. Ye're dying inside, lad. You're not cut out for polishing brass and taking orders from some fat captain who hasn't set foot in a dinghy since Trafalgar! That's no life fer the likes o' you, Robbie. Ye was always yer own man! An' I'm offerin' ye a chance t' be yer own man again. Ye jist gie me yer *aye* an' I'll make ye the first mate o' my own *Sea Tiger!*"

Robbie exhaled a deep sigh. "This is my life now," he said, trying to force conviction into his tone that was not in his heart. But how could he muster any conviction when every word Pike had uttered was true? He didn't feel like a man anymore. His life was no longer his to control. He had to grovel before a power-hungry commander who seemed bent on destroying any sense of worth he might possess. What did it mean to be a man if he had to take such abuse and was powerless to stand on his own two feet?

"Ach! Ye dinna mean it, lad!" boomed Pike. "I ask ye again, what kind o' a life is it?"

"We need more ale!" declared Robbie, finally putting some urgency into his tone. He jumped to his feet and went in search of Lucy.

When he returned with three frothing pints in his hand, Pike relentlessly picked up the trailing end of the same conversation.

"One look at the *Sea Tiger* an' ye'd change yer mind in an instant."

"What if I don't *want* to change my mind?"

"Then it wouldn't matter one way or the other. So what do ye hae to lose? Come an' see her—shouldn't do ye no harm if what ye say be true. Though I suspect ye *do* want to change yer mind, but ye jist don't know it yet!" Then Pike's eyes narrowed to a sly glint, indicating his unabashed challenge to Robbie's insistence, as he said, "If ye're truly happy servin' in Her Majesty's Navy, then a wee look on me own good fortune couldna hurt ye none, now could it, lad?"

"Then I wouldn't mind if I did, in that case," replied Robbie. "Just to have a look, that is. As long as we understand each other."

"O' course! O' course!" insisted Pike, the ghost of a smile discernible on his grimy and grizzled face.

Later that night, while Robbie was back in his quarters, sound asleep on his cot and none the better for his evening out, the conversation continued in a different vein at the *Rum Runner*.

The place had quieted considerably, with only a handful of the most wretched of the merrymakers remaining. Lucy and Barbara were doing their best to turn away two drunken newcomers at the door, and hoping to get the rest out too, so they could close. Thus, they did not pay much attention to the conversation at a back table, now cast in shadows as the fire in the hearth died to mere embers.

"Five shillin's!" said Kerr, biting down on one of the coins to test its genuineness, though his teeth appeared none too capable of carrying out their part of the arrangement. "You tol' me ten."

"That's when your job is done."

"Now wot've I gots t' do?"

"You see that he gets out to the *Sea Tiger*."

"The bloke's goin' t' get suspicious," argued Kerr. "You said yoursel' t' make sure he don't go suspectin' nuthin'. An' I tell you he's goin' t' wonder if somethin's up wi' me gettin' so fren'ly all of a sudden."

"I'll worry about that. You just get him to the ship. It'll be worth a quid to me instead of just the extra five shillings."

Kerr scratched his head.

"You that sure he's goin' t' join up wi' ye?"

"Never surer of anything. Now get out, and make a good job of it!"

"Don't see why ye're so set on him nohow," mumbled Kerr as he rose and ambled away from the table and out the door.

Pike leaned his chair back on two legs and rubbed a rough and dirty hand across five days' worth of gray beard. The night had gone well—exceptionally well. If Kerr would keep up his end and not botch things, he ought to have everything pretty well sewed up in a few days. But time was no problem, for the *Sea Tiger* would not be ready to put out until the middle of February. That gave him a month. Still, Pike had enough other things to worry about without having to sweat over this at the last minute. But even if it did take some extra effort, he was set on having Robbie Taggart as his first mate. It had been sheer luck that he'd found him in the first place after all these years, and he wasn't about to let such a golden opportunity like this pass.

Pike grinned broadly.

Lady Luck had indeed been more than generous with him lately. First of all, meeting up with the blokes at the Cathay Mercantile Company—Cranston and Dempster—had been a boon as not many sailors could boast. They had said he was just the man they needed, and, of course, he'd be the last to disagree. An offer as they proposed seldom came to a middle-aged, one-legged sailor. Pressing his luck to the limit, he had insisted on a partnership in the deal and, surprisingly, they had agreed. It was obvious they counted him too valuable to lose. Whether that fact was the result of his experience or his dubious character, Pike did not ask.

Then to top it all off he had chanced to meet Kerr one night in the *Rum Runner*. While discussing old shipmates, Taggart's name came up. That was the moment Pike realized just what a streak of good fortune he was on. And he felt in his bones that things were only going to get better. For once in his life, he—Benjamin Pike—would have a few things *his* way! He *deserved* it and by heaven, he'd get it—get it all, he would!

Pike lowered his chair with a resounding crack through the now deserted dockside pub. He pushed it from the table and lurched to a standing position. As he walked toward the door he took no notice of Barbara's disgusted glance at his half-leg, its wooden stump grinding into the floorboards with each forceful step. But if he had seen the girl, he would merely have given her a scornful sneer, probably enough to send even that hardy woman into a faint. He was well used to people's stares, but he never let them pass without rebuttal.

He deserved that, too, and let no man or woman try to rob him of that right.

5

A Surprise Meeting

The next week gave Robbie not a spare moment. Though Barclay could have known nothing of his evening out, it seemed as if he were making him pay for it nonetheless.

By week's end he had to get away once more. For all his talk to Pike of the Navy "not being a bad life," he knew the words were empty and meaningless. His taste of independence in his younger days had ruined him. Now he was stagnating while others moved on up the ladder. That very morning a new promotions list had been posted, and as usual his name was nowhere to be found. Several of his equals, however, had received their due; one, who had entered the service at the same time as he and who had grown to be one of Barclay's favorites, was made commander.

Robbie pushed back from his desk in the little cubicle that had grown to be representative of his tenure in Her Majesty's service, and knew that he was ready at last to make his stand, whatever that would be. This emasculating life could not go on forever—at least not for him! He was a man, and would take his stand as one!

His first act of defiance was to stride resolutely from the office building. He was off duty for the weekend—officially. However, Barclay expected all his men to report to him prior to their departure. Robbie decided to ignore this little ritual. He knew his commander was certain to find some reason to detain him, and he was in no mood for it just now. But beyond such reasonings, Robbie himself was no doubt unaware of his full intention in this minor act of confrontation. As a man standing on the gallows, though fearful of death, yet only wants the execution to be done with and the awful tension relieved, so Robbie instinctively realized that things could not go on as they were. If forcing the issue would bring it to a head—whatever the result—perhaps that was for the best.

So he flung his coat over his shoulders and pulled his hat down tightly over his forehead in anticipation of the threatening storm. The clouds that had hung low over the city for days had lifted a bit in the last hour, though one could never tell what they might do. For the moment the streets were dry, and for that Robbie was thankful.

Once he found himself striding down the street, Robbie realized he had no particular destination in mind. The thought of the *Sea Tiger* had never been far from his mind that week, but—if he could admit it—he was somewhat afraid of Pike's words and the challenge they had contained. At the same time, however, he yearned to look upon that craft as any man would who had once been intimately associated with such a vessel. He longed to feel the creaking timbers of her deck beneath his feet, to stand looking up at the glorious heights of her masts, to run his hand along her polished oak rails while listening to the river lap lazily against her hulls. He didn't dare allow his mind to picture her with sails full as she raced with the wind down the channel toward the open sea. Such a thought would have undone him.

No, he could not let himself give quarter to Pike's tempting offer. And seeing the ship sitting in the harbor would be the worst thing for him right now! Instead he turned from the direction of the docks. It didn't matter where he went, so long as he was far from the temptation of the *Sea Tiger*.

In forty minutes he found himself near Hyde Park. He smiled ironically to himself, for he had certainly been successful in finding as great a contrast as possible to the docks. Here were neat little houses, all in stately rows that hadn't changed for years on end—nor had their occupants, most of whom regarded change of any kind with disdain. They awoke at 7:00 sharp every morning, breakfasted on an egg (cooked precisely three and a half minutes), and buttered toast while reading the morning *Times*. The men took the 8:15 to their offices and the ladies lunched with their garden clubs and took tea precisely at 4:00. For variety, an evening at the theater was permitted.

Suddenly Robbie caught himself, ashamed of his mockery. Only months ago he had been willing to become one of them for a chance to win Jamie. But even had she accepted his love, he wondered if he could ever have adjusted to such a life.

It was doubtful. He was not made of the same stuff as a country squire or a Westminster businessman. And the Navy was strikingly similar. The military presented glamour and shine and polish and excitement on its surface, while beneath, the sole purpose was to convert all manner of divergent individuals into a single, nonthinking, unified mass—each part identical to the other. Individuality, any deviation from the accepted norm, resulted in punishment and ostracism. And again the question came to his mind: *How can I be my own man when every move toward individuality is repressed?*

46

When he had entered the Navy four years ago, he had been optimistic. The Navy had seemed like such a chance in itself—a grand new experience to add to his vast repertoire of memories from around the world, and one with new potential for growth and advancement and travel. He had soon been purged of those false assumptions. Perhaps he had not been wrong originally. It *was* certainly a new experience. In after years, he would doubtless look back and say that he had learned from it. What if his frustration came, not because of the Navy life itself, but because he had mistakenly considered his joining the Navy as permanent? Perhaps it had played itself out, and now he was ready for another new experience. He was not bound hand and foot to the Royal Navy. He was, after all, still his own man—they could not take that from him!

His thoughts had been so occupied as he walked along that he hardly noticed the passing coach, nor first heard when his name was called from inside. But as the coachman pulled the horses to a stop just ahead of him, he could not help but wonder, a reaction that increased tenfold as his name was again called out.

"Robbie . . . Robbie Taggart!"

At the sound a surge swept through his entire body. *It couldn't be!* But his heart gave a leap in spite of himself.

"Robbie!" came the voice again, and this time there could be no mistaking the sweetly familiar sound. It fell upon his ears more welcome to his aching heart than a brisk sea breeze.

He hastened forward to the coach and took the dainty, gloved hand offered out the window.

"Jamie," he said, "it *is* you! Dear Jamie MacLeod!"

"Oh, Robbie! I could hardly believe my eyes when I saw you on the street!" said Jamie. "Seeing you makes my visit to London complete!"

"Then you are only visiting . . . ?" Robbie tried not to let the sound of disappointment creep into his voice.

"Yes. I suppose you might even call it honeymooning." A flush crept up into her delicately creamy features. "Edward wanted me to see the city. And he had some business besides."

"So you are Lady Graystone now! I'm happy for you!"

Though Robbie had not been happy for himself lately, his words were genuine. He loved Jamie enough, with the right kind of love, to be able to rejoice in her having found her heart's desire.

"Won't you come join us, Robbie?" she said, glowing with pleasure, for her love for Robbie was also of the right sort. "We are on our way to meet Edward for luncheon. He would enjoy seeing you again."

Robbie recalled that Graystone had been none too enthusiastic upon their last meeting. But the situation was quite altered now—they were no longer rivals, and that made all the difference. And how could his friendship with Jamie possibly conflict with the relationship between a husband and wife? She was a dear friend, perhaps the best friend he would ever have—but that was all. Everything became plain now that he saw her again. And how glad he was that she had come back into his life just then, for he needed a friend so very badly.

Just then a golden head poked out the window next to Jamie's.

"Look, Mother, a soldier!" exclaimed a child of six, whose lively eyes glinted with enthusiasm for everything around him.

"I'm a sailor, lad," corrected Robbie. "Blue for the Navy, red for the foot soldiers."

"Do you have your own ship?"

Robbie's grin faded briefly, but with a jocular tone he glossed over the chagrin caused by the innocent words. "And what else would you expect a sailor to have, lad? Now, who might you be, young man?"

"I'm Andrew Graystone," returned the boy proudly. "Can I see your ship?"

"Andrew," said Jamie, "you have only just met Lt. Taggart—"

"I don't mind, Jamie," cut in Robbie. "It does me good to see such youthful excitement."

"Are things well with you, Robbie?" asked Jamie. He knew her question was more than a polite pleasantry. Her concern was prompted by a depth of friendship that noted something amiss in the tone of his voice. It was also a question that required an answer reflecting like depth—an answer Robbie was not quite yet prepared to give. Even he did not know the answer to it.

"Oh, I suppose they could be better," he answered lightly. "But isn't that always the case with Robbie Taggart—never quite satisfied with the spot where his feet choose to alight?"

"Robbie . . . Robbie—always the soldier of fortune. That's the real you, isn't it?" said Jamie with a tender smile.

"Robbie Taggart, Highland sailor—that's me! Not like you, I'm afraid, content always to remain in the lee of your dear mountain. In fact, it surprises me to find you so far from Donachie and the Highlands."

"London was one of the grand cities my father spoke so often about," replied Jamie with a distant look in her eye, "a place at the far end of the world that I so longed to see. But it's taken the years and insights of adulthood for me to begin to see what my grandfather meant when he would say, 'Why lang fer the rest o' the world when ye hae the best richt here on oor ain Donachie?'"

"Then you'll be glad to return to Aviemere?"

Jamie sighed.

"We won't be returning to Aviemere." She explained that Derek Graystone had lodged his hereditary claim to the estate, and Edward had chosen to depart from his beloved land, no longer willing to serve his brother's interests.

"I am sorry," said Robbie when she was through. He took her hands comfortingly in his. "You loved the estate so—and your dear Donachie is gone also."

"They are not gone, Robbie," replied Jamie. "God doesn't take back his good gifts, though sometimes He sends us on to new things, and more often than not, much better things. As it is in our case. I'm content, Robbie, for my joy doesn't rest in things, but in life. God has given me all I want, or could hope to want."

"I've always admired your faith, Jamie."

"But not enough to espouse it yourself?" she rejoined with a smile and a good-natured twinkle in her eye despite that the words came from the depth of her heart of love.

"I shall leave that to you and Andrew here."

"Is that to say that the things of God are best confined to women and children?"

"I suppose not . . ." he hedged. "But then I doubt God needs to be bothered with a healthy, strapping man who can take care of himself."

"Oh, Robbie, if you only knew! Do you think that your manhood would somehow be lessened if you admitted that you needed God?"

"Perhaps. I've always prided myself on being independent since I was just a kid. For a woman like you—"

"You think it's different for women?"

"Well, isn't it?"

"No, Robbie, No, it isn't. Women are just as independent as men. And we each have just as great a need of the Lord in our hearts. That's how I discovered what it truly meant to be a lady. And I venture to say that's the only road to true manhood as well. But I'll not preach at you. I care about you too much to try to convince you of something only God can reveal to you. 'Tis best you find out in your own way and in your own time—and I know you will!"

Jamie gazed out the small coach past Robbie, then closed her eyes for a minute. To Robbie she appeared homesick, saddened by the dreary scene of the city sidewalks and cobbles and brick and stone. He would never have guessed that at that very moment Jamie was praying for him, asking her Lord that no matter where Robbie's restless feet led him, He would reveal to him the strength and humility of true manhood, known through the saving truth of God's love.

Wanting to lighten the heavy mood he judged had fallen upon the unexpected reunion, Robbie slapped his thigh, and, grinning with a new rush of enthusiasm, said, "I've just had a splendid idea!"

Jamie opened her eyes and smiled back. It was good to see the old sparkle in his eyes again. For a moment she felt as she had that day so many years ago, tramping along the snow-covered road with Robbie, on their way to Aberdeen and new adventures.

Yet they were both such different persons now. Lady Graystone possessed a much keener insight and sensitivity than had the naive shepherd lass known as Jamie MacLeod. And since the instant she had laid eyes on Robbie this present morning, she had sensed a change even in the carefree Robbie Taggart. His laughter did not seem to flow from that natural fountain of bravado he had always displayed—it was forced, having a desperate quality, as if he must maintain it at all costs. Of course, only Jamie would have noted such a change.

"Well now," Jamie replied, attempting to equal his enthusiasm, "what is this wonderful idea of yours? I hope you don't plan to carry us off to Tasmania or the South Seas?"

"Not when you and Lord Graystone are on your first trip to London together," Robbie laughed. "I shall wait for another time for that."

"Oh, *now*, Lt. Taggart . . . now!" begged Andrew, hardly understanding anything of the adult conversation, but sensing innately that this blue-clad sailor could offer nothing but grand adventures for a boy of six.

"My idea is almost as good," said Robbie. "Maybe even better. How would you like to come with me and see a real sailing ship?"

"Hooray!" cried the boy, clapping.

"That *is* a wonderful idea," agreed Jamie. "To tell you the truth, there hasn't been a great deal here to amuse Andrew. But Edward is waiting for us."

"I'm afraid I may not have another free day," said Robbie. "But why don't I take the boy with me now, and you can go ahead and meet Lord Graystone?"

"Wouldn't that be asking too much of you?"

"Not at all!" Robbie replied. "You know how I love to brag about the sea, and here is a fresh new audience for all my tales!"

"Please, Mother!"

"How can I possibly refuse you both?"

"I shall see to it that he has lunch," said Robbie, adding with a mock sheepish grin, "in a reputable establishment, I assure you!"

Jamie laughed. "I trust him with you, Robbie, as much as I trusted myself with you back in Aberdeen. Just have a grand time."

She opened the door and set little Andrew outside the coach, gave him a parting hug, and after some arrangements about where to meet, she watched the two stroll jauntily down the walk. Robbie doffed his fine uniform cap and set it on top of Andrew's blond curls. The boy turned, beaming, and gave a final goodbye wave to his stepmother.

What a pair they are, thought Jamie! Hand clasped in hand, one would hardly have guessed they had only just met.

6

Dreams and Delusions

The London docks at that late morning hour were a swarming hive of activity. Robbie and Andrew had hired a coach to the Naval yards, but had abandoned it some distance away in order to see everything up close.

Once on the ground, however, much of Andrew's view was blocked by stacks of crates and bales of cargo and barrels of everything ranging from oil to whiskey to fresh water for lengthy sea voyages. When he was nearly knocked off his feet by a busy dockworker oblivious to all but his labors, Robbie bent down and hoisted the boy onto his shoulders.

That made a view too grand for words! Andrew could hardly contain his agitated boyish enthusiasm at all the wonders his eyes beheld. Rows upon rows of ships of every kind, every size, and every nationality lay before him. To his left, a man, small and wiry like a spider, was climbing aloft on the rigging and Andrew beheld him, wide-eyed at the sight, fearful lest the daring sailor lose his balance, yet at the same time enchanted at the very idea that a man could be up so high. On another ship, huge bales of cotton were being hoisted overhead, having just arrived the day before from Manchester, the cotton capital of the North, where they were then dropped unceremoniously on the dock with a soft resounding thud. Everyone with them was busy about some task or another, all scurrying about in different directions. Andrew had never seen the likes of it—what a lot of men there were! The clothing was bright, sometimes outlandish, colorful, varied, dirty; yelling voices, strange, wonderful noises and unusual smells. Some of the men sported long moustaches, a couple wore golden rings in their ears! And there were foreign tongues shouting with all the rest amid the throng—black-skinned Africans, dark brown Indians, fair-skinned Chinese. Many possessed not the most welcoming of countenances, but the boy took no notice of that, though when one gave him a toothless and crooked, yet friendly grin, it nearly startled him out of his wits. In the fascination of it all, the energetic atmosphere of the place struck deeply into the boy's heart. Whatever fears the unknown may have held were swallowed up in a fascination that penetrated far deeper than words or conscious thoughts.

As they walked, Robbie pointed out various ships they passed, explaining their tonnage, rigging, and whatever interesting anecdotes he happened to know of their histories. Andrew, of course, understood little, but what he remembered in later years was the sound of Robbie's voice, acting as backdrop for the new and unusual sights that his mind's eye would always remember.

"There's the steamer *Rangoon*. Look at the fine lines of her hull, and she's a full 3,000 tons!"

As he pointed toward the ship, even the most casual observer would have noted that the tour guide was every bit as wide-eyed as the lad propped upon his broad shoulders. "And there's the *Sardinia*. They cut her down to a barque rig, but she was a beauty in her day. Tis said she made the passage from London to Shanghai by way of the southern tip of Tasmania in only 101 days. Over 20,000 miles! But who's to say if it's only a legend?"

"Hey, Andrew, over there's a new one!" exclaimed Robbie all at once in a new tone. "I wonder if she's got one of those triple expansion engines I've heard so much about. I read that the passage to Melbourne via the Cape could be as little as forty-five days in one of them."

On it went, with Andrew interrupting frequently with questions or to point out some new wonder. Such was their absorption in the salty scene that they scarcely noticed the old man leaning lazily against one of the crusty wooden pilings that bordered the dock they were walking along, until they had nearly stumbled over him.

"Pardon me!" apologized Robbie, as he set Andrew on his feet in order to steady the old gentleman. "We weren't paying attention to where we were going."

"Ha, ha!" croaked the man in an ancient voice. "It'd take a stronger wind than the two o' ye landlubbers t' blow me o'er!" In truth, the man appeared so seamed and weathered that if he were one of the ships he had been gazing so steadily at, he would never have been counted as seaworthy for as much as a sail to the other side of the Thames.

"Is that your ship?" asked Andrew, oblivious to the limitations of age, who beheld only the man's captain's hat and woolen pea coat, complete with brass buttons. He was too young to note the significance of the missing and tarnished buttons, and the patches on the coat that did little to allay its generally frayed appearance. He only knew that here was another sailor—a man who had set foot on distant lands and laid eyes on wonders untold.

"Aye, laddie," said he, a Scotsman by tongue, as he focused his rheumy eyes on the fine brig and ran his gnarled old fingers through his thick white beard. "They're all mine, they are . . . they're yers too, lad, if ye dream hard enough!"

Andrew wrinkled his smooth brow, puzzled by the man's cryptic words.

"He's a bit young to understand your meaning, old-timer," said Robbie.

The man looked up from Andrew to Robbie, and for a brief instant his eyes seemed to come into clear focus. "But *ye* unnerstan' me, dinna ye though, yoong man?"

Robbie hesitated. "Yes. Yes, I suppose I do," he answered slowly, but looking away as he spoke, unable to return the man's intense stare.

"Oh, ye ken my meanin', an' that's a fact," said the old sailor. "I can tell. An' 'tis not by yer outfit that yer mind's open t' me—'tis in spite o' it. 'Tis in the way ye're gazin' at them ships. I can see the look in yer eye. 'Tis a look I ken weel mysel'. An' ye'll teach the laddie here, ye will."

"He's but a friend's child, and not my own boy," replied Robbie lamely, as if this bit of fact would break the spell of the old man's words.

"*They that go down t' the sea in ships,*" quoted the sailor, the focus now gone from his eyes and a distant tone in his voice, "*that do business in great waters; these see the works o' the Lord, an' His wonders in the deep.*"

"We'd best be on our way," said Robbie uncomfortably.

"I'm but an auld man," continued their new acquaintance as if no one else had spoken. "I'll see no more of the deep—dreams is a' Cap't Smollet's left anymore." The old man, apparently named Smollet, laid a heavy hand on Robbie's shoulder. "Maybe ye'll ken all aboot that one day, too. But the laddie here"—he gestured with a hand toward the ships and perhaps beyond—"they're all *yers* fer the askin'."

Robbie bid the old captain goodbye, and, hand in hand, he and Andrew walked on, though Robbie found himself not quite so talkative as before.

"What did he mean?" asked Andrew.

"'Tis hard to tell," Robbie replied pensively. "Perhaps that you can have whatever you want in life—it's just up to you, that's all. That you can sail to whatever distant shore you choose, that any ship bound for anywhere can be yours, if you decide to make it so."

He paused, not even sure he knew what he meant himself. He found himself wondering what Jamie would say in response to the old man's words.

"Mother always tells me that it's the Lord who directs our ways," said Andrew innocently.

"Well . . ." Robbie cleared his throat somewhat awkwardly, "your mother is right, of course. Always do as she says. Maybe the Lord is captain of all the ships, and we simply have to decide which one to sail on. Perhaps that is what the old man meant."

Robbie didn't know why he said it; somehow it seemed appropriate, even if he didn't understand it himself. But it seemed to satisfy the boy.

"Do you think it's true, Lt. Taggart, that those that go to the sea in ships will see the works of the Lord, like the man said?" asked Andrew after a pause.

"You have a very good memory for a boy of six!" said Robbie. "But I don't know, Andrew. He was a very old man, and I'm not sure but that a few of his sails were reefed. And besides," he added on a lighter note, "he was a sailor—and you know what they say, you can't always trust a sailor!"

"Mother said she could trust you."

"Oh well, that's different, son. I'm Robbie Taggart!" Here Robbie laughed, and the boy laughed with him, never questioning his reply. For not only was he at an age where trust was instinctive; he sensed too by the security he felt with Robbie that the words came from a character that was true.

Before long they had arrived at the Naval yards, and there came to the H.M.S. *Landmark*. It was not Robbie's ship, of course, but he had been on fairly good terms with one of the officers, a certain fellow lieutenant by the name of Robertson. He hoped his friendship would insure them a welcome, even though it was all too clear that he didn't belong here. If Barclay had known of his whereabouts, he would probably have had a better chance of being invited aboard one of Cap't Smollet's elusive vessels.

As they approached the ship, suddenly Robbie realized that to go aboard the *Landmark* was almost as bad as a visit to the *Sea Tiger*, a temptation he had studiously avoided. Perhaps it was worse, for the *Landmark* represented what might have been for him—and all that was being so unjustly withheld, though it had once seemed so close within his grasp.

The old sea captain had said, "They're all yers too if ye dream hard enough!" But what were Smollet's words but visions of hope spoken to entice a young child to see beyond the horizon? What meaning could they possess for him? For Robbie knew all too well the pain of dreams unfulfilled.

"Ahoy, Lt. Taggart!" came a shout from the *Landmark's* deck. It was Robertson.

"Ahoy, Robertson!" returned Robbie. "Might my young friend and I have permission to come aboard?"

"On official business?" asked Robertson with the hint of a grin.

"No. I'd just like to give the lad a bit of a tour."

"I see no difficulty with that. I'm sure the captain won't mind—permission granted."

For Andrew the next hour proved as awe-inspiring as had the walk along the docks. They left not an inch of the royal frigate unexplored, inspecting everything from the boiler room to the galley. And in the galley the cook gave the boy a taste of "bully beef," the tinned meat introduced at the beginning of the century from France. It perhaps was not on a par with anything he might have been served at the Regency, where he and his parents were staying, but to Andrew it was indeed a gourmet delight.

For Robbie's part, nothing on this particular day could have pleased him more than to show off his world to the enthusiastic child. And it was no small pleasure besides to be held in such reverence by Andrew, nonetheless because he was now Jamie's son. But an unconscious bitterness insisted on nagging at him, as he found himself confronted over and over, at each turn of a new narrow corridor onboard the ship, that the *Landmark*, nor any like it, would ever be his. But by the time they climbed above deck again into the clean, fresh air, he managed to successfully—if only temporarily—shake the bonds of that depression.

He was standing on the deck, watching Andrew run down its length, while enjoying a pleasant conversation with Robertson when all at once he glanced up to see, less than ten yards away, Commander Barclay walking up the gangway to board the *Landmark*. His instinctive reaction was that the meeting must be somehow less than coincidental, but the look of surprise on Barclay's countenance to match his own assured him that their paths had indeed crossed by chance.

Barclay had been speaking to the captain as they boarded, but his words faltered perceptibly when he raised his eyes in Robbie's direction. He spoke a few more words to the *Landmark's* captain; then the two strode across the deck to where Robbie stood with Robertson.

"Good afternoon, gentlemen," said Barclay crisply, leveling his gaze directly at Robbie as the two lieutenants snapped to attention and saluted.

Even Robertson was noticeably cowed by the commander, though he was not directly answerable to "wee Bonaparte." But Robbie did not flinch, and returned the commander's cold stare, finding himself unaccountably steady. Perhaps the growing sense of futility, which had led to the morning's feeling of abandonment as he left the compound without checking in, had boosted his confidence to stand firm.

"Mr. Taggart," Barclay went on after returning the salute, continuing his custom of refusing to recognize Robbie's commission and addressing him as he would a civilian, "I do not recall assigning you any duty relating to the *Landmark*."

"No, sir, you didn't. I was merely visiting—on my free time."

"I see . . ." Barclay drew the words out meaningfully, though Robbie could only guess at what sinister meaning they might hold; " . . . then that must explain the presence of a child aboard a royal warship."

Barclay and the captain exchanged glances. The captain was about to say something, when Robertson spoke up: "I gave my permission, sir. I saw no harm—"

"It is obvious to me," stated Barclay, "that Taggart here must certainly have given the impression he had the assent of his superiors in this request."

Robbie's mouth shot open in preparation to make a heated denial. But he stopped himself abruptly. To say anything further now would only draw Robertson into unnecessary trouble, and no doubt place him in an awkward position having either to defend his fellow or protect his own standing. He would have to take care of himself without anyone's support, even against an unjust accusation that only Robertson could confirm.

"I'm sorry," he said instead of what he had initially intended. "I wasn't thinking." The words barely made it past his tight throat.

Even as he spoke, something deep within told him this was probably the end. Barclay now had the excuse he needed, no doubt to demote Robbie if he chose to press it. But even if he let it pass, he knew within himself he could take no more of Barclay's persecution, nor that of the Royal Navy. Something had to give.

"I will see you in two hours in my office, Taggart!" said Barclay.

"Yes, sir!"

Robbie about-faced, and with his fingers resisting a clenching motion, he strode away. He called Andrew, who had been happily oblivious of the interchange, and together they disembarked the H.M.S. *Landmark*.

7

Decisions Weighed

In the drawing room of the Graystones' suite at the Regency, Robbie paced the floor feverishly, not even aware he was doing so. Jamie and her new husband had taken the exhausted little Andrew to bed in the next room.

He was still striding with a vengeance across the thick carpet when Jamie stepped back into the room. He stopped short when she appeared, and tried gallantly, though futilely, to recapture some of his old carefree form.

"You best watch that son of yours, Jamie!" he said jokingly. "I think the lad's got the sea in his blood!"

"A day with Robbie Taggart can be dangerous!" Jamie returned, laughing. "And I should know! Why, I might have gone to sea myself had I been a man!"

"And a bonny sailor you would have made too!"

"Not so fine as you, Robbie," Jamie replied earnestly. "I am, and I have always been so proud of you. And proud to know you."

Robbie looked away and unconsciously began pacing again. Jamie took several steps toward him, then laid her hand on his arm.

"Dear Robbie . . . what is troubling you so?"

He paused and turned to face her. Searching her eyes, he saw more vividly all at once something that had only begun to dawn on him last year when had asked for her hand in marriage. Back then he had chiefly been struck by her loveliness, by the dazzling contrast she represented to the child he had left at Sadie's. But now a greater depth to her loveliness was becoming more and more apparent—a sensitivity and wisdom and peace of a woman far beyond her youthful years. Oh yes, the lively twinkle still shone from her emerald eyes, and the determined set to her chin was still visible, which gave her delicate features an unusual strength. But all these surface observations only heightened the conviction of something most lasting that dwelt within. She spoke often about her faith in God. Was that the cause of the change Robbie sensed?

It was too bad he could not consider such a faith for himself, especially now when he felt weaker than at any other time in his life. But he was different, he argued with himself. Different from one like Jamie who could accept these things more easily. He told himself he required a freedom that the constraints of such a faith would smother. He was already being suffocated too much of late to welcome another potential despot, be it God or anyone else. Let Jamie have her faith. It might provide a rich focus for her life, and be desirable for many others. But for an adventurer like Robbie, taking the step of embracing it would be too great a risk.

"I'm not pleased with the Navy," he finally said bluntly, almost as though he expected an argument in response.

"I wondered," Jamie replied quietly.

"Do you know me better than I know myself?" he sighed, running a hand through his thick black hair. "I'm doubting it's the life for me. I should have been smart enough to see that four years ago. I don't know why I ever accepted the commission."

"God has a plan for everything, Robbie. But we don't necessarily always have to understand it at every step of the way."

"A plan for an infidel like me?" He laughed a short, hard laugh. "I'm afraid anything he might have had in mind for me would have been a waste of the Almighty's time, Jamie." He didn't know why he was being so callous with her all of a sudden when all she wanted was to give him the understanding he had longed for. But because he could not accept the only answer she had for him, he tried to pretend he hadn't really wanted an answer after all.

"What else might you do with yourself then?" Jamie asked after a lengthy pause. She had been well aware of the growing resistance in him, and thus drew back so he would not erect a wall that would bar her completely from his life.

"There's a merchant ship—an old sea clipper." Even as he spoke the words a familiar spark began to flicker once more in his eyes. "The captain's a friend of mine from the old days."

"I can see you're excited about the possibilities," she smiled.

"That's where I belong, Jamie—on the sea! That's what I was made for, not a stuffy naval office in London!"

Another short pause followed.

"But I have to get back. My commander's expecting me," said Robbie.

Just then the door of the other room opened and Edward entered, closing the door softly behind him. "Well, Lt. Taggart," he said, "little Andrew is full of tales of your afternoon together!"

"I'm glad he enjoyed it. I was just leaving," he added, approaching Edward and extending his hand. "Thank you for your hospitality, Graystone. You have a wonderful family. I envy you." For a moment the two men held each other's eyes; then Edward nodded and gave Robbie's hand an additional firm shake.

"Our prayers will go with you, Robbie," he said. "You mean a great deal to my wife here, and to my son also. Therefore, I will always consider you my friend as well. Our home is always open to you. Wherever your travels take you, we will expect you to keep in touch."

"Thank you," replied Robbie. "That means a great deal to me."

He made toward the door, but stopped. Then, as if his resolve was suddenly settled, he turned back into the room, took off his naval cap, handed it to Edward, and said, "I don't think I'll be needing this again. Please give it to Andrew. Perhaps it will make up for my not saying a proper goodbye to the boy."

He turned toward Jamie and caught her eye. She smiled and approached him with open arms. They embraced warmly, bid one another goodbye; then Robbie turned again and left the room, shutting the door behind him.

"I will pray for you, Robbie," Jamie murmured. She could not escape a certain heaviness in her heart. This parting was so different from all the others, for Robbie was not the same as he once was. His bravado contained less security, and a cloud of uncertainty hung over him. Part of Jamie regretted the passing of the old Robbie, for his lusty, merry nature had been a strength to her once, in her own time of uncertainty. But now the tables were turned, and she knew he looked to her for strength; but the strength she had to give he could not receive. But as she began to pray Jamie realized why Robbie seemed so burdened down now. In the old days he had not been fighting a battle with an unseen and all-powerful Adversary. God had not yet reached out His hand to draw Robbie into His fold. But now—it was so plain, Jamie wondered that she had not seen it sooner—God was calling Robbie, and the noble sailor was squirming and wrestling because he did not want to give up his independence to follow the voice of the Lord.

But Jamie knew Robbie. He was a man of tender heart, and whatever it might take, she knew the love of the Everlasting Father would win him in the end. She realized too that the path before him would not be an easy one. The very qualities that made of him a good and honorable man would likely be the final obstacles in the way of his realizing his need for God.

She lifted her eyes and met Edward's gaze. She sighed, and he understood her. "He's very troubled," she said at length.

"God is dealing with him," replied Edward softly, "and for that we can be thankful."

"I fear it will be difficult for Robbie. He has known so little trouble in his life. The stalking of his heart by the Lord could well prove a long journey."

"Our prayers will be a protection for him."

"And God will be faithful."

Jamie reached up and took her husband's hand. Who better than she knew intimately the faithfulness of God, and she comforted herself that Robbie could not be in better hands than the very hands that loved him into being.

Robbie's thoughts at that moment were not in the least on the God whose gentle but unseen hands were guiding his steps. Instead, as he entered his barracks, his only thought was that a great weight had been lifted from his shoulders. But as free as he felt at that moment, Robbie yet knew nothing about the true freedom for which all men have been created. And though he turned his back on what he considered his present bondage, he still could not escape the most dangerous bondage of all—that is, slavery to self. His only point of reference to date was his own being. Though Jamie's words of faith had sown seeds within him, they had not yet sprouted into personal reality: he had no concept of a personal and immediate Friend, only some vague ideas of a distant Power people called God.

Thus, Robbie saw only surface problems, and sought only temporal solutions. His present position was unfair and unfulfilling. He was taking abuse that a man should not have to endure. The answer, so far as he could see, was simply to remove himself from the source of discomfort. Yet God's hand still guided, and would mold his action—however selfishly motivated may have been its origins—to fulfil His divine will.

He reached Commander Barclay's office feeling rather too lighthearted. He rapped confidently on the door, heard the voice on the other side, stepped inside, and greeted his commanding officer with a smart salute.

"I am reporting as instructed, *sir*!" he said.

"You are out of uniform, Lieutenant!" returned Barclay, directing his sharp eyes to Robbie's uncovered head.

"Yes, sir."

"You no doubt have a perfectly plausible reason for reporting to me in such a condition?"

Robbie's hesitation lasted only a moment. When he spoke it was with a natural boldness that had scarcely surfaced during his entire tenure in the Navy.

"The time has come, I'm afraid, when I can no longer wear the uniform of Her Majesty's Navy with pride."

This unexpected response took Barclay so completely by surprise, as did the almost cocky tone of Robbie's voice, that he had no ready rejoinder at hand.

"You, you—what?" he stammered, incensed at young Taggart's audacity to speak to him thus.

"Did you really think that your humiliating tactics could make me submit to a system where men were judged not for their virtue but their birth? You have only served to weaken any respect I may have had for you, and for the Navy."

"You are a fool, Taggart!" said Barclay, finding his voice at last; but it was icy cold with undisguised hatred. "Don't you know what I can do to you?"

"You can do nothing to me, Barclay!" replied Robbie. "I have come to give you my resignation from the Royal Service."

"You are more of a fool than I took you for, Taggart. I must say, this comes as something of a surprise, even from you." Barclay was struggling to maintain his composure, but his eyes betrayed the fire burning within. The young fool was threatening action that would take revenge out of his hands. And to find himself powerless was unendurable to one such as Barclay.

"Does it?" said Robbie. "A surprise, you say? Perhaps . . . but doubtless not a disappointment. This is what you have hoped for, is it not?" he asked, his voice calming.

"If you are bitter about your years in the service, you have only yourself to blame."

"Have I?" said Robbie with raised eyebrow. "Perhaps you're right. I am to blame for putting up with such treatment as I have for so long."

Robbie paused momentarily. It was useless to argue further. He had said too much already. He had served honorably, and now he would leave with honor as well.

"As you say, Commander," he continued tersely. "I have no desire to debate with you. I will tender my official resignation tomorrow. I trust there will be no difficulty in waiving the remainder of my enlistment, knowing what a relief it will be to you to have me gone from your command?"

Barclay hesitated. Than a cold gleam crept into his eye. "I could block your resignation, you know, Taggart. I could make you stay, and could make life positively unendurable for you."

"But you won't, will you, Commander? The thought of having me gone will outweigh whatever delight you would take in crushing me still further under your thumb. I know you hate me, Commander. I could never understand why, until recently. But now I see it is because I represent a life you can never have—a life not bound to rank and privilege and station. And though you have been determined to destroy me, mine is the kind of spirit small men like you can never overpower. Though you would love to punish me further, in the end you would rather see me gone. The daily reminder of your own bondage to a system from which you cannot escape would be too great a trial for you. And when I am gone, Commander, it is I who will have been victorious, not you. For I shall be free."

Robbie stopped, as surprised by the eloquence of his passionate outburst as Barclay must have been.

The commander stared at him for a few moments with a look Robbie had never before seen in his eyes.

"I believe we can make satisfactory adjustments in your absence," he said at length. "As you indicated, to remove an unsightly blemish from the noble officer's stock is a greater good than for me to indulge the pleasure it would give me to see you chastened as you deserve."

Robbie turned without a salute, walked to the door and outside, without once looking back. As the fresh air again assaulted him, a great smile spread over his face. If his hat had still been on top of his head, he'd have tossed it into the air in delight. At last it was over!

Tomorrow would be a day of new beginnings, a new adventure! Where his steps would lead, in his wildest thoughts he could never have imagined. It would be a beginning that would take him upon a course that even he, in all his global sophistication, could not have charted. His journey would take him toward what his God had been preparing for him since the dawn of time—a life of growth, a spirit of wisdom, and a personhood of completion and fulfillment.

For as much as young sailor Robbie Taggart thought he was free, the true freedom of his manhood was still awaiting him. And it was toward this freedom—a freedom all men yearn for but few allow themselves to find—that his footsteps were now pointed.

Part II

Sea Tiger

8

The *Tiger's* Complement

When Robbie set foot upon the gangway of the *Sea Tiger*, he felt as though he was coming home. To a restless wanderer such as he, it was fitting that *home* should be a vessel capable of taking him anywhere, of reaching the ends of the earth, but with no port to call its own.

As he walked slowly up the thick wooden planks, Robbie concluded that no finer home had ever been his, even beneath the brilliant Highland stars of Scotland. The *Tiger's* mast towered majestically in the harbor, and added the suggestion of power to the graceful lines of her hull. At her prow was carved the figurehead of a Mandarin dressed in fiery red robes, carrying a scimitar in his right hand and gazing out on the glassy harbor with eyes that were indeed as fierce as a tiger's. With such an imposing figurehead, she could have been a warship, but she was built to do battle with the sea and the mighty elements of nature. And no soldier had ever faced a more merciless foe.

He stepped onto her shining teakwood deck, so absorbed in the glory of the ship that he hardly noticed that there was neither captain nor boatswain to greet him. He paused for a moment to feel the gentle movement—it was a good feeling, one he had missed. He moved slowly forward, taking in every familiar detail, pleased that he had forgotten nothing in his years away from the square-rigger.

His eyes picked out each line of rope and sheet, and quickly followed them to the sails they controlled. The seeming maze of complicated rigging was as clear in its integrated complexity as each finger on his hand.

Robbie gave a sigh, relieved. He had not been too long away.

"'She walks the waters like a thing of life, and seems to dare the elements to strife,'" came an unexpected, however melodious, voice from astern, disturbing the inner quietude that had stolen upon Robbie. He turned sharply to face the speaker, who sounded too much like an oracle to be thus found anywhere in the regions of London's shipyards. And what he beheld appeared indeed more a poet than any kind of seaman Robbie had ever seen, though he thought he had seen every conceivable type.

"Byron," said the man. He was several inches shorter than Robbie and appeared ten or twelve years older, but was in fact only thirty-four. His dark eyes studied Robbie momentarily with an odd mixture of mockery and sensitivity, holding for a moment on Robbie's face, then twitching quickly to find a temporary rest at some point over his shoulder. As Robbie drew closer he detected the unmistakable odor of whiskey about the man's person.

"Good morning, Mr. Byron—" Robbie began, but before he had the chance to utter another syllable he was cut short by the man's sudden burst of laughter.

"'There were gentlemen and there were seamen,'" the man quoted again through his mirth, "'in the Navy of Charles the Second. But the seamen were not gentlemen; and the gentlemen were not seamen.' That was Macaulay," he added.

"I see," said Robbie, unperturbed. "And I take it the first was from *Lord* Byron?"

"Correct you are! And please forgive my laughter. I thought a gentleman such as yourself—"

Now it was Robbie's turn to laugh. After four years of striving unsuccessfully to fit into a gentleman's world, how ironic it was that the first person he met in the world where he rightfully belonged should take him for a gentleman.

"I am better acquainted with rigs and sails than poems," said Robbie. "I am no gentleman, believe me."

"Then the pleasure is all the greater in meeting you," said the quoter of rhymes, thrusting out his hand. "I myself loathe the breed . . . Elliot Drew is the name."

Robbie took the offered hand, which looked slender, almost effeminate, but with hard calluses upon its surface.

A shout from the stern brought their conversation to an abrupt halt as they turned their attention toward it.

"Hey, Vicar!" said the newcomer. "Who you gots there?" As he was speaking the man lithely swung a bulky frame down the companion ladder from the raised quarter deck and approached the two.

"I'm not quite certain," answered the one called *Vicar*. "But if he wants a berth, I'd say give it to him. He looks like a good man."

"And what'd ye know, ye lubber!" the other replied roughly. "Ye wouldn't know a seaman from a wet rat."

"Perhaps because there's so little difference," rejoined Drew.

The newcomer merely grunted, then brusquely pushed the Vicar aside and approached Robbie face to face.

"I'm Jack Digger, Bo'sun[1]," said the large man, unsmiling and without the least inflection of welcome. He did not even offer one of his fleshy hands to Robbie. "If ye got business on the *Sea Tiger*, 'tis me ye'll be speakin' to."

This last was spoken almost like a reprimand for his interchange with Drew.

"There was no one on deck when I came aboard."

"Well, what's yer business?"

"I'm here to see the ship's master, Benjamin Pike."

Digger sized Robbie up and down with eyes that appeared as mere slits in his thick face. Robbie wondered that this cumbersome man could function on a ship in any capacity. However, he appeared fit, and the enormity of his bulk was by no means given over to fat. And his agile negotiation of the companion ladder gave indication that his size was no hindrance to him.

"What's yer name?" asked the bo'sun.

"Robbie Taggart."

"Taggart, eh?" His look and tone left little doubt that he was singularly unimpressed. "So ye're the new mate."

Robbie had not seen Pike since that night at the *Rum Runner*; was the old seaman so confident of Robbie's final decision that he had actually spread the word of his coming?

"Is the skipper available?"

Digger cocked his head toward Drew. "Run below an' fetch the cap'n," he ordered.

Drew complied, and soon disappeared down the main hatch. Robbie and the boatswain stood silently together. Digger peeled off a sweat-soaked bandana tied around his forehead, and with strong fingers squeezed it nearly dry.

---

1. Boatswain—petty officer who has charge of the deck crew and rigging.

"I'll be headin' back to work," he said at length, turning to leave.

"Tell me," said Robbie, and as he spoke the bo'sun stopped, "is that other fellow a member of the crew?"

"Just barely," said Digger with a smirk; "he's an ordinary seaman. Now if ye don't mind, I gots me work." Without waiting further leave, he swung away, scrambled up the ladder of the quarter deck where he had apparently been engaged in some activity at the back of the deck house.

Robbie tried to return his attention to the ship, but now his thoughts were filled with these two men he had just met. Two more dissimilar characters he could not hope to encounter. He wondered what the rest of the crew would be like. As first mate, Robbie would be required to command them all. And though he did not fear leadership, he knew that every man was capable of presenting his own special kind of problems to someone in authority. He was not left to ponder his fate long, however, for within a few minutes Pike climbed into view from the main hatch.

"Robbie—ha, ha! You son of a sea cook!" Pike's barking laugh compensated for in volume what it lacked in merriment. "I knew I'd see yer ugly face afore long!"

"I suppose I knew it too." Robbie drew the words out thoughtfully. Then he laughed lightly: "Well, where do I sign on?"

"No need for that, laddie. I'll show you around the ship an' we can end off in my cabin an' have a drink on it." Pike threw his arm around Robbie's shoulders, and they started off.

Pike launched immediately into a detailed and comprehensive description of his ship, such that would have bored most laymen. But to one like Robbie the words felt like spring water to the mouth of a thirsty man, and he listened to every detail with fascination. The *Sea Tiger* was an Aberdeen-built clipper, first launched in 1869. She was 930 tons and had distinguished herself nicely in eleven years of life. During six years in the China trade she had acquitted herself well, twice making the homeward passage with the new crop of tea in under a hundred days. But speed was not her only strength. When steamers making passage via the Suez Canal began to monopolize the tea trade, most lovely clippers had been relegated to long distant voyages to Melbourne or Sydney or South America, picking up whatever cargos were available. But the *Sea Tiger* still demonstrated her great stamina and had weathered the torturous gales of Cape Horn three times since then, and though dismasted once on that run, she had managed to limp into port only a week behind schedule. She was one of the few clippers still able to compete strongly in the changing world of late 19th-century shipping. She was well-seasoned now, yet still very much in her prime with many voyages left in her.

Robbie liked what he saw. There was something comfortable and friendly about the *Tiger*, yet at the same time sturdy and reassuring. Out in the middle of the ocean a man trusted his life to the worthiness of his ship, and Robbie could feel—as if through the creaking timbers themselves—that such a trust would not be misplaced aboard the *Sea Tiger*.

"What's her cargo?" asked Robbie as he climbed down into the hold of the ship. The air was thick and stale and too humid for comfort, yet to Robbie it only added to the mystique he had been missing for four years.

"General is all," answered Pike. "Sheet iron, copper, yard goods— nothin' interestin'."

Robbie slapped his hand on a large wooden crate. "This one's not marked," he said casually.

"Them cursed loaders!" Pike exclaimed. "Can't do nothin' right. I'll get it taken care of!" Pike seemed suddenly nervous on account of the unlabeled crates, and hurried Robbie off in another direction.

"Will we pick up tea in Shanghai?" asked Robbie as they continued through the hold.

"Ha!" barked Pike scornfully. "Them days is over, laddie. All we get is trinkets now—matting, paper, rattans, feathers!" He spat the last word out bitterly, as an ugly vision of a tea-laden steamship crossed his mind, all but blotting out memories of the glory days of the tea runs from the East.

Robbie wondered about the great riches Pike had promised. This hardly seemed the sort of cargo that would make a man wealthy. Had he been exaggerating merely to entice Robbie aboard? Yet what could be his purpose in that? They had never been *that* close as friends, so as to justify such efforts on Pike's part to lure Robbie away from Her Majesty's service.

Robbie shrugged off the question. He was, after all, a good sailor, a hard worker. Perhaps that was reason enough.

"But why go to China at all?" he asked.

"The owners of the Cathay Mercantile are old die-hards, I'm sup- posin'," answered Pike. "They won't give in t' the new ways without a fight. They're still tryin' to play by the old rules. An' the *Sea Tiger*'s worthy o' the attempt. But if we can't pick up a cargo in Shanghai, I've orders to swing down t' Melbourne."

Pike swung up the ladder almost effortlessly, slinging his crutch over his shoulder by a leather strap, then pulling himself up with extraordinarily strong arms. "As I recall, laddie," he said with a grin, "ye was always fond of the galley . . ."

Robbie laughed. "Show me the way!"

The master of the galley was an elderly Chinese man whose unpronounceable name had been Anglicized years earlier—no doubt originally somewhat tongue-in-cheek—and the name had stuck. Ever since he had been known simply as Johnnie Smith. At seventy, the man was tough and sinewy, dressed in a combination of seaman's attire of canvas trousers and peaked cap, and an oriental silk shirt. When he turned away from them, Robbie saw that he wore a braid stretching down most of the length of his back. He greeted them in a stream of Chinese which, working in combination with his furiously waving hands, gave the distinct impression of anger toward the intruders.

"Shut up, Johnnie!" spat Pike coldly. "You want something, you bloody well better learn to speak like a civilized human being!"

Pike's outburst was met with another verbal barrage. Robbie would soon learn that words from Johnnie's mouth hardly ceased from morning till night.

"Foreigners!" growled Pike scornfully. "But he can cook. I ne'er knew a ship's vittles t' be so good. The only man ever could match him would be mysel', but then it wouldn't do for a captain to be putterin' about the galley, now would it?"

"It's just as well," quipped Robbie. "I don't seem to have the same memories of your cooking."

"You know how to hurt a man, Robbie," he said, attempting a laugh to accompany his humor, but the effort fell short. Then turning to Johnnie, he yelled, "Fix us some vittles!"

Johnnie replied in Chinese that sounded as if it were the equivalent of, "Not on your life, you one-legged blag'ard!" But notwithstanding his outburst, he immediately began gathering the ingredients to a first-class captain's lunch.

"He can understand you?" asked Robbie.

"The ol' devil! He understands every word you an' I are sayin' an' can probably speak better English than either one o' us. But he's a stubborn ol' Chinaman!"

While they waited for their food, another crew member poked his head into the galley. His round, perpetually sun-burned, fair-skinned face was topped with thinning blond hair. In his early fifties and short of height, the man was broad of chest with long muscular arms. Pike introduced him as Torger Overlie the coxswain.[1]

"Glad to meet you," he said after he and Robbie had shaken hands, his thick Norwegian accent contrasting colorfully with the cook's, and his grin revealing a perfect set of straight, white teeth. "We have da new fittings in and ready to inspect," he said to Pike.

"I'll be right out," replied the skipper.

When Overlie had departed, Pike shook his head dismally. "More foreigners," he said. "I'm glad ye joined us, Robbie."

"And what's your trouble with foreigners, Ben?" asked Robbie. "Aren't Scotsmen considered foreigners down here?"

"And what makes you think I'm a Scotsman, lad?"

"I always took it for granted. You *sound* enough like one, at least most of the time."

"Purely feigned, my boy! I put on whatever tongue suits me best—a bit o' Cockney, a bit o' Scots."

"You're a remarkable man, Ben, I have to admit! You've got more sides to you than an African diamond!"

When they had finished lunch, the best Robbie had ever enjoyed aboard a ship, Pike led the way back to the top deck and fresh air. Robbie breathed deeply and looked around him with satisfaction.

"The rest of the crew'll be comin' aboard soon," said Pike. "Sixteen in all, countin' you."

"A bit on the small size to run a clipper, isn't it?"

"I'll take sixteen *good* men any day over fifty dullards!"

Pike's so-called "good" men proved to be a thorough hodgepodge of characters, of which those he had already met were a typical introduction. Robbie wondered if the captain could have selected a stranger lot of shipfellows. Already he'd met the genteel Drew, the surly bo'sun Digger, the talkative Chinese cook, and the grinning Norwegian coxswain. But the bunch ushered aboard that afternoon by Digger made these Robbie had first seen ordinary by comparison. Unkempt and bleary-eyed, they had probably been picked by Digger at the various boardinghouses for sailors after a long night of carousing.

As they shuffled on board, at least half of the ten men looked not just willing, but in some cases eager to pick a fight with anyone who might cross them. The look of one was particularly alarming, yet he seemed on friendlier terms than the rest with the bo'sun, sauntering next to him

1. The coxswain steers the ship.

apart from the others. Robbie later learned he was the ship's carpenter, a wiry, swarthy-skinned Arab who was known as Ahmed Turk. It seemed he was accorded some authority among the group, and, as Robbie learned soon enough, both Turk and the bo'sun exerted considerable influence over a certain contingent of the crew. The bo'sun did so by the sheer might of his imposing being and his position of responsibility in the hierarchy of the ship's authority structure. But Turk leveled his influence with one piercing glance from his black eyes that looked out in evil stare from a face scarred with evidence of fights innumerable.

Immediately Robbie could sense the man meant trouble. Never had he beheld such scars. They ran from forehead to cheek, two in particular perfectly bisecting each eye. Robbie didn't want to even consider what awful rite or battle could have inflicted such wounds. Moreover, he didn't want to think of the possibility of opposing the man who had survived such an ordeal. Yet if he was to be first mate, having to be in charge of the whole motley crew, how would it be possible, in months at sea, to avoid an impasse with Turk? He hoped it wouldn't come to that.

At first glance these new arrivals hardly seemed worthy to fulfill Pike's boast, and if Robbie had been in the habit of praying, he might have prayed that his initial estimation was wrong. As if to confirm the worst of his fears, Robbie's eyes gave him another surprise when they reached the end of the line. Wondering to himself why he didn't see Kerr walking on board, considering his apparent and puzzling intimacy with Pike, Robbie looked up to see one Jeremiah Lackey, whose presence seemed always cause for alarm. Robbie knew him well; he had sailed on the *Macao*. He had to be nearly seventy by now, and looked every day of it, with a face as lined as a map, leathery and toothless. But his yellowed eyes were bright and alert. He was one of those ageless creatures who always seemed to haunt the sea and anything that sailed upon it, and though he looked ancient, he did not appear a day older than when Robbie had last seen him nine years earlier. It was very likely he had always looked seventy.

"Why, bless me!" he croaked like a piece of old rigging, "'tis little Robbie Taggart. If we dinna sink or flounder or mut'ny betwixt ourselves, we'll do all right!" But the moment his feet touched the deck, his wrinkled countenance sagged. "'Tis a rum ship! I can feel it! Saints preserve us!"

Robbie had never forgotten the man's capacity for instilling gloom and fear. By Lackey's estimation, any ship that dared wet its hull was always on the verge of some catastrophe visited upon it by an angry Providence. He had taken upon himself the role of prophet of doom. And if none of his prophetic pronouncements ever came to pass, it hardly mattered.

Seamen were a superstitious lot, and he could always find plenty of timorous souls willing enough to listen, and to fear the *one* time when his words just might turn out to be true.

9

Midnight Visitations

Robbie was surprised to learn they would sail the next day. When he commented to Pike on his good fortune to show up when he did, the unlikely captain merely responded with a mysterious half grin, as if he knew luck had nothing to do with it.

Sleepless in his bunk later, Robbie tossed about restlessly. Finally around midnight, attributing his lack of sleep to anticipation of the following morning's departure, he rose and made his way topside, hoping a stroll on deck might soothe his nerves into slumber.

He climbed the companion ladder to the forehatch, and had only just poked his head above deck when he saw three shadowy figures crossing up the gangway. Robbie would have given them little thought except by their very stealth, with many covert glances over their shoulders, and their obvious attempts to remain quiet, the men drew the attention that Robbie instinctively felt was the very thing they wanted to avoid.

Two of the men carried a crate, hoisted above their shoulders, strikingly similar to the unmarked containers he had seen earlier in the hold, and were followed by another man limping along after them. Robbie was about to call out when he realized that the third man was Pike himself. He decided his best course of action was to remain silent. Curiosity was not one of Robbie's strongest characteristics, be it virtue or fault, and he was content to shrug off the incident as none of his concern and of little sinister significance. If Pike had private belongings he wished delivered to the ship under cover of darkness that was his business—he was master of the ship. But whatever their intent, Robbie judged it better to pause several moments until the trio had descended down the aft hatch leading to Pike's cabin before he completed his exit onto the deck.

The crisp February air stung Robbie's face and invigorated him rather than offering promise of sleep. He remembered a brace that had been troublesome that afternoon, and wandered to the foremast to have a look. Forward of the mast he noted Drew perched somewhat precariously on the capstan puffing on a pipe, attempting to effect the perfect smoke ring, but finding each of his efforts immediately whisked away by the gentle night breeze.

"Evening, Drew," said Robbie, climbing the ladder to the raised forecastle where the capstan was located. He was quite willing to forget the brace in light of an opportunity to chat with this odd mixture of sailor and poet known as the *Vicar*. For of all the assorted assemblage he had viewed that day, this one intrigued Robbie the most.

"Ah, 'tis the first mate," replied Drew. "Out for an evening stroll, or were you perhaps investigating our late night visitors?" Drew's words were slightly slurred and his eyes bloodshot. Robbie suspected his condition was not entirely due to lack of sleep.

"Only out for a walk . . . I couldn't sleep," Robbie replied.

"Sleeping with one eye cocked, as you sailors like to say, will do you no harm on this little cruise."

"What do you mean by that?"

"Well, 'tis plain to see that Captain Pike—and I use the term *captain* only for the present. I don't know about you, but *I've* never heard of a man in his condition being given his own ship! Makes me wonder, Taggart— but, as I said, 'tis plain to see that he did not recruit his crew from any Church of England congregation, no, nor a Dissenting one either."

Drew took a long draw on his pipe before speaking again. "And those late night deliveries—this was not the first."

"A master has a right to his personal ventures."

"True, true," agreed the Vicar, blowing out a long stream of smoke. "And I'm the last man with a right to judge his actions, for we are told not to judge our neighbor. But there is still the matter of the crew—of which, I might add, you are rather the anomaly."

"I was thinking the very same thing about you," replied Robbie with a friendly grin. "And what do you mean by *you sailors*? What do you call yourself?"

Drew laughed dryly. "Certainly not a sailor! I just humor the men I work for by going along with their little games of pitting their masculinity against the powers of the sea. It's all futile, you know. You can't win.

The *Powers*"—and as he spoke the word he gestured grandiosely toward the darkness of the sky above—"of the heavens are infinite beside our puny little selves."

"If you can't win, and you're no sailor," said Robbie, "then why are you here?"

"Oh, I said *you* can't win—you sailor types. Men like me, we're the only ones who *can* win, because we recognize the futility in the universe." He laughed again, but there was almost a pathetic ring to it. "Don't you see, Taggart? It's all a gigantic, cosmic game! But you've got to know the rules! And most of your sailors—they don't know what they're up against. But," he added, in a softer tone, almost as if it pained him to make the admission, "I fit in more than you might suppose, Taggart. I do my job, and try not to let my past interfere in any other way than through the sayings that seem so bent on coming out of my mouth."

"And where do you hail from?"

"From Glasgow, where else? Ye mean ye canna tell me Lalan's dialect frae the rest o' 'em?"

Robbie laughed. "No, to tell the truth. Your English is as perfect as any born Londoner."

"That's what Oxford will do to a man. But as for yourself, I still detect a ring of the Highlands about you—Grampian, I would say. Perhaps Aberdeenshire."

"Bravo!" said Robbie. "But my father traveled about so much that we never settled in on the speech of any one place. I suppose that's why I'm just a conglomeration—a true Britisher!"

"So you may say. But once a Highlander always a Highlander, or so I've heard."

"You're not so far off the mark there, Drew! Well, it is nice to find a fellow Scot among this aggregate mass of the world's peoples!"

"Ah yes—Scotland, the fairest homeland among all homelands," he said with overstated feeling, before launching into verse:

"'O Scotia! my dear, my native soil!
For whom my warmest wish to Heaven is sent!
Long may thy hardy sons of rustic toil
Be blest with health, and peace, and sweet content!'"

quoted Drew, with just enough sarcasm to his voice to rob the poem of all sincerity.

"That is—" he began to add, but Robbie interrupted.

"I do know Burns, Mr. Drew," he said, recalling their meeting that morning.

Drew laughed again, the laugh with which Robbie would soon become quite familiar. Like Pike's, it held no merriment, but unlike the skipper's, it did contain a good deal of humor—though not always of a pleasant sort.

"Of course," he said. "Every Scotsman knows 'Robbie the great bard,' if nothing else." Then he quickly added, "No offense intended!"

"None taken," replied Robbie good-naturedly. Folding his arms over his chest, Robbie leaned against the forecastle rail, warming to the man despite his propensity toward cynicism. "Might I ask how you came by the label of *Vicar*?"

"Oh, that," Drew said, waving his hand carelessly. "Nothing but a nasty rumor circulating that I was once a man of the cloth."

"Only a rumor?"

"Come now, Taggart," he replied. "One look on my unesteemable and decrepit person ought to answer that question." Then he deftly changed the subject. "There are likewise rumors circulating concerning you, to the effect that you resigned a commission in the Royal Navy to join this rat-trap."

Robbie caught Drew's evasive ploy, and though disappointed to get nothing more from the Vicar, decided to let the matter pass. "*That* rumor is indeed true," he answered. "I gave up the constriction of a prison for the freedom of this . . . rat-trap, as you so unjustly call it."

"Was it not Samuel Johnson who likened the life of the sailor to that of a prison? His comment, preserved for all time in the annals of our country's literature, was that being in a ship was to be in jail with the chance of being drowned to top it off. Moreover, a man in prison has more room, better food, and commonly better company to boot."

"Is that how you see it, Drew?"

"A man is his own prison, Taggart." With the words he reached into his coat and withdrew a small flask. "'Tis a cold night—I could use some warming for the innards. Won't you join me?" He uncorked the flask and held it out to Robbie.

"No thanks," Robbie replied. "I don't wish to trade one prison for another."

Drew laughed. "Well said, my friend! You've a wit to match your amicable nature." He had a swig from his flask, then wiped a grimy sleeve across his mouth.

"You know, of course," said Robbie, nodding his head toward the flask, "there will be none of that after we set sail."

"To be sure . . . to be sure," answered Drew lightly. "All the more reason to indulge now before the dawn breaks. But have no fear, Mr. Royal Navy Taggart, I'm a perfect teetotaler at sea." He lifted the flask once more to his lips and drank long and greedily. When he finished, he turned the bottle upside down, showing it to be quite empty. "It's gone now. I'll behave myself from here on." He jammed the cork back into place with morose finality, and dropped the flask into his coat pocket.

"Good night, Drew," said Robbie. "I've enjoyed our talk."

"You are too kind, Taggart. Especially when I can see our talk has disturbed you."

"You are a difficult man to understand," Robbie answered truthfully enough, for he realized their conversation had only deepened the enigma of the Vicar.

"Then don't try. 'A double-minded man is unstable in all his ways.' So beware, Robbie!" He knocked his pipe on the capstan, then slid to his feet. "I shall join you, for I see no point in prolonging the dread coming of morning any longer."

As he gained his feet, he swayed dangerously, his knees almost buckling under him. Robbie jumped forward and caught him, then slung the Vicar's arm around his shoulder, and led him all the way to the crew's quarters below. At the doorway Drew paused before staggering to his berth.

"You're a good Scotsman, my friend," he said, with an intensity that Robbie decided could be as much from the alcohol as from sincerity.

"Get to bed, Drew. Tomorrow's going to be a busy day."

"And I think you should know," Drew continued as if Robbie had not spoken. "All those nasty rumors . . . they are entirely true. A *stickit minister*, that's me, with all the privileges and mockeries thereof." He wheeled around and disappeared into the darkness of the cabin, where the snores and movements of his sleeping shipmates accentuated the lateness of the hour.

Robbie turned and found his way to his own cabin. He was no nearer finding sleep than when he had left an hour before. The entire conversation with Drew replayed itself in his mind, and he found the man no less puzzling now, lying in bed, than he had seemed in the chill air on deck.

As sleep eventually began to overtake him, a new thought caught hold in his mind. But just as quickly as it flitted into his consciousness, he quickly and willingly let it go, for it was not something he wanted to dwell on. He and the Vicar were, oddly, very much alike.

10

The *Tiger* Sets Sail

Robbie awoke the next morning refreshed despite only four hours sleep.

Johnnie was already busy over a pot of gruel in the galley. He tossed the cook a cheerful "good morning" and set about doing what would have naturally fallen to a first mate before Pike came above deck. All the gear would have to be cleared or secured for running, the hatches battened down, the sails prepared for trimming, some of the anchor cable brought in. Enthusiastic at the mere thought of being at sea, Robbie's buoyant countenance was greeted with scowls by Digger and Turk as they came on deck.

By the time Pike came up, the fore and mizzen yards had been trimmed and the ship was ready and waiting for the skipper's final commands. He appeared none the worse for his late-night activities. But Robbie knew well that if anything, Pike was tough. Life at sea was not an easy life for any man, and Pike had survived that life for nearly thirty years with only one leg. Robbie knew few of the particulars of Pike's accident, or what struggles he had faced as a result afterward, for he was extremely private concerning his personal life. But Robbie did know that Pike had been very near to making his first mate's certificate when it had occurred. He had no doubt cherished hopes of achieving a master's license by the time he was thirty. Yet those hopes had been amputated along with his leg. A seasoned and proven master might well be kept on—handicap or no. But a young man just breaking into command had little hope of being given a fair shake. Yet the sea was the only life Pike had known since he had shipped aboard an East Indiaman at the age of ten.

After the accident he had knocked about from ship to ship, a deck hand here, a cook there. He had been sweating in the galley of the *Macao* when Robbie met him. Probably in consideration of his friendship with Robbie's father, Pike immediately took the novice sailor under his wing.

Pike had been fortunate, indeed, to have achieved his present position. Robbie had never imagined Pike as a leader of men. Even now the thought of him as a captain was incongruous to everything Robbie had ever known of the man. He was a loner, even surly at times—though not often to Robbie. As a seaman he was certainly adequate, perhaps even above average. But commanding a ship required so much more. This would be his second run as master, and Robbie had heard of no ill reports from his first voyage. Thus Robbie refrained from passing judgment. Benjamin Pike deserved a chance, even at this late stage in his life.

Setting sail would be but the first test of Pike's mettle. Yet it would be a vital one, and would go a long way to set the tone of his command. Everything had to be timed to perfection for a smooth departure. If the anchor was raised before the sails were properly set, the ship might lay to helplessly; but if the sails were set before the anchor came up, the ship would heave forward, causing the anchor to grip even more firmly to the bottom. Such a rough, disjointed beginning was as portentous of evil to follow as embarking on a voyage on a Friday, an absolute taboo among sailors and a fact certain to be made much of by a doomsday prophet such as Lackey.

Robbie walked to the forward end of the *Tiger* to supervise the raising of the anchor. But when he arrived, Digger was already standing on the forecastle deck, apparently in complete control, in none-too-subtle defiance of the mate's traditional position during cast-off. It was foolish to make a row of such a small thing on the first day of the voyage, and Robbie's initial reaction was to relinquish him the position. Perhaps he had merely forgotten.

Yet as Robbie glanced quickly around, he realized that the eyes of the other men were fixed upon him. The time had come, sooner than he had anticipated, when he would have to prove his strength. This was a test of wills, and he knew that the men would subconsciously follow the one who emerged as strongest. No man in his position could hope to command respect and obedience if he retreated from such a simple and yet flagrant act of insubordination. Already Digger had his contingent of followers, a half-dozen or so men who had made it clear, albeit silently, that they were only following Robbie's orders because Digger had given them leave to do so. They were humoring the newcomer, and still seemed to regard him with the sort of skepticism they would accord an eighteen-year-old novice. If Robbie bowed at this point to Digger's defiance, he would no doubt lose even further the respect of the rest of the crew.

Robbie approached and focused a steady gaze on Digger.

"I believe you have the starboard watch, mate," he said coolly.

For a long, tense moment Digger did not budge. Robbie could feel the mental processes working in the man's thick head.

Finally he opened his mouth. "Now, just you—" he began, then stopped abruptly. "I must've gotten confused," he said after a pause. But even as he stepped down, he shot Robbie a piercing glance of defiance, almost as if to throw down the gauntlet with a glare.

Robbie swung up on the forecastle deck, and as he turned he caught a trailing glimpse of Pike hobbling away from behind the main mast. So, Robbie's apparent victory had in reality been but a superficial one; the muscular boatswain had only succumbed under the scrutiny of the captain. The incident had been nothing but a stand-off, and there would inevitably be another confrontation, more than likely at sea—the most dangerous place of all for such a showdown. Robbie had known plenty of men like Digger; the only strength they knew was measured by the might of their fists and the intimidation of others.

But such thoughts of impending trouble were shoved out of Robbie's mind almost immediately; the work before him was demanding enough at present, made more so by his inexperience of recent years. And if Digger's challenge had been observed by the men, how much more would they be watching his ability to command the weighing of anchor? In the end, if the *Sea Tiger* made a perfect departure, the first mate could be praised no less than the captain.

Robbie fell to his work with gusto. He knew his ship, even in the short time he had been aboard her. And he knew his work.

"Ready on starboard?" he called to the men on the right side of the ship.

"Ready on port?"

"Prepare to cast off!" he called, then he jumped down and ran to where Elliot Drew was having difficulty managing his sail assignment in the rising breeze. "Steady, Drew," said Robbie, correcting the angle. "Now . . . you got it?"

Drew nodded, but said nothing.

Robbie ran back to the forecastle, surveyed proudly the scene before him, visually checked each man's position and that of every sail, then called out:

"Weigh anchor!"

Almost immediately he felt the first tentative, jerking surges of the great clipper beneath his feet as it floated free from its encumbrance. But there was not an instant to lose. "Sails, men . . . now!" he called out.

Immediately the great flapping sound of the wind against the unrolling of the magnificent white canvas sails filled the air. *What a grand and glorious sight*, thought Robbie!

Gradually the enormous white wings filled with air. Robbie left his post again and ran aft, where he grabbed up a slack rigging and held it firm. As he did so, his eyes were on Drew, but the Vicar now seemed to have his assignment in hand. As soon as he had the rope secure he hurried around checking all the rest of the sails, from the poop deck to the fore. By the time he again took his position on the forecastle, she was well underway. He paused a moment to relish the feel of the rolling deck beneath him.

What a supreme pleasure it was! And though the speed was not yet up to two knots, the gentle breeze fanned his face as he peered forward in the direction of their course. The day was perfect for his first sail as a free man again. High white clouds scattered across the sea of blue above; below, turbulent whitewater was churned up under the *Tiger's* prow. Robbie breathed deeply with satisfaction. He had done it! They were underway, and he had not disgraced himself.

It mattered little to Robbie who received the praise, for what was important was that the *Sea Tiger* had again made a good account of herself. It would not have done to make a grand ship as theirs a laughingstock. But she had demonstrated her nobility that day, just as a living steed with good bloodlines would have. Her sails unfurled and filled with the wind, she gradually increased momentum and sped away from Gravesend, where they had lain at anchor, toward Southend with great purpose, and out to the Channel. Robbie did not want to leave the deck—he could have viewed that sight for a lifetime, he thought. But he had matters to discuss with Pike, who had retired to his cabin for a rest from the rigors of the morning. Eventually Robbie tore himself away, walked along the deck, descended through the hatch, and made his way into the bosom of the ship.

Robbie had just lifted his hand to the door when he stopped short; the bo'sun's voice from inside arrested his attention, raised well above propriety.

"It's a bloody rum deal, I tell ye!" he barked.

"You was out of line up there, Digger," returned Pike. "I told you how it was goin' to be."

"Well, I don't like it!"

"Ye made that clear at the beginnin'," rejoined the skipper, "an' I told ye that you'd do it my way or not at all."

"It don't make sense."

"I got my reasons."

"What'd ye want the blimey bluejacket for anyway?"

"That's my business. Yours is to do what I say."

"I just better be gettin' my usual cut."

Robbie turned and left the door, wanting to hear no more. Whatever Pike's mysterious words could mean he did not know, nor whether they were spoken in reference to him. Was there something more here than Pike's initial assertions when they had met at the *Rum Runner* about Robbie needing the freedom of the sea?

He quickly let it go, perhaps unwilling to think ill of a man who had been in a sense his mentor and his father's friend. Loyalty had always been something of a code of honor with Robbie, one that usually stood him in good stead. But there were times when his fealty could blind him to realities that others would have been able to spot in an instant. Pike had always been good to Robbie, whatever his reputation with others. Robbie had heard him called crazy, and worse. And he had occasionally seen flashes of, if not insanity, certainly a lack of stability and balance. But Pike had been through a great deal, Robbie told himself, and he could excuse his eccentricities. It was Pike who had visited him every day on his sickbed after the accident on the *Macao* that had nearly killed him. Visited him, that is, until he suddenly shipped out on another vessel.

And Pike had also made an effort to find him all those years after they had been separated. He owed something to the man for that alone, notwithstanding that Pike and his father had once sailed together—no little thing among comrades of the sea. So Robbie went a long way to gloss over Pike's faults, of which there were more than a few, even if they did seem sometimes to border on lunacy. Whatever had been the implication of Pike's words to the bo'sun, Robbie refused to attach any sinister meaning to them. And, as if to cement the validity of Robbie's decision in his mind, in the days that followed, Pike treated him with a respect bordering occasionally on deference, as if Robbie himself were captain of the ship.

As the days passed, almost without his noticing it at first, Robbie gradually developed his own contingent of loyal followers, those who saw in the young lieutenant not only strength of limb but a seasoned savvy in practical matters of ocean travel and a sensitivity to each individual under his command. These saw in Robbie one they could trust; and they did trust him, refusing to be cowed by Digger's size, brute strength, and position of authority under Robbie, or by Turk's silent menace. Though Robbie had not set out to exert his position over the men of the crew, most who observed him in action could not fail to see his ability. It was clear, whatever other motives swirled beneath the surface of his complex and cynical face, Pike's choice of first mate had been well made. But it was not only Robbie's grasp of the ship and its workings that made him a first mate worthy of any crew member's trust—though at sea such an understanding is vital. The men who followed him could also not fail to appreciate his fairness and honesty and sympathy to those about him. Robbie was, in a word, a leader.

As greatly as Robbie despised any splitting of a crew into factions, knowing that such divisiveness could prove fatal on a deep-sea voyage, he could not seem to do anything to prevent it aboard the *Tiger*. Try as he might to gain the respect of the boatswain and those closest to him, it was not long before he accepted the inevitable—that for the present a reconciliation was next to impossible. And if Digger and the others were bent on resisting him, perhaps it was for the best that he possessed a loyal following of his own.

11

Harmony at Sea

Fair seas accompanied the *Sea Tiger* through the Channel. The wind held steady off their port quarter, the skies remained clear, and on the Saturday evening of their first week out, the dark evening canopy boasted stars as large as party lanterns. The moon would be rising in the east before long, and even now a strange, ghostly light on the horizon portended her golden coming. Below there was nothing but water. The phosphorescent whiteness from the caps of the waves and from the turbulence of the ship's prow cutting through the blackness lent an eerie luminescence to the night; it seemed as if the stars and the glow from the water's surface were somehow reflections of one another. If there were other vessels across the watery void, they could neither be seen nor heard, as the wind-borne ships cut silently through the water, each on her own individual course. The masts of the *Tiger* were at their full height, and though the mainsail was loose, the foresail and jib were both full, and she ran before the wind as if hungry for the unknown infinite spaces that lay ahead.

Two hours later, the moon had risen to reign glorious in the heavens. Her light dulled the stars, but cast an energizing glow on a wide swath cut across the waters between herself and the *Tiger*. And that mystery of mysteries of the moon and the sea, the reflection remained ever the same, yet was ever changing as the *Tiger's* relentless motion coursed through the night.

As Robbie stood on the poop gazing out on the wondrous sight, breathing deeply of the salty, watery sea air which is life to the lungs of a sailor, he had to admit that he felt good. He had made the right decision. This was the life he was made for, not some Naval office!

There was, despite favorable winds and clear skies, always work to be done in plenty. Robbie took pride in the ship, even though it was not his own, especially in that Pike at times seemed woefully neglectful of maintenance. Robbie had set the crew to scrubbing, scraping, polishing, and mending, along with general ongoing repairs which were always part of any ship's required health.

But tonight he had taken the helm, set a lookout on the forecastle, and sent Torger Overlie to fetch his harmonica. And it was clear the eight men of the watch appreciated this opportunity to sit back and relax.

The men of the evening watch reclined here and there on the poop deck at the *Tiger's* stern, while Torger began the familiar strains of "The Bonny Sailor." Robbie chuckled to himself at the fact that the old Norseman was so well versed in British tunes. After the Norwegian played it through once, the men joined with the words:

> Fair Sally lov'd a bonny seaman,
>> With tears she sent him out to roam,
> Young Thomas lov'd no other woman,
>> But left his heart with her at home.
> She view'd the seas from off the hill,
> And as she turned her spinning wheel,
>> Sung of her bonny seaman.
>
> The winds grew high, and she grew pale,
>> To see the weather cock turn round,
> When, lo! she spy'd her bonny seaman
>> Come singing o'er the fallow ground.
> With nimble haste he leapt the stile,

> And Sally met him with a smile,
>> And hugged her bonny seaman.

A few of the men tried to harmonize, others croaked out in their crusty monotones, and the breeze carried their strangely melancholy voices off through the night as if they might be meant to linger eternally in the air, perhaps to greet other sailors whose ships would one day pass through these same waters.

Nothing can compare to an evening like this! Robbie thought. Everything was in perfect accord. When the sea was friendly and the winds favorable, all was well. Robbie noted that even several of the bo'sun's crowd, who happened to be in Robbie's watch, had joined in with the others, not so inclined toward antagonism when they were out from under the influence of Digger or Turk.

> This knife, the gift of lovely Sally,
>> I still have kept for her dear sake;
> A thousand times, in amorous folly,
>> Your name I carv'd upon the deck;
> Again the happy pledge returns
> To tell how truly Thomas burns,
>> How truly burns for Sally.
>
> This thimble thou didst give thy Sally,
>> When this I saw, I thought on you.
> Then why does Tom stand and dilly dally.
>> When yonder steeple's in our view?
> Tom, never to occasion blind,
> Straight took her in her yielding mind,
>> And went to church with Sally.

Robbie sang along, for he knew the old song well. It was hardly surprising, he thought, that while at sea—the place most of these men loved better than any other—they would sing lovingly of home and sweethearts. It was a lonely life. But each had—for his own reasons—pledged himself to the sea. Yet the memories came more readily on a night such as this, and cast their merriment into nostalgic and pensive tones. Neither was it strange that hard-bitten men whose solitary existence was often predicated on the supposed strength derived from keeping their feelings and emotions to themselves would, when led by such a simple device as a harmonica, break into song as if they were children.

Torger had just begun "Fan Left on Shore" when Robbie heard soft footsteps approach from behind. He turned and saw Elliot Drew.

"I heard you singing," he said. "Why don't I take the helm and you can go down and join them?"

"I'm enjoying it well enough from here. Thanks, Drew, but there's no need to keep you from the festivities."

"You'd not be keeping me, to be sure," replied the Vicar, leaning back against the stern rail and folding his arms across his chest. If he meant to effect a swagger, it was quite lost on his slender and wholly unathletic frame. Only his eyes, full as they were of their customary sarcasm, came close to the image he may have wanted to convey. "I don't quite fancy singing songs about women just as well left on shore. These blokes sound almost as if they *wanted* to settle down with the girl they left behind!"

"Perhaps it's true," said Robbie, staring ahead at the moonlit wake left by the running ship.

"Ach! They'd go crazy—the whole lot of them," laughed Drew scornfully. "Besides, for all their songs and poems of love, they'd never find her waiting once they got there. Women!—they're an unfaithful lot. And most of these men are just sea-bound drifters. What woman'd have a one of them?"

"Again it seems you think none too highly of your fellow comrades."

"And what's the use of it? But what about you, Mr. First Mate Taggart? Do you have a young woman waiting on shore?"

Drew's voice carried almost the tone of a challenge to Robbie to dare answer.

"No," replied Robbie, drawing the word out thoughtfully. "There is no one waiting for me."

"But there *is* someone who fills your thoughts." The Vicar's words were a statement, not a question.

"I suppose you're right," said Robbie.

"Ah ha! Just as I said."

"But she is married now—to another man. She fills my thoughts only as a pleasant memory. But not as you might think. I love her still, but I respect her new husband and bear them both but the best of wishes."

"Ah, Taggart! Spoken like a true stoic gentleman! No tears of remorse for you, eh? Stiff upper lip and all that?"

Robbie said nothing. For once Drew's cynicism fell on unwilling ears. He decided it was time to turn the tables. "And you?" he asked meaningfully.

"I stand with my brother, the Apostle Paul, who said, 'To the unmarried and widows, it is good for them if they abide even as I.' *He* was a confirmed bachelor, you know."

"But you sound more like you despise the whole of the weaker sex, rather than objecting on any more utopian grounds related to bachelorhood."

"I loathe them. Why else would I have condemned myself to this monastery upon the water?"

"Why indeed?" echoed Robbie, feeling only part of the story must have been revealed. "From your words it is apparent that you loathe women *and* men, and disdain your fellow seamen. Is there anything you *do* like?"

"Hmmm . . . how perceptive of you, Taggart. You find the old Vicar out, down to his vilest secrets!" He paused, rubbed his unshaven chin for a few moments, then quoted, "'For no man ever yet hated his own flesh; but nourisheth and cherisheth it . . .'"

"So, you like yourself," said Robbie. "That's how you answer my question. I suppose that is something."

"'Tis nothing at all!" countered Drew quickly. "What kind of moron would care what happened to a wretch such as this?" he held out his arms to indicate himself.

Robbie studied him a moment, the shabby clothing, the day's growth of beard peppered with gray even at his young age, the bloodshot eyes, the tremulous hands. He had no doubt been drinking on the sly despite Robbie's admonition the day of their departure. Beneath it all, however, seemed to reside a gentility that could not be disguised, though it appeared Drew's objective was to obliterate it completely.

"I'm afraid," Drew went on, "that the Apostle and I will have to part company there. It *is* possible to hate even oneself."

Robbie had no reply to give. The words were spoken so lightly that they took a few moments to sink in. And as they did, Robbie could not help but feel a great pity for this unfortunate man.

"Don't look so forlorn, my friend," said Drew with an unsuccessful attempt at a comforting grin. "I'm not the first man to admit his displeasure with his own person, though perhaps the first to admit it in your hearing."

"I don't know whether to believe you or not," Robbie said at last. "I wonder if you are merely trying to shock me."

"You think I have sinned by making such a statement?"

"I'm hardly the one to ask. That's the business you were in, Vicar."

"Well, I doubt that God will lay it to my account."

"Don't be too certain," said Robbie. "I have a friend, the young lady

I mentioned, who would tell me that God *loves* you. By your reasoning that would make *Him* a moron."

Drew laughed heartily. In the right mood, he did love a good debate.

"So, we've a closet theologian in our midst! But though you jab your dogmatical sword at what you perceive as my hypocrisy, you don't accept the tenets you espouse yourself. You are undone, Taggart! A nice ploy, but one that holds no water! Ha, ha! ha!"

"I made no claim for myself. I was only saying that your reasoning was flawed."

"Ha, ha!" laughed Drew. "Ah, Taggart, you have given me a good laugh. We should be calling *you* the Vicar! But don't you see, you're in no position to make such a statement because you have nothing to offer in its place. My statements of faithlessness are more consistent than yours."

Robbie did not reply.

"But I can see you are confused by my arguments. To return to the original question at hand, the sin of blasphemy, as you so correctly uncovered, is one I will accept." His words were almost merry, as if he were not speaking about his immortal soul. "But not the sin of self-hate. Whatever you say, I do not accept that as a sin, but only the inevitable result of a life of failure."

Robbie peered earnestly at Drew. "Then you do not love God, is that it?"

"Ah, Taggart. Your youthful naivete is so refreshing! What is love . . . what is God?"

Though Robbie had never thought of the question of love for God in reference to himself, a fact all too painfully clear to Jamie, it was still incredulous to him to hear one talk thus who had once been a cleric, a so-called man of God. What could have happened to cause him to abandon the very rudiments of his faith? But Robbie was in the tenuous position, as the Vicar saw so clearly, of expecting another to cling to a theology that he did not accept for himself. If the God of Christianity was indeed a God of love, then that love was meant for *all* men, not just a drunken ex-Vicar and a Highland lass he had once loved, but even for Robbie Taggart himself. But Robbie's time had not yet come.

"Listen!" said the Vicar, bringing them back to the reality of events before them. "They've finally come to their senses."

Robbie had all but forgotten about the men singing, and now suddenly their voices woke again in his ears.

The Vicar had picked up their conversation as one of the seamen had called out to the coxswain, "Torger, div ye ken *Ratcliffe Highway*?"

"Ya," drawled the Norseman in his thick accent, "been dere mony times."

"Not the *place*, ye dimwit, the song!"

"Ya, I know dat too," laughed the good-natured Overlie. He cleared his throat and set the mouth organ once more to his lips, while most of the others followed with the words.

> You jolly sailors list to me
> I've been a fortnight home from sea,
> Which time I've rambled night and day,
> To have a lark on the Highway.
> > *Listen you jovial sailors gay,*
> > *To the rigs of Ratcliffe Highway.*
>
> Some lasses their heads will toss,
> With bustles as big as a brewer's horse,
> Some wear a cabbage net, called veil,
> And a boa just like a buffalo's tail.
> > *Listen you jovial sailors gay,*
> > *To the rigs of Ratcliffe Highway.*

The men laughed as they struck up the next verse. Perhaps they were thinking of their own adventures on that disreputable street in London, or on similar avenues where sailors congregate while enjoying shore leave.

Robbie's merry mood had left him; the Vicar's comments had unconsciously disturbed him. His sympathetic nature was drawn to pity the man, but not a small part of him was vexed with the pleasure Drew seemed to take criticizing everything about him.

Why should he pity the man? Drew refused to acknowledge anything good about life, and thus brought his troubles upon himself. Why, Drew possessed enough self-pity for both of them! He didn't need Robbie's besides.

He was angry, too, that Drew had spoiled his jolly mood. The evening had started out so well. But he wasn't going to let it slip away because of a broken down, doleful ex-preacher.

"On second thought, Drew," he said, in a tone that would have belied his next words, "maybe I do feel like singing. At least I can give it a try. Take the wheel."

He started to descend from his post, then stopped and turned around. "And try not to run us aground," he added caustically. He turned again, and joined the rest of the watch at the other end of the poop.

But the evening had lost its allure. For Robbie the melodies were forced; even his usually light heart could not pick itself back up. And clouds began to tumble in upon the lovely moon-bathed and star-studded sky.

12

Accusations

By the following morning Robbie's vexation had shifted onto himself for letting himself get frustrated with the Vicar. His naturally sanguine nature had returned; once again he was able to look optimistically at life. And almost without noticing it, he found himself seeking an opportunity to reconcile with the Vicar the tension with which the evening had ended.

It disturbed Robbie to see how most of the crew treated the Vicar, sending him to fetch a bit of gear or another cup of coffee or a bucket of water for them. Yet Drew obeyed like a whipped pup. Not with a willing exuberance as did Sammy the cabin boy, but rather with a heavy sigh, as if this were no more than he deserved, though he retained the right within the privacy of his own mind to despise them all for it. But Robbie believed that if Drew were treated with something akin to respect, he might rise out of the hole of self-abuse in which he continually seemed to be wallowing.

Robbie found the Vicar sitting in the midst of a pile of canvas, mending an old sail, just as Jenkins, one of the able seamen, was calling to him from the forecastle. Robbie approached unnoticed.

"Hey, Vicar!" called Jenkins. "Me blade on this trowel broke. Why don't you be a good chap an' run below an' get me a new one?"

Drew glanced up, opened his mouth momentarily as if to protest, then thought better of it, rose, and sauntered away toward the hatch, passing Robbie on the way.

Robbie fell into step beside him.

"Elliot," he said, "if you want that treatment to stop, you have to stand up to them."

"What in heaven's name do you mean?" asked the Vicar, as if the thought had never occurred to him.

"I mean," replied Robbie with forced patience, "that if you showed a little backbone, they might stop pushing you around. I'd step in myself if I didn't think that would only make things worse for you in the long run."

"The vertebral portion of the anatomy was never my strongest asset."

"Drew!" exclaimed Robbie, frustrated with the ex-cleric's sarcasm. "Why can't you just once look a problem straight in the eye without turning it into a joke?"

"If you only knew what you asked, Robbie Taggart."

By now they had reached the forehatch, and Drew yanked it open with a jerk. He turned back toward Robbie with a smile that looked almost sincere. "I appreciate your concern, my friend. But don't waste your time trying to reform me. It's not worth your trouble. After all, even God couldn't succeed in that area. So it's doubtful you will be able to either."

"He must have once."

"That was a *very* long time ago." With the words, Drew ducked into the hatchway and disappeared.

A few minutes later the Vicar returned, humbly delivering the required tool to Jenkins. As Robbie observed the remainder of the proceedings, he could hardly fathom what could be at root in the heart of such a weak soul. He had always been the sort of person himself who would fight for his rights, who would stand up for what he believed in. Drew, on the other hand, seemed to shout out his weakness like an oracle proclaiming doom. Yet Robbie could not escape the conclusion that there was more to the man than the apparent cowardice he seemed bent on portraying. What he was hiding, what he was afraid of, Robbie could only guess. If it was true cowardice, that would be unfortunate. For Robbie was good-natured enough to accept almost any other kind of man but that.

Still wondering what other motives might be able to account for Drew's peculiarities, Robbie walked slowly to the chart house. He had been there about a quarter of an hour when suddenly he heard a great clamor forward. He hurried out to see Turk at the forehatch screaming in an unintelligible mixture of Cockney and Arabic.

"What's the trouble?" Robbie shouted, trying to make himself heard.

"Robbed!" screamed the Arab. "I am robbed!"

"Thievery's a serious crime aboard a ship. What makes you think so?"

"I tell you," replied Turk, calming enough to make his English coherent, "someone's been rifling through my locker!"

"Is that all?"

"That's enough, ain't it?"

"But was anything taken?" As he spoke Robbie could see the rest of the crew gradually gathering about the scene. He glanced up at them as if to find his answer there.

"Nothing, as I can see—*yet!*" returned Turk. "But a man's locker is sacred, and someone was in mine! If ye got no trust on a ship, ye got nothing!"

Robbie was struck with the incongruity of words about trust coming from the man on board he would trust less than any of them.

"So, Turk," said Robbie, "what proof do you have to make such accusations?"

"Proof! You want proof!" shouted Turk, his rage starting to boil over again. "Well, I gots it! The lock has been broke on my locker, so I tied a len'th of hemp roun' it. And I used a special knot! The dirty thief retied it so's it *looked* like my knot. But it wasn't the same! That's how I *know!*"

"I know what he's talking about," put in Jenkins. "We used to call that one there a thieves' knot. It's just like how if you tie a square wrong, it won't hold. I know the knot Turk ties. But not many know it, even many sailors. Most blokes try to imitate it. That's what they're tryin' to tie, and it looks the same, but won't hold. I seen other blokes make the same mistakes. One fellow I knowed tied a knot like that in the rigging once when his wife's lover was climbin' aloft. Killed the bloke . . . couldn't hold his weight."

Robbie could not refrain from an involuntary shudder at Jenkins' story. His own accident aboard the *Macao* had been similar. He had been climbing up a ratline to secure a top gallant during a heavy squall when one of the lines gave loose. A fall from aloft was nearly always fatal, whether the man fell into the sea or on deck. In Robbie's case the fall was broken by some webbed rigging that slowed him down, and thus his final free-fall to the deck had only been some twenty feet. A few bones had been broken; even that could have proved fatal had they been far out at sea. However, fortune had it that they were near port and had reached a doctor within two days. His recovery had been complete, even though at the time it had put him out of commission for several months.

His was an accident though, and Robbie recoiled at the thought of such a mishap being contrived, though it was no secret that seamen were a hard and rowdy lot. The kind of life they lived required it. Yet there remained a certain unshakeable honor—an undefinable camaraderie—even among the worst of them. Every once in a while one showed up who was rotten through and through, but Robbie had rarely encountered such. Even two men who might come to blows in the rigors of sea life would probably lay down their lives for one another if crisis demanded it. He was certain even men such as Digger and Turk would demonstrate their loyalty to the rest of the crew, even him, if put to it.

Thus the slightest hint of robbery among mates caused Robbie a sense of revulsion. But he would give any suspect fair play until proof was conclusive. Turk, however, was not so benevolent.

"The skipper taught me that knot," he was saying, "an' I'll wager there ain't a handful of you that knows it. But it's the one who *don't* know it as was in my stuff. An' I'll say right here—I seen the Vicar go below not twenty minutes ago."

"What a minute, Turk!" said Robbie.

"Don't you go tryin' to coddle him now, Taggart. I didn't see no one else go up or down in the time since I last checked my gear."

Several voices at once agreed with Turk, and Drew was gradually isolated from the rest of the crowd as they eased away from him.

"What have you got to say for yourself, Drew?" asked Robbie.

The Vicar stood in silence for some moments, as if he were mulling over the consequences of various replies in his mind. But before he had a chance to speak, the coxswain pushed his sturdy frame through the group.

"I yust heard what is happen here," he said breathlessly, for he had jogged there from his post at the helm. "An' Mr. Turk be mistaken about Mr. Drew's being da only one to go below. I vent dere mysel' only about half an hour ago."

"That's right," said another, suddenly recovering his memory. "An' ain't the skipper himself down there right now?"

A trickle of laughter spread through the group, for whether the men respected Pike or not, they knew the notion of his involving himself in petty theft, or even *attempted* petty theft, was inconceivable.

Robbie laughed with the rest, glad for the release of tension.

"Well, Turk," he said, "it appears we have three suspects now. Whom will you accuse?"

"You're protecting him, Taggart," objected Turk, his menacing eyes seeking Robbie's with unspoken threat. "I ain't heard no denials yet."

Torger merely laughed at the very idea. Drew remained silent. Fearing he might incriminate himself just for the sake of doing so, or with some obscure quotations whose meaning remained hidden to all but himself, Robbie quickly cut in.

"So . . . we have two denials," he said. "And I presume you will agree that we will most likely receive one from the captain as well. However, if you would like to question—"

"So that's how it is, is it, Taggart?" exploded Turk, seething. "Take care of your babies, and to blazes with the rest of us!"

"Now you listen to me, Turk," said Robbie firmly, but maintaining his calm. "You cannot prove a theft has been committed, and I will not lay such a serious charge against any man on board this ship without hard evidence. All we know at present is that your cords were tampered with. It may well be that someone found them loose and, as a good deed, tried to re-tie them."

"Then why won't he admit it?"

"It is doubtful at this point that you'd believe any explanation. If I had done it myself, I think I'd hesitate saying anything after seeing the fire in your eyes. I grant that the situation bears watching. But I'll not punish a man without proof."

"I'll take it to the skipper!"

"Do that," said Robbie confidently. "But you'll get no different response."

As assured as Robbie sounded, however, in reality he was not at all certain just how Pike would react. He was not an easy man to understand, perhaps with more undercurrents of conflicting motives than even the Vicar. His mood had a great deal to do with his response to any given situation. Till now he had been completely supportive of Robbie. But who could tell what the stress of the sea might bring?

Turk spat at the deck and stormed away. He did not, however, go below to Pike's cabin.

The men slowly dispersed, and by and by the work around the ship resumed. But Robbie continued to mull the incident over in his head. Was it possible there truly was a thief aboard? And worse, *could* it have been the Vicar? Heaven only knew he didn't appear to have the guts for such an act—especially against a ruthless character like Turk. On the other hand, sneaking about while no one was watching might just be something he would do. Could he have been looking for whiskey?

When Robbie finished up his business in the chart house, he decided it was time to find Drew and get to the bottom of it. He had taken quite a chance in standing up to Turk on Drew's behalf. And if it turned out he was in truth a common burglar, he'd keel-haul him.

But before he ran across the Vicar, Robbie encountered Pike.

"I heard there was some trouble," said the skipper, limping toward him from the forecastle.

"Just some accusations," Robbie replied, determined to keep talk about the incident as understated as possible.

"That Vicar bears watching."

"Oh, I think he's harmless enough. Turk worries me more."

"How much do you know about him, Robbie?"

"Who?"

"The Vicar."

Robbie slowly shook his head. "Not much, really."

"Well, I hear he nearly killed a man once, and that's why he's been exiled from his fancy Hyde Park life."

"I find that too incredible to believe!" replied Robbie. Yet even as he spoke he recalled Drew's words the night before they departed England: *I fit in more than you think, Taggart.*

All at once Pike stopped, turned, and faced him, then said, jabbing a long, crooked finger into Robbie's chest to accentuate his words: "Things ain't always what they seem, mate!"

It was the first time Robbie had ever taken close note of the hard glint in Pike's sallow eyes. For the briefest of moments he wondered that he could have considered himself friends with such a man.

Almost as if reading Robbie's inner hesitancies, Pike broke into a great rolling guffaw. Were one to regard his face closely, he would have seen that glint still present, but the uncharacteristic laughter made Robbie forget—at least for now. There were too many real problems and dangers at present for Robbie to occupy his mind with imagined fancies about their skipper. If he let himself dwell on such fleeting notions, before long he'd start believing himself caught on some ill-fated ship of doom bound for a fate unknown.

The vessel ran smoothly the following morning, as if she were not aware of the potential for strife she carried. Their pilot disembarked at the Isle of Wight where they were held up several hours with blustery weather and contrary winds. When they sailed the next day, none aboard had any idea that their number had suddenly increased by one, nor that this particular addition would likely light the already short fuse of conflict aboard the *Sea Tiger*.

13

Stowaway

They were met with strong headwinds off the Channel Islands, and it seemed as if an end had come to pleasant seas.

The yards and sheets required constant attending as Pike attempted to tack his way through the weather, veering more north than he would have liked. After twenty-four hours they'd made but little headway, though each man was exhausted. Finally the winds eased up, and the next afternoon they caught sight of the Lizard. But its significance was not dulled with the delay.

The Channel lay behind them now. From here on it would be open sea.

Torger, as if to celebrate their last sight of English soil and the swinging about of the winds, went below after his harmonica.

But after several minutes absence he returned with quite a different prize.

"Look vat I gots here!" he exclaimed, with a bemused expression on his broad, friendly face as he emerged topside.

Grasped firmly but gently in his large, fleshy hand was the slender arm of a most unlikely sailor—unlikely, that is, in that his reluctant charge was a feisty, squirming young girl of not more than fifteen or sixteen. In all other aspects but her sex, she appeared more a sailor than young Sammy, or even the Vicar for that matter. Atop a long mass of tangled brown curls sat an old captain's cap, complete with faded gold braid. This cap had been pushed back on her head during the brief scuffle with Torger, revealing a face which, beneath the smudge and grime of two days in the hull of the ship, showed promise of one day becoming rather pretty. The tough scowl which at this moment framed her pale gray eyes, however, hinted prophetically that if she did not take care, those features that contributed to her youthful attractiveness now could, as the years passed, make of her a hard and bitter woman. Dressed in several layers of breeches, shirt, vest, heavy coat, and thick woolen scarf, she looked as if she carried her entire wardrobe on her back, which indeed she did.

It was Digger who chanced to be nearest the receiving end of Torger's announcement. He stopped at the hatchway, first with an angry grimace across the hardened features of his face. But on closer scrutiny of the coxswain's find, his mouth widened into a lecherous leer.

"Ha! ha! Who says this be a rum ship?" roared the bo'sun as he grabbed the girl's chin in his thick paw to inspect her closer. "Now wot's a pretty little thing like yersel' stowin' away aboard a crate like this fer?"

The girl's sole response was to jerk her chin from his sweaty grasp, shooting as she did a fierce look at him from her pale, thickly lashed eyes.

"Don't you touch me!" she hissed vehemently.

"Well, what'd ye expect aboard a freighter, missy?" replied Digger, in mingled anger and amusement. He would not be put off so easily.

"I can take care of myself, an' I don't care *where* I am!"

Just as Digger reached toward her again, Robbie walked onto the scene, quickly stepping between the bo'sun and the *Tiger's* uninvited passenger.

"Leave the girl alone, Digger," he said; "can't you see she's afraid?"

"It don't look like fear in them eyes to me," Digger replied, glowering at his adversary. "And who made her your business anyway, Taggart?"

"Whatever happens on this ship is my business. The sooner you accept that, Digger, the sooner we're going to start getting along."

But one look at the girl, as she shook her tangled mane and straightened her shoulders proudly, told any observer that perhaps Digger was right—fear was the last emotion her defiant carriage exuded. Her present look of belligerence hardly seemed appropriate for a nonpaying sneak, by rights a criminal aboard the *Sea Tiger*; she stood facing the three men as if she were rather the owner of an entire fleet.

If Robbie had first thought he had come upon another Jamie MacLeod, innocent and unstudied in the ways of the world, that look in this girl's eyes quickly dispelled the notion. It was clear, as she said, that she did indeed know how to take care of herself, and had been doing so along the southern coast of England for several years. Whether she was an orphan, or whether her parents had merely cast her adrift in their poverty, even she did not know. Nor had she yet reached an age where she often questioned her background. She took what came her way, manipulated people and circumstances to suit her, and had through the years fallen into a lifestyle with which she could be content. Her independent nature taught her to go where she chose, to answer to no one but herself; she was still young enough to find the lack of family constraints a blessing rather than a cause for loneliness.

"So, vat ve going to do with you, missy?" said Overlie as both Digger and Robbie sized up the situation in their own minds.

"Digger, go tell the skipper what we've found," said Robbie. "In the meantime I'll take her down to the galley. She looks as though she could use a meal."

"I found her first!" protested the bo'sun loudly, if not entirely truthfully.

"That's an order, Digger!"

The bo'sun's fingers knotted into fists as he glared at Robbie for a long, tense moment. Finally, seeming to think better of a confrontation at that juncture, he said, "You're goin' to go too far some day, Taggart," then spun around, muttering as he stalked away.

Ignoring the threat, Robbie turned his attention to more urgent matters, namely, what to do about the *Tiger's* young stowaway. "I think you can safely release the young lady, Torger," he said with a hint of a smile in his eyes. "She can't run very far," he added for the girl's benefit.

"Now, miss," said Robbie to the girl, while Torger transferred responsibility for his temporary charge and made his escape, "I'm Robbie Taggart, first mate here. Who might you be?"

She folded her arms firmly across her chest, resigning herself to whatever fate might be in store. Though the imperceptible softening of her features indicated her growing realization, judging at least from the looks of the man in front of her, that she might not be in for such a bad time of it after all.

"My name's Kitty," she answered.

"Short for Katherine?" asked Robbie, thinking it rather too-fine sounding an epithet for so ragged a girl.

"So they tells me."

"They?"

"People—you know. Besides, it was a long time ago."

"Have you a family?"

"*I'm* my own family, and a long sight better than some whole broods I seen round and about!" She paused, then added, "So if ye're thinkin' of some do-gooder thing like sendin' me home, you can forget it, 'cause I ain't got none. You may just as well keep me aboard."

"Hmm," said Robbie, rubbing his chin thoughtfully, "the captain'll have to decide that. In the meantime, you must be hungry after two days in the hull."

"I am at that," she answered, thawing still further toward this good-looking first mate.

Johnnie was none too pleased at having to mess up his spotless kitchen at such an hour. But since it was Robbie making the request he put forth only mild protests. The fare was simple and cold, for Johnnie had banked the fire in the stove, but the young misfit fell to it with relish nonetheless.

"A merchant vessel is hardly a fit place for a girl," said Robbie as she ate.

"Ah! I'm a natural sailor! Look at me—I feel great, though it's only my second day out."

"But aren't you the least bit frightened?"

"Me?" she said, looking up coyly from her meal. Then after a pause, she added, "I suppose there ain't much left that could scare me."

"Been on your own a long time?"

"Long enough. All the more reason to keep me; I can take care of myself." She paused, stuffing a crust of bread into her mouth. It took several moments before she could continue. "'Sides, you don't look too awfully fearsome to me." As she spoke, her voice seemed to take on the hint of a sweeter, higher-pitched tone.

Before Robbie could respond further, Pike made his belated appearance. He eyed his new passenger with disgust, and not a little contempt. Delays due to weather he could tolerate; they were to be expected. But now because of this fool girl, he would have to lose another two or three days putting her ashore.

"All right, ye little harpy!" he said without prelude, putting his most menacing tone to full use, "what have ye to say fer yerself?"

"I'll pay you your money!" she shot back defiantly. Robbie noted her confidence with an interested glance; it was no small matter to stand up to men like Pike and Digger.

"Likely story!" snorted the skipper. "No doubt ye'd rot in the chokey first!"

"Come on, Ben," put in Robbie, "go easy on her."

"She's done a crime, and jail's where she belongs!"

"In the meantime, we have to decide what to do with her till we reach port."

"Put her in irons!" sneered Pike, then added with a wink, "as much for her sake as for ours, if ye take my meaning, Robbie."

"I can work," said Kitty quickly, for Pike did not appear the sort of man who made idle threats.

"Ha!" scoffed Pike at the idea. However, by the following morning Robbie had convinced him to let her share Sammy's work, for he had more than enough to do as cabin boy. Kitty was relieved not to have to spend any more time in the dark, rat-infested places on the ship. Robbie gave her his quarters and took up temporary residence in the aft cabin with the other men of his watch.

Kitty tackled her assignments with the same vigor with which she had consumed her meal. She appeared enthusiastic, and her surly disposition was soon replaced with a contented smile. With good reason too, for she had succeeded in securing a place of acceptance aboard the *Sea Tiger* when she could well have found herself handcuffed to the rail. Now she just had to find a way to convince her benefactors to keep her on for the duration of the voyage.

When she'd decided a few weeks ago to make her break from merry old England and expand her horizons in the directions of the rest of the world, she hadn't realized how difficult it would be for a girl, capable though she was, to find a place on a ship. But once Kitty set her course, she was not easily deterred. The idea to stow away, while perhaps not the most creative of notions, was nevertheless the solution she had settled upon. She'd figured that once at sea, she could depend on her wit and cunning, not to mention her immature feminine wiles, to *keep* her aboard. She had hoped to delay her discovery until they were far out on the open sea, at least past Gibraltar. But when she made her untimely venture out of her place of hiding, thinking the coast was clear for a few minutes to stretch her legs, her plans were suddenly altered by Torger Overlie's unexpected appearance.

Still undaunted, she knew she would find some other way to achieve her ends. From what she could judge thus far, the first mate would be easy to maneuver. As she scrubbed down the deck she reflected on the fact that the nicest blokes were never a problem.

Kitty was but sixteen, but during her short life she had managed to pick up a fair understanding of how to use the lines of her body and the smile on her face to optimum advantage. The times were not few she had been told she was a pretty young thing, and when she put her mind to it she knew she had what it took to charm and beguile an unsuspecting sailor, even if he was a dozen years older than herself. If only she had something more in the choice of a wardrobe! Well, she'd just have to be resourceful.

Her next problem would be the captain and that bo'sun who seemed to hold some power aboard the ship. The bo'sun was a brute, to be sure, and not overly bright. But she thought she could handle him. It was the captain who worried her. She didn't relish the idea of tangling with him. Or having anything to do with him for that matter. Though she was an expert at concealing her fears, he was a man who could make her quiver. There was something in the evil stare of the man's eyes. She didn't like it!

"Well, no need to bother with him," she told herself. "I'll just concentrate on the mate and the big man called Digger."

She squeezed out her mop and dumped the bucket of dirty water over the side. But she reminded herself as she gazed out at the gray, turbulent sea that she had been found sooner than planned, and that the *Sea Tiger* was barely underway. There were still any number of European ports that would not be greatly out of their way. That meant she would have to work quickly if she hoped to secure her continued presence on this particular ship. If she couldn't prove herself, Captain Pike would make as fast as he could to the nearest convenient port to discharge his unwanted passenger.

And Kitty was determined to prevent that if she could.

14

Designs

Two mornings later Robbie stood at the forecastle rail looking for a break in the contrary weather. But all that greeted him were heavy gray skies and persistent winds coming from the west. Luckily they were northerly enough to allow them to tack down the coast. But progress was slow. He did not even notice that Kitty came up behind him.

"I love the movement of the ship," she said. "I've always wanted to see distant lands."

Robbie turned to face her. "I know what you mean," he replied in a kindly voice. "No sailor can be contented for long without that rocking under his feet. But I'm afraid, Kitty," he went on, "that France is going to be the farthest land you see on this trip. The skipper's going to put you off first chance he gets."

"Aw, doesn't he know I can be a help? Wouldn't *you* like to keep me on?" she said, inching closer.

"A ship's no place for a young girl."

"I'm not really so young." She stood very close to Robbie now. "An' what I might lack in age, I more'n make up for in *experience*. Why, I've been accepted for eighteen—even twenty, many times."

"I suppose it's been rough for you, having to grow up faster than most," said Robbie sympathetically.

"It ain't been easy. Not that I'm complainin', mind you! But . . ."

Here she let her voice trail away dreamily. When she began again it was with a melancholy sigh. "I hoped that jist maybe if I got away, you know, to someplace new—that I might be able to get a new start."

She paused again. "You won't laugh if I tell you somethin', will you?" she said after about a minute.

When Robbie shook his head in reply, she continued. "I always dreamed that somethin' grand would one day happen to me. Every girl does, I suppose. But I've felt that deep down it *could* really happen to me. Who could tell but what I'm supposed to go to a far-off country an' meet a prince who'd fall in love with me—an' make me his princess—"

She stopped and looked up quickly. "You ain't goin' to laugh, are you?"

"If I've learned anything," answered Robbie wistfully, "it's not to laugh at other people's dreams. They sometimes do come true. I knew a girl who was very much like you, Kitty—homeless, penniless, unlearned. Jamie was just a ragged shepherd girl when I found her. Now she's Lady Graystone, of one of the noblest families in northeast Scotland."

Kitty's eyes glistened eagerly with Robbie's words. "See!" she exclaimed. "It *does* happen! An' it can happen to me—I'll make it happen—!" But she broke off sharply, realizing all at once that she had begun to reveal more of herself than she had safely intended.

"Kitty, you can't always *make* such things happen. Jamie didn't. It just came her way."

"Well, maybe this Jamie is the lucky type—but I don't like to leave things to chance."

They fell silent a while, watching the movement of the sea, each deep in private thoughts. From the tone of Robbie's voice, Kitty thought, he must certainly have once been in love with this Lady Graystone. If he meant what he said about her reminding him of Jamie, then this Mr. Taggart no doubt had a weakness for the helpless type.

The *Tiger* suddenly lurched to one side, but it took Kitty less than a fraction of a second to seize her opportunity. She stumbled sideways, falling against Robbie. As she had hoped, he instinctively reached his arms up to catch her.

"I guess I'm not as accustomed to the sea as I thought," she said, making no move to pull away from him.

Robbie relaxed his arm to loosen his hold, but she quickly laid her hand on his arm.

"Robbie . . ." She turned toward him, slipping her own arm around his waist. "I can call you Robbie, can't I?"

"Kitty—"

"It must get mighty lonesome for you out here." She leaned her face closer to his.

"Kitty," said Robbie, gently pushing her from him, "I'm not your prince—"

"Oh, Robbie," she replied tearfully. "Can you blame me? I ain't ever met anyone like you before."

"That's because you're still young. You will one day, maybe just like you said."

"I'd give up all them dreams for you, Robbie!"

"Don't give up your dreams, Kitty. Someday—"

A clattering behind them interrupted Robbie's sentence, and he turned to see the Vicar climbing up the companion ladder to the raised deck where they stood.

Relieved and embarrassed, Robbie turned to greet Drew, while Kitty fell quickly back, flustered by the untimely intrusion.

"I'd better get back to work," she murmured, giving Robbie a coy smile as she turned and walked off.

"Making progress with the young thing already, eh, Robbie?" said Drew with a wink.

"Hardly that, my friend! Hardly that," replied Robbie. "If there's one thing I don't need right now, it's the problems a woman brings."

As Kitty resumed her tasks, Robbie's last word still rang pleasantly in her ears. *Someday* . . . he had started to say. And from that single word she was able to build all sorts of airy castles in the sky as to what he might have meant. In truth, her vain imaginings were worlds different than what Robbie had intended to say. Even a Sadie Malone, cut out of the same cloth as she was, could have warned young Kitty that her sights were set much too high. But in her childish innocence, Kitty went away encouraged, and began making preparations for her next conquest.

Later that day Kitty was busy sweeping out the forecastle cabin where the stores were kept. Sammy stopped at the door.

"Need any help?" he asked.

"Thanks, but I'm doin' fine," she answered. Then she added as if the idea had only just occurred to her. "Sammy, maybe there is somethin' ye can do for me, if ye was of a mind to?"

"Anything ye say, Kitty," replied Sammy, the only crew member so far to have succumbed to the young stowaway's charms.

"This room's a mess, an' maybe if I do a real good job cleanin' it, it'd impress the first mate—ye know, so's he'd convince the captain to keep me on."

"That'd be fine, Kitty!"

"Could ye keep the mate away till I was finished, then, say in about twenty minutes, bring him by—just casually, ye know—so I can surprise him? Ye see, he was sayin' this mornin' as how this place needed cleanin'."

"Sure! You can count on me!"

Sammy ran off. The moment he was out of sight, Kitty set down her broom and set off herself. She found Digger not far away, supervising repairs on the capstan.

"Mr. Digger," she called in the sweetest voice she could muster.

Yes, the bo'sun was *quite* willing to give her a hand in moving the heavy cartons in the cabin. Why, *no*, he wasn't too busy at all. It was *much* too strenuous a job for her alone. In point of fact, Jack Digger had not been so willing to do something for another person in a very long while.

"Oh, Mr. Digger," said Kitty some fifteen minutes later, as he was in the midst of lifting a heavy box of iron fittings, "I ain't never seen a man as strong as you are." She used what she judged to be her most alluring tone, and though it fell far short of what she had intended, it helped that Digger was not particular. "Why, just look at them arms!" she added, laying a hand on his thick forearm.

Digger paused, his brow knit with a puzzled expression. Only the day before yesterday this little snip had hissed at him like a she-cat. But why should he question such feminine attentions? It had probably just taken these two days for her to realize what kind of man he was. Quickly he shoved the carton aside, and as Kitty picked up the broom to resume her work, he grasped her shoulder in his hand.

"It ain't sweepin' ye really want to do, now is it, missy?" He let his hand slip from her shoulder, taking her into his arms.

"I got my work to do," she answered faintly, as if she did not mean it.

"Yeah, but there's somethin' more important than work, eh, missy?"

"I wouldn't want no trouble."

"Don't ye worry about a thing."

Digger moved still closer, pressing her slight body up against the wall of the bulkhead.

"But you might get in trouble with the captain or the mate," said Kitty, thinking to herself that Sammy should be back by now. How long could she hold this brutish man off anyway?

"Ha! Fools, both of 'em! I do wot I wants around here!" Digger declared. "Nobody tells Jack Digger wot to do!" Then, as if to emphasize the validity of his words, he planted his lips against hers.

Kitty cringed at the awful sensation of the man's kiss. For all her claims of worldly experience, she had in fact been kissed only once or twice, and that by boys no older than herself. And certainly never like this! To make matters even worse, this man smelled! But she tried to still her revulsion. She had to keep him here until Robbie arrived.

"Hmm. Mr. Digger," she sighed, in a small but determined voice.

"Ye liked that, did ye, miss . . . ?" He grabbed her up in both his arms and brought his lips once more to hers.

Sturdy girl that she was, Kitty felt faint and sick. But before her growing fear had a chance to master her, she heard the door open. Robbie saw exactly what she had wanted him to, and to insure his proper reaction, Kitty immediately began to whimper and squirm helplessly.

"You've gone too far now, Digger, you no good low-life!" yelled Robbie as he burst through the door. He grabbed the bo'sun's shirt in his fists and flung him away from Kitty.

"Why you . . . !" cried the enraged bo'sun. "I'll kill ye for that!" He lurched toward his prey, but Robbie was quicker, and, stepping aside, sent Digger stumbling against the wall. Fuming and blustering loudly, Digger swung around as he rose, making ready for another attack. But he never saw it completed, for Pike, just then passing the cabin, had stepped in to investigate the tumult.

"I knew ye'd be nothin' but trouble, ye little vixen!" he said, leveling his cold gaze on Kitty, while keeping Digger at bay with his crutch.

"B—but I—"

"She'd be far less trouble," put in Robbie, "if Digger showed her some respect! She's a mere child."

"Aw, she was askin' fer it."

"From what I could see," Robbie went on, "she was trying to get out of your clutches."

"Why, you dirty—!"

"You get out of here, Jack!" said Pike. "Cool yourself off. I'll talk to you later."

"Me!" exclaimed Digger. "An' wot about him, actin' as if he owned the bleedin' ship!"

"Get outta here!" hissed Pike, "before I lays ye on the deck."

Grumbling noisily, Digger stalked away, momentarily at bay, but by no means confessing defeat. The next time, he swore to himself, even Pike wouldn't be able to stop him.

But Pike had already forgotten his boatswain, now directing his wrath at his passenger. "I should 'ave locked ye in the hold the first time I laid eyes on ye. But we're puttin' in the first chance we get—Lisbon, if I can manage it—and till then I don't want to see yer little face above this deck, ye hear?"

Kitty nodded submissively.

"Now get outta here!" Pike added with an oath.

Kitty was gone in less than a moment. Robbie started after her, but Pike caught his arm.

"Lock 'er in the cabin," he said. "'Tis the only way any of us'll be safe."

"She's but a child, Ben," said Robbie.

"That's yer problem, Robbie," said Pike, "always seein' the good in everyone. Don't be so naive—you've seen her flaunt herself around here!"

"She's too young to understand half of what she's doing. We are grown men, and ought to be able to act accordingly. She could be a help around here."

"Maybe so . . ." Pike said, rubbing his chin thoughtfully. "On the other hand," he added with a sly wink, "maybe ye'd jist like to save her for yerself, eh, Robbie!"

He laughed in a knowing manner. "Don't worry, Robbie, I'll keep Digger out of the way fer ye!"

Disgusted, Robbie turned and left the small cabin without another word.

15

A Stop at Lisbon

Kitty knew her chances were pretty well ruined. But when Robbie knocked on the door of the cabin, she tried to answer sweetly.

"Come in," she said, not moving from where she lay sulking on the bunk.

Robbie opened the door and stepped inside.

"Digger didn't hurt you, did he?"

She shook her head. "You came along jist in time."

"It was quite a stroke of luck," replied Robbie in a meaningful tone. "I mean, that Sammy came for me and brought me back to the cabin at just the right moment."

"I don't take yer meanin'," she said innocently, but shifting uncomfortably in the bunk.

"Kitty, I don't know what you hoped to achieve, but you can't use people like that. Not only does it hurt others, but someday you'll hurt yourself too."

"I don't need no moralizin' speech," she rejoined, with a flicker of ire in her tone.

"I don't much like giving them either, so that's as much as you'll get from me. But I want you to know I think you're a fine girl, Kitty. I'd hate to see you get yourself into a fix you couldn't get out of just because of one foolish little action. Don't spoil your chances for a good life over a man like Digger."

"Oh, Robbie, I'll never have a good life, not unless I get away, get out and see the rest of the world!"

"I wish I could help you."

"Convince the captain to let me stay on."

"That would be impossible after what just happened. Besides, you'd never be able to control Digger. He's a mean one."

"You'd take care of me, I know you would!" She stood and approached him, hoping one last time to make him take notice, like Digger had. But he backed away, sadly shaking his head.

"It wouldn't work, Kitty," he said, more aware than ever that it would take far more than a lecture from him to make the *Tiger's* young stowaway see the error of her designs.

"You're my only hope, Robbie," she pleaded, longingly looking into his eyes.

"No, I'm not, little Kitty," he said gently. "I think you're the kind of young lady who will always land on her feet. And you might find your prince, too, if you have a little patience—with a little wisdom thrown in for good measure."

"You're going to let them dump me off in a strange city?"

"I have no choice. It's not my ship. But we'll book passage back to England for you." Kitty slumped back onto the bunk and said nothing.

Robbie turned to leave the cabin, saddened that he could not get through. He did not even hear the fierce kick the temperamental young waif aimed at the door once it clicked shut.

As the winds gradually swung around from the north, the *Tiger* made more consistent progress, and within a week put in at Lisbon, the sailing capital of the world several centuries before. Robbie took charge of Kitty. Pike would have simply thrown her ashore and have done with it, but Robbie made arrangements for her return to England on a British vessel and paid the captain for her passage. They remained in port a day and then made ready to sail once more. Kitty's departure would follow a day or two later.

Resigned to her fate, Kitty had softened once more toward Robbie. He walked her down the gangway for the last time.

"I hope you'll consider me a friend, Kitty," said Robbie.

"Small good that'll do. I'll be stuck in England and you'll be off to see the wide world."

"Sometimes friends meet up again," he answered. "In the meantime, it's always nice to know you have a friend out there somewhere."

She smiled, "Well then, good-bye, Robbie Taggart," she said.

"Goodbye, Kitty. I'm glad our paths crossed, even if only briefly."

"You won't change your mind?" she asked half-heartedly. Even as she said the words, she knew he was not meant for her.

Robbie laughed. "You'll do just fine, Kitty. I know you will. I hope you do meet your prince."

She returned his smile with growing assurance. "And you your princess!" she called out to him as she watched Robbie make his way back onto the deck of the ship. Stowing away on this ship had been a bad idea, she thought. But something else would turn up, some other way to get out of the rut she was in—and she would find it somehow.

She waved one last time at the *Sea Tiger* as the wind and receding tide carried it away, then turned expectantly toward Lisbon where she would have another day or two before her return. *Hmm*, she thought to herself as she walked away, *I wonder if I could cash in the ticket Robbie bought for me? I might just like to stay here for a while.* Her step took on a lilt as she picked up her stride. *Not a bad idea at all!*

Robbie leaned against the aft rail of the *Sea Tiger*. Lisbon harbor was nothing but a distant blur; he could no longer see Kitty waving from the dock. He could not help wondering if he'd done the right thing. But it hadn't been up to him anyway, he thought. If he had been captain, perhaps he would have given her a chance. But even then the voyage would not have been what she was hoping for. He had been like Kitty once—young, looking for a dream over every horizon. And over the years he had seen many of those exotic ports and the men and women who populated them. But in not one in a thousand had he found the kind of happiness Kitty was searching for. No princes, no princesses. He was still looking, and he'd been at it a lot more years than Kitty.

He couldn't blame Kitty for her dreams, though. For he had dreams himself. He sighed deeply. Yes, he thought, everyone had his dreams—of princes and princesses, of adventure, of travel to faraway places.

"So there you are," said a voice behind him. It was the Vicar. "Not pining away after our little stowaway, are you?"

"What?" replied Robbie distractedly, caught off guard by the unexpected comment.

"You look as if perhaps the ship might be headed in the wrong direction."

"You're jesting!"

"No regrets at leaving the girl behind?"

Robbie laughed. "Even if I were of a mind to fall in love with a sixteen-year-old, it wouldn't have been with her. Kitty was a bit much!"

"A foolish notion, I'll grant. But I dare say she was no different from most females, weaving their tangled webs of deceit."

"You, Elliot, are the wrong man to talk to on the subject," said Robbie, half in jest. Then he paused, deep in thought. "I suppose my problem is that my friend Jamie has spoiled me for other women," he began again. "I will always measure others against her, and I'm afraid they will always fall short."

"Well, I say you are a better man for it, if it keeps you free of such entanglements."

"Am I?"

"O course! You're a free man. Savor it, my friend!"

"I was willing to give all that up for Jamie."

"A passing moment of insanity, no doubt," rejoined the Vicar.

"I don't know . . . yet as much as I loved her, in the end a part of me was glad to still possess my freedom." As he spoke Robbie gazed intently into the gray horizon. "But I sometimes wonder if there isn't someone out there, someone whom I could love and for whom I'd have no reservations about giving up the roving life."

"The princess you will kiss who will turn all life into a fairy tale!"

"Do I detect sarcasm in your voice?"

"You want a perfect woman, Robbie; believe me, she doesn't exist."

"Perhaps not. But maybe there is one who is perfect for me."

"Dream on, lad!"

"Well, even if I never reach the end of my dream and find my princess, the life of a bachelor isn't so bad, is it?"

From Lisbon the *Tiger* pursued a course almost due west, swinging out between the Azores and the Canary Islands. Then they ran in ballast with a northeast tradewind for the better part of a week. Each morning and evening the set of the sails had to be tended, but for the remainder of the day it seemed the *Tiger* practically ran herself—but for the man at the helm. Had it not been for the early strife, it would have been the sort of beginning every seaman dreams of. And though storms and squalls would come, and tempers would no doubt flare again, as well as winds turn against them, while they lasted, such fortuitous conditions were welcomed, and almost made Robbie forget about his run-ins with Digger altogether.

16

Calm

Once well out into the wide expanse of the Atlantic, the *Sea Tiger* ran smoothly in front of favorable winds—as smoothly as possible with such a diverse crew aboard. The following weeks, past Madeira off Africa's west coast, and south beyond the Tropic of Cancer and into the tropical regions, were without incident.

They continued on past the equator with sunny weather and stiff breezes. Then, on their thirty-seventh day out, halfway between the Equator and the Tropic of Capricorn, Robbie and Pike were on deck inspecting the condition of the newly repaired foremast clew lines. Throughout the morning the wind had been gradually dying. At first no one had even noticed, though by degrees the ship's momentum had grown slower and slower. The fair weather had nearly lulled the seasoned sailors into a false security.

Now, however, as if by common instinct, Robbie and the skipper realized that as they stood, everything about them was deathly still. The sounds of motion had fled. The *Tiger* was sitting dead in the water.

A calm is like waking death to a seaman.

For four days the *Sea Tiger's* sails banged hollowly against the masts, hanging limp and impotent. At first Robbie had been able to adjust the rigging in order to gain a slight advantage from the faint breath of air that remained. But before the first day was out even that was gone, and nothing Robbie's skill could conjure would help. The mighty clipper may as well have been sitting in the middle of a tiny inland lake.

Tensions quickly rose. Pike did not leave the bridge except to sleep. It was the most anyone had seen of him above deck since the voyage had begun. Grumbling and growling about his ill-fortune and the schedule he had to maintain, he paced back and forth, his crutch and wooden leg beating out an ominous rhythm on the poop deck. More than once his crutch shot out in frustrated anger, whacking whoever happened to be close by. His most likely victims were young Sammy, who didn't know enough to stay away from the skipper in his present mood, or the coxswain who had no choice since he had to remain at the helm even though there was nothing to steer.

Others grew similarly edgy, and petty arguments flared up all over the ship. Robbie found his position as referee almost a more vital assignment throughout the calm than whatever he had to do as mate. Jeremiah Lackey was in his glory, shuffling up and down the decks, prophesying imminent doom.

"We'll sit 'ere forever!" he cried in despondent and eerie tones. "Thus sayeth the Lord, 'They shall 'ave no wind to blow at their backs.'"

"Shut up, you old fool!" yelled Digger.

"There'll not be any more grain nor water in all of Egypt!" went on Lackey. "We'll sit 'ere till our stores be gone. Thus will the doom of heaven fall upon us!"

"The old blowhard," muttered Drew. "Wouldn't know a scripture if it jumped out and bit him!"

By then Sammy was in tears, and Robbie finally had to confine Lackey to his quarters. But that could not stop the old sailor. Even ten feet away Robbie could hear him wailing morbidly, "You'll see . . . we'll all see . . . we'll rot 'ere—we're doomed, says the Lord!"

He had considered slugging the old man to keep him quiet. Robbie liked this calm no better than anyone else. But they had to get through it as best they could.

The air hung heavy and oppressive about them, so thick it seemed you could cut it. The sky was dim and colorless about the horizon. Even at night the stars were dull and sulfurous, like worlds about to burn themselves out. Yes, there was a tension hanging over them all. Robbie hated the doldrums too, but not because of Lackey's portentous ramblings. A calm was bad enough in itself. But this one seemed to hold another even more terrifying element, one which added a dread to the quiet. He felt it palpably in the stagnant air: a storm was coming.

He suggested to Pike that they haul in the Royals and topgallants, but the skipper sneered out his reply:

"You ain't gettin' lily-livered on me, are you, young Taggart?" pausing only a moment in his restless pacing. "I thought ye was made o' better stuff!"

"No, I'm not getting soft, Pike!" retorted Robbie tersely, angered mostly that Pike's assessment might be true—or at least looked that way. He stalked away, reproaching himself for succumbing to the miserable atmosphere and to Pike's verbal jab.

On the fourth day Robbie found Pike missing from his constant vigil on the bridge. He thought nothing of it throughout the morning, but shortly after lunch, when he still had made no appearance, he asked Overlie where the skipper had been. Torger merely shook his head with concern, and when he said, "He's gone below," it was not with his customary grin.

Robbie swung around and headed for the stern hatch. All too common were the stories of captains both literally and figuratively going over the edge—more frequently in calms than storms. Others, unable to withstand the pressures and stresses, but without the wherewithal to jump, merely sat in their cabins and drank themselves into oblivion. Even when on deck, Pike's presence had been of concern to Robbie. His pacing had been like that of a caged animal, his eyes wild, his emotions taut, as if waiting to break like the gathering storm Robbie felt in the air. Almost unconsciously he had been keeping his own vigilant eye on the skipper, and now wondered if he had finally cracked.

He hurried below and met the Vicar halfway.

"Has the skipper been this way?" he asked.

"I'd leave the old man be if I were you," replied Drew. "He's in a fit. I expect he's more than half-drunk by now."

Robbie closed his eyes in momentary despair. It might well be that Pike was not the most fit master, but it saddened Robbie to think that he might spoil even this small opportunity he had to prove himself a capable ship's captain.

"It has always puzzled me," the Vicar was saying, "why you have so taken to that man. Of course, I might ask the same question regarding myself. I suppose you are the kind who cannot refuse a stray or degenerate."

Robbie shrugged, but said nothing. He didn't even have an answer. Neither did he need Drew's cynicism now. "The skipper is an old family friend," he said at length. "And," he added somewhat defensively, "he's been decent to me."

"Well, you must be a minority of one in that category," remarked Drew.

Without commenting further, Robbie pushed past the Vicar and walked on down the corridor. He knocked at the captain's door, and waited a long moment before there was a response.

"What d' ye want?" came the skipper's voice. It was more than clear from the tone that he had been drinking.

"It's Robbie. Might I come in?"

"Can't a man get no privacy!" shouted back Pike. Then, after another long pause, added testily, "Oh, come in! What d' I care?"

Robbie stepped in, closing the door behind him. In the time he had been absent from the bridge, Pike had degenerated considerably—even for one whose normal appearance bordered on that of a vagrant. He sat slouched in his chair, his brass-buttoned coat hung open, and in one hand he held a nearly empty bottle of brandy and in the other a half-full glass. He glared up at Robbie, cursing out a sound that could be little distinguished from an angry snarl.

"So!" growled the skipper, "did ye come here just t' gawk at me, or do ye 'ave some business?"

"I was concerned," Robbie replied. "No one had seen you on the bridge, and even Torger—"

"Playin' the nursemaid are ye!"

"No, Ben. This calm has got to everyone. I only thought maybe you—"

"Ye thought ol' Benjamin Pike had gone looney, eh? Well, he ain't! He can still run this ship 'thout no help o' yers! Calms come an' calms go just like storms an' fair win's, an' I don't need the likes o' a young ne'er-do-well t' hold me hand through any of it!"

"I know that, Ben."

"Oh, look at you!" Pike leaned forward and leered at Robbie as if to take his own advice. "Ne'er a ruffle in ye, is there? Just like yer father! Yes, you could command this ship—better'n me, too; I'd wager my crutch on it!"

With a shaky hand he emptied the brandy bottle into his glass. "Yes, you could," he repeated, "and ye'd like that, too . . ."

Suddenly his face twisted into such contorted hatred that Robbie gasped audibly in surprise. Never had such a look been cast upon him. "But you ain't!" screamed Pike as he hurled the bottle toward Robbie.

Robbie recovered from his shock in time to dodge. The bottle grazed the side of his head before crashing into pieces against the door. The next moment the door itself burst open and the Vicar entered. He rushed into the room, looking apprehensively about, as if he expected to be greeted by some sordid scenario.

"Another nursemaid—is that what we gots?" yelled Pike defiantly.

"Skipper, what's gotten into you?" said Robbie, rubbing his bruised head.

"As if ye didn't know!"

Robbie shook his head dismally. "I don't understand."

All at once, with more speed and skill than Robbie could have imagined from a man in Pike's condition, the skipper leaped up, knocking his chair to the floor. In the hand that a moment earlier had held the lethal bottle, he now wielded a knife.

"Maybe this'll put some understandin' into that pretty fool head o' yours!" cried Pike, waving the weapon about wildly. "Ye walk around here so high an' mighty. It's time ye got yersel' mussed up a bit—brought down to the level o' the rest o' us commoners!"

He leaped at Robbie, deftly upon his one leg, but Robbie deflected the blow easily, grasping the knife-bearing hand in his. Then as quickly as the attack had begun, Pike sagged back and fell away, still, however, glowering at the man he had so recently praised in order to make him his first mate.

"Get out of here—the both of you!"

Robbie stood where he was, dumbfounded. The Vicar grabbed his arm and, with as much force as his strength could muster, led him from the room. Outside, Robbie stopped, coming to himself, then turned back toward the captain's quarters.

"Let him cool off a bit," said the Vicar.

"I don't believe all that happened," said Robbie, his tone reflecting the daze still showing in his eyes.

"What did you say to incite him to such violence?"

"Nothing . . . nothing at all! That's what's so puzzling. It sprang up out of nowhere."

Robbie shook his head again, and rubbed his hands over his face. He winced as his fingers scraped over the spot where the bottle had struck, growing more tender by the moment and swelling slightly.

"Is it bad?"

"No, I'm fine," replied Robbie. "I just need some fresh air."

"You'll not find any topside," said the Vicar.

With the words Robbie remembered what had provoked the incident in the first place. Notwithstanding, he turned and climbed the ladder, leaving Drew alone in the corridor.

The heavy, stifling air met him as he emerged onto the deck. By now even a hurricane would be a relief. Whatever had been eating at Pike had obviously been stirred by the calm. Perhaps it would all be forgotten once the ship and crew got to work again.

Robbie walked to the ship's rail and looked out on the placid sea. So smooth and so tranquil was the water, it seemed incredible that it could cause so much tension. Yet here they were in the middle of the Atlantic, the nearest land days off, and they could not move. They were totally at the mercy of nature. Small wonder that Pike reacted as he did—it was not part of his nature to sit helplessly by. Even with his handicap—and perhaps because of it—he was a proud and independent man. Robbie had never once seen Pike seek assistance from another. Possibly that had been the cause of the flare-up; he had taken Robbie's concern as an indication of weakness. *I should have said nothing,* thought Robbie.

He turned his eyes toward the dull sky. There were no clouds, not even the hint of a breeze. But something was out there. He could sense it coming, and he didn't know whether he should fear it or welcome it.

Against his own advice, the Vicar returned to the skipper's quarters, bearing a dinner tray and a pot of one of Johnnie's special brews. The alcoholic tremor in his hand was markedly pronounced as he raised it to knock on the captain's door; Elliot Drew knew he shook as much from fear as from drink. He had no idea why he had embarked on this mission of mercy. Some sick carryover from his past life, no doubt. Well, someone had to get the skipper back on his feet, and it looked like Robbie could only do so at the peril of his own life.

"I said get out—and stay out!" came Pike's response, more feeble now, completely spent of its previous passion.

As if he didn't hear, Drew opened the door and entered. Pike had regained his chair, but now his head and upper body were sprawled over the small round table he occasionally used for dining. He lifted his head at the sound of the Vicar's footsteps, and peered at him through half-closed eyes.

"I said—"

But Drew interrupted quickly. "Johnnie sent down some food. You may as well eat it—you know how furious he gets when his crockery is sent back full."

"Why should I care a blasted farthing about that Chinaman?"

Drew set the tray on one corner of the table and began pouring the brew into a cup. As its aroma wafted up to him he wondered, as he always did, just what it was made of. For he had never seen the like of it for clearing the effect of alcohol. Its flavor—herbs and roots, no doubt, but who could ask a man like Johnnie?—was at once soothing and wretched, and despite the fact that it was positively nonalcoholic, Drew always found it quite pleasant. He hoped Pike was of the same opinion as he pushed the cup toward him.

"What're you about here?" Pike asked, as if noticing Drew for the first time.

"Only on Johnnie's errands."

Pike snorted disdainfully, then grabbed at the cup, spilling half before the brew reached his lips. He drained the remainder, then grimaced sourly, and held the cup out for more.

"Why'd I do it, Vicar?" Pike asked miserably, after taking another long swallow from the cup.

"I don't know," answered Drew. "Neither does Robbie."

"Why should he . . . ?" The skipper squinted as if he were trying to remember something. "Why should he?" Pike repeated. "He were just a baby . . ."

He shook his head and took another drink. "I could've killed the boy."

"I doubt you would have."

"What do you know?" There was a return of the sharpness to Pike's voice that seemed to indicate more suspicion than questioning.

"It would be a wicked man indeed who would intentionally try to harm one so kindhearted as Robbie Taggart," replied Drew.

"Wicked . . ." mused Pike. "Wicked . . ."

Then in a voice that was almost his normal tone, he asked, "You're a religious man, Vicar. So tell me, don't the Bible say 'an eye for an eye, an arm for an arm, a leg for a leg,' that sort of thing?"

This sudden new line of thought caught Drew so off guard that when he had fully absorbed it, he had to smile, not so much at the question itself, but that it should be addressed to *him*.

"*Religion* aside," replied Drew lightly, "I doubt that Robbie knows the meaning of the word revenge."

"He wouldn't!" shot back Pike oddly; he sounded disappointed, and Drew could not help wondering if they had the same thing in mind.

"At least you've nothing to fear from him," said the Vicar. "But it wouldn't hurt for you to apologize to him. Confession is good for the soul, you know."

"I ain't got no soul, and I don't want one!"

"You would, no doubt, be much better off were that the case," mused the Vicar. "But I would venture to say that your flicker of remorse might indicate otherwise, whatever you *say*. Thus, if you fancy a good night's sleep, you'd do well to make it up to Robbie. He's not a friend you'd want to lose lightly."

"How well I know it, Vicar. How well I know it," moaned Pike. "Get out now," he added unceremoniously with no word of thanks. "I gotta rest."

When Drew had made his exit, Pike rested his elbows on the table and dropped his chin into his hands as if he were indeed going to sleep. But he could neither rest nor sleep. He merely sat there grinding his teeth together, rocking back and forth.

"Oh yes," he mumbled to himself, "you're a good man, Robbie Taggart."

He then picked up the empty brandy glass and eyed it regretfully, hungrily, his fist tightening around it.

"So—so good!" he said through gritted teeth. "*So good!*"

Suddenly the glass smashed within his grasp. But even then he did not move, his bloodied fist still clenched about the lethal shards of broken glass.

17

The Squall

That night Robbie paced the forecastle throughout his watch. His, however, were not the wild, irrational ravings of a caged animal. He was instead pensive, perhaps confused, and his steps were slow, as if with every stride forward he was searching out some new territory.

He had spoken to Pike after dinner.

Pike had approached him, and had seemed a different man than the one who had nearly attacked Robbie earlier. Whether the change was due to Johnnie's brew, the lunch, or some repentant twist to his heart—who could tell? He had given Robbie a friendly slap on the back, accompanied by what was a passable attempt at a laugh.

"Lor'! if the wind don't blow soon," he had said, "we're all gonna go crazy, eh, Robbie?"

"It'll blow," replied Robbie. "Then we'll all be wishing for this calm again."

Pike tried to laugh again. Robbie forced himself to join him, but he keenly felt the hollowness in the skipper's merriment, and could not so easily forget the bitter hate in his eyes before.

"So," said the skipper after a pause, "you still think a storm is brewing?"

"Pure intuition."

"You've got a good feel about the sea, Robbie, an' I don't doubt that you're right." He slapped Robbie's shoulder again, and then Robbie first noticed the bandage wrapped around his right hand.

"What happened there?" asked Robbie, indicating the bandage.

Pike looked at his hand, puzzled for a moment, then replied in a faraway tone, "Oh, nothin' . . . nothin' at all." Then, seeming to snap quickly back to the present, added, "I ain't been myself lately. But you know I don't mean half of what I say."

"Sure," said Robbie, "I know. It's this rotten weather."

But now, alone, gazing on the dark still sea, reflecting on the day's events, Robbie was not so sure after all. Did Pike only mean half of what he said? He didn't know what to think. How could he respond to a man like Pike?

The seeming hatred in his eyes would perhaps not have hounded Robbie so incessantly if he only knew what he had done to deserve it. Yet was he guilty himself of not being straightforward, of not asking Pike right out why the man looked at him so? Or was all this now unnecessary in light of Pike's most recent act of reestablishing their camaraderie?

In his frustration Robbie kicked the capstan as he passed it, reminding him of his talk with the Vicar that evening when he had felt very much like he did now. He wanted to sympathize with Pike. Yet why did Pike—or the Vicar, or anyone—deserve his sympathy? *He* had been the one to bodily attack him. What sympathy could go out to an act like that!

Though he could not have realized it, Robbie's anger and frustration, in truth, stemmed from being caught in such complex human situations. He liked things simple—black and white, spelled out with no room for misunderstandings. But both the Vicar and Pike seemed, by their very natures, bent on drawing him into that dreaded relational predicament where you just didn't quite know where you stood. Robbie could bear anything but that. He didn't like uncertainties.

So occupied were his thoughts that he barely felt the faint breath of air when it came, but when it did, it came as a relief. He could understand the shifts and movements of the sky and sea, and though he knew he could not control them, he felt at least some measure of power knowing he did understand. It was altogether unlike the helplessness he felt in the company of the complex characters into whose lives he had been thrown.

What a welcome sound were the first tentative flaps of the sails as the wind gently kissed them! Heads began poking through the hatch, even those not on watch. The air was filled with a sense of expectation, though perhaps foreboding at the same time. The sky was black, yet toward the horizon off the starboard bow there was a deeper blackness—felt if not actually seen. And the blackness was drawing closer.

Everyone knew the stagnant calm had come to a sudden end when a bright streak of lightning ripped through the dull sky, illuminating the oncoming blackness. The following crack of thunder shook the yards. The man jumped to their stations in preparation. Within twenty minutes the clipper was well underway, her sails filled again with the wind, bearing her before the approaching storm. But she could not outrun it. A quarter of an hour more and great drops began to pelt them. And still the wind rose.

The movement of the *Tiger* was glorious! They rode on the crest of the increasing wind for an hour. In the midst of the falling rain, Robbie stood on the forecastle, watching the sails swelled with life, letting the delicious wind and water beat against his face. *This is the life of the sailor!* he thought. It was for moments like this that he had left the Navy!

Still the winds increased their velocity, gradually shifting to the port quarter, and seeming—though the storm was coming from behind them—to push the *Tiger* into the very heart of the heavenly turmoil. The swell rose, and soon twenty footers were crashing against the *Tiger's* hull; the storm above and the storm below tossed the tiny craft about as though it were a mere toy. It was time to adjust the yards and haul in the royals and topgallant sails. Robbie required all of his and most of Digger's watch. Over the lashing wind he shouted his orders, rallying every man, save the helmsman, to the mainmast. However, a quick assessment of his manpower showed that someone was missing.

"Where's the Vicar?" he yelled, reminded of his previous frustration with the man.

"Went below an hour or two ago," replied Jenkins.

"What! I gave him no permission to do so!" yelled Robbie. "Go get him! I need every hand!"

They fell to their tasks immediately, and he barely took notice of Drew's arrival a few minutes later. It was just as well, for he shuffled on deck with a decided stagger, and the odor of whiskey followed him closely.

The first necessity was to adjust the yard to point into the storm so the wind pressure would be spilled from the sail. This done, they had to haul at the braces. It was backbreaking work, and dangerous, for the deck was slick with the falling rain and the sea breaking over the rails. But there was no rest even when this was done, for they still had to man the sheets and the crew and bunt lines for hauling in the sail. First came the mainmast, where Robbie took one sheet and put Jenkins, his best man, on the other, dividing the remainder of the watch between the other lines.

"Let go!" shouted Robbie.

He and Jenkins released the sheets in perfect timing, while the rest of the men began hauling on the other lines. All the men save one pulled with all their might with even tension. But the one line developed slack and began to tangle.

"We're losin' the sail!" yelled Jenkins.

Robbie looked up and saw it immediately; it would be blown to shreds if action wasn't taken immediately.

"Haul, man!" Robbie called out. The slack line was Drew's.

"My hand slipped," said the Vicar lamely, and even in the rising storm Robbie could hear the drunken slur of his words.

Another order, one that would not have been so kindly spoken, was about to come from Robbie's lips when a cry diverted his attention back to Jenkins just in time for him to see the sheet snap from his grip. Robbie shot a glance upward and saw that the sail had taken control. There was no time to think of that now, for the force of the sudden release of the sheet had flung Jenkins against the starboard rail. He would likely have been lost to the angry sea had the ship not hit a trough at that precise moment, lurching suddenly to port, and sending Jenkins sprawling across the slippery deck.

"Grab that bloody line!" Robbie yelled at the Vicar. There was no pity for the man in his voice now, only wrath. He had almost caused a good man to go overboard.

Later, despite the gusty wind, Robbie climbed aloft with half the men of the watch to secure the sails. But even the heady exhilaration of hanging eighty feet above the raging sea did not cool his fury against Drew for his incompetent behavior.

When a lull finally came in the work, Robbie found him at the rail facing the wild storm. His face was pale; he appeared sick, and he had obviously been retching over the side.

"You've been drinking!" Robbie shouted.

Drew made no response. Robbie grabbed his shoulders and shook him violently. "Tell me, you dirty coward!"

Still there was no response from the Vicar. Robbie gave him a final shove, spun around, and stalked to the forehatch. He scrambled down the ladder, and when he reached Drew's quarters he kicked open the door. He went straight to Drew's cot and tore apart the bedding. Having no luck there, he attacked the Vicar's gear, flinging clothes, books, and miscellaneous mementos across the tiny cabin. He did not hear Drew approach, and only became aware of his presence when he gasped as Robbie found what he had been seeking. Holding up two bottles of Scotch whiskey, one of which was half empty, he turned to glare at the culprit.

"How could you!" As he spoke, Robbie's voice was now barely above a whisper. Even in his fury on the deck, somehow he had hoped his assessment was wrong, that somehow that depth of character he felt lay somewhere in the Vicar might have triumphed. Therefore, even as he spoke, Robbie's anger was laced with disappointment.

"You—you can't expect me to face each day cold, stone sober," the Vicar replied lamely.

"You have a job to do!"

"I do my job."

"Not when you're full of drink! You almost killed a man!"

Drew covered his face with his trembling hands. He would have wept, but he had used up all his tears many years ago.

"I suppose you think feeling sorry somehow makes up for it! Well, it's not enough!"

With the force of his righteous anger, Robbie flung one of the bottles against the bulkhead.

"No!" screamed the Vicar in a pathetic wail, but he was too late. The glass shattered and its amber poison dripped down the wall.

"You deserve to look every day in the eye and be forced to see what kind of cowardly wretch you are!" said Robbie, hurling the second bottle after the same fate as its mate.

Drew stumbled to the wall and piteously touched the dripping liquid with his fingers. "What have you done?" he whimpered, bringing his wet fingers to his lips. "What have you done . . . ?" His mournful tone sounded like an injured child.

"I'm trying to make a man of you."

"I told you not to try to reform me," replied Drew, his old voice gradually returning.

"It's gone beyond that, Drew," Robbie replied, his anger abating. "Your drink has endangered both ship and crew."

"It wasn't the drink," countered Drew. "I've worked far drunker. My hand just slipped. It could have happened to anyone."

"It could have. But it didn't! It happened to *you*. You can't deny that you were drinking. Just like you couldn't deny Turk's accusations the other day."

"If you thought I did it, why did you defend me?"

"I don't know," replied Robbie, shaking his head. "I wasn't sure about you—till now. I hoped you had more self-respect than that. But now I see I was wrong. You were looking for whiskey, weren't you? So, you are a drunkard *and* a thief. Could you sink any lower? Oh yes, you still have murder."

Robbie paused, then with a questioning furrow in his brow, added, "Or have you done murder too?"

"Please, Robbie, don't hate me," begged Drew pitifully, dodging the thrust of Robbie's question. "You're the only friend I have. I used to be a man. I used to be able to face things. But now I don't even know what a man is. Don't blame me if I can't face life anymore. It's not my fault."

"Who's fault is it then, Elliot?"

The Vicar was silent.

Robbie turned to go.

"I'll do better in the future," pleaded the Vicar after him. "Please . . . give me another chance."

If the hard, cynical Drew frustrated Robbie, this groveling, sniveling one disgusted him. Yet how could he turn his back on him? A man like Robbie, although he counted many as his friends and needed no others, could not turn his back on one who had none but him. He did not hate Elliot Drew. How could he? Only the most heartless kind of man could hate one so pathetic.

"We still have the storm above," said Robbie. "Are you able to finish the watch?"

"Yes . . . yes. I'll finish," replied the Vicar.

Robbie strode from the cabin. He didn't know if he was being too soft on the man for not confining him to some discipline in his quarters, or if he had been too hard on one so fragile. He only hoped his actions would not in the end prove harmful, even fatal, to anyone on the ship.

Drew padded after Robbie. When they reached the ladder, he laid a hand on Robbie's arm to detain him. Robbie stopped. Drew pulled him aside, looked about to make sure there were no listeners.

"I want you to know one thing," he said, and as he spoke his voice took on an uncharacteristic edge, reminiscent of a sense of pride. "I am no thief. Yes, I went into Turk's chest—but not to steal anything. Not for myself at least."

"What for then?"

Again Drew looked about down each corridor before speaking.

"Several days ago," he began, "we were on watch. I came below to—well, to have a drink. I passed by Turk's cabin, and when I heard a noise, I stopped to look in. The door was open, but Turk had not seen or heard me. And there he was rummaging through his chest. I saw him pull out a pistol. At least, that's what I thought I saw. One of those old kinds. Just what you'd expect an Arab to carry. He replaced it quickly, and I couldn't be—you know, my eyes were a little blurry— exactly certain. I know it was foolhardy, but the first opportunity I got, I knew I had to have a look and be sure. This crew makes me nervous enough—but to think of one of them—and a man like Turk; he's no one's friend I can tell you that, except the bo'sun's—to think of one of them carrying a weapon. Well, I thought I should have proof before I made accusations."

"Very wise," agreed Robbie. "And what did you find?"

"Nothing. It was gone. But I did find these." He reached into his pocket and held up several slugs.

"I don't recognize the caliber. They almost look like the balls from an old dual-flintlock pistol," said Robbie.

"I couldn't be sure."

"And you said nothing?"

"My word against his."

"I appreciate your telling me. This is something I should know."

"I had to," replied Drew. "Perhaps I'm not a total loss."

"No. Perhaps not." Robbie's mouth curved up into a reluctant smile as he turned to climb up the ladder.

The instant they emerged, the storm whipped against Robbie's face, reminding him of immediate realities. Yet he could not so easily forget all he had just heard. Once again Elliot Drew presented himself an enigma, a man of deep contrasts, as indeed did their skipper. Both displayed remarkably divergent personalities. One moment Drew was groveling at Robbie's feet begging forgiveness, the next was braving the dangerous wrath of Turk to solve the mystery of a gun that might not even exist.

Of even more concern to Robbie were his own unsettled reactions. Again his emotions found themselves stretched from pity to anger to something almost like friendliness toward the man.

Again, that fleeting half-formed thought he had had on the night of their departure intruded upon his brain. He and the Vicar were perhaps more alike than he wanted to realize, each in his own way struggling to attain something—perhaps an elusive dream, or some part of himself hidden so deep that neither could readily identify it.

Both were seeking meaning. However, one was doing so by running from it, or attempting to obliterate it at every opportunity. He feared that perhaps it was lost altogether, but feared even more lest it should be found, and he be forced to face the awful consequences. But the other, Robbie Taggart himself, seemed to wear his masculinity across his broad chest, as if that were all there was to life—as if he believed he had no further to look.

Robbie, unlike the Vicar, was aware of no fear in himself, and thus he was perhaps in greater peril than his crewmate. For where there is no sense of need, there is no seeking after deeper knowledge of self, and no search after the One in whom all needs are fulfilled, whether known to us or not.

The blast of the storm was welcome to Robbie, for it released him from the wearisome task of introspection. Even working beside Turk on a troublesome sail for three-quarters of an hour was more pleasant than the train his thoughts might otherwise have embarked upon. The hard work, the lashing wind, and the driving rain cleared his brain. He could not focus on the more manageable reality presented by the sinister man, made even more so by the suspicion that he carried a firearm.

18

South Past the Cape

The gales drove the *Sea Tiger* for five hours more, with a force of ten winds. She was driven on her beam ends for an hour and shipped water until her decks were flooded.

The watches were abandoned as the entire crew labored against the squall. Every man worked to his limit, groaning at the pumps or hauling in sail. The main topgallant and the mizzen royal were lost, and twice little Sammy was nearly washed overboard.

Still Lackey found opportunity, in spite of the amount of work pulled out of him, to wail, "This is the end, saith the Lord of the wind. The power of the air seeks its revenge on a sinful race! You will be lost before you round the Cape, says the servant of the Most High!"

"I can't think of a more fitting end to it all," countered Drew, walking past Lackey. The prophet of platitudes had for the most part regained his old cynical self and indulged himself by poking fun at the ship's prophet of gloom. The Vicar labored valiantly alongside his mates—almost bent, it seemed, on acquitting himself of his shameful behavior.

It was Drew who spotted Sammy's danger in the midst of the boy's second dangerous foray with the torturous sea. Sammy had been making his way aft, carrying a large coil of rope. It had taken the boy nearly twenty minutes to traverse the length of the ship, hanging on to swinging rigging or stationary rails when available. He was aft the mainmast when a fifteen-foot wave broke over the port rail, knocking him from his feet. Momentarily rendered senseless by the fall, he slid across the flooded deck and could not gain his feet before the next crashing wave hit. His body slammed against the rail, and in the lurch of the ship that followed he would almost certainly have been washed over. Drew caught him just in time, however, and, hanging on to the boy with one arm and the rail with the other, he struggled to keep them both on board while still another torrent from the sea did its best to overwhelm them.

Witnessing the struggle, Robbie managed to get a length of rope to Drew, and, waiting for a break between the swells, hauled the two to safety.

He ordered Sammy below, helping him through the hatch, then turned to the Vicar.

"You saved his life, Drew," he said simply.

"Please. No laudation of glory and honor," scoffed the Vicar. "What I did was from reflexes alone."

"I doubt Sammy will believe that," returned Robbie, wiping a fresh splash of sea-spray from his face.

"In the evening a coward, by morning a hero—is that it?" said Drew with a raised eyebrow. "Come now, Robbie, no one changes quite that quickly."

"I agree," replied Robbie, "which only makes me wonder—"

"Well don't wonder," rejoined Drew sharply. "Your estimation of me earlier was the correct one. A man cannot be what he isn't, not even after a well meant lecture by a friend. I tried that long ago—being what I wasn't cut out to be. I battered my head against the natural flow for a long time, but it was all futility. God said he'd make a new man of me— or so they told me—but it never happened. Perhaps even God himself wasn't up to such an undertaking. Or perhaps, though he *could* have, he just wouldn't. 'Many are called but few are chosen,' you know. Yes, that's it, I was a lost cause from the beginning. So don't you go trying to plant any hope in me, Robbie. I won't have it."

"I doubt God gave up on you," returned Robbie. "I think you must have given up on yourself. I don't know as much about God as you do, but something tells me that he wouldn't turn his back on anyone, even the likes of you."

"Well, if there's any repenting to be done, I'll undertake the project on my own," rejoined Drew.

"If you get any leanings in that direction," laughed Robbie, "it wouldn't hurt if you brought some of the rest of these scalawags with you!"

About noon Pike and Robbie managed to get the *Tiger* before the wind, and were finally able to heave-to on a starboard tack. They had covered nearly two hundred miles in winds as fierce as sixty miles per hour. Heavy gales continued to assail them the rest of the day and through the night, but gradually moderated. And by the following morning they were able to trim all the sails, replacing those that had been torn or ripped apart in the storm.

Once the storm had completely subsided, the *Tiger* encountered the southeast trades and ran close-hauled for two weeks against strong headwinds. This took them at last to the Cape known as Good Hope, but it was not hope it seemed bent on giving the *Tiger* on this particular voyage. The winds remained so contrary that Pike decided to take the *Tiger* much further south than usual in order to catch the more favorable westerlies.

They swung wide and south, past latitude 50° and almost to 55° before encountering the winds that would take them northeast through the Indian Ocean. Though they were now well into April, this southerly detour took them so far south that they ran into groups of stray icebergs and air so frigid that ice lined the yards, the weight on one occasion nearly snapping the bowsprit in two. It took two men on the forecastle, and a man on mid-deck to relay instructions to the helmsman, in order to negotiate the treacherous path during the nighttime hours in and out of icebergs, during which time the sails flew at only partial strength to keep their speed to a minimum. Beyond issuing the occasionally necessary order, Pike remained in his cabin throughout most of the perilous escapade. It was left to Robbie to guide them through the hazardous path, a fact which by this time most of the men greeted with a certain relief. And though Robbie by this time had his sea legs and ship's wits firmly under him and about him, and felt competent enough for the responsibility, he did not feel altogether comfortable in the position. Pike's words during the calm were still etched harshly in his memory— "Yes, ye could, *an' ye'd like to* . . ." Nor could he forget the look which had accompanied them.

Two weeks after passing the Cape they swung north and once more toward the warmer latitudes. With the wind at their backs and the *Tiger's* sails full, it was but a week back to Capricorn and the eastern shore of Madagascar.

One morning Robbie went into the chart house and there found Pike bent over a map making some calculations.

"When do you figure we'll reach the Sunda Straits?" Robbie asked. "We seem bearing a bit too much north for Indonesia." Though he loved the open sea, he had begun to anticipate a day or two on land for a change, and the Straits were the gateway to Jakarta, the China Sea, and many exotic ports that had long remained indelibly imprinted in his mind from his younger days.

"Oh, did I forget to tell ye, mate?" replied Pike offhandedly. "We'll be stoppin' by Calcutta first."

"Calcutta! No, you didn't tell me! That's four thousand miles out of our way!" Robbie was perturbed not only at the oversight, but because he strongly suspected why Pike had never mentioned India in connection with the voyage. Calcutta and Bombay were the major opium market places of the East. And while the drug trafficking trade with China had been legalized since the Opium Wars of the forties and fifties, it was nonetheless abhorrent to Robbie. Legal or not, drugs brought no good to those who dealt in them. From Pike's tone, Robbie was certain the skipper must have recalled the youth's outspoken opinions of the trade years ago. Why else would he have kept quiet about such an important layover?

"Not if we take our way south through the Straits of Malacca and by way of Singapore."

"You know better than that, Pike," insisted Robbie. "That would save us only five hundred miles, or less, over Sunda. And wouldn't be as safe."

"Well, suit yourself. We'll go through Sunda. But not until we've stopped in Calcutta!" His eyes for an instant took on a glow Robbie did not want to recall.

"I don't like your keeping me in the dark!"

"No need to get touchy, laddie," said Pike.

"You said nothing because you knew I wouldn't sign on if I knew you were dealing in opium."

"Well, ain't it true?" But before Pike gave Robbie the chance to respond, he hurried on. "'Sides, I wouldn't waste my time on opium. China grows her own now an' there ain't enough money in it. Oh, I expect to pick up a couple chests of the stuff; ye can still make a sale now and then. But I got somethin' bigger to attend to in Calcutta."

"Which is?"

"Guess there ain't no harm in ye knowin' now, seein's how ye can't jump ship on me. Well, I gots me a connection in Calcutta what's got a high grade strain of a similar drug. But 'tis purer an' stronger than any opium ye ever seen. We got us a distributor set up in China—an' they're payin' big money for it. You ain't opposed to makin' a bit of siller, are ye, lad?"

"You know I don't care about that," replied Robbie flatly.

"That's right, I forgot." Pike drew out the words to gain the maximum sarcastic effect. *"The noble Taggart breed—"*

"That's not the reason, Ben, and you know it."

"It's always been true! Ye was always better'n the rest of us, eh, laddie?"

Though Pike's tone seemed congenial enough on the surface, the cutting edge of his words were no less evident. Again, one look into Pike's eyes told Robbie that he was not imagining the glare he saw there. In them was the same look they had contained when he had attacked Robbie—cold, cruel, and chilling. Robbie looked away, an involuntary shudder passing through his body. The Benjamin Pike of those eyes was not a Benjamin Pike he knew—nor wanted to know.

"I wish you didn't think that," Robbie tried to reply, but his voice was hesitant. It was difficult to form a logical reply to such words. What was Pike harboring against him, anyway? And if there was something, why had he been so determined to make Robbie his first mate?

"I'm sorry if I've done something to give you such an idea. Whatever I've done, Pike, I didn't mean any harm."

Suddenly Pike's demeanor changed and grew softer. He threw an arm around Robbie.

"Of course ye didn't, laddie!" He seemed completely in earnest, a different man. "But ye can see, can't ye? I had to go to Calcutta. Ye're like a son to me, laddie. An' once I seen you again, I couldn't sail without ye."

"I suppose I can understand—"

"Ye ain't gonna jump ship, are ye?"

"No," replied Robbie, his tone indicating, however, that he was still not fully resolved to Pike's Calcutta scheme. But what could he do about it? And he could not so easily abandon his loyalty to the ship or his father's friend. "Let's just forget all this happened," he said finally.

Pike flashed a relieved grin, but as Robbie slowly left the chartroom, he found he could not quickly forget his recent interchange with the skipper. It left him with an eerie feeling he could not shake. The man was out of balance, or so it seemed, displaying widely divergent personalities at different times. His propensity to outbursts of violence worried Robbie. Whether he was just suffering from the stresses of the voyage, Robbie could not tell.

Nine years ago it had been the same way with Pike. He *had* been able to forget that, though now bits and pieces began to come back to him out of memory. He had been just as puzzled then by the man's erratic behavior. And now he saw another dimension to it that had escaped him before. It was not so much what Pike always *said* that was troubling, but rather what the man left *unsaid*. And more—*how* it was left unsaid. It weighed so heavily upon him now that Robbie wondered how he could ever have forgotten.

19

The Vicar's Attempt

Several mornings later, Robbie lay on his bunk relishing the last few moments of repose before he would have to spell Digger and his watch. The winds had been favorable and the skies mostly clear, and had he thought about it he might have known some new episode was due on board this ship of seafaring eccentrics. But he was hardly prepared for it when it came. It was the last thing he would have expected.

Gradually a voice bore in upon his waking consciousness. At first he paid little attention, but as the voice persisted, even grew louder, he could not ignore it. The sound was apparently coming from above deck. There was a monotonous ring to it, a droning sound as if a lecture were being read. Getting to his feet, Robbie could not imagine its source. He opened his door and proceeded down the corridor, and by the time he reached the ladder up to the hatch he knew well enough the source of this oration. The voice was the Vicar's.

Robbie climbed onto the deck.

Around the forecastle were gathered a half-dozen or so of the men whose watch would be ending soon. Above them, perched on a section of the foremast, which he had appropriated for a makeshift bench, sat the Vicar, waxing eloquent as he must once have from his own pulpit.

"And so, my friends," he was saying as Robbie approached, "I tell you once more that the time has come for you to listen to the Lord of Hosts. For He would tell you that the season of your transgressions must draw to a close. The hour is nigh when He will visit His wrath on a perverse and faithless generation, even yourselves, who, though your raiment not be fine as the Scriptures say of the godless, yet nevertheless the Lord looks not on the outward appearance of a man, but upon the heart. And what will He see when He looks upon your heart, my friends? What will He see when his eyes—"

"An' wot will 'e see in yer own 'eart, Vicar!" shouted one of the men.

"Ah, He will see a heart soiled as filthy rags," replied the Vicar, unperturbed by the interruption. "My own heart is stained and unclean. I admit it. But that must not keep you from inclining your ear to the voice of the Most High. His hand is knocking at the door of your heart. Do not clothe your hearts in the soft raiment of the Pharisees of old, but rather open your eyes to behold that your righteousness is as filthy rags in the sight of a pure and holy God to whom all sin is an abomination."

"*All* sin, Vicar?" asked another of the men, with a knowing wink at his fellows, who chuckled at his wit.

"That's right, my friend. The Lord of Hosts visits His righteous wrath on the iniquities of the just and the unjust, even as the rain falls from heaven on a merchant clipper and a pirate ship with no respect of persons. The great God, even the Lord of Hosts, speaks to the generations of men, calling them to repentance. The moment is at hand to decide whether you will be one of the brood of vipers, or one of the chosen, the Elect, foreordained since before the dawn of time to share in the blessings and righteousness of the Lord of Hosts. Now is the appointed hour. The valley of decision lies before us. Multitudes are gathered. With which of the mighty armies will you side, as they wage war in the heavenlies? For the battle is not against flesh and blood, but against principalities and powers of darkness. The battle is nigh thee and—"

"Hey, Vicar! What'n blazes is a preencepality?"

"Yeah, Vicar, I hain't ne'er heard o' none o' that brood o' vipers. What're ye ravin' about, anyway?"

"These are no ravings of the man you once beheld in your midst, a man timid of step and slow of tongue. This is the voice of the Lord speaking through his oracle, as Jonah of old sailed the waters of the Mediterranean, first resisting the voice of God to him, but then proclaiming the truth boldly. So I come to you on these waters, as one who first resisted but now sees the light and calls you likewise to repent of your folly and turn—"

"Aw, Vicar! You ain't seen no light 'cep' the golden glow o' yer bottle o' whiskey since we left England!"

"I tell you, my brothers, I have—"

"Come on down off o' there, Vicar," said Digger finally, "afore ye fall an' get yerself all banged up."

"No, wait, my friends," called Drew, as a few of the men began to wander back toward the chores they had left.

"Gone plumb looney!" muttered Digger to no one in particular.

"Drunken fool," said Jenkins, who, though he was on Robbie's watch, had risen before the first mate and had come up topside to see what was going on.

Others were even less kind in their appraisal of the Vicar's sudden foray into the unknown waters of repentance, and took his attempt at soul-saving as the final sign that he had lost his mind.

"Throw him over the side!" said Turk, still harboring a considerable grudge over the matter of the mis-tied knot. "If the maniac is so anxious to meet his maker, I say we oblige him!"

"Wait, my brothers. I speak only the truth!" called Drew, in a last-ditch effort to save his congregation.

"Hear him . . . hear him!" wailed Lackey. "Hear him, ye brood of vipers! The doom of the Lord is coming, even as Jonah foretold, we will be shipwrecked and swallowed by great beasts of the deep! The next storm will be our last, ye brood of vipers . . . hear him! . . . hear him . . . ye ill-begotten brood of snakes!"

"Come down, Elliot," said Robbie at length, stepping forward.

"I tell you, my brothers," called Drew after his retreating flock, " . . . wait! Robbie Taggart . . . tell them—tell them I'm a changed man!"

"Come down, Elliot," said Robbie. "Then we'll talk."

Drew looked around, as if bewildered, then slowly abandoned his perch and climbed down to the deck beside Robbie.

The Vicar followed Robbie along the deck in silence, staring down so as to avoid any stray glances from the men, some of whom regarded him with pity, others who were still chuckling among themselves over the ill-fated impromptu sermon. He trailed the mate, almost as if being led away to some disciplinary doom, his head hanging low rather than erect in the triumph of his victory over self.

Robbie led him down the hatch and back to his cabin where he pointed to his bunk.

"Lie down for a while, Drew," he said. "Cool off a bit. Let your head clear."

"It is clear, Robbie! I saw everything so clearly—what a miserable fool I've been! I thought . . . I thought I could somehow . . . you know, make it better. Make up for the past, you know."

"But you won't make up for the past by spouting off a bunch of stock religious phrases."

"The words of the Lord," corrected Drew.

"For all I know, you're right," consoled Robbie. "Maybe they are the words of the Lord. But none of the men understood a word you were saying, Vicar. What good do the words do if no one can understand you?"

"But they taught us to speak the word, and let the Lord reveal understanding to the heart of the hearer. They told us not to worry whether people understand."

"But how can the Lord give understanding to your listeners if you're talking what to them sounds like nonsense? Even I didn't understand a fourth of what you were talking about."

"So I've failed again!"

"Maybe you should look upon it as a time of learning," said Robbie. "Might there be some other way to make up for the past, as you say?"

"What other way?"

"I don't know. You're the Vicar. Is standing up in a pulpit the only way to validate whether your faith means anything?"

"What faith?" shot back the Vicar, the old cynicism creeping back into his voice. "I never had any faith to begin with! That's always been the problem, trying to talk about something I had nothing of inside!"

"I'll cover for you on watch an hour or two," Robbie said. "Maybe you'll feel better then."

Slowly Robbie turned and left him alone.

Three hours later the Vicar had still made no further appearance on the top deck. Deciding it might be time to check on him, Robbie again sought his small cabin. The door was closed, and his knock was not greeted by any sound from within.

He tried the door. It was not locked. Robbie pushed into the room, his nostrils immediately assaulted by the pungent smell of alcohol. The Vicar half lay on his bed, snoring soundly in a drunken stupor.

Robbie sighed deeply, pondering what to do.

He stood a moment—annoyed, frustrated, yet perplexed. Had the time finally come for some stringent disciplinary action toward the Vicar? He had, after all, broken a command by falling so dismally off the wagon. He was absent from his watch. Robbie had every right to punish him severely. Or was this another time to exercise patience? The man was obviously caught in the midst of a painful personal crisis. He might come out of it on his own if just given the time. But if pushed, the poor man's distraught emotional and spiritual state could cause him to collapse altogether.

He did not have long to reflect upon his decision, however, for almost immediately from behind him he heard the sound of rapidly approaching footsteps. The voice that accompanied it was ranting angrily.

Robbie spun around to find Ahmed Turk racing toward him, wildly shouting half-intelligible accusations and threats.

"You get . . . my way, Taggart . . . no more this time! . . . my turn now . . . I kill blag'ard!"

Robbie stepped forward and held up his hand to stop him.

"Hold on now, Turk," he said. "Whatever this is all about, we can—"

"You no more protect thievin' liar, Taggart!" he yelled, swinging a wild fist in Robbie's direction.

Robbie grabbed his arm and arrested it in mid-flight with his powerful grip. Turk's eyes filled with hatred as he wrestled away, freed himself, then retreated a step. "I'll kill him, Taggart!" he repeated. "And you, too, if you try to stop me!"

"Just tell me what it's about, Turk," said Robbie again.

"That lyin' phony of a preacher's been in my gear again, stealin' this time! Now, you gonna move out of my way?"

"You're going nowhere, Turk, until I get to the bottom of this!"

"He's broke in, I tell you!" yelled Turk savagely. "And I'll prove it. You just stand outta me way!" Again he rushed toward Robbie, but still again Robbie prevented him from passing.

"What's missing, Turk?"

"Nothin' you need know about, you pandering Navy man!"

"I won't do a thing about this unless I know all the facts," said Robbie, trying hard to keep his calm.

Suddenly Turk retreated several steps, then pulled his gun out from somewhere among his layers of strange clothing. At the same moment more footsteps could be heard tramping along the corridor. It was Jack Digger.

The moment he saw his Arab compatriot with his long pistol pointed at Robbie, he stopped.

"I told you not to try to stop me, Taggart!" said Turk, his voice now calculating and sinister. "But you wouldn't listen! You had to try to play the part of loyal mate, defending your scum of a crew."

"Now hold on, Turk," said Digger behind him. "Put away the pistol, an' we can—"

"Back off, Jack! This is my fight now. This sap's never been my first mate! And he's tried to protect that thievin' preacher once too often. Well, I'm gonna give him somethin' to bleed about now!"

"What are ye talkin' about, Turk?" said Digger, inching closer by degrees. Turk's eyes were riveted on Robbie some ten feet away, but out of the corner of one he perceived the bo'sun's design.

He turned quickly toward Digger. "You stay where you are, Jack! I told you this is my fight—"

But as he turned, Robbie seized the fraction of a second his eyes left him to lunge toward the adjoining corridor, and behind a partition out of line from Turk's weapon.

Seeing a flash of movement, Turk spun back toward Robbie and fired, discharging both barrels. A resounding crack reverberated and echoed throughout the ship as the bullets ricocheted off the cabin walls. Robbie dodged the gunfire, smacking his head against the bulkhead in the process.

Digger grabbed Turk, screaming and flailing wildly, and wrested the gun from his hand, throwing it to the floor while holding the Arab fast.

"He stole my Vodka, Jack," wailed Turk.

"Killin' the first mate's no way to get even, man!" shouted Digger. "Now you go back to yer cabin! An' don't ye leave it till I come fer ye!"

Slowly he released Turk, who sulked back down the corridor the way he had come. Then the bo'sun approached Robbie.

"I'm sorry, mate," he said. "The bloke must 'ave lost his 'ead for a minute."

"For a minute! The lunatic's stark raving mad!" Robbie retorted angrily; he didn't notice, nor did he care, that Digger seemed to making a conciliatory gesture. He didn't like being shot at and he was sick of being the brunt of everyone's hostilities. He pushed past Digger in the direction Turk had gone. But Digger laid a hand on Robbie's arm.

"Ye better leave him be, Taggart," said Digger. "I can 'andle him."

"You've hardly handled him yet, Digger. He's deranged!"

"He were jist protectin' his possessions."

"By committing murder?" rejoined Robbie. "Did you know about his having that gun?"

"What's it to ye, Taggart!" replied the bo'sun, losing what little patience he may have had. "What I know's me own business! Ye ask too many questions! I was in charge here afore ye came along. An' we 'ad our own way of runnin' things. So don't ye go tryin' to change them! Ye hear me?"

"I hear you, Digger," said Robbie. "But if you let Turk get away with keeping a concealed weapon aboard this ship, then you're as much to blame for what happened as that demented Arab!"

"But the Vicar's thievin' is jist fine, is that it, Taggart?"

"It doesn't even compare with what Turk tried to do, and I'm not going to let him get away with it."

"What do ye mean by that?"

"Wild men who fire guns don't belong on this ship," replied Robbie tersely. "It's not up to you anymore, Digger. I'm the mate and we're going to do things my way now!"

"We'll see, Taggart! We'll see!"

The huge boatswain turned and stormed back down the corridor after his friend.

Instead of immediately following the bo'sun, Robbie made his way back to Drew's cabin where the Vicar still lay as he had left him, sprawled across the bunk unconscious. Robbie looked about, spotted the three quarters empty bottle, cork securely in place, held tightly against the Vicar's chest with his fingers still wrapped firmly around it, like a favorite childhood toy he had taken to bed with him. He didn't want to admit that Digger might be right or that his anger toward the bo'sun was misplaced. Well, petty theft was a far cry from attempted murder. It was as if Digger and Turk had been baiting him, *asking* him for a confrontation.

"Oh, Drew, what have you started?" Robbie murmured to himself.

He reached down, took the bottle, and with a look of determination spreading across his face, he exited into the corridor. Spotting the pistol still lying where it had fallen, he stooped to pick it up and made his way up the aft hatch to the top deck.

The crisp, breezy air stung Robbie's hot cheeks. He breathed deeply of the cool air, walked from the hatch over to the starboard rail, and without a moment's hesitation flung the bottle of clear liquid over the side and into the deep blue of the Indian Ocean. A second more and the pistol followed it.

That done, Robbie turned again, descended the hatch, and made his way in a firm resolve to Turk's cabin. As he suspected, he found Digger there as well.

Robbie burst in without knock or courtesy.

"I'm here to search the room!" he announced without introduction.

"And what right do you have to—"

"The right of my position, Turk!" shouted back Robbie. "The right of your attempted murder this morning!"

"I warned you, Taggart," said the bo'sun, standing now and approaching Robbie. Sensing that a greater battle was at hand than his puny frame would be able to keep clear of, Turk said no more and slunk into the farthest corner.

"You warned me, all right, Digger," replied Robbie, "and I told you that I was the first mate now!"

Without stopping, Robbie walked straight toward Turk's chest, unlocked now, with the securing rope untied and lying in a heap beside it. Before either the Arab or the boatswain had a chance to object, Robbie had thrown it open and taken another full bottle of Vodka into his hand.

"Jack," wailed Turk, "it's me last bottle. Stop him, Jack!"

"Don't, Digger," said Robbie, thrusting the bottle, which he held by its slender neck toward the bo'sun's protruding belly. "You try to take this bottle from me and I'll bash it over your head!"

"What do you intend to do with it, Taggart?" said Digger, warily keeping his distance, but his eyes clearly indicating his readiness to pounce at the first slackening of Robbie's defense.

"It's going the way of its mate and the way of the pistol—over the side to Davy Jones!"

Robbie ran from the room, Turk wailing in suppressed agony over the loss of his liquor. Digger sprang after him. Robbie reached the top deck about ten seconds ahead of the puffing boatswain. Digger emerged through the hatch just in time to see the bottle hurled in a wide arc into the sea.

"Ye shouldn't 'ave done it, Taggart," he said with intimidation in his deep voice. "Ye 'ad no right! Just like ye had no right to interfere between me an' the girl."

"I had every right, Digger! And you know it."

"So ye think. But this was my ship afore ye came along, an' now I'm thinkin' maybe ye'd like to be joinin' those bottles yerself!"

He strode forward, his eyes full of suppressed wrath.

Jenkins observed the proceedings from farther down the deck, and when he heard the shouts from the forecastle, Overlie hastened toward the trouble. But neither man dared interfere. They knew the mate and bo'sun had to settle their differences according to the law of the sea, where the strongest must be in command, for the good of the ship.

Robbie stepped back.

"I've got no argument with you, Digger," he said. "Don't be a fool for the sake of the Arab. He's not worth it."

"It's between you an' me now, Taggart," replied Digger, still approaching like an enraged bear. "It's time this was settled once an' for all!"

"There's no need for it, Digger."

"Ye yellow-livered coward!" laughed Digger, still approaching.

"I'll give you one more chance to keep your record clean, Digger. Don't be a fool and do something you'll regret!"

"I'll never regret throwin' ye to the sharks!" laughed Digger.

"This is your last chance, Digger. When we get to Calcutta, you get rid of Turk. Send him back to England on another ship. Do anything you see fit with him. Just get him off the *Tiger*. You brought him on. You get rid of him. He's a danger to the rest of the crew. Do that and I'll keep this act of insubordination off your record."

"Ha!" spat Digger. "You weak-kneed Navy boy! You expect me to turn out a friend?"

"He's no friend of yours, Digger. He'd slit your throat in a minute if there was a sovereign in it."

"I won't double-cross him!"

"Then you'll leave me no choice but to turn you both out in Calcutta, and you'll go down as insubordinate besides. You'll never get work on another ship."

"You won't be around to do anything in Calcutta!" growled Digger, finally losing patience and lunging toward Robbie in unmasked hatred.

Robbie jumped backward, but not before Digger's massive hand had closed around his wrist. Robbie struggled to free himself, but the bo'sun laughed a cruel laugh, then bashed his left fist into Robbie's midsection, releasing his wrist with his right as he did.

Robbie staggered back, slamming into the rail, gasping for breath.

The bo'sun came toward him again, like a shark at the first taste of blood. Digger swung, this time for Robbie's head, but Robbie eluded the blow. Angered, Digger came on, swung again, this time grazing Robbie's forehead. In size the fight was a mismatch—like a dog against a raging bear. But Robbie was quicker on his feet than the bo'sun, rendered even more flatfooted by his unleashed fury, dulling his perceptions.

He reached out, trying to lay hold of Robbie to hoist him over the rail. Robbie hit at Digger's outstretched hand, catching the bo'sun's fleshy forearm with the knuckles of his closed fist. The pain was more an annoyance than a serious deterrent to Digger, but it stopped him for a second, enabling Robbie to regain his footing and take a breath of fresh air.

The next instant, however, Digger was on the attack again. His great arm jabbed out from his body and dealt Robbie a punishing blow along the left side of his head. Immediately blood began to trickle from Robbie's ear. A left followed to the chest, and once again Digger tried to seize Robbie with both hands to lift him up and over the side.

Just as Digger approached, Robbie, with his back to the railing, quickly lifted both legs. Hanging on to the rail with both arms locked around it, he pulled his knees to his chest, then sent his feet into the bo'sun's approaching midsection in full extension. The bo'sun, taken by surprise, was thrown backward, reeled for balance, and fell on his back.

Sobered and incensed, he struggled to regain his feet.

"Last chance, Digger!" shouted Robbie. "Send him away in Calcutta!"

"Go to the devil, Taggart!" replied the bo'sun feverishly, again with his legs under him. He lurched forward, swinging wildly, while Robbie parried the blows as best he could. Another shot landed against Robbie's forehead, sending him reeling backward. As Digger lunged again, Robbie stepped aside and, grabbing him as he passed, threw the bo'sun against a barrel standing near the bulkhead.

Robbie quickly retreated to firmer ground and awaited the next attack. The bo'sun got to his feet, but his reflexes were beginning to slow. Robbie had succeeded in buying enough time to make a fair fight out of it. This time when Digger approached, therefore, Robbie was prepared.

With a rapid left, Robbie diverted Digger's initial attempt, following it with a solid right directly on Digger's jaw. The bo'sun shook his head in disbelief, only to feel an equally painful jolt follow almost immediately on his left cheek just below his eye.

He struggled to raise his arms to protect himself from the sudden onslaught by the first mate he had apparently misjudged. But they had grown heavy, and he could not get them up before still another devastating fist hit squarely between his nose and mouth.

By now his eyes were full of sweat and tears of pain. If he could only see the first scoundrel, he'd finish him off with a single blow, and make shark bait out of him!

From Digger's blind side Robbie mustered all the strength of his powerful right arm. His fist found its mark in the pit of Digger's massive stomach. The blow sent Digger staggering backward, gasping for air. His vision went black as he fell with a resounding thud to the deck senseless.

An immediate cheer went up from Overlie, followed by shouts from several of the others who had gathered around.

Robbie heard nothing, however. He walked over to where the unconscious bo'sun lay and knelt down beside him to watch for the first signs of wakefulness. After a minute or two, the stunned bo'sun began to stir. Still Robbie waited.

At last Digger opened his eyes and glanced around, his mind in a fog. As he caught Robbie's eyes at length, he stared in dazed unbelief.

"Calcutta, Digger!" Robbie said in a deliberate, slow precise tone. "I meant what I said. I don't want to see the man again. As for you, I'll leave your fate up to the skipper."

He rose without another word, disappeared down the hatch, and again sought the Vicar's cabin.

Drew still lay as he had left him.

He paused a moment, then murmured to himself, "And what am I going to do with *you* now?"

20

Calcutta

The remainder of the passage to Calcutta transpired without serious incident. Word of Robbie's victory over the bo'sun spread quietly throughout the crew, and as a result none dared further challenge. Digger kept to himself, did his job, and if he nursed thoughts of revenge he did not show it. Turk sulked about, showing venom in his eyes, but apparently afraid to make any moves without Digger at his side. Whether he was told by his friend of the first mate's order with respect to his future employment aboard the *Sea Tiger* remained unknown to Robbie. He said nothing further about it himself, awaiting their arrival in port. When he told Pike of the confrontation with Digger, the skipper insisted he be kept aboard.

"I can't be havin' ye gettin' rid of half my crew," he said. "Bad apples or not, we need every strong man we have."

"Turk's never been worth that much anyway," countered Robbie.

"Ye're right there, I suppose, laddie. You can get rid of him if ye've still a mind to. But the bo'sun stays. I'll watch him."

"No need, Ben," said Robbie. "I can handle myself."

"You be careful. He's a dangerous man."

Robbie left Pike's quarters more pensive than ever. Something still didn't feel right about the whole thing. Pike and his boatswain must have something going on that he didn't know about. He'd almost forgotten that first conversation he'd overheard between them in Pike's cabin. With Pike's insistence on retaining Digger on board, suddenly it all came back to him.

In light of the recent conversation in the chart house and Pike's unexplained assault, more and more Robbie was coming to feel trapped in a maze of unknowns. Three men of the crew had already attacked him, and who could tell when one of them might be successful? Pike's erratic treatment of him, alternately like a son and an adversary, frightened Robbie.

Fear was not an emotion Robbie was well acquainted with, and its unknown quality only added to the enigma of this voyage. To be afraid of a visible assailant was one thing—a foe who stood before you face to face. That was a fear to be handled; courage could overcome it. But to fear the shadows of the night, not knowing what danger awaited its opportunity, that was a fear Robbie Taggart had never before known.

He thought he had known himself before—known his strengths, his limitations. Indeed, his fortitude and intuition as a man had always stood him in good stead. He had always been able to land on his feet, whatever life happened to throw at him. But now he found himself faced with uncertainties that his strength as a man was ill-prepared to deal with. His anxieties over Digger and Turk were only part of it. Pike remained a mystery. And he had never felt so incapable of dealing with an individual as he had with the Vicar.

Notwithstanding his newly aroused sensitivities and anxieties—perhaps because of them—Robbie worked hard. The Vicar sobered up, heard what had transpired on his behalf from other lips than Robbie's, and as a result seemed more deferential than ever to his first mate. But he and Robbie spoke little.

In three weeks the *Sea Tiger* was in Calcutta. When they docked and the men began to disembark for shore leave, Robbie caught Digger's eye and held it in a firm, though not angry stare. Two hours later Robbie saw Turk, carrying a canvas bag over his shoulder, walk toward the gangway and start down it. Halfway toward the dock, he stopped, seeming to feel Robbie's eyes on him. He turned, and with a menacing look of fury in his eyes, shook his fist defiantly in the air and shouted, "I shall not forget you, Taggart! I will have my revenge!"

Robbie did not see him again.

Calcutta had not changed in the years since Robbie had last seen it. The streets were just as filthy, teeming with every conceivable example of the lower levels of humankind. Alongside Pike the next day, Robbie shouldered his way through the mass of humanity, trying not to look too closely at all he saw. In his carelessness he nearly stumbled over a legless beggar perched against a wall holding a tin cup. The man's lips spread into a lopsided toothless grin, and Robbie dropped a coin into the cup before hurrying on, repulsed. The poor wretch couldn't help his condition, but Robbie nonetheless felt the unsettledness of one who has taken his own wholeness for granted.

Ahead two men were screaming at one another, haggling over the price of a dirty crust of bread. Others joined the fray, for apparently the seller had been guilty of price-gouging in the past and this was their opportunity to get even. Shouts passed to blows, and Robbie and Pike had to gingerly skirt the edge of the street to circumvent the melee.

They had nearly succeeded when a small, dark-skinned Hindu grabbed at Robbie's arm.

"English!" he shouted over the din.

Robbie stopped. "What do you want?"

"Big English," said the little man, "you help. Very bad merchant. Steal every day from starving people."

Before Robbie could respond, Pike turned and thrust his crutch into the man's belly, sending him flying into the angry crowd.

"Leave us be!" shouted Pike, limping quickly away.

Robbie paused just long enough to see that the man had not been trampled by the brawlers, then followed Pike.

"You could have hurt him," rebuked Robbie when he caught up with his skipper.

"Ah, laddie, ye're too soft! Ye got to show these people who's boss, an' what we British are made of. They're all thieves an' liars! I'd check my pockets if I were you."

Instinctively Robbie's hand shot to his trouser pockets, but finding all his valuables still on his person, he admonished himself for his mistrust of the pathetic little man they had just left. He had never been one to judge a man by some artificial standard of race. Nor was he given to flaunting the might of the British Crown, even if she were the most powerful nation on earth. He met the people he encountered on their own terms, and thus was usually able to make friends with any man. Pike's bigotry disgusted him, no matter that it seemed the prevalent attitude by which most people deported themselves toward their neighbors.

As they walked through the narrow, crowded, smelly, muddy streets, Robbie threw Pike a sidelong glance.

The man is strange, Robbie thought to himself. *Yes, and fearsome too.* Everything taken together disturbed him—an odd look here, an unguarded word there, a hollow grin, a brief explosion followed by contrition. The man was unpredictable at best. And at worst . . . ? Robbie didn't know what he was. There was something inside Pike . . . something hidden—something gnawing away at his mind. There could be no other explanation for such erratic swings of mood and such outbursts of violent behavior. He was hardly the man to captain a merchant ship!

It had not been until the attack, followed by the peculiar conversation in the chart room, that Robbie's eyes had begun to open to the true sort of man Pike was. He had been wary, even a little distant since then. But Robbie had to admit also, he had been distant toward Drew and everyone, not just toward Pike. Yet despite his suspicions, he still could not resolve all this with the decent treatment he had received from the man, though even Pike's congeniality toward Robbie was not without its edge. It had all been so clear during those brief moments in the chart house when his eyes had belied his smooth words.

He was beginning to wish he had come ashore in the morning with Drew instead of waiting for Pike. Perhaps he could prevent the Vicar from becoming inebriated, though if his new resolve of alcoholic repentance—pledged to Robbie on the gangway as he left that morning—was to mean anything, it would have to come as a result of his own strength, no one else's. But even Drew, he thought, would provide more companionship than Pike's cronies he was to meet about the chests of drugs to be loaded onto the *Tiger* that evening. Robbie should never have come, despite Pike's insistence. He didn't believe in what Pike was doing—it wasn't right, even if it *was* legal. How many more of these mysterious "cargoes" might Pike be planning to pick up? *This is not why I left the Navy,* thought Robbie. Friend of the family or not—and what did he *really* know of Pike's supposed friendship with his father? Pike's company was growing tedious, and hazardous as well.

But in the middle of his reflections, Robbie saw that Pike was turning into a narrow doorway, and he continued after him. They strode down a dark corridor a short distance until Pike came to another door, which he shoved open. They were immediately assailed by the noisy clamor, smoke, and sickening reek of one of Calcutta's lesser known public houses. It was not the sort of place most visitors from London were very likely to see.

Elbowing their way through the press of bodies, they came to a table where several of the *Sea Tiger*'s crew were reposing in various stages of drunkenness. There were no empty chairs about, and it seemed almost a small miracle that the men had procured the ones they had. However, by the battered look of a couple of them, they had probably not come by them peaceably.

"Hey, Newly, Jenkins," said Pike, "go fetch us some ale."

"Ye don't need two of us for that," argued Newly, unwilling to risk the loss of his seat.

"Says who?" countered Pike, and his ever-ready crutch speared at the recalcitrant Newly.

The sailor dodged the thrust in time, but lost his seat in the process. Without hesitation or compunction, the skipper settled his worn frame where Newly's had been.

"Here," said Jenkins, standing and shoving his chair toward Robbie.

"I don't feel like sitting," muttered Robbie.

"Sit down, you lubber!" shouted Pike. "An' get that ale!" he added to Jenkins. "Ye'd think this were a church meetin' or somethin'!"

Robbie sat down heavily in the vacated chair. All at once he did not like the idea of being Pike's so-called protégé, following him about, doing his bidding. Why had he been so eager to sail with him in the first place? The question brought to mind his boring, oppressive life in the Navy. At least Pike was no Commander Barclay!

"Hey, ye lubbers!" bellowed Pike, to no one in particular, "don't drink yerselves balmy. We still got business later. I need ye able to stand on yer feet!"

Robbie drank his ale slowly, little enjoying it, though the cold was refreshing after the searing heat of the city streets. Robbie looked about. Notwithstanding the turbaned Hindus and other exotically garbed patrons, as well as the loud mix of languages, this place looked little different from any pub to be found on London's docks. Dark-skinned Indians were not a rarity in an international port like London, nor were fair-skinned British soldiers in their familiar brown khaki attire altogether unusual in this city of the central British Province.

Robbie leaned back in his chair, but he could not relax. The heat of the place was even more stifling than it had been out on the dusty streets, despite the large, slow-turning circular fan overhead barely stirring the stale air. But heat had never bothered Robbie in the past, and he knew that was not the problem now. A disquiet had stolen upon him in recent days, and it was now weighing especially heavily on his mind. Though he did not recognize it as such, it was the disquiet that comes from a growing dissatisfaction with oneself. Things were slightly out of step within the heart of Robbie Taggart. He felt its effect, but did not know its Source. He searched for fulfillment but was able to find none. When fulfillment finally came to his troubled soul, it would come from an unacknowledged and unfathomable Power.

To Robbie's mind it seemed a good part of the problem stemmed from Pike. But there was more to it than that. He could handle Pike. He had handled Digger and Turk. He was man enough to face any opponent. But this was something else, something he couldn't pinpoint. Was it the same unrest that had plagued him during his final year in the Navy? The day he stepped on board the *Sea Tiger* he had believed all that was behind him.

How could Robbie have perceived, in his present state, that the seeds of unrest are always planted by the divine hand? Had Robbie been able to confide his confusion to Jamie, she might have illuminated to him that it is the Lord who stirs men's souls. But in his gloom Robbie was not now thinking of Jamie, nor of the mysterious God she always spoke of to him. He was instead thinking of himself, and there is no quicker or surer way to deaden the divine influence than that.

Life to Robbie Taggart had always been a lark. He had spent his years purposefully—indeed, artfully—avoiding any path that might bring friction or confrontation or serious self-analysis. He did not want to think, least of all about the meaning of life, of selfhood, of what purposes there were to being. The larger questions of life were for the philosophers, for the Jamie MacLeods and the Elliot Drews of the world. But not for Robbie Taggart. Life was to be lived—not morosely analyzed!

Then what had happened to such a lighthearted philosophy? Where was the Robbie Taggart of old?

In a tunnel, it seemed. A dark, dank, stifling passageway, as uncomfortable as that Calcutta pub, and without beacon lights to reveal direction ahead or illuminate the walls to each side. His brain had grown dark, and in every direction he turned his thoughts, there was only darkness.

All tunnels end, but for those stuck in their midst, however bright the light at its end, all remains blackness. Light was on its way to Robbie Taggart from the Father of Lights, who was sending His answer to His son, even before prayer for it had gone heavenward. When that light came, it would bring joy and freedom such as Robbie could not presently imagine, in comparison with which his former free-wheeling self would seem but a pale shadow.

In the meantime, Robbie's eyes could not perceive the destiny to which he was being called. But even as he sat wrestling with his own anxieties, out on the streets of the city was waiting an innocent victim of the world's poverty. Unknown either to Robbie Taggart or to the little Indian maiden, she had been sent from on High, to pierce the first blow through the masculine armor of Robbie Taggart. Thus would begin the process of the breaking of that tough exterior shell into fragments—fragments of a former self to place on the altar of sacrifice, out of which a tender and more purer manhood could emerge.

After sitting in Jenkin's chair in silence for some time, Robbie suddenly lurched to his feet. He had to have air, even if it stank with poverty and mid-day heat.

"Where ye goin', mate?" said Pike.

"Out. I'll see you back at the *Tiger*."

"Hey, we got our cargo to pick up."

"You've got plenty of men here to help you."

"I want you with me, Robbie."

"I'm going back to the ship."

"Robbie . . . Robbie!" called Pike after him.

But the skipper's first mate was gone.

21

An Angel Unaware

Loneliness was not a sensation Robbie Taggart had often felt. And today it felt all the more peculiar to him in the midst of scores of people pressing at his elbows.

The open-air market swarmed with shoppers, and the heat continued to beat relentlessly on the city, even though it was late afternoon. It resembled so many of the markets Robbie had seen in the Far East over the years. Fruits and vegetables, half of them already past the point of no return, and various other fried meats, fish, and assorted foodstuffs, were heaped unappetizingly upon broken-down, dirty tables, drawing more attention from flies than the passers-by, who looked too poor to afford even the most pitiful of the offerings. Even more pathetic to him were the women squatting by their homemade pottery or ceramics or dry goods—finely handcrafted handkerchiefs or shawls or porcelain figures or cups or bowls—selling them for a pittance. Robbie could imagine them having worked weeks or months on their meager assortment, but they would be happy if they earned enough from the items for a bag of rice. The poverty was so close, so real, so overpowering in a place like this. And yet no matter how much a single man might try, what could he really do to stem its tide?

The women he passed held out their things to him, beseeching him in any number of Indian dialects. But he didn't have to understand their language to know what they were saying. He was a wealthy Englishman.

Big English, the fellow an hour ago had called him. Surely it would not hurt him to part with a small portion of his silver. In return he would possess some fine item of local distinction, and with it the heartwarming satisfaction of having helped stave off starvation for another day.

Robbie walked on. This was not the moment for him to begin a one-man crusade against the squalor of Calcutta's slums. Even if he were wealthy, he'd not long remain so if he bought every trinket or scrap of leatherwork or statue in sight. Pike had accused him of being soft, but that could only go so far. There was a fine line between softness and foolishness.

It did not take much walking for Robbie to realize that if he had come outside to relieve his morbid mood, it had been a bad idea. There was nothing here to lift a man's spirits. If anything, these miserable surroundings made him even more aware of his inner struggles. Seeing these creatures in the marketplace pulled him in two opposite directions—from pity to loathing. But pity in a place like this was a dead-end street. Better to toss a coin in the cup and hurry on, unfeeling, as he had with the legless beggar, than to allow tenderness to arise, and thus consume him. A man could not be swayed by sentimental sympathies; he had to be strong.

Suddenly he found himself bending over a woman's wares. He had not planned to do so, but he picked up an embroidered handkerchief, then tossed her a coin—three times what she was asking, but not a fourth of what the needlework would have been worth in Piccadilly Circus in the heart of London. Then he scowled at himself for the impulsive act, stuffed the silly thing in his pocket, and hurried on. What he'd ever do with it he couldn't guess—give it to some pretty girl, no doubt. Maybe he would send it to Jamie, or his mother.

Who was he kidding? It didn't matter what he did with it. That wasn't why he had bought it—the whole thing was nothing but stupid sentimentality.

All at once Robbie smiled. He was growing just as complex and bewildering as Pike and the Vicar!

The smile quickly faded, however, the moment he saw the child.

Leaning against a building, dressed in a soiled and faded Indian sarong, she was probably seven or eight; though she was poor and dirty and probably hungry, her countenance did not bear the listlessness he had seen in so many starving children. Her large dark eyes held an awareness that spoke of intelligence and courage, while mingled with sufficient sadness to cause the tall, broad-shouldered British sailor to stop cold in his tracks the moment his eyes met hers.

"What do you want?" Robbie asked, though he knew she could probably speak no English anyway.

She said nothing. Her eyes appraised his slowly, eyes that might well have been beautiful had they not been surrounded by such a scrawny, impoverished frame. She gazed up at him with a kind of mournful awe, as if he represented some wonder, some being from afar, one that could never be part of her world.

Feeling awkward as the object of the child's gaze, reproaching himself for not going on his way, Robbie continued to stand as one transfixed. But he could not rush on, perhaps because he knew those eyes would continue to follow him no matter how far away he got. Not knowing what else to do, he jammed his hand into his pocket and pulled out a coin. Perhaps that would break the strange bond which had reached out to him unawares, and now held him, as one powerless, in its grip. But as he held out the money, the child shrank back, as if she would force her way backward through the wall that supported her.

Well, she is no beggar, thought Robbie. *But I should have known that from her first look.*

"What do you want?" he asked again, more harshly this time, though he did not feel harshness in his heart toward her. "Why are you staring at me?"

Immediately he regretted his tone. In that city of hundreds of thousands, she stood there . . . alone. Was she not—in a distant sort of way—a bit like him? His mind flew back to another day, seemingly so long ago, when he had met another waif and rescued her from a Highland blizzard. Jamie MacLeod had also been desperately alone, orphaned, in need of a friend. Robbie had not feared the look of her searching eyes. He had opened his heart to her, had taken her under his wing— not spoken harshly or tried to dispose of her quickly with a handful of money.

What is happening to me? he thought heavily. *Have I fallen to this, that I am intimidated by a helpless little child?*

He stooped down to one knee. "Are you lost?" he asked more gently. Still there was no reply.

"What is your name?"

A smile slowly crept to her lips. But still she spoke no words.

"My name is Robbie Taggart," he said. Then he remembered his purchase. He reached once more into his pocket, but this time he took out the handkerchief from the market. He held it out to her.

She cast her lovely, sad eyes down at the fine cloth Robbie held, drawn especially by its lace and embroidered flowers. She raised her eyes back to Robbie's face.

He smiled. "Take it. I want you to have it."

Tentatively she reached out a tiny brown hand to lay hold of the handkerchief. Even at her young age she grasped the difference between begging and accepting a gift from a friend.

"Oh, *there* you are, Mira!" said a voice behind Robbie, jolting him out of the trance into which he had fallen.

Robbie turned quickly and saw that the speaker was a woman of about fifty. Though dressed in a sarong, she was fair-skinned, and by her flawless English he surmised she was British.

"We thought we'd lost you, dear," she said with the gentle admonishment of one who is more joyful than angry.

Then the lady looked at Robbie. "I hope she hasn't troubled you, sir."

"No! No, she hasn't. Not at all," replied Robbie rising. She had in truth troubled him very deeply. But not in the way the woman meant.

The child—called Mira—held out the handkerchief for the woman to see, glancing at the same time toward Robbie.

"That was very kind of you, sir."

"It was nothing," Robbie answered. "I'll not even miss the coin I spent to purchase it."

"That is the way of life here, is it not?" said the woman thoughtfully. "Even our poverty would be riches to some of these people. And though you hardly felt the cost of the little thing, it shall have interminable meaning to her. May God bless you, through your simple act of charity, with great riches."

"I don't care about being rich," said Robbie.

"I am not speaking of money, or worldly wealth, but of the riches of the spirit. I will pray Him to give you the riches of the Lord's kingdom. I can tell you are a man of God."

"I'm only a sailor," said Robbie, embarrassed by the woman's words.

Her face broke into a smile, for indeed it was her whole countenance and not merely her lips that participated in the action. "Even a sailor can be used of God," she said.

"I just happened to be passing by," he replied. Then in an attempt to steer the conversation in a new line, asked, "Why doesn't she say anything?"

"She is mute. We believe she has been so since birth, though she only came to us a month ago. We found her in the streets, alone—orphaned or abandoned. Who knows how long she had been roaming about?"

"She looks intelligent, perceptive."

"She may not be able to speak, but she can still think," answered the woman. "She may well be smarter than you or I."

"No doubt," Robbie smiled.

"Would you like to come visit our mission? We would be honored," said the woman.

"Oh, no . . . thank you. But I really must be on my way."

"It's not far from here. The children would so love to see a real sailor."

"I really have to get back to my ship."

Robbie shied away from the invitation not entirely because he did not want to go. A certain aspect of his nature—the old, happy-go-lucky Robbie Taggart—was curious. That Robbie would have gone in a second, and would have made every child happy by his own boyish enthusiasm and zest for life. But at this particular moment, a new Robbie Taggart was struggling desperately against a new host of unknown fears. Thus the greater part of him was afraid of what such an encounter might do to his already shaky sensibilities. He could easily tell—from the aspect of the unusual child named Mira, and from the woman who was her guardian and who radiated an aura of utter peace and a countenance of genuine humanity and warmth—that this mission she spoke of would likely be no ordinary slum kitchen.

He had left himself unguarded long enough; he was not ready to open up to any more of the unknown.

Robbie bid the woman good-afternoon, then paused, and stooped down again alongside the child, taking her hand in his.

"Goodbye, Mira," he said, so unprepared for the alarming development that his voice had grown husky with emotion.

She looked down at her tiny hand grasped by such a huge manly one, then smiled up at him, while tears spilled from her, making tracks down her cheeks through the grime on her skin.

Why she should react thus, he could not tell. Had she understood his words? Did she perhaps realize instinctively that, though they had perhaps briefly become friends in a way that transcended all barriers, they would never see one another again?

Or were they simply tears of joy from the gift, and the small respite from her poverty that their meeting had given her?

In any case, whatever feelings beat inside her own heart, the fact was that Robbie Taggart had been deeply stung. And though he could not know it yet, and though its visible result would not surface for some time, the blow would prove to be lethal to his former self.

With a jerky, hurried motion, Robbie stood, then turned and strode quickly away, hoping he had been quick enough to hide the moisture filling his own troubled, sea-blue eyes.

22

The Call of the Highlands

Pike managed to get his dubious cargo to the ship without Robbie, though when Robbie arrived back, after another hour or two of wandering, and pitched in to help with the loading, the skipper was uncharacteristically silent.

The *Sea Tiger* then made good passage down through the Indian Ocean and through the Sunda Straits. They put in at Anjer for orders, which remained unchanged, and to take on some additional cargo—this time perfectly ethical goods. A throng of Malays swarmed aboard, and, dressed as they were in their bright native costume, combined with a bizarre assortment of western garb, the place for an hour or so resembled more a carnival than a ship. When the loading was done, the men bought various trinkets from the natives, and flirted with scantily dressed women along dockside, and were not altogether pleased with having to set sail early the following morning without shore leave. Several grumbled and talked about jumping, but nothing came of it.

It was mid-May when they sailed into the China seas, met by the southeast monsoon. With winds often contrary, they made slow passage through the South China Sea, which in itself was hazardous enough. Dotted with treacherous reefs and many islands with confusing channels, it was often the most difficult stretch of an ocean voyage to the East.

But Pike had been this way many times in his fifty years at sea, and was perhaps as good as any pilot. He often boasted, "I can make me way through here blindfolded!" Yet since leaving Calcutta he had resumed his habit of remaining below, and Robbie suspected he usually had a bottle for company.

Robbie was almost glad Pike had been keeping to himself. Since Calcutta it had been difficult to face him. It was as though his eyes had been opened, and now he perceived in all its stark reality the chilling bitterness in the man. Whether it had been there all along and he was only now noticing it, or if the skipper had been overtaken by some new mood swing, Robbie couldn't tell. But whatever the case, Robbie sensed that Pike's sour disposition was aimed directly at him. There were still occasionally friendly moments, but they were so exaggerated as to be obviously hollow. Had they always been thus? Had Robbie only imagined a friendship that was not really there?

When Robbie had all but decided his imagination was making more of the problems with Pike than really existed, another argument flared up that only cemented its reality more firmly in Robbie's mind.

A few days beyond the Karimata Straits south of Borneo, Robbie was supervising cleanup after a minor leak had been discovered and pitched in the forward cargo hold. Several crates had had to be moved to avoid water damage, and Robbie had his shoulder squarely against one when Pike burst through the hatch. He saw the activity about the unmarked crates that had been the object of the midnight delivery before their departure from England.

"What's going on here?" he bellowed.

Robbie looked up, brushing a sleeve across his sweaty brow. "We just ran down a small leak," Robbie replied, panting with the weight of the crate.

"Why wasn't I notified?"

Robbie shoved the crate into place, straightened up his sore back and faced Pike. The skipper looked a wreck, worse than Robbie had yet seen him. His hair was tangled and matted with perspiration, his eyes a sick mixture of yellow and red, and his clothing had been neither washed nor changed for days. A surge of pity rushed through Robbie at the sight of the wasted, one-legged man.

"You were—" Robbie began gently, "—that is, I didn't think it was necessary to disturb you. Your cargo from Calcutta is safe and dry in the rear. I checked it earlier. And there was nothing here but these crates. I didn't think you'd—"

"I bet you didn't!" Pike growled, seething. He poked his crutch at the crate Robbie had been trying to shift to a better position. "What're ye doin' with that?" he spat.

The question hardly seemed necessary, with the floor wet from the leak. "We've got to shift things around as best we can to prevent water damage," said Robbie.

Even as they spoke two of the other men were approaching with a like crate hoisted on their shoulders. Anxious to finish and have done with the job in the stifling hold as soon as possible, they were hurrying more than was advisable, and lost their balance as they tried to place their load on top of the other crate. They stumbled forward, the crate slipping from their grasp.

Robbie jumped immediately to their assistance, while Pike struggled to get out of the way, but even Robbie could not prevent the crate from crashing to the deck. The wooden box split open and the contents spilled out onto the floor.

Robbie gasped. Three carbine rifles slid from the opening in the box. After a moment he pulled his eyes away from the weapons to meet Pike's gaze.

"Ye done yer work here!" Pike shouted to the other men. "Get back up on deck!" He waved his crutch to emphasize his order, which was obeyed without question.

Robbie did not budge.

"These aren't on the manifest," he said calmly. Still his strong sense of loyalty would not let him think the worst.

"Don't you start moralizin' with me!" warned Pike, pushing past Robbie and attempting to shove the guns back into their carton with his crutch. "You think anyone makes money these days haulin' sheet iron and cloth!"

"Is money that important to you, Pike?" asked Robbie. "You're jeopardizing the whole crew by dealing in this contraband. Or am I the only one in the dark about this?"

"No one's in *jeopardy*! Ain't nothin' dangerous about it!"

"At least opium's legal. This is—"

"So what're ye plannin' to do about it?" Pike stepped close to Robbie, forcing his back up against the wooden crates.

"You won't get this past Chinese customs."

"Ah, 'tis perfect for ye, ain't it, laddie!" Pike's tone was filled both with ire and irony. "Ye'd like nothin' better than to sing like a bird to them."

"Ben, how can you say that? I've been loyal to you."

"Oh, ye've been wantin' to get at me for years . . ." Suddenly the old man's hand shot up, grasping the dagger he had once used against Robbie. He tore it from its scabbard at his side and before Robbie realized what was happening had its deadly tip pressed against Robbie's throat. "It ain't enough you took my leg—"

He broke off suddenly, his voice shaking with passion.

Even with the knife so dangerously close, Robbie could easily have overpowered him. But he stood as one stunned, and could not move. He felt a small trickle of blood running down his throat where the razor-sharp dagger had sliced the skin. Yet there was no pain, and still he made no move.

The sight of the blood seemed to sober Pike back to reality. He stared horrified, and stepped back.

"Ye're just like him," he muttered. "What am I supposed to do?" But the skipper's words were not addressed to Robbie but rather to himself, or to some unseen demon hovering at his shoulder. He jerked around, still mumbling unintelligibly, and stumbled away, climbing awkwardly from the hold.

Robbie made no move to help him, still too benumbed to move from where he stood. He hardly noticed that for the first time Pike was not his agile self. He looked like a decrepit old man hobbling on a crutch and wooden leg, hardly a threatening adversary. Yet the madman had come within an inch of killing Robbie.

Mechanically he brought his trembling hand to his throat. It was bleeding more than he had realized. Still he stood, until his practical nature came suddenly awake and realized it must tend to the damage the dagger had done.

As he made his way above deck, Pike was nowhere in sight. Robbie descended again and headed toward the galley, hoping he would encounter no one en route. But rounding a blind corridor, his instincts too dulled to react quickly, he almost ran into the Vicar.

"Good Lord!" Drew exclaimed. "What happened to you?"

"Nothing," Robbie replied in a dry, taut voice. "Just a little accident."

"It's the skipper, isn't it?"

Without answering, Robbie brushed past him and into the galley. Drew followed close on his heels. Johnnie was not there, and for that, at least, Robbie was thankful. He was in no mood for the cook's constant chatter, and was relieved not to have one more source of rumors to head off. He opened a cupboard and fumbled about unsuccessfully through boxes and containers.

"Let me help you," said Drew, his voice stronger than Robbie had ever heard it. The words sounded like an order. He nudged Robbie aside, then quickly found the proper supplies. Soaking a piece of cotton in some pungent liquid, he reached up and began to clean Robbie's wound.

Robbie winced, but offered no further objection, passively accepting Drew's ministration.

"He's going to kill you someday, Robbie," said the Vicar, applying a bandage once the wound had been cleansed.

Robbie made no reply.

"And you'll continue to take it, because of your inane sense of loyalty, until suddenly it goes too far," Drew went on. "My advice to you is—"

"I didn't ask for your advice," cut in Robbie sharply.

"Well, you're getting it anyway! You'd better desert at the next port and just pray you make it *that* far."

"That would be *your* advice," replied Robbie sarcastically.

"I've never denied my cowardice. And you can think of me what you will. I deserve your scorn. But your situation has nothing to do with courage or cowardliness. It would simply be downright foolhardy to stay aboard a ship where the master has made two attempts on your life, not to mention the boatswain."

"It wasn't like that with Pike."

"Then what *was* it like?"

Drew expected no answer to his probing question. And Robbie was not willing to form one. There could be only one answer, and that was to be found in Benjamin Pike's face. Robbie shuddered still when he thought of his look. And he knew, though he might not be willing to admit it, that there was indeed murder in Pike's wild eyes.

For the next several days he avoided both Pike and Drew. When he did run into the skipper, Pike seemed to have forgotten the entire sordid incident. But he had not been able to erase the Vicar's words from his mind: *You'd better desert at the next port and just pray you make it that far.*

It would not be long before they would be making port. In Shanghai he'd have no problem signing aboard another vessel, a foreign one, perhaps—German or American. It didn't matter which or where it was bound, as long as it was far from Pike and, if he was lucky, away from some of the mental confusion of late. He wouldn't be the first sailor to jump ship, and many with far less cause.

Late one evening Robbie went on deck to try to clear his thoughts. He stood for several moments on the forecastle, then walked across to the rail. It was the midnight watch, and all was quiet except for a brisk breeze playing along their starboard quarter. The *Tiger* made her way *with a bone in her teeth*, as they said, the white water at her bow shimmering fluorescent in the light from the half-moon. There wouldn't be many more days like this with the prevalent southeast monsoon. He had not even noticed the mournful tones of Torger's harmonica. But now the soft sounds began to filter across the night into his ear.

How could Overlie have so accurately probed his present mood, thought Robbie. And how did he always manage to know the perfect Scottish or English tune?

The minor-key melody was familiar to Scotsmen the world over, carrying the melancholy lament of their own favorite poet throughout the ends of the earth. *Ah, Mr. Burns*, thought Robbie of his famous namesake, *how could you know so well the heart's call of a roving Scotsman?*

The harmonica's tone was louder now. Did Torger know what he was thinking, wondered Robbie? Had he sensed his homesickness? Or was he merely an unknowing instrument in some divine plan of which he knew nothing? A lump rose in Robbie's throat as he turned his gaze back out to the sea, the words to the sad pibroch stinging his brain out of memory for his beloved homeland:

> My heart's in the Highlands, my heart is not here,
> My heart's in the Highlands a-chasing the deer,
> A-chasing the wild deer and following the roe—
> My heart's in the Highlands wherever I go!

Yes, it would be easy to desert right now. Eventually he'd find his way home . . . to Scotland . . . to the Highlands. Oddly, he had never realized how much home had meant to him. Scott had been right when he had penned the words about a man's soul burning within him upon seeing his native land after "wandering on a foreign soil." Though Jamie had taught him a deeper appreciation for many things, and for the land of his birth through her own veneration for her beloved mountain of Donachie, somehow tonight it seemed more real than ever. Now that his world—the world he loved, a world of travel and adventure and excitement—appeared to be crumbling around him, Scotland seemed a refuge.

Oh, how he longed for those grand Highland hills at this moment— always solid and barren and unchanging!

> Farewell to the Highlands, farewell to the North,
> The birth-place of valour, the country of worth!
> Wherever I wander, wherever I rove,
> The hills of the Highlands for ever I love.

How many times had he, unthinking, unfeeling, bid farewell to that dear land, that place of his birth? In all his youthful years he had not quieted his restless heart long enough to feel the security of his roots. He was, after all, a world traveler, a seeker of adventure, a roamer his mother had called him. Robbie Taggart, Highland sailor, soldier of fortune! But where had his lust for adventure brought him now? Standing on the deck of the *Sea Tiger*, Robbie Taggart was more lonely of heart than he had ever thought possible to one such as himself.

Oh, what he wouldn't give at this moment to be able to stoop down and grasp a handful of black Highland peat, to twist off a tiny branch of blooming heather from its wiry root to give to a passing child, to look upon the homey face of a country woman tending her small garden of "tatties" and kail outside her cottage of gray granite blocks and black slate roof. What wouldn't he give for just one pass through the streets of Aberdeen! Or one glass of ale from the hand of Sadie Malone!

There he had known no confusion, no loneliness, no deception. There everything had been simple.

> Farewell to the mountains high cover'd with snow,
> Farewell to the straths and green valleys below,
> Farewell to the forests and wild-hanging woods,
> Farewell to the torrents and loud-pouring floods!

Robbie closed his eyes and sighed deeply, still fighting that strange sensation in his throat. He could picture the very stream old Robert Burns must have been writing about! There was just such a one near his mother's house. In the spring, the amber, peat-stained water rushed down from the rain-soaked mountains with a vengeance, boiling and frothing white, as if to impress the very life of the rugged Highlands into every inch of land below. He had foolishly tried to swim the raging torrent the last time he was there, and had been nearly frozen as well as dashed to bits against the rocks in the swirling tide. What a frightening and glorious memory it was! Oh, for a splash of that crisp, icy water against his face! Could it be possible that it was even more delightful than sea spray?

Robbie sighed again. The memory only deepened his sickness for home. But he knew, as certainly as his feet were perched on that gently heaving deck, that he would not soon lay eyes on his Highland home. Whether it was for loyalty, misplaced perhaps as the Vicar implied, or whether it stemmed from his own insatiable desire to roam, he would not desert the *Sea Tiger*, nor her perilous master. He did not know what he should do, if anything, about Pike's larcenous business dealings. Nor did he know what to make of Pike's bizarre treatment of him. Whether he was actually capable of murder, Robbie could only guess. It seemed Pike hated him one moment, loved him as a son the next. He had asked himself a hundred times what was the root of Pike's seemingly possessed behavior. But still no logical answer presented itself. Perhaps, too, it was because he had to find the answer to that question that he was compelled to remain aboard, and loyal to the very man who might one day kill him.

> My heart's in the Highlands, my heart is not here,
> My heart's in the Highlands a-chasing the deer,
> A-chasing the wild deer and following the roe—
> My heart's in the Highlands, wherever I go!

As Torger's harmonica drew out the final strain and then faded into silence on breezes of the night, Robbie's heart was pierced through with the pain only a wanderer could know—the longing for something he knew he would never have, for something he was not even certain he'd be happy with once it was obtained.

Robbie was being borne on the winds of the sea toward a land he did not yet know, toward a future he could not foresee, toward a place which would satisfy the longing of his heart. His new homeland would little resemble the rugged land of his birth. It was a Kingdom not made with the hands of men toward which he was bound. And thus it was Homeland for all the people of the earth, of which the roots of one's earthly fathers and mothers are but a faint and nostalgic echo.

23

Typhoon on the China Sea

The favorable weather did not last.

Three days later, toward sunset, a great bank of clouds appeared off the starboard bow. They rushed up to meet the ship as if on a headlong collision course, heedless of the wind which seemed going in the very opposite direction. The brilliant sunset of yellow and orange was quickly swallowed by the approaching blackness, and in less than an hour after the storm's first sighting, the *Tiger* found itself engulfed in a vortex of wind and sudden driving rain. They would soon be caught in the midst of a dreaded Asian typhoon.

It took mere moments for the crew to come alive in a frenzy as if their lives depended on their every action, which in very truth they did. Some manned the lines to haul in sail, while others scrambled aloft to fasten down the canvas. Johnnie killed the galley fire and bustled from his private domain to give a hand with the foremast clew lines. The winds had already risen to such force that an Ethiopian by the name of Suderia, whom they had picked up in Calcutta to replace Turk, was knocked into the angry sea.

Robbie immediately issued an order to lower a boat. But already, even before the lines could be unhitched, the African was lost to his sight in the gathering darkness as the ship continued to race furiously ahead. Not only would there be no hope of finding him, the lifeboat would not stand a chance in that sea; additional lives would be lost and the rest of the crew and the *Tiger* all endangered.

He rescinded the order with a sickening feeling in the pit of his stomach.

Yet there was no time to lose weeping over one man if they hoped to save the rest from following him.

One moment the ship seemed about to be swallowed at the bottom of a great ice-green valley with infinite walls of water on each side, the next suddenly heaved to the very top of one of those mountain-walls, to perch precariously for a moment before tumbling back down the other side into the next trough. Hoping at least to save the sail, Robbie scrambled up the mainmast of the heaving and pitching clipper.

But it was too late. The sail was already gone. Below, Digger was having trouble securing the topgallant. Robbie shimmied down the mast to assist him.

"Get on yer way, mate!" barked the bo'sun. "I don't need none o' yer help!"

"We all need help!" Robbie shouted over the deafening wind, "and I'm not about to lose any more good sailors because of your stubborn pride!"

Digger vouchsafed no reply. Together he and Robbie managed to bring the sail under control and secure it. Digger said nothing more, only offering a disgusted snort whenever communication was required.

Carefully they descended the mast to the deck. Digger stalked away. If Robbie had been capable of despair, it would have overtaken him at that moment, for how could they possibly hope to survive if the crew were not united as a team, and instead were battling each other as well as the storm?

Robbie carefully made his way aft—no easy matter in the wind with the deck treacherously slippery—to inquire about the status of the helm. The winds and seas had already wrought so much havoc on deck that the ship was unrecognizable. Ladders had been washed away, along with two of the four lifeboats. The galley was flooded, and a huge section of the forecastle cabin roof had been smashed to pieces. Before Robbie reached his destination, he heard the awful cry through the howling wind:

"Man overboard!"

He rushed ahead to the site of the calamity, looked over the rail along the line where Jenkins was pointing. Already the ill-fated crewman had fallen half a furlong behind the ship and disappeared from sight.

"Who was it?" Robbie shouted.

"Collins."

Robbie rubbed the rain from his eyes and sighed. With two boats lost, he could not give thought to risking another on the hopeless attempt. Two men gone was no small loss. But with their already meager crew, to lose another two or three men and a precious lifeboat besides would be suicide for those that remained. Such was the seaman's life. The potential for tragedy always lurked nearby. But there was no time to grieve. The *Tiger*'s peril still lay very close.

"I told you all!" wailed Lackey. "I told you when we left—she's a rum ship! We're headed down!"

"Quiet, Lackey!" yelled Robbie. "Why aren't you at the pumps?"

"It's a lost cause."

"Shut up! Move to your station or I'll throw you over the rail!"

At length Robbie reached the poop just as a huge violent wave gathered itself to crash over the front of the ship, sending the aft-section breaking down into the momentarily created trough unprotected. Even in the noise of the storm he heard the distinct snap of the rudder as it was wrenched from its pintle, before the next instant the ship rose with the great heave of water. Torger was whipped to the deck as the helm suddenly lost traction.

"We lost the rudder!" he shouted, but the coxswain's announcement was hardly necessary as the already rolling ship nearly lurched to her side.

The next moment Pike and Digger made their appearance.

"What's happened?" asked Pike, his gravelly voice hardly distinguishable from the sounds of the windy fray.

"The rudder's gone," answered Robbie.

"Lor'!" exclaimed Pike, suddenly heedful of Lackey's evil pronouncements.

"The fool Lackey must be right," muttered Digger.

"We don't need that from you!" said Robbie harshly.

"Yeah! An' what do ye intend—" But his threat remained unsaid.

"We gots to make port!" interrupted Pike.

"You know we can't make it," Robbie replied, struggling to keep his head. He thought a moment. "The same thing happened to *Cutty Sark* in '72 on a run to Melbourne."

"I remember it," said Pike, calming a bit. "She was in a race with *Thermopylae*. She lost, after what happened, but there never was a finer piece of seamanship."

"We can do what she did!" said Robbie. "They built a jury rudder from spare parts, and fit it right at sea."

"Ye're crazy!" put in Digger. "This ain't no squall; this is a full-blown typhoon. Those are hundred-mile-an-hour winds hittin' us!"

"We can do it—it's our only chance," argued Robbie. "You got any better ideas to see us through this! Now, go get Jenkins on cutting the spars. And we'll need a forge—"

He stopped suddenly and shot a glance at Pike, realizing he had rushed ahead without the skipper's approval.

Something ominous flickered through Pike's eyes, but almost the same moment the ship lurched violently, reminding him sharply of their imminent peril and the utter futility of his personal vendetta at that moment. He gave a jerky, half-reluctant nod of his head to Digger, who swung hotly about in pursuit of Jenkins, angrier at having to take orders from the naval clown, as he still considered Robbie, than fearful of the sea's power to take his life. Robbie watched him go, hoping he would be able to give himself fully to the tremendous battle that lay ahead of them.

The seas washed out the forge several times, but Jenkins was a good carpenter. Despite his grumbling about the impossible conditions, eventually he managed to construct a fair substitute rudder. Then came the awesome and dangerous task of attempting to fit the huge, cumbersome instrument, measuring sixteen inches in diameter at its gunstock end, and a good four feet at its fullest width. Attaching it to wires and pulleys, manned by most of the men situated at various key positions, it was lowered over the stern of the ship.

Huge combers continued to sweep over the poop, knocking the laborers sprawling. Eventually they arrived at a system of trying to anticipate the rhythm of the waves. In the ten to twenty seconds respite while lying in a trough, the men lowered the rudder before taking what refuge they could in preparation for the next crusher. The second it was past, they sprang again to action, lowering their cables farther, attempting with each successive effort to bring it a little closer to its final destination. Battling the wind and sea and a ship out of control, it took more than two hours to lower it into place. A slight lull in the onslaught of waves allowed Robbie, secured by multiple lines around his waist, to be lowered over the side, remove the broken rudder and afix the new one into place. It took several tries, and was not without great risk, as the waves could dash a human body to pieces against the side of the ship if Robbie failed to secure himself in advance. But between them he eventually set it in place, and when he yanked on the line and was raised back up onto the deck, a great cheer went up from the exhausted men of his crew.

The storm beat on them another day, but the makeshift rudder held fast, and Pike decided to beat it past Manila, the nearest port, and chance a run to Shanghai with the present setup. In the night the makeshift rudder began to show signs of strain, and by the second morning was only barely doing the job. The *Sea Tiger* listed like a crippled bird, at the mercy of the unfriendly sea.

It was time to reevaluate their course. The *Cutty Sark* had traveled eight thousand miles in a similar condition, but she had been commanded by a first-rate master. Robbie possessed no vaunted ideas about his own abilities, nor Pike's. They had nearly a thousand miles yet to go—a small enough distance relative to the entire voyage of some eighteen thousand, but far enough with a malfunctioning vessel. They had already shipped the new rudder aboard once for repairs and strengthening, a demanding job when added to the grueling labor of handling the rigging during the final lashing tailwinds of the abating typhoon. The short-handed crew was exhausted, and Robbie feared he might have a mutiny on his hands if they had to ship the rudder even one more time. Nothing would have pleased Digger more, he was sure of that.

He found Pike in his cabin, and with trepidation opened the door and went inside to confront the skipper. At first he had hoped he could broach the subject subtly, even making it appear it had originated with Pike.

"We're going to lose that rudder again," said Robbie.

"We'll ship her aboard again," replied Pike, as if it were no concern of his.

"It's wearing the men out."

"They're a lot o' lazy babies!"

An angry return rose to Robbie's lips. He had himself been skeptical of the crew when he first laid eyes on them, and half still resembled pirates at first glance. But they had proved themselves able sailors, and had labored remarkably for their ship. Two had given their lives. But this was no time for a confrontation with Pike. At the same time, there was now no further need to be subtle.

"Listen, skipper," he said, "Amoy isn't that far from our present position—I think we can keep her going until then. But for another week . . . I just don't know if she'll last."

"We're not putting in at Amoy," replied Pike firmly.

"What about Foochow then? Or even Hong Kong, though it would mean some backtracking."

"No."

Robbie well knew that Pike would never agree to a stopover in a port where his contraband cargo might be discovered. In Shanghai he had no doubt already cultivated connections, and more than likely had already made arrangements with his local people for the bribing of the customs officials in advance. It would be too great a risk for him to enter an unfriendly port with such a stash of guns aboard, not to mention the cost of having to pay out more bribes to new officials.

Robbie rose to leave, seeing no further advantage to be gained from arguing the issue, when Pike got up slowly out of his chair and limped to a table where a map was lying.

"Right here," he said, tapping the map with his forefinger.

Robbie approached the table and saw he was indicating a group of islands just north of Luzon in the Philippines. He did not know much about them, except they were notorious for their coral reefs and poor harbors. He said as much to Pike, who simply snorted his disregard for such practicalities.

"There's a spot," said Pike mysteriously. "I remember it so well. During the Opium wars when we couldn't get through with our cargo and sometimes had to dispose of it till things cooled down, we found a harbor, right here—"

Again he indicated the map.

"It ain't great. But it'll do the job. We can at least lay over long enough to fix the rudder proper."

Robbie sighed, relieved that he had been spared an unpleasant argument. If they didn't crack up on the reefs, they still had a chance.

He smiled to himself as he left Pike's cabin. He was starting to sound like old doomsday Lackey!

Later that night the winds began to abate. The worst appeared over, but heavy seas and strong winds continued to hamper them.

When the lookout shouted *Land Ho!*, there was not a man aboard the *Sea Tiger* who did not rejoice.

24

Unscheduled Layover

Fighting a headwind, it took the remainder of that night and most of the next morning before they had drawn close enough to the island to look for a suitable anchorage.

The sea-surrounded strip of lava and earth could not have been more than ten miles long, and three or four miles across at its widest point. A narrow sandy beach was lined with coconut palms, but inland the island rose to a rugged height of over 2,000 feet of volcanic rock. With the storm now played out, Robbie could feel the tropical heat rising in the air. But there was still sufficient wind to carry them around to the northern side of the island. They dropped anchor about four furlongs out in a small natural harbor. If another typhoon sprang up, it offered little protection against the ship being blown to bits. But if the calm held, it should afford them what they needed.

Robbie wasted little time. There was work to do, and he was anxious to explore this tiny piece of the world he was seeing for the first time. He had been to the Philippines, but never to any of her outer northern islands. One of the two remaining launches was lowered and half the crew embarked, including Robbie, Digger, Overlie, Newly, Drew, Jenkins, and Pike. The thought of leaving Lackey aboard, walking the decks with a captive audience, was not without humor, thought Robbie as they pulled away from the *Tiger*'s side. The small craft heaved up and down over the swells, but with each mighty pull on the oars, the island drew closer by degrees.

"Is it deserted?" asked Drew.

"Was twenty years ago," said Pike. "Or so we thought."

"We'll find out soon enough," added Robbie. "But most of these islands have native tribes on them. Perhaps we'll encounter some locals."

They beached the boat on the warm, white sands. All seven men—even those who never allowed their emotions to show—stood still for a moment in a kind of awe. An intense quiet hung over the place, broken only by the dreamlike rustle of the leafy tops of the coconut palm trees towering a hundred feet overhead. A gentle breeze played across the beach, and it was impossible to imagine that only yesterday the same typhoon that had crippled their ship must have raged over this peaceful setting. Visual reminders of the storm lay strewn about, however—broken palm branches, scattered driftwood thrown ashore by the crashing waves, and one entire coconut tree fallen on the sand. But there was no sound now, as if the storm had washed all life from the island.

Robbie felt strangely as if they were the only living creatures left in the world. The only sound was the gentle lapping of the ends of the waves against the sand, set in harmony against the breezes in the trees. Several of the men glanced back at the anchored ship, as if to assure themselves that they had indeed not been utterly abandoned and left to Crusoe's fate.

Suddenly a flurry of sharp screams and great chattering pierced through the silence. Even Digger's stern countenance paled momentarily.

"Nothin' but monkeys!" he said, as much to ease his own mind as the others'. Almost immediately several of the noisy creatures appeared, swinging in the trees. And directly after the appearance of the monkeys, out of the undergrowth stepped six or eight islanders.

The launch crew had by necessity come ashore armed, having no idea what dangers might be encountered in the untamed tropics. At the first stirring of the dense growth lining the shore, Pike and Digger and Newly shouldered their weapons.

"Keep those down!" ordered Robbie instinctively, notwithstanding that he was speaking to his own captain.

The natives were smaller in stature than the intruders to their tiny isle, though their bare, bronzed torsos revealed sinewy muscles. Their bodies stood tensed for fight if necessary, and their eyes were fierce and distrustful. Each carried some primitive weapon—a bow, a spear, a hand-hewn axe. For a tense moment they stood dead in their tracks, some thirty feet from the crew, each of the two groups of men sizing up the capabilities of the other.

Whether they were friendly or hostile could not be told from a quick glance. But Robbie wanted no bloodshed. He knew Pike's attitude of superiority all too well toward races and origins other than his own. A quick glance in Pike's direction confirmed Robbie's fears; the man's knuckles were white from the tight grip on his rifle, and his lip was curled in disdain. He would have to act quickly before some stupid accident turned this chance encounter into a brutal slaughter.

Hastily Robbie stepped forward with his hands extended in a gesture of friendship.

"We mean you no harm," he said. Though he doubted they could understand him, they could not mistake the friendly inflection of his voice. Under his breath, back toward the crew, he said, "Put down those guns!"

The men, standing behind him now, did not move until Pike added, "Go on—do as he says!" Instantly they relaxed their weapons.

One of the islanders stepped toward Robbie. His black hair was peppered with gray, and his sun-darkened face, lined and creased, projected an image of great venerability. His spear lowered and he held it perpendicular to the ground. He spoke a few words in his own language, not exactly a friendly welcome, but neither in the tone of a war cry.

"We must make repairs on our ship," said Robbie, gesturing with his hands to add meaning to his words as best he could. "We need only a few days, and then we will leave peacefully."

Seeming to gather at least a hint of Robbie's meaning, the islander gestured with his hands, making the unmistakable sign of a gun, then furiously shaking his head.

"Yes . . . of course," Robbie replied with several exaggerated nods. He pulled his sidearm from his belt and threw it in the sand beside him. Turning toward Pike, he said, "He didn't ask, skipper—he *told* us!"

Reluctantly Pike tossed down his rifle, and the others quickly followed suit. The islander barked an order and one of his men scurried forward, none too pleased, by the look on his face, to have to draw so close to these suspicious white aliens, and gathered up the weapons.

Then the leader, for the graying native could be none other, looked back toward Robbie, pointed toward the sun, then stopped and laid three small sticks of driftwood side by side in the sand. His message was clear—the crew of the *Sea Tiger* had three days to make their repairs and be gone.

They spent the remainder of the day setting up a camp on the beach, bringing supplies from the ship, and building a hastily assembled forge. Early the next morning Robbie and the Vicar struck out into the forest to try to locate some appropriate trees that would provide wood for their needed repairs. They set out east, where the island rose in elevation, hoping to discover some hardwoods. Even an hour or two after sunrise the temperatures were stifling. Within thirty minutes they had abandoned their sweat-soaked shirts, and the sun beat relentlessly on their backs.

"If we stay out in this sun we'll turn into natives ourselves," said Drew.

Robbie laughed. "After three months aboard ship, our arms and backs are nearly there already!"

As they continued on, the raw primitive quiet of the place began to impress itself upon them. It was different than the hush that had met them upon their arrival on the beach. Now the jungle was filled with the movement of animals, the call of birds, even the rush of a stream in the distance. But such sounds were an intrinsic part of the quiet itself. The only alien sound was the plodding of Robbie's and the Vicar's heavy boots.

All at once, without warning, they stumbled into a clearing and found themselves face-to-face with a small group of native women and children. The women gasped and, clutching the children to them, shrank back, their faces filled with terror.

Again Robbie extended his hands in peace. "We won't hurt you," he said gently. But the women stepped back farther, clearly afraid for their lives.

The Vicar began fumbling through his pockets until he had retrieved a handful of bright coins he had picked up in Calcutta. He held them out to the women. "Go on," he prompted when they made no move in this direction, "gift . . . for you."

At last one of the more bold from the group stepped haltingly up and took a coin from Drew's hand. She looked it over, seemed pleased, and smiled. Taking heart from her success, and safety, one-by-one they came up to Drew until his hand was empty. Then, like a flurry of birds, they turned and departed from the clearing.

"A nervous lot, aren't they?" commented Drew as the two men resumed their trek.

"Yes, and it makes no sense," said Robbie. "I'm sure we're not the first white men they've seen. Their fearfulness just doesn't conform to what I've heard about people in these regions."

"Perhaps that's the problem," returned Drew. "Maybe they've had other encounters that weren't so pleasant."

Robbie shrugged, a puzzled furrow in his brow. Though he had a broad worldly experience, it had largely been positive. He simply had not nurtured the sort of cynicism Drew bore. But Drew had a point—something was wrong here. He could sense it, almost feel it in the hot air. There was more going on around this island than met the eye.

They made their way up a sharp ascent toward the volcanic peak Robbie had seen from the *Tiger*. Here they came into an area less dense with overgrown jungle, forested with a kind of mahogany. These trees towered over them branchless until, like the coconut, they spread out into a leafy canopy. The leaves above interlaced so tightly from one tree to the next that little sunlight penetrated to the forest floor. Robbie examined the trees and nodded his head in satisfaction. He had seen specimens of this type in Manila and had learned that they were strong hardwoods, extremely resilient.

"These ought to do fine," said Robbie, breaking the long and deep silence. "We'll bring the men back here and should be able to get all we need."

But when Drew turned to go back, Robbie added, "I'd like to climb to the top of the peak before we return."

Drew brushed an arm across his sweaty brow, heaved a tired sigh, and followed. They had already climbed a good deal of the way, and twenty minutes later Robbie crested a ridge, followed soon thereafter by the Vicar.

Robbie gazed around him, beholding the spectacular view of the entire island, lush and green, surrounded by the shimmering sapphire sea.

"We're no nearer the peak than we were when we started!" exclaimed Drew.

"All I really wanted was a view from up here," said Robbie. "I think this is just as good as we'd have from up higher."

But when he gazed toward the east, a sight—more puzzling than beautiful at first, then alarming—met his eyes that he had not expected.

"Look," said Robbie, pointing; "a ship."

"Of course. It's the *Tiger*, isn't it?"

But then even before he had completed the question, Drew found his bearings, and glancing left beheld the *Sea Tiger* resting peacefully in the little northern harbor.

Had he been as acutely aware of such indicators as Robbie, Drew would have noticed almost immediately that it was no British vessel sitting off to the east of the little island, nor even European. It was a Chinese junk, three-masted with great bamboo sails, nearly as large as the *Tiger*.

"It appears we have company," commented Drew dryly.

"Or rather, the natives do," corrected Robbie. "This may account for the look of fear on the faces of those women, and the rather hostile reception we received on the shore."

Robbie rubbed his chin thoughtfully. Why had the Chinese ship anchored on this eastern side of the island when a far better harbor existed just to the north? If they had only just arrived, why seemingly avoid the harbor where there was another ship present?

Something seemed to tell Robbie they were not new arrivals, however. An unsettled feeling in the pit of his stomach warned him to beware. He turned suddenly to Drew.

"Let's get back to camp," he said, already striding rapidly down the slope.

25

Sea Pirates

The night promised to be an ideal tropical evening. A full moon shimmered above the palms, whose great branches swayed gently in the light breeze overhead. The sands shone fluorescent, and waist-high breakers rolled lazily against the beach in never-ending succession. All the crew, save Torger and Lackey who were minding the ship, had come ashore. They were sitting around a huge fire on the beach roasting a wild boar Digger had shot that afternoon. It was the first fresh meat they had smelled in weeks, and the mere thought of what it would taste like put everyone in a festive mood. Even Pike passed around a cask of grog he had secreted aboard the ship. The night air filled with rowdy laughter, accompanied by the telling and retelling of everyone's favorite seagoing adventures, most exaggerated beyond recognition from the original facts.

Joining merrily in the revelry, Robbie was happy for an opportunity to blow off a little steam and release his mind from the troubles that had been plaguing him. Without the aid of Overlie's harmonica, the singing was notably bad, worsened further by the effects of Pike's alcohol. But the emotional good was still squeezed out of it, notwithstanding the Vicar's derisive snorts whenever a love song was begun.

This was the kind of place that made forgetting easy. It was clean, unaffected, pure. It was the kind of paradise more than a few sailors had jumped ship for. Though the lure was not quite that strong on Robbie, he could not keep out a few idyllic fantasies about staying here forever. Why not find himself a wife among the lovely brown-skinned women and make a life and future here? He could stroll every day upon the beach, plant rice and pick coconuts. Here his fantasies usually ended, however, because Robbie could not think of a more boring existence than sitting waiting for crops to grow. He was made for adventure, for new horizons!

His laughter grew louder. One too many draws off the cask of grog aided him in the delusion that he was indeed having a fine time and that this was the essence of the adventuresome life of the fun-loving sailor.

The party was suddenly and unceremoniously interrupted by a hard, high-pitched laugh.

"Ah, ha! So here are our visitors from pretty English vessel!"

Even in the shadows the speaker's coarse, evil voice could readily be discerned, made all the more sinister by his heavy accent. As he walked slowly into the light of the fire, Robbie saw that despite the Chinese heritage of his large and burly frame, he was dressed in typical western seaman's attire—blue canvas trousers, loose linen shirt. Strapped to his ample midriff was a thick black belt, from which hung an ornate blunderbuss pistol and a shiny steel cutlass. The handful of men at his back were similarly clad, although some were adorned with silk oriental shirts instead of the linen. All were heavily armed, though mostly with old-style weaponry.

Immediately Robbie sobered. Traders occasionally carried weapons for protection, as had their own landing party the other day. But it was obvious these men were not traders, and Robbie instantly grew wary. Robbie held his peace however, waiting to see their intent.

Pike pulled himself up with his crutch and leveled an uncompromising stare at the speaker.

"We are that," he said with cool defiance. "An' just wot might *ye* be yerselves?"

The question was unnecessary, for Robbie had reported his discovery of the Chinese junk lying at anchor on the other side of the island. But the verbal sparring might buy them a little time, and Pike did not ask it in a manner that required such a straight-forward answer.

"Seamen. We be seamen—like yourselves. I am Chou Gung-wa, commander of *Kiaochow*," replied the hefty man, trying to pass as an innocent Chinese sailor. "Our vessel damage in storm. We seek refuge. Like yourselves, eh?"

"That's our business."

"Ah, yes . . . of course." Then Chou held out a porcelain flask. "We come sociable. See . . . bring gifts. Good drink. English sailors partial brandy, eh?"

"Well, ye're welcome to our camp," acquiesced Pike begrudgingly, knowing there was nothing else he could do. "But I see no need for all that hardware." He cocked his head toward the weapons.

"One never knows what wild things one will meet on untamed islands," said Chou.

"But as you see, we are carrying none . . ."

Chou barked an order in Chinese to his men, and immediately, though not without some grumbling, they dropped their swords and gun belts in the sand.

"See," said Chou, with a lopsided grin, "we men of peace!" But his cold, cruel eyes, hardly visible in the flickering firelight, told a different story.

Robbie edged to the fringes of the group, found a piece of driftwood in the shadows, and sat down against it. Skeptically he observed the proceedings, especially the increasing rowdiness and drunkenness of the *Tiger*'s crew. Chou's men were hardly the sociable type. Something did not ring true about this so-called peaceful visit.

Robbie was as willing to make new friends as the next man. But he had sensed trouble from the moment he had spotted the junk from the mountain top. He had warned Pike, but the skipper had laughed it off.

"Let the blag'ards come!" he had shouted. "If they mean trouble— then, by Jove, we'll give it to them!"

But it was a toothless boast, for there was no telling how many besides the present handful were on the *Kiaochow*, and the *Tiger* was down to fourteen besides the skipper. Of that, one was a child and two were old men. Even with their archaic weaponry, Robbie doubted the *Tiger*'s crew could put up much of a fight against the Orientals, even the few gathered around the fire.

A casual observer, however, might have questioned Robbie's misgivings in light of the apparent free flow of camaraderie between the two groups, though only two or three of Chou's group could speak recognizable English. And the look on Johnnie's face would not have indicated that a dangerous situation was brewing. It would have appeared merely that two crews of shipwrecked sailors were having a good time together.

Gradually two voices rose above the rest. The boatswain had taken a noisy interest in an antique pistol belonging to one of the Chinese sailors. It was of a Persian make about 18th century, with a stock inlaid with bone, turquoise and brass. The butt was of pure ivory. *No doubt booty from some overpowered ship*, thought Robbie, though he prayed he was wrong.

"Not a bad piece," said Digger, sighting down its barrel.

"*Very* good gun," said the Oriental, nervously eyeing his gun in the hands of this white barbarian.

"Well, it ain't *that* good! Pretty, I'll grant ye, but probably too old to be accurate." Digger was drunk, and perhaps thought things had become a bit too congenial. A good fight, in his distorted inebriated mind, could only represent an improvement. "I bet ye couldn't hit a coconut at ten feet in broad daylight with this pea shooter!"

"Hit what aim at," returned the Chinese, roughly reaching out and retrieving his gun, then leveling it dangerously at Digger himself.

"Why you dirty—"

But Digger did not bother to finish his verbal insult, and instead leaped at the sailor, a tiny man half his size.

His adversary nimbly jumped to his feet and stepped aside, sending Digger sprawling into the sand. Jenkins and Johnnie tried to calm him, but, spitting and sputtering, he knocked them aside.

"Lemme at him, the dirty Chi—"

But Pike broke in. "Get out of here, Digger! Go cool your head in the sea! We don't want trouble."

Digger fell back a step, muttering to himself, "Just one o' those *English* rifles in the hold an' I'd—"

He never had the chance to finish his statement. Pike's crutch shot up, landing a punishing blow to his jaw. Digger fell to the ground unconscious.

"Fool!" breathed Pike, before turning again to the merrymakers. "We gots work to do tomorrow!" he shouted. "Time to break up this tea party!"

But the damage had been done. And Pike knew it.

26

Attempted Negotiations

Benjamin Pike did not like traipsing through tropical forests at all, least of all in the dead of night. His fool leg kept sticking in the soft earth, and even with the moon, he could hardly see his way.

But something had to be done, and quickly, if he intended to save his neck, and that of his crew. Not to mention his two shipments of highly profitable cargo.

If Chou had mingled with the natives at all—and the possibility seemed undeniable that he had—then he must know that the *Tiger* had three days to make her repairs and clear out. That meant Chou would have to make his move sometime tomorrow, perhaps even this very night, in order to prevent the *Tiger* from making a fast getaway. For whatever he may have *said*, from the moment Pike laid eyes on the Chinaman, he knew he had robbery and pillage on his mind.

The only way to deal with scoundrels like Chou was to beat them to the punch, seize the initiative, cut a bargain if you could, or better, intimidate them—that is, if you possessed anything that would put fear into them. The guns in the *Tiger's* hold would no doubt have held off three crews the size of Chou's. But that would have taken ammunition, and unfortunately that had not been part of the cargo. So Pike, the veteran negotiator, swindler, and sea-faring privateer, would have to try another tack. He hoped Chou would be dutifully impressed. At least enough to leave them alone.

Pike well knew the strength of crew a junk like the *Kiaochow* was likely to possess, for Digger was not the only one guilty of a little ill-advised boasting that night. They outnumbered the *Tiger's* men at least two to one, maybe more; if they had succeeded in buying off the natives, or cowing them into submission, the odds would be far worse.

Pike had never been afraid of a fight. He had been in many in his time. But this would be nothing short of a massacre. He was already missing a leg, and he did not fancy losing his neck to boot! At the same time, he had no intention of losing his cargo either. Ten thousand pounds sterling worth of guns, not to mention half that in opium, or whatever the stuff was—he would not give up these riches without giving up his life in the process!

The only way he could see to keep both was to confront Chou, and try to cut a deal with the pirate. He did not relish the idea of getting his throat slit. But he was not fool enough to walk into enemy territory without some insurance.

The long trek through tangled underbrush with only one good leg was a grueling undertaking. He was lucky to find his way. And Pike was no longer a young man. When at last he reached the fringes of Chou's camp, he stopped and leaned a few moments on his crutch, breathless. They were a confident lot, he thought. No sentry even posted. He walked on until he could see the glow of a smoldering fire.

A sharp challenge suddenly rang through the night. It was in Chinese, but he knew the intent of the words.

"I come to see Chou," Pike replied. "You tell him I'm the captain of the *Sea Tiger*. And I too bring a gift." He held up his last bottle of brandy—worth ten of the cheap rum Chou had passed off on them.

A long pause followed, after which the lookout motioned him forward. From the look of the place, Chou and his men had been there for some time. If their story about weathering there during the storm for repairs was true, then this was not the first time they had been there. More likely, thought Pike, they used this place as a hideout after their raids. And it was indeed a fine setup—located in a clearing in the jungle, far enough from the beach to be obscure, but near enough to spot any visitors, however unlikely they might be on this treacherous eastern side of the island.

The camp itself was large enough to accommodate fifty men comfortably. Two shacks had been erected at either end—of bamboo and sturdy lauan. If they had weathered that last typhoon, they would have to be considered permanent! Between, at scattered intervals, lay the individual bivouacs of the crew, and by the look of it, their boasts had not been hollow. A quick count revealed some twenty sleeping bodies, not counting the lookouts, the men still on the junk, and Chou.

The guard led Pike to one of the shacks, obviously Chou's quarters. After a sharp knock and several brief words, followed by an even sharper reply from inside, Pike was instructed to enter. He was met immediately with the heavy, sickening odor of opium mixed with rum.

"You Englishmen have strange social custom," said Chou dryly. "In China, we pay visits more seemly hours."

"There is a time for everything, as they say," replied Pike as he settled himself on a low cushion opposite the Chinese leader. An opium receptacle stood between them, and Chou offered Pike a long, cylindrical pipe.

"No, thanks," said Pike. "I like to keep my head clear."

"Do not make mistake of underestimating clarity of honorable host's head."

"Thank you for warning me. I wouldn't think of it."

"So, have you come for business, as you English say, or pleasure?"

Pike offered up his brandy. "Perhaps a little of both, I hope. No need for it to be otherwise."

Chou took the bottle, and while he poured each of them a serving in two fine porcelain cups, Pike took in his surroundings. Silk tapestries hung on the walls of the shack, all of ancient Chinese scenes—emperors and deities and pagodas. A bed at one end of the room was encased in mosquito netting and more silken tapestries, and the cushions on which Pike sat were of thick, rich velvet. *Chou knows how to live well, if nothing else*, thought Pike. *He must do well in his business!*

Brandy in hand, Pike raised his for a toast. "May we find mutual interests and prosper in them."

They drained their cups and Chou refilled them.

"I am intrigued, Captain Pike," said Chou, with what might have been taken as a cunning grin.

"You and I both know," Pike said, following the train of thought his host had begun, "that a man . . . such as yourself, might—and who could blame him?—find a cargo such as the *Sea Tiger's* very tempting."

"How should I know of your cargo?"

"Come now, you heard the boastings of my foolish men as well as any. You do not need to be coy."

Chou laughed outright—a high-pitched sound that was hardly in keeping with his great, burly frame. This was the first time the fly had come right into the spider's den to try to talk his way out of the inevitable. "So," said the pirate after a moment, dabbing the corners of his eyes with a silk handkerchief, "you have come to beg mercy."

Now Pike returned the laugh, matching the pirate's in harshness and cruelty. "I have come to *warn* you to tread lightly where the *Sea Tiger* is concerned."

"*Warn* me!" exploded Chou in a momentary rage. "Warn Chou!"

He stopped, suddenly struck with the humor of what he had said.

"Ha, ha, ha!" he laughed, his anger diverted for a moment. "You English dogs are so amusing!"

Suddenly he whipped his cutlass from its scabbard and pressed its point against Pike's chest. "What, tell me, would prevent your venerable host from taking whatever he pleases—including your groveling life? Ha, ha!"

The suddenness of Chou's intimidating threat took Pike by surprise. "I . . . I . . ." he tried to speak, but further words stuck in his dry throat.

"Aha! So the English pig is not so confident at end of sword!" Chou gloated. "*Warning*, indeed!"

Pike cleared his throat and attempted to regain his composure. "You would do well to take heed, *pirate!*" Pike spat out the word defiantly, though his voice still carried the hint of a tremble. "You would not dare cross the buyer of my goods."

"I do what I please!"

"Have you no familiarity with the name Wang K'ung-wu?"

The moment the name fell from Pike's lips, the pressure of Chou's cutlass immediately decreased. Slowly he dropped it from Pike's chest.

"So . . . you *have* heard of my client," Pike went on in a steadier voice, regaining his confidence. "And you know he would not be happy to find his precious cargo tampered with, or lost upon the high seas."

"You English barbarians have saying—Dead men tell no tales!" Chou smiled at his own wit, but Pike was not through yet.

"Wang knows the cargo, knows my schedule, it wouldn't surprise me if he already has me being watched—somehow! The man is unscrupulous! Wang will know if anything happens, of that you can be certain!"

Pike paused a moment, letting his words sink in. He knew Wang K'ung-wu's reputation would do more than anything he might say. His was a name to shoot fear into even a pirate, however ruthless, throughout the whole Far East.

"Have you ever seen Wang angry?" he went on. "Why, I have seen him cut off a man's fingers for taking his drink, or gouge out a man's eyes for looking upon his woman. How many men he has killed by his own hand, I wouldn't even guess. Don't think you will escape lightly for trying to rob him, my friend. Which is what he will take it to be if harm comes to me or my ship."

Chou leaned back and, weaving his fingers together, rested his hands against his large mid-section. "Yes, that may be so," he said slowly, a self-satisfied grin spreading across his devilish face. "But it could well be that he honor man who bring him cargo—*at no cost.*" He threw his head back and roared in laughter. "He Chinese. He not trust likes of you, Pike. He pay you for guns, but still mistrust you. If I bring him guns . . . as *gift*—he happy!"

Again he laughed uproariously.

Pike swore silently to himself. He had never thought of such an angle. The pirate could indeed steal the guns, then ingratiate himself to Wang by turning them over free of charge. These idiot Orientals would be just fool enough to do such a thing! But he would not relent just yet.

"Only a fool would harm a friend of Wang's," he said.

"Friend! Bah! Wang have no friends!"

"Before you are so hasty about it, you had better ask him about his old comrade Benjamin Pike."

Chou was thoughtful a moment, apparently weighing Pike's words, eyeing him carefully while sheathing his cutlass. Still he wore his smug grin.

"Perhaps I spare you, dog," he said at length. "Would be curious to see how friendly Wang *is* to you, no? Perhaps I take you to him myself."

Pike swallowed hard. While it was true he and Wang had done some business together, he knew Chou was right. Wang K'ung-wu hated foreigners. At best this little ploy might buy Pike some time—and perhaps a different locale for his death.

"Now—get out of here, dog!" cried Chou. "Go warn crew their doom is near—very near!"

Pike heaved himself up from the floor, wondering what might happen if he killed Chou right here and now. He could do it. But escape would be a lost cause. He quickly gave up the idea. It would be a stupid act. He wasn't ready to die just yet! He hobbled out of the shack without another word.

As he made his way through the blackened jungle, he did not feel altogether defeated, even though he had not exactly attained his objective. Perhaps Chou was too confident. He let Pike walk away. He considered him a stupid, barbarian dog. *That was fine!* thought Pike. Just so long as it kept the pirate confident enough to trip over that filthy grin! And he had at least given him something to think about by throwing Wang into the discussion. If he did try to seize the *Tiger*, Pike was sure it would not be without some serious soul-searching—if the savage even had a soul!

There was one other thing Pike had working in his favor. Chou knew the *Tiger* had been given three days to make repairs. But that night around the fire, Pike had subtly let it be known that they would never be ready by then. He let word slip that the rudder was nowhere near completed and that they could well be up to a week. In reality, however, they could sail within hours. With difficulty—yes. But it could be done.

Suddenly Pike stopped still in his tracks.

He'd heard something in the forest—no natural sound, but rather what sounded like booted feet. He could not have been followed from Chou's camp.

All at once, Robbie stepped out into Pike's path.

"Well, laddie," said Pike, relieved, "fancy meetin' the likes o' you here!"

"What are you doing out in the jungle?" asked Robbie, somewhat sharply, for he too had been startled by the other's appearance.

"I'm thinkin' I could ask the same of you," returned the skipper coolly.

"Yes, I suppose you could." Lately Robbie found himself suspicious of nearly everything Pike did, and now he wondered if these were the same kind of thoughts that were responsible for Pike's odd behavior toward him. It chilled him to think that he might be falling into the same pit of mistrust as the old sailor.

"Well, we ain't gots time to be passin' the time of day," said Pike, shaking off any accusations that might have risen to his lips. For the moment they would each have to lay aside their personal suspicions at finding the other in the forest in the middle of the night.

"What's wrong?" asked Robbie.

"I'll tell ye what's wrong." He lowered his voice to a whisper. "We're getting out o' here—tonight."

"That's impossible. The ship—"

"Quiet, man!" Pike nervously looked this way and that. "I said we're gettin', an' we're gettin'. Chou is preparin' to attack us, an' our only chance to save our necks is to sail tonight. You got to run back to camp—they'd massacre us before I got there on this crutch! Rouse the men, break up camp. Get the rudder an' half the men to the *Tiger* first an' get that blasted rudder on!—I don't care if you got to hold it on yersel'! The rest o' us'll come wi' the supplies in the other boat. We'll be there afore ye're finished with the rudder."

Robbie studied Pike a moment, saw the dead earnestness in his words, and broke into a full run back to camp.

27

Sobering Questions

It took Robbie less than a quarter hour to haul the rudder aboard one of the two lifeboats and set across the narrow stretch of the sea with Jenkins, Digger, Newly, Drew, and Johnnie. Pike, with the remainder of the crew in the other boat, were less than thirty minutes behind.

When Robbie jumped aboard the *Sea Tiger* in the middle of the night and divulged the skipper's departure plans, the first to speak was Lackey.

"It's Friday!" he cried, bewailing an old sailor's taboo. "'Tis an ill-fated vessel indeed that tries to hoist its sail before the Sabbath!"

"Another word from you, Lackey," remonstrated Robbie, "and I'll lower *you* into the water to hold the rudder in place!"

Lackey pouted his way into silence. He detected a note of urgency in Robbie's voice. The young mate was no doubt finally cracking under the pressure of it all. No use tempting fate. He would keep silent until they set sail.

The next three hours required Herculean efforts on the part of every member of the crew. Along the decks, above and below, running feet and shouts could be heard, everyone pulling together in great unified effort. Without anyone's actually voicing it, each seemed to know he was quite literally working to save his life. Half the crew, under Robbie's direction, worked to install the new rudder. The others, with Digger barking out orders, readied the masts and sails for the winds they were likely to face during their final run for Shanghai. In three and a half hours they were ready to pull up anchor.

Slowly the sails went up, filling the night air with their ghostlike flapping, and gently the *Tiger*, urged forward by the wind, left the harbor and the island behind in the darkness. When the sun rose two hours later, the skies were clear; the winds, while not altogether favorable, enabled them to steer a course north toward the mainland, and there was no sign of land in any direction.

But even with several hours' head start, it was unlikely they could outrun the junk in their makeshift condition. If the Chinese craft had truly sustained damage during the storm—which was unlikely—they might have a chance. The situation was all the more perilous in that Chou knew their condition, knew their necessary course given the winds, and knew their destination. He would have very little trouble finding them, and no difficulty overtaking them.

By Robbie's estimation their best chance was to catch the southeast monsoon and run their easting down all the way back to Hong Kong. He didn't care about customs officials or Pike's precious cargo. What mattered now was the survival of the ship and crew.

At his first opportunity alone with Pike, he told the captain his plan.

"We're bound for Shanghai!" insisted Pike intractably, "an' that's where we're going!"

"We'll never outrun Chou in this condition."

"An' wot are ye goin' to do about it, laddie—mutiny, an' take the ship from me?"

The very word was loathsome to Robbie. It grated painfully against his strong code of loyalty. They might all lose their lives, but he would not lead a riot, even against one so incapable of command as Pike.

He spun around and stalked from Pike's cabin.

On deck Robbie took several deep gulps of the warm sea air. He loved these seas! It was only too bad they had to be sailing under such conditions. But he was only the first mate, not the captain. Therefore, he bent his attentions to the supervision of the rigging and hourly checks on the rudder. *That* was his job, and he determined that if they must make for Shanghai, then he would see to it that they made it there as quickly as possible, and hopefully in one piece. So far, the coxswain reported the rudder functioning capably, though the sea had not tested its vigor yet. If they could keep this pace, they could make the Chinese coast in two or three days, Shanghai in probably six. Maybe . . . just maybe, it would be possible.

He climbed up onto the poop and gazed out astern—no ships on the horizon, no Chinese junk, no Chou.

The Vicar ambled up. The two had hardly spoken recently. Now, however, Drew seemed inclined to renew their old dialogue.

"We are going on a broken sail and a prayer—is there not a saying somewhere to that effect?"

"More one than the other, I fear," replied Robbie grimly.

"'The prayers of a righteous man availeth much,' you know," quoted Drew. "Unfortunately we are in short supply of righteous men here aboard the *Tiger*. I cannot think of a single one other than yourself, Taggart."

Robbie laughed, hardly taking note of the Vicar's heavy sigh.

"Ah, you should have seen me in the old days, Robbie," he went on. "I could pray up such a storm. You wouldn't have had a thing to fear with the Rev. Elliot Drew aboard. No Jonah or Paul could have served a ship so well!"

"'Tis no storm I'm wanting right now, Elliot," said Robbie. "Not even of prayer. Though I would turn nothing down from that direction."

Now it was Drew's turn to laugh. "A simple westerlie, perhaps," he said. "As easy as that!" he snapped his fingers, still laughing. Then suddenly he turned sober. "Sad to say . . . the Rev. Drew is no longer with us."

"Why do you torture yourself so, Elliot?" asked Robbie, turning to face the Vicar, still wondering why a man would intentionally put himself through such punishment.

"Ah, Robbie Taggart. You are a more astute judge of human character than to have to ask that! Why, beyond myself, you are probably the closest thing we have to an intellectual aboard, though you try to hide it with that strong image of the rough sailor. But you don't fool me, Robbie! I'm sure you know me as well as I know myself. It can't have escaped you that I thrive on my own plight. I suppose I gather a certain amount of morbid satisfaction in making myself miserable."

Drew sighed and cast a long gaze out over the sea toward the horizon.

"However, none of that will help the *Tiger*, will it?" he said at length. "I am impotent! And the really sad part of it is that I was impotent then, too. Only I was too foolish to realize it."

"I didn't know you then, Elliot," said Robbie, "but from the looks of it, I can't help but wondering if you didn't have more then than you do now. At least you had something to believe in, no matter how pitiful it may have been. And perhaps if you'd stuck it out, who knows what might have happened. You might have discovered something real, like my friend Jamie did."

"Your friend who believes that God loves all men?"

Robbie nodded, surprised that Drew, in his state of mind, could remember such detail from a conversation so long past.

"Well," the Vicar continued, "I have often thought of that. Perhaps one day I'll meet your friend and she can tell me where I went wrong. Or where the world went wrong, and why God was powerless to prevent it from happening. Maybe she could tell me why a well-meaning young preacher—"

He stopped suddenly, choking over the words, took a shaky breath, then tried to go on, "Maybe she could tell me why her God of love—"

But he broke off again in a strangled sob, and closing his eyes, he paused for a long time, unable to speak.

Robbie remained silent. He did not know what to say, what to do.

He found his thoughts all at once drawn back to Jamie. She had not entered his mind for a long time, almost as if she had ceased to exist, except in some dreamlike fairy tale. *What would she say to the Vicar?* he wondered. *What would she do with this sad, lonely, disconsolate, cynical man?* He could almost see her gazing deeply into the Vicar's face with her penetrating emerald eyes, and saying, "God has a plan for everyone, dear sir, but we do not always have to understand it. Of only one thing you can be sure—that is that He loves you intimately, and means nothing but good for you." And with the words, her voice would mirror that very love which she attributed to her God.

But Robbie had no such words for the Vicar. And he knew that if he tried to spout Jamie's in order to comfort the man, they would be empty and hollow, and would fall on the Vicar's starving ears like the empty words of peace the pirate Chou had spoken. Robbie had nothing to give, for he was no nearer an understanding of Jamie's words than the Vicar.

And yet, the very words Jamie had spoken to him that day in her hotel room in London seemed more real at this moment than they had then. Back on that day he thought he had licked all his problems. He was going back to sea—the *real* sea! Everything was about to come up roses for him. He couldn't have imagined then that the footloose Robbie Taggart could be so caught up in doubts and events and frustrations that he would turn downright melancholy! He still had difficulty believing it. This wasn't him!

Jamie had freely shared with him all about her relationship with God, as she called it. But it had fallen on the ears of a self-satisfied man. He remembered back in Aberdeen when he had first seen the "new" Jamie MacLeod—and fallen immediately in love with her.

The changes in her were visible to all. And he had fallen in love with the visible, surface alteration. She was beautiful, she carried herself with poise and grace . . . she was a lady!

But he knew, too, that the change in her had gone deeper than her clothes, deeper than her face, deeper than her graceful demeanor. Her *heart* had changed. And *that* was the reason for the glowing smile on her face. Peace and an inner contentment and confidence had replaced the uncertainty and discontent of the shepherd girl he had found all alone in the blizzard.

She had attributed all this to God. "He has changed me, Robbie," she told him. "He has shown me the love in His heart for me, and made me complete." But at the time Robbie had not wanted to change—he felt just fine as he was.

And now?

Well, he'd be fine now if it wasn't for Pike . . . and all his ridiculous talks with the Vicar . . . and this seemingly fated ship old Lackey continued to pronounce doom for.

But what about God? wondered Robbie.

He hadn't done much for the Vicar. But there was so much more to the man Drew than Robbie could fathom. He knew very little of the man's actual background. Even he said it wasn't God's fault he had turned out as he had. How could God's love—supposedly the same for everyone—fail with someone like Drew and at the same time work such marvelous changes for good in one like Jamie?

What if *he* turned out to be one of God's failures? What if he turned out in the end to be a drunken, bitter fool, like Drew? Or worse—what if he turned out like Pike? Was it possible to even speak of God *failing*? Or did the responsibility lie elsewhere?

Robbie did not want to think of such things! Especially now, when there were dangers much more close to home to be faced.

He particularly did not want to think about what the cost a step toward God might entail. Yes, he supposed it could turn out to be wonderful as it had been for Jamie. But most of the so-called *religious* men he'd been acquainted with in his life were hardly "men" at all, as Robbie defined the term. Retiring and slender of frame, weak and effeminate—that's what it seemed to take to be religious, thought Robbie. It was different for women. Women could be religious without giving up their womanhood. But Robbie could not envision being a religious man without giving up a good portion of his virility—the robust, strong athletic masculinity he was proud of.

That wasn't for him! Maybe for others. But he was a man's man and didn't want to be any other way!

He knew how Jamie would reply—she would say the risk would be worth it. And that whatever he might have to give up would be repaid ten times over. Perhaps the risk *might* be worth it, if only—

"Look!" Drew's voice broke the deep silence. He had recovered his composure, and was now pointing toward the horizon. "Is that only a fog bank, or could those be storm clouds?"

Robbie was relieved to have a diversion from his thoughts. At the same time, however, another part of him felt a momentary hint of disappointment.

He almost sensed that if he had thought it out a minute longer, he might have gained a great prize. But the moment was now past.

He turned and gazed over the starboard quarter where Drew was pointing.

28

They That Go Down
to the Sea in Ships

It was not fog Drew had spotted. That would have been welcome.

"Another storm front!" exclaimed Robbie. "And moving this way!"

He leaped instantly to action. It was time to lay aside any further philosophical quandaries, for the *Sea Tiger* was in no condition to meet another storm, even a light one. But if one was coming, he would do everything in his power to use the winds to their advantage.

Robbie quickly ordered the royals hauled in. All the other sails he left trimmed. If the rudder held, they could ride the storm, and then nothing could outrace the *Tiger*. They would leave Chou's junk far behind.

The clouds had overtaken them in less than an hour. And even before that the winds had increased considerably. How long they could stay at the storm's front was the question. For a long while the *Tiger* flew through the water, making a good eighteen knots. The storm was their ally, even though Robbie knew it could not go on indefinitely. He hated to drive his ship so; each groan, each straining creak of the boards sent a shudder through his body. Yet he had already felt the grand nobility in her frame. If any clipper could do it, it was the *Sea Tiger*—if the rudder held.

The squall belched rain from above and stirred up the sea from beneath for another full day. It was not nearly so severe as the typhoon, though in their crippled state the effect was nearly the same. The main hatch stove in and water poured in below, twelve inches deep, until the pumps finally cleared it out. The forecastle roof, which they had fixed on the island, blew completely away. But miraculously, the rudder held.

During the next night, however, the wind shifted, and then indeed might Lackey have correctly prophesied disaster. The change would not have been significant under ordinary circumstances. It was only a few degrees. But with a weak rudder having difficulty keeping the *Tiger* aligned properly, the sudden difference between broad reach and beam reach was enough momentarily to snap the sails back. The sharp pressure cracked the fore topmast, and with a horrifying crash, hauling sails and rigging with it, the mast fell to the deck.

So concerned with the rudder, Robbie had never expected catastrophe to strike from above. But everything had happened so suddenly that nothing could have been done to prevent it. Pike, who had been astern, hobbled quickly to Robbie's side. Together they stared hopelessly at the wreckage. When their eyes met a moment later, Robbie perceived such a depth of despair in the old man's sinking heart at seeing his dreams vanish before him that instantly he forgot all his animosity. He laid a comforting hand on the skipper's shoulder.

"We'll make it through this, Ben," he said gently. "Come on, the men will need us. We have to clean up and make what repairs we can."

Pike stared at him blankly, as if he had not heard such a crazy notion in all his long life. But Robbie gently urged him forward. He knew a dose of hard work would be the best medicine for the heartbroken old sailor.

Robbie fetched a box of tools, then began cutting away at the tangled mass of sail, mast, and untold hundreds of yards of rope and rigging. Suddenly an agonized gasp escaped his lips, and Robbie jumped back, staring as one looking on death for the first time.

It was scarcely any wonder that he had not first noticed the bodies, half covered as they were with sail, and with rain and wind pelting him in the face. But now that he saw them his heart suddenly went sick. He turned away and gagged violently.

Young Sammy's foot was tangled in a coil of rope. He had apparently been part way up the rigging when Jenkins tried to free him. But he had not been in time to save either of them before the mast toppled over, taking them both to their deaths beneath it.

A half-choked, screaming sob broke from Robbie's lips, followed by a hot rush of tears escaping from his eyes. He clenched his teeth together to try to stop, but it was no use.

"*Oh, God, why! Why is life so cruel to those who deserve it least!*" he yelled into the wind.

Sammy had so loved the sea, had spoken dreamily about becoming a captain one day. "But don't worry, Robbie," he had said. "I'll never give up a clipper for steam!" They had laughed heartily. After all, they were true *sailing* men! Suddenly the boy was dead, before his first voyage was half over.

And what a good man Jenkins was! How could they possibly continue without his strength and know-how? If Robbie could have felt glad about anything at that moment, it would have been because the able sailor had died heroically. If anything could give back an ounce of hope, and could enable the men now to do what they had to do in order to keep the *Tiger* afloat, it would be the memory of that hero's death, giving his life trying to save another. Therefore Robbie turned with renewed vigor to the task of clearing the deck and caring for the dead. The bodies were wrapped in canvas to await burial at sea when the weather permitted a proper service.

It took the remainder of the night to sort through and clear off the debris from the deck, while the rest of the meager crew hauled in all the sails. There would be no way they could run now, especially after Torger delivered his report that the rudder was weakening. They would have no choice but to heave to and sit the squall out.

By the first gray light of what passed for dawn, the winds had abated somewhat and the seas had quieted enough for a brief funeral.

As the dead were brought to the rails, everyone seemed to look to Robbie for some kind of eulogy. Pike, even as captain, seemed out of the question for such a role. But any words Robbie tried to force out only stuck in his throat. Could he say that their brave comrades and faithful shipmates had given their lives because of their skipper's greed? Could he say they had given their lives for a worthy cause—shipping contraband to Chinese outlaws?

All at once something sprang into his mind. It seemed ages since he had heard the words from an old sailor; in truth, it had been only a few months since that day when he and young Andrew Graystone had walked happily along the London docks.

"They that go down to the sea in ships, that do business in great waters; These see the works of the Lord, and His wonders in the deep."

Robbie paused. That was all the old man had said. It didn't seem like much of a sendoff for these two shipmates. Then a quiet voice from the rear of the small group spoke, taking up the scripture where Robbie had left off:

"'For he commandeth, and raiseth the stormy wind, which lifteth up

the waves thereof. They mount up to the heavens, they go down again to the depths: their soul is melted because of trouble. They reel to and fro, and stagger like a drunken man, and are at their wit's end. Then they cry unto the Lord in their trouble, and he bringeth them out of their distresses. He maketh the storm a calm, so that the waves thereof are still. Then are they glad because they be quiet; so he bringeth them unto their departed haven.'"

A great hush fell over the group when Drew stopped as quietly as he had begun. For the first time since Robbie had known him, the Vicar spoke of God with neither cynicism nor bitterness. The words of Scripture had been spoken with apparent sincerity, even if with the sincerity of a man who believes a thing though he himself cannot personally espouse it.

But as amazing as were Drew's words and the almost prophetic look upon his face as he spoke, even more so was the sanctified hush that fell on the rest of the crew. Hardly a man of them had ever before made so much as a mention of God. Yet now even the roughest of them bore upon their tough, weather-beaten countenances a look of reverence lovely to behold.

The verses reminded them not only of the realities of the sea, but also of its mercy. They well knew what a haven, a safe harbor in a time of storm, was. And they were reminded now that death also could be a haven from the stormy cares of life. As they stood there, some of the men, in the quiet of their own hearts, found themselves repenting of past hardness, either toward God or their fellowmen. It is difficult to predict what the Vicar's reaction would have been had he been told that *his* words had served to draw some of these men a few steps closer to their Maker. The lady from the mission in Calcutta had said, "Even a sailor can be used of God," and her words must also apply to an embittered ex-clergyman.

The timing of that Godly intervention could not have been more perfect, for many of these men would very soon find either their final haven or tumult, as their hearts would reveal when the time came.

In that reverent atmosphere the bodies of the dead were discharged into the sea. Then as God had given Noah the rainbow for a sign, He seemed to give to these men a sign of His presence also. A great bright streak of light broke out above the back of the mass of gray clouds. The dawn had boldly made itself known, forcing back the darkness of the diminishing storm.

All at once the reverie ended with a shout.

"A ship!"

All eyes turned astern. There against the dark, murky horizon, where the water and sky met together in a dull blend of gray, the shadowed outlines of a ship in full sail appeared. A great cheer arose from the crew of the *Tiger*. Each one of them well knew they could not have gotten much farther in their condition. Even though land was only five, perhaps eight, miles west of them as they skirted the Chinese coast, without the main mast it might as well have been a hundred.

Only Robbie did not join in the jubilant cheer of anticipated rescue. He remembered, if they did not, that not all vessels met in these waters were necessarily friendly. He also vividly remembered the different look in the cut of sail between an English clipper and a Chinese junk.

29

Final Port of Call for the *Sea Tiger*

The shouts aboard the *Tiger* quickly fell the moment the ominous outline of the *Kiaochow* could be clearly distinguished. Most of the men merely stood gaping, as if they had been cheated by their false hope.

But Robbie sprang into action.

"Digger!" he shouted, "break out the weapons! The rest of you, let's trim what's left of these sails!"

Unquestioningly the men obeyed. But Pike, who had been moving about in a daze, laid a hand on Robbie's arm. The act was not resistant, nor were his words spoken out of authority. He asked a simple question, as one might to his commander: "What are you doing?"

"We'll either fight them or outrun them!" returned Robbie.

"You know we can do neither."

"We have to try! We can't just sit here."

"We can give up, and hope we are spared."

Robbie appraised Pike for a long moment. Was he truly suggesting giving up, or was there some unseen ulterior motive in his statement?

This hardly seemed the same Pike who was such a short time ago willing to brave all manner of hazards to save his valuable cargo. Was it possible that he knew his cargo, and perhaps himself as well, *would* be saved, and in actuality he cared not a thing for ship and crew?

Robbie could not even force himself to believe his own thoughts.

Now was not a time, however, to deliberate with himself. There was only time to act on gut instinct. And his instinct told him that there was little hope a man like Chou would spare them. Then came Pike's quiet words, as if he knew he no longer carried the right to determine the fate of his ship. "Do what you can," he said, then spoke no more.

Even before the *Kiaochow* was within the *Tiger's* range it began to fire, though these blasts fell far short. But these initial forays with cannon fire were merely intended to intimidate, for Chou was after the cargo and would not dare chance damaging it. As soon as they were close enough, the cannons were replaced by guns, and a volley of handfire between the two ships ensued. Though some of the Chinese weapons were archaic, others were not, and within ten minutes three more of the *Tiger's* crew were dead and Chou's hoard had been diminished by only a handful.

Chou waved a flag of truce and the fire on both ships ceased. It was not truce he wanted, but surrender.

"Give up at once," he yelled across the water, "and you may yet find mercy!"

Even as he spoke of mercy, Chou stretched his arm to his left indicating his cannons, manned and ready to fire.

Robbie turned back to gaze upon his own meager crew. There were but nine of them left, as well as Pike, who had retired to the chart house to await his ship's final fate. Robbie was silent a moment, then said, "What'll it be, men? You have the right to choose how you will die."

"I say fight it out if we have half a chance!" cried Overlie.

"We might not have even that much," said Robbie solemnly.

"Give 'em the bloody cargo!" said Digger.

"Yeah, what is it to us?" added another.

"We may do so and still find ourselves on the end of their swords," said Robbie.

"But if we don't give it to them, they'll kill us all first, then take it anyway!"

"Look at 'em! There must be fifty men still on that ship!"

A general clamor of agreement arose.

"What do we have to lose? The cargo's as good as lost. We can't hope to win in a fight."

"That's right! The only chance is to let them have it!"

"It may be no chance at all," said Robbie.

"But it's the only one we have!"

At last Robbie realized that the men were no longer prepared to lose their lives for a skipper for whom they had lost their respect. Especially when giving up seemed to offer their only hope—however slim—of survival. Facing certain death, it became easier to put their fate into the hands even of a pirate.

Slowly Robbie raised his weapon into the air, took one last look toward his men as if to ask, "Are you sure this is your decision?" Then with great effort of will, he flung the gun into the water. His men immediately followed the lead.

Within moments, notwithstanding the substantial breezes and that the sea was by no means calm, the *Kiaochow* had moved alongside the *Tiger*. The junk's crew had obviously had a great deal of experience of this very kind.

Chou was the first to step aboard, wearing an ugly, triumphant grin. One look at Robbie, and Chou thrust an evil finger toward the first mate.

"Hold him!" he ordered to several of his men. "He looks as if he is not fully convinced of the wisdom of his decision."

Three bare-chested Chinese stepped forward and held Robbie fast. He now had to look on, helpless, as the remaining hoards of pirates swarmed aboard his ship. A half dozen of the marauders held guns to the crew, while another thirty or forty went below to begin relieving the *Sea Tiger* of her cargo. The task was no small one, and it was noon before the contraband of rifles and other items was stowed aboard the junk.

When the task was completed, Chou sent three of his men to ferret Pike out of his hiding place. They found him half drunk, and dragged him before their leader.

"So, where do great sea captain's *warnings* leave him now?" laughed Chou.

"You dirty, yellow-eyed—"

But Chou's fist rammed Pike viciously in the stomach, cutting off further insults as the captain crumbled to the deck.

"Go ahead, put up good show, Mister Captain Pike," jeered Chou. "But do not worry. You need barter but once with me to save skin. Your words on island suffice."

"What the—!" exclaimed Digger. "You tried to make a deal with these savages!" he cried at Pike. "Why you double crossing, no good—"

Digger burst free from his captors and threw himself at his traitorous skipper. He reached Pike and had his hands around the older man's scrawny throat when a shot rang through the air.

The huge bo'sun dropped heavily to the deck.

Robbie fought to break free, but he could not budge. He could not help, anyway. Digger was already dead.

Then he became conscious of Chou's wicked laughter ringing through the air as the echo from the shot died away. More even than pillage and murder, he seemed to take great delight in turning men one against the other, watching mate betray mate in a final hopeless effort each to save his own skin.

"It might prove better sport," he said, still laughing, "to leave you to mercies of own men, eh, Pike? But no, I would not miss watching you squirm before Wang K'ung-wu."

He motioned to his men. "Take him aboard *Kiaochow*!"

Staring straight ahead, Pike hobbled away between his captors. He looked neither to the right nor left, refusing to catch the eye of any of his crew, all of whom stared after him silently. Robbie's gaze followed him all the way, still hoping that in the end Pike would turn and say something to reassure them that he had not sold them out. But it looked as though he would never know.

The moment Pike was aboard, Chou led the rest of his pirates off the *Tiger*, though not before they had crippled its two remaining lifeboats. Any relief the men may have felt at seeing the devilish junk pulling away from its hull was short-lived. For within moments Chou gave the order and the cannons of the *Kiaochow* began firing. The first ball fell short, but the next two hit the *Tiger* broadside, and a third and fourth blasted apart a large portion of the interior deck. A fire was soon raging amidships from the explosive charges.

The wind swiftly carried the junk away. The *Tiger* was now shipping water at an incredible rate from more than a half-dozen gashes and rents in its once-proud hull. Black smoke poured into the sky as the bright orange flames from the burning sails licked the masts that had once mightily held them against the world's winds. Slowly it began to reel toward port, as the stern sank deeper and deeper into the rising sea.

The men who remained of the crew began leaping over the side of the ship so as not to be sucked into the vacuum-like pull of the sinking vessel. Robbie waited a moment before jumping, thinking, as for an instant he surveyed the tragic end of a proud craft, that it had probably been some mercy of Providence that young Sammy had been taken as he was. He quickly counted six heads bobbing up and down in the water.

There should be another, he thought. But the seas were turbulent enough that anything could have happened to the other man. Then he spotted the Vicar, clinging to the side of the slanting starboard deck farther toward what had once been the bow of the ship. Robbie ran up the deck toward him.

"Jump, man!" he shouted.

Still the Vicar hung tightly to the rail.

"Jump, or we'll go down with her!"

"I . . . I can't swim," said the Vicar, almost pitifully.

"That hardly matters now, Vicar!" said Robbie. He grabbed at Drew's hands, struggling to unwrap them from their panicked grip, then half shoved, half pulled the Vicar, and the two of them leaped over the side and into the water.

When they sputtered to the surface, with his left hand clutched around the Vicar's shoulder, Robbie swam furiously to escape entanglement in the ship's rigging and to distance himself as much as possible from the sinking ship.

When he could swim no more, he stopped, just in time to watch the sea swallow the last of his noble *Sea Tiger*. The tears that rose in his eyes would never be seen by another man, for the ocean washed over them freely. But Robbie was too exhausted to care—they were going to die; what else mattered?

A great wave washed over them, then another. But Robbie could not give up. Each time he struggled to the surface he pulled the nearly unconscious Vicar with him.

"Isn't the third time under supposed to be the last?" gasped the Vicar. "Let me go and let me die! They say drowning is the most peaceful way of all."

Another wave crashed over them and Robbie kicked and fought once more to the surface.

"I'll not let you go, Vicar!" Robbie tried to shout.

Another wave interrupted him.

"If we go . . . we both go together!"

A moment later and they were under the surface again. Each time they seemed to remain under longer. This time Robbie's grip on the Vicar began to slip. His lungs ached for air. His legs were numb from the cold and the ceaseless kicking and the added weight of the Vicar's body.

What would it be like to drown? Robbie wondered. With the thought came a momentary relaxation of his strength. He could not fight much longer. And what was the use? They could never make land—the ship was gone, the Vicar couldn't swim. Why not just give in to the sea? Why not just let it wash peacefully over them. *Relax,* he thought sleepily. *Just let the water sweep over . . . rest . . . just rest.* It would all be over soon . . .

Suddenly his head broke through the surface and he again felt air on his face. He gasped violently for oxygen, then felt himself smack hard against some object in the water with them. Vicar! Where was the Vicar! Oh no! The Vicar was gone! He'd let go of him! . . . What was that floating in the water?

Robbie's mind was not thinking rationally. He could not focus on what was happening. He could not distinguish between the Vicar and what he had bumped into and the delicious air his lungs were frantically trying to fill themselves with. Instinctively his one hand grabbed the floating object while his other beat about around him for Drew.

"Drew!" he gasped. "Vicar . . . Vicar . . . where are you?"

Robbie's foot hit against something soft.

"Vicar!" cried Robbie.

He reached down with his free hand. His fingers closed around a shred of clothing. He pulled with all the might left in his weakened arm. In a moment the Vicar's head broke through the surface.

"Vicar!" cried Robbie, "hang on . . . take hold of this . . . I've found something from the ship . . . grab hold . . ."

He put Drew's arms around the floating timber from the *Sea Tiger.* Gradually Drew began sputtering for air, and as he did so, his limp arms felt the wood and tried to grab it.

"Hang on to it, Drew . . . hang on!"

An hour later, Robbie and the Vicar were still alive, still clutching the spar—for it was the mizzen topgallant yard from the *Sea Tiger*—and still fighting off the bitter cold from the sea. Drew lay with his arms around it like one already dead, and still Robbie was paddling with what strength remained to keep them both afloat.

Hours seemed to pass. Still the sea did not overwhelm them. Occasionally Robbie wondered about the rest of the crew, whether they were out there clinging for their lives to other pieces of the ship. But he could see nothing, and had scarcely the strength to lift his head even if he could have seen beyond the next wave. The whole world consisted of him and the Vicar and a broken yardarm and the pounding sea.

He tried to think of their bearings. The *Tiger* had covered a lot of ground during the storm. Perhaps they were not that far from shore. They had been running parallel to the coast because of the rudder. What about the tides and currents? He had no idea of their direction.

But it was all an empty hope! They could not hope to swim one mile in these seas!

Were they about to die? What would come then? Would he see heaven? But of course that was impossible! He would be one of the damned. What about the Vicar? Would this be their final parting—the Vicar to the place above, and he to the place below?

Desperate for the sound of a human voice, he tried to speak.

"Elliot," he gasped, "Elliot . . . are you afraid?"

The Vicar merely made a soft gurgling sound, which was as close as his dispirited mind could come to a laugh.

"I never thought I'd be afraid to die," Robbie continued, his words labored. "Being afraid frightens me almost . . . almost as much as dying."

"A new sensation . . . fear . . . something Robbie Taggart hasn't known, eh?"

"I've rarely been afraid—until now."

"Don't worry, Robbie—you'll get used to it."

"But what's going to happen to us? I don't want to go to hell. I feel I should repent . . . or something, but—"

Another wave caught him full in the face, and his open mouth took so much water that he could not speak for some time.

"Repent because you're dying?" said the Vicar, his passion for discussion undaunted even in the face of death. "That's the worst possible reason for repentance."

"What are the *right* reasons?"

"I used to know some . . . can't think at the moment. Now shut up . . . so I can die in peace."

It was just as well. Robbie could talk no more. He couldn't think straight. Would God have mercy on him even though he hadn't repented? He didn't even know what repentance meant.

It was just so cold . . . he could kick his legs no longer . . . did not even realize it when the seas gradually began to calm. Repentance . . . the *Sea Tiger* . . . Jamie . . . the face of Benjamin Pike—they all loomed in his mind: words, faces, feelings, memories . . . jumbled into confusion.

On he floated in waking unconsciousness, no longer even aware of the Vicar, wondering occasionally if he'd drifted off and into the sea and into some peaceful final sleep.

Only vaguely did Robbie feel the strong hands yanking and pulling at his body. Were they taking him out of the sea to warm him by the fires of hell? Was he dead? There seemed to be a dry surface underneath him, but it continued to rock and undulate like the sea. Was hell nothing more than an continuous experience of the moments of your death?

Then came the sound of voices floating in the air above him—the voices of angels or demons or some other beings he could not see. They reminded him of the voices of his Highland home—warm and earthy and reassuring. He could understand nothing of what they said. It sounded in his memory like the strange and rhythmic Gaelic tongue spoken by the natives in the hills of his homeland.

In his exhausted and delirious state, Robbie could not tell that they spoke not the Gaelic of the Scottish Highlands, but indeed a rather similarly melodious dialect of Chinese.

Part III

China

30

The Mission

Robbie opened his eyes. All was darkness.

His first thought was that he must still be unconscious. Then came the terrifying question: Was he in some black afterlife limbo?

One thing was sure: He was no longer in the icy, turbulent water of the East China Sea. He tried to move; sharp pain rippled through his body. He winced. He must not be dead. Somewhere in the room a fire radiated warmth toward him. Reassured, he closed his eyes again and tried to let the warmth lull him back to sleep.

All at once the thought of the Vicar came into his hazy mind.

"Drew . . . Drew!" he tried to call out, but his voice could only manage a whisper. He tried to sit up, ignoring the pain coursing through his body. But he could not. And even as he fell back down, a gentle hand reached out and touched his shoulder.

"Shhh," said a soft voice. "Your friend is alive."

It was a tender, musical voice, at once grave and yet joyful, but very hushed as if it were part of the night and had itself come out of the warm glowing fire. "You must rest."

Robbie struggled where he lay to find the face that went with such a voice, but the room was very dark and his eyes extremely heavy. He had no inclination to argue. He had no idea where he was nor what had become of him, but he felt oddly secure. The Vicar was safe, they were both apparently alive, and all other questions seemed to dissolve for the moment. He lay back and let the peace of the darkness, the warm fire, and the invisible ministering angel surround him again.

Bright light and searing heat woke him several hours later. He was drenched with perspiration, sticky and uncomfortable—and so very thirsty! The vague sense of darkness and peace and a soft voice from the previous night lingered discordantly with these new sensations of wakefulness, and he decided the former must have been a dream. He tried again to pull himself to a sitting position and discovered with the first flexing of his muscles that at least the aches had been no dream.

"Good morning, Robbie!" came a jaunty, familiar voice.

Robbie turned in the direction of the sound. "Drew!" he exclaimed, "you old sea dog!"

"My, but you seem to take the privileges of your position seriously," said the Vicar, looking worn in the bed beside him, but otherwise none the worse for his recent ordeal. "I thought you were going to sleep away the entire morning!"

"If this place is a hospital, isn't that what we're supposed to do?"

"No doubt. And I shall overlook it this time, since it seems you swam for two in our recent adventure."

Suddenly Drew's voice lost its familiar flippant quality and turned earnest. "You saved my life, Robbie. At first I didn't know whether to curse you or thank you. But I've decided on the latter. You could have drowned yourself on my account, but you didn't let go of me. I shall never forget that."

Robbie made no reply. A long pause passed between them.

"Where are we?" Robbie asked at last. As he spoke he stretched his neck up so his eyes could sweep in his immediate surroundings. Now first he realized how weak he was, for after a few moments he fell onto his back exhausted. The room he saw was not as small as he had imagined during the night. It was rather quite large, with two rows of beds, three against each wall, of which he and Drew were the only occupants at present. Though very rustic, it was clean and orderly, and he realized it must be a small hospital of some kind, as he had guessed.

"I don't know," said Drew in response to his question. "I've seen no one. I just awoke—"

At that moment the door at the far end of the room opened, followed by the entrance of tall man who, though Occidental in all his features, was dressed in Oriental fashion with a long, black cotton high-collared and loose-fitting trousers to match. He appeared in his mid-fifties, and his thick black hair, combed severely back from his forehead, was amply laced with gray. Not a bulky man, his narrow shoulders and slight frame contrasted sharply with his overall look of gravity. In his hands he carried a tray containing bowls, a teapot, cups and various utensils. He moved into the room with deliberate, measured steps as if even the trivial movements of his body were of worth and not to be wasted.

"Praise be to the Lord!" he said with quiet intensity, his voice slow and methodical as were his movements. Each word seemed to have been given great consideration before spoken. "God has returned your lives to us. You gave us quite a fright when they brought you in. How thankful we are that you are conscious again."

Though the man's tone conveyed that he was truly thankful, and that the loss of these two strangers would have grieved him deeply, both men—though for entirely different reasons—were put off by his somber religious tone.

"I am Dr. Wallace—Isaiah Wallace—the director here," the man added after a brief pause. As he spoke he extended his hand, a small but browned and work-worn one, to each man in turn. When his hand and the Vicar's clasped, Robbie could not help seeing the comparison—they were both the hands of scholars, who, for whatever, reasons, had been called to physical labor also. He then set the tray on a nearby table and began to arrange things for a meal for his patients.

"We are indebted to you, Dr. Wallace," said Robbie, clearing his throat and trying to speak clearly. Whether it was the residue of his hours at sea, or something about this man before him, he had difficulty finding his voice, and felt somehow like a child before his schoolmaster.

"It is not myself to whom you should be indebted, young man," replied Wallace, not sternly, but with firm conviction in his tone, "but rather give your thanks to God who brought you out of the water like Moses—the name with which we have dubbed you in lieu of your real one. He was drawn out of the water to new life and new purpose, as I believe the Lord also intends for you. And for Jonah here, also." As he spoke these final words, he indicated the Vicar, who squirmed under his gaze. "Give your thanks to God who alone is worthy, and who alone can save, both from the sea and from ourselves."

For a rare instant in his life, Robbie found himself daunted. He had never met a man quite like this, and he wasn't sure he liked it. He felt as if his gratitude had been thrown back in his face in a pompous and condescending manner. *A mere "You're welcome" would have sufficed*, thought Robbie, *in place of all this religious gibberish*. He did not doubt the man's depth of sincerity. This was no hypocrite, no weak-kneed buffoon like the churches back home were filled with. But notwithstanding his good intentions, he could have used a little simple tact.

During the pause that followed, Robbie noted for the first time the outlandish long white gown he was wearing. He looked like an old man in nightclothes!

"Your own clothes will be returned to you directly," said Wallace, noting Robbie's grimace. "They were quite wet."

"Yes, of course," replied Robbie, adding, "I'm not very accustomed to hospitals."

"That is obvious, young man. I should guess the last, and perhaps the only time you have been in one was when you broke your shoulder—some years back, by the look of it."

"How did you know?"

"I am a doctor, remember." Wallace motioned toward the table. "If you are up to it. Otherwise, you can take your meal in your beds. You were both very weak. You will need to spend a good while recuperating."

Robbie and Drew both stood beside their beds, realizing for the first time how weak their legs, indeed their entire bodies were. Gingerly they walked toward the table and sat down to the simple meal Wallace had set before them.

"Now," Wallace continued, "though Moses and Jonah are no mean names to be lightly set aside, I am certain your own would be preferable to you." Although there was nothing overbearing about the doctor, there was something in the tone of his voice, and in the penetrating gaze of his small, deep-set eyes, that commanded respect.

"I am Robbie Taggart, and my companion is Elliot Drew," answered Robbie. "We are of the British clipper, *Sea Tiger*. We were wrecked by pirates some . . . well, I have no idea how long ago. We went down June the tenth."

"Quite incredible," said Wallace, nodding his head as he drew out the words. "Today is the thirteenth and the fishers found you very early yesterday in the Hangchow Bay. You must have been in the water well over twenty-four hours, perhaps thirty-six. That is nothing short of a miracle. Praise be to God! I see that the pseudonyms you were given are even more apt than I first thought."

Wallace paused and seemed to meditate a moment on this insight. When he spoke again, it seemed an effort for him to concentrate on more mundane matters when he would rather focus his attention on deeper things of the spiritual realm.

"You are now at Christ's China Mission station in Wukiang, about ninety miles from Shanghai. And, I add with utmost sincerity, you are most welcome here, and may feel free to remain with us as long as you wish. We will do all we can to care for you and speed your bodies back to health."

He paused, rose slowly but purposefully from the chair he had taken, and then added, "I will take my leave of you now so you may finish your meal in peace. Please remain in bed for the rest of the day. It may take some time for your strength to be restored. You were quite near exhaustion when they brought you to us. Perhaps this evening, if you would like, we could arrange for a short walk, maybe a tour of the compound."

"Thank you very much, Doctor," said Robbie.

Wallace made no rebuffing comment to Robbie's second expression of gratitude. He walked to the door, and there turned to add, "A young lad named Ying Nien will be your attendant. Please feel free to call on him whenever necessary."

Alone once more, Robbie and Drew sat in silence for some time, slowly eating their meal, while reflecting on all that had happened and the unexpected turn of their fortunes.

"A mission!" exclaimed the Vicar at last. "Of all the nasty chance."

"I should think you'd feel right at home."

"Don't be cynical, Robbie. That's my role, remember?"

A mission was certainly not the most peculiar place Robbie had ever stayed, and he was willing to take the new adventure in stride. But he was not sure he cared for this Wallace, a religious fanatic by all appearances. Drew was apparently thinking along the same lines.

"You will keep the *Vicar* business quiet?" said Drew. "I wouldn't want to cause—ah, any undue awkwardness . . . to the good doctor, of course."

"Of course," replied Robbie, but his voice grew distracted as another personality suddenly entered his mind. Had Pike indeed betrayed them, or was he too a victim? Had his secret meeting with Chou been an attempt to save the *Tiger* and her crew, or was he merely bargaining for his own skin? No doubt Pike was somewhere in China at this very moment. Alive or dead, who could tell? Whatever the case, Robbie would have to find him. He had to know what had really happened.

"You're thinking of the skipper, aren't you?" said the Vicar.

Robbie nodded. "If he did betray us . . ." Robbie's voice trailed off into thought. Then a moment later he added, "But on the other hand, what if that wasn't the case? What if he needs our help?"

"I doubt Chou would keep him alive past his usefulness to him."

"You're probably right," said Robbie. "Still, the man is our skipper."

"Who just may have gotten us into this fix! But vengeance is mine, says the Lord!"

Robbie merely smiled at another of Drew's hollow quotes. The sea water did not seem to have affected his memory!

When they were through, a polite Chinese youth entered and cleared away the dishes. In broken English, he bid them follow the honorable doctor's orders and return to bed.

They did so. Robbie slept the remainder of the morning and most of the afternoon. When he woke, evening shadows slanted across the room, and the sun had already begun to set beyond the distant mountains to the west. He tried to swing out of bed, and though the motion was slow, he happily noticed that his limbs did not ache nearly so much as they had that morning. He was ready for some fresh air! Then his eyes fell upon his nightshirt. That would never do for a stroll about the mission. What was the name of that nurse? Ying . . . something. Robbie was about to seek him out when he spied his clothes, laundered and neatly folded, lying on the chair by the table where he had eaten breakfast. He dressed quickly, and only as he was about to leave did he notice that the Vicar was gone. *Well*, thought Robbie, *I hope he hasn't already found passage to Shanghai. I'll miss the old cynic.*

A gentle breeze met him at the doorway and made him realize for the first time how stuffy the room had been. It was not yet dark, but many stars had already shown their bright faces.

All at once Robbie was struck with the realization that he was in China . . . alone . . . with nothing but the clothes on his back . . . and with no future. The words of Isaiah Wallace crept into his mind, though he had hardly given them more than a thought when they had first been spoken:

"He was drawn out of the water to new life and purpose. . . ."

Of course the doctor had the tendency to overdo things a bit, adding dramatic religious overtones to everything he said. But as he stood there in a new country, in a place he'd never been before, with no future to look toward, the words somehow seemed appropriate. Though Robbie could barely grasp their superficial significance, much less the more profound spiritual implications, he could yet sense the possibilities all around him.

Possibilities for adventure—yes. But there was something more here. He could feel it! He wasn't sure what it was, or whether it would all be to his liking. But as a man always welcoming newness, Robbie Taggart was ever ready to step boldly forward to meet whatever came his way.

31

The Rabbit and the Swan

The evening was warm and sultry, but a light breeze offset the intensity of the summer heat.

Looking about, Robbie saw a small cluster of buildings—three in all. These made up the mission compound, though they were not walled off as was generally the case with missions. They were, however, set apart by about a stone's throw from the nearest row of village houses. The mission buildings in construction were very much like those of the village, rustic with an air of poverty, and each with the traditional pagoda-style roof that stood in peculiar contrast to the large wooden cross adorning the largest of the three buildings.

The village itself had grown up around the juncture of two streams, and most of the houses fronted these waterways. In reality they were small rivers on which the villagers traveled by boat, and on whose banks the women pounded out their wash. The mission stood on the northern bank of the larger of these, and being at the farthest end, Robbie could stand on the bridge over this stream—some seventy five feet long, and ten to twelve feet above the level of the water at its midpoint—and command a fine view of the entire village. It was quiet all around him. A woman was carrying a pail of water on a small wooden yoke over her shoulder, a few children occasionally darted in and out among the houses, and down the river a man was mooring his junk to a stone platform in front of his house. Over it all as if from the starry twilight above, and through the melodic sounds of the stream tumbling by him, a peace prevailed over the place, unbroken even by the faint barking of a dog somewhere in the distance.

Robbie wandered toward the middle of the bridge. It was itself as rustic and seemingly flimsy as the fairy-tale houses in this picture-book setting. But though it creaked a bit beneath his weight, it was sound and had been so for years on end. Robbie looked down at the dark ripples passing by underneath him. He loved the water, and his near-fatal experience on the sea would never alter that.

On the opposite bank of the river, about a hundred and fifty yards away, Robbie saw Wallace conversing with another man. Robbie would have given it scarcely more than a glance except that the doctor's companion was rather alarming in appearance to pass off casually. He stood in complete and total contrast to the peaceful village surroundings, and, even from Robbie's limited contact with the villagers, he could see in an instant that this man did not fit. He was a brawny Oriental, garbed in leather breeches and vest with high-top heavy boots. His shaven head sat upon a thick neck and was topped with an ill-fitting cloth cap.

But what alarmed Robbie most was the dagger and pistol strapped to his belt. He immediately thought back to Chou's men, for the image was identical. Could they have possibly traced him here? But why would they have bothered? He meant nothing to them. Yet what else could such a man want in a place like this?

Whatever the answer to that question, one thing was apparent— Wallace would not easily allow him to have his way if it was in conflict with the purposes of the mission. Even in the poor light, Robbie could see the doctor's austere features as stern as ever. However, there was with them something of the beseeching quality as well. It was very possible the missionary was trying to spare his flock from the attentions of some marauding gang of bandits. Whatever the case, even in the short acquaintance Robbie had had with this place, he realized what a desecration it would be for such a man as Chou to touch it.

He then looked up and down the river, trying to pull his attention away from the disquieting scene—he had had enough of discord for a good while and desired only to drink in the tranquil setting all about him. A saying he had once heard about "borrowing trouble" came to him.

He could not help smiling.

If there was any trouble, it would find him soon enough without his having to dream it up from a simple conversation between two men off in the distance. He let himself relax, and the quiet feeling he had sensed earlier washed over him once more. He forgot about ships and cities and pubs, but in a restful way was perfectly content to be right where he was at that moment. He found himself wondering what these people were like who had spent their entire lives here, beside these two streams that emptied farther down into the great Yangtze River.

At length he felt constrained to return to the mission lest his benefactors grow concerned over his absence. Just as he did so, a figure stepped onto the bridge from the south bank, apparently coming from the village on the other side. Not wanting to appear rude, he paused. The girl who approached him was of diminutive stature and delicately featured, dressed in a light blue ankle-length skirt and white, short-sleeved Oriental jacket, both of a homespun cotton. Her thick black hair was pulled back from her lightly tanned face, plaited into a silky braid that reached the length of her back. Her oriental facial features at first appeared somewhat taut and drawn, as if she were in the midst of some unpleasant dilemma. But when she saw Robbie, these softened into a warm smile. Robbie returned the greeting.

"Good evening," she said in perfect, though accented English. "It is good to see our Moses restored to health enough to get out of his bed."

Robbie had nearly forgotten the two biblical appellations the doctor had given them. But the first thing that came to Robbie's mind was that this girl before him was certainly the owner of the striking voice he had heard in the night. He felt suddenly shy and awkward.

"Yes, I am feeling much better, thanks to the doctor," he replied, "and perhaps also to you . . . ?"

She colored slightly. "I did not think you would remember. I did very little, really. I was merely a sentinel instructed to run for my father should your condition worsen. We thought you would die when they brought you in; you were nearly dead already. My father prayed over each of you for an hour after he got you dried and to bed."

"Your father?" queried Robbie.

"The doctor."

"Dr. Wallace?"

She smiled again, more amused by Robbie's reaction than disturbed. "Yes," she said, "in every way but by birth."

"I'm sorry, I didn't mean—"

"It is a common response. But I am honored to call him father, and I hope he is proud to call me daughter."

She paused and looked out upon the lazy current of the stream. In many respects her eyes were like the doctor's, despite the fact that they had no common blood. They were intense like his, looking out on the landscape as if they perceived so much more than simply what presented itself on the surface. But they also contained a kind of serenity, an easy joy he had not readily noted in Dr. Wallace's incisive gaze.

Robbie could tell she took pleasure in what she saw. But when she spoke again, he realized it was not about the countryside alone that she had been thinking. "Please forgive me," she said, turning her gaze upon Robbie. "I have made you uncomfortable."

"No," he replied quickly. "Well, at least not so much that I cannot recover. I could have been more tactful—after all, I am the stranger here."

"Then I hope you will not always remain so. I am Hsi-chen[1]."

She bowed slightly, then smiled. "Welcome to Wukiang. May you find here, as your Western saying goes, a home away from home, as long as you are with us."

"That is the only kind of home I have ever known," said Robbie. "But I am afraid I may have some difficulty getting used to this place, for I am used to a bit more activity."

"Yes, Wukiang must seem rather subdued to a world traveler such as yourself. But there is a peacefulness in this little valley that may grow on you, as my father puts it, or grow *in* you, as my people would say. Who can tell, you may end up liking it and want to stay forever."

"I can hardly imagine any place doing that to a wanderer like me."

"We have a tale of just such a thing happening, and not far from this very place."

"I love a good story," said Robbie.

"You see! Already you have something in common with us, for China is the land of proverbs and legends."

She paused, and when she spoke again her voice took on a deeper, more resonant quality, and became imperceptibly more formal. It carried the tone of a storyteller.

This is a legend about an occurrence that took place long ago in old China when the beasts could speak and the birds had voices, and when some say that God had given of His wisdom to be lived out among the animals so that it might be passed on to us in ways sometimes difficult to see. The story is of a rabbit, Liu Ken, who had lived his whole life in the Hill country. One day he was out foraging for food and he traveled farther than usual from his home because the ground had been stubborn that year and food was scarce. So intent was he on his hunt that he had traveled many hours before he realized he was in a strange country. The soft, wet ground first alerted Liu Ken to his folly, and when he looked up he saw streams and lakes and marshes, but no hills! Frightened, he hopped this way and that, but he had no idea which path to take that would lead him home. In despair, he sat down upon his hind legs and wept.

Now there lived in a nearby lake a swan named Yu Hua, and she heard the quiet sound of Liu Ken's weeping, and swam to the edge of her lake to see what it was all about.

"Please, sir," she said kindly, "do you need some help? You look very sad."

1. Pronounced *she-chen*.

Liu Ken wiped a furry paw across his teary eyes and said, "I am lost and very far from my home, and I do not know how I will ever get back."

"I am sorry for you," said Yu Hua, "but I know no other country but this, and I cannot travel far from my lake or I would help you find your home."

"What shall I do, dear Swan?"

"You are welcome to come to my house," said Yu Hua. "You can rest and have supper and perhaps things will look better then."

"Where is your house?" asked Liu Ken, his crying now stopped, but still somewhat apprehensive.

"Right here by the side of the lake. It is very cozy, not too hot or too dry, and there is shelter from the wind in the lee of the mulberry bushes."

"But I do not like water," protested Liu Ken. "Rabbits were not made to live near the wet places."

"I am sad to say it is all I have to offer," said Yu Hua. "Sometimes when you are far from home, it is necessary to change your ways."

Liu Ken was a polite little rabbit, and so he went with Yu Hua, both so as not to hurt the nice swan's feelings, and because he didn't know what else to do. At first he felt rather out of place in that watery home. But after many days he found that food was plentiful there and that even in winter there was no snow or ice to make the ground barren.

He even learned to swim, a great rarity among rabbits!

As time passed Liu Ken wondered how he could ever have lived in the hot, dry hills, and he gave up looking for his old home, because he knew he could never again be happy so far away from the water. Many years went by and one day Liu Ken awoke, feeling very odd indeed. When his dear friend Yu Hua saw him she could only sing with joy. But he could get no explanation from her. He went down to the edge of the lake as was his morning custom, bent toward the water for a refreshing swim, then stopped in amazement. The reflection that stared up at him was not that of a brown, furry rabbit.

Liu Ken had turned into a grand white swan!

When Hsi-chen finished her story, Robbie gently laughed with approval. "It's wonderful!" he said. "And well told! We will have to see if it is the same for sailors cast out of water as it is for rabbits put into it."

Hsi-chen laughed with him—an unassuming laugh, almost humble, but musical, and full of merriment.

Then they continued their walk back across the bridge toward the north shore and the mission. As they went, Hsi-chen pointed out various interesting features of the place and told him more about the village of

Wukiang and the peasants who lived there. It was clear she possessed a special fondness for the place, and Robbie could not help but recall to mind Jamie's love when she spoke of Donachie. He was surprised to learn that Hsi-chen had not been born in Wukiang as she said nearly all the other inhabitants had. She had come to the village some thirteen years ago, at the age of nine. She and her mother were alone and homeless and had sought refuge in the mission.

"What happened to your home?" asked Robbie.

She turned pensive a moment, showing that same look he had first seen in her; then she said lightly, "One lengthy story in an evening is enough."

By now they had come into the mission compound and Robbie started to turn in the direction of the hospital. He considered inquiring about the man he had seen with Wallace, but on second thought decided it might be meddlesome of him. If it had anything to do with him, he'd find out quickly enough.

"Please," said Hsi-chen, "if you are not too tired by your outing, my family would be honored to have you join us for our evening meal."

"Is it . . . expected of me? And there is my friend—?"

"Your friend is welcome also. More than an expectation, it would be a pleasure."

Robbie had hardly anticipated encountering someone so intriguing in this provincial little peasant village—especially after his first impression of the mission left by the austere Dr. Isaiah Wallace. He thus entered the third building of the compound at the far end from the hospital rather buoyantly, anticipating the pleasure of new faces, and possibly more interesting tales.

32

Dinner at the Compound

The moment Robbie entered the front room of the living quarters of the mission staff, he noticed the striking blend of Oriental and Western furnishings. Woven bamboo-leaf floor coverings, one or two lovely silk tapestries and bean-oil wick lamps, combined with three handmade rocking chairs, small tables upon which the lamps stood, and two large bookshelves, all of which together gave the place a warm but uncluttered atmosphere. Whether the room was simple by design or by poverty, Robbie could not tell. He decided it was most likely somewhere in between; for though the furnishings were nice enough, they were old and well-worn and used. Even the tapestries were frayed and fading.

At the far end of this large room sat a long dining table, also hand-made. Eight chairs, four on either side, lined the table, which was already set for dinner.

"Please be seated," said Hsi-chen decorously, indicating one of the rocking chairs. "I must go and give assistance to my mother."

Instead of sitting immediately, Robbie ambled over to the bookshelves and scanned the titles, more for something to do than from interest. They were mostly theology, with a few historical works, and one Chinese grammar. This last he took down, but, quickly thumbing through the pages, discovered that he would need more than a book to teach him the language. He was about to replace it when Wallace entered the room.

"I see you have found our meager library," he said. "I have a few more volumes in my office, and if you are of a mind to, you may avail yourself of them, Mr. Taggart."

"I don't really read much," admitted Robbie.

"There is much wisdom to be found in books," replied Wallace, striding to the bookshelf. "However, there is often heresy also, as well as human error. One must read with discerning spirit. The wisest choice is always God's own inspired Word."

"Yes . . . yes, you are quite right there," came Robbie's obligatory, awkward reply.

Wallace responded with a smile, the first Robbie had seen from the man. It was by no means a ready, natural smile, yet it could not be called forced. It appeared sincere, but like everything else about him, it was methodical, well thought out.

"You need not strike an air of forced agreement with me, Mr. Taggart," he said quietly and without rebuke. "I am as capable of accepting an unbeliever into my home as a brother. I would not be in China otherwise. I have sensed from our first meeting that you have stepped into alien territory. There is no shame or wrong in that. The wrong would be in hiding it, and trying to be something you are not, and thus losing a great opportunity to discover the truth for yourself. Does not the

Word of God say, 'How then shall they call on him in whom they have not believed? and how shall they believe in him of whom they have not heard? and how shall they hear without a preacher?' So you see, if you hide your disbelief, how will you ever come to believe?"

"Well, I *do* believe!" replied Robbie defensively, misunderstanding the depth of Wallace's words. "I'm no heathen, for heaven's sake!"

"For *heaven's* sake, I sincerely hope you are not," said Wallace. "There may, however, be something other than belief as you are acquainted with it and sheer paganism—something considerably more personal and—" but before he could finish his thought, the front door opened, and their attention was momentarily diverted in that direction.

The new arrival was a middle-aged English woman whom Wallace introduced as Elizabeth Trumbull, the mission schoolteacher. She was very tall, in fact, nearly as tall as Robbie himself. Her shoulders drooped forward, the obvious result of many years of attempting to minimize her height. Her brown hair was streaked with gray, pulled back in a tight bun. Robbie guessed immediately, even before she spoke, that she was English, not only by her clothing—the only Western attire he had yet seen—but mostly as a result of her bearing, which was very proper and stiff, and would have fit perfectly into any Victorian drawing room. It seemed, however, rather out of keeping here in this faraway setting. Yet her smile was pleasant and friendly, and her handshake firm.

Robbie greeted the woman with a smile, though he was still somewhat affronted by the doctor's remarks. The usually sparky and congenial Robbie Taggart found himself in a very uncharacteristic and uncomfortable position of being treated like an outsider. He wasn't sure he at all liked being lumped together in Wallace's mind with a bunch of Chinese pagans!

But before Robbie had the chance to dwell on his perturbation further, the entire remaining retinue of the mission had gathered for dinner, all except for Hsi-chen and her mother, who were still in the kitchen. Besides Miss Trumbull, the only other Westerner connected to the staff was Thomas Coombs, assistant pastor to Wallace, who acted as both senior pastor and physician to the mission. Coombs was twenty-two, of fair skin and blonde hair, a youth who hardly appeared even to have begun shaving. Of stocky build and an inch or two shorter than Wallace, he was several pounds heavier, and openly deferred to the older man in all things. Wallace was clearly the patriarch of the mission, its heartbeat, the man everyone looked to for direction and initiation. Robbie's first reaction in observing Coombs, and then the others, was that they all must feel intimidated by Wallace. How else would he have been able to command such unquestioning loyalty, obedience, and apparent respect? Why, the man almost reminded him of old Commander Barclay!

The Vicar soon joined the group, arriving with the young medical attendant, Ying Nien, an orphan who lived at the mission in exchange for his assistance in the hospital.

The group took their seats at the long table, and a moment later, Hsi-chen appeared, carrying a steaming bowl of rice. With her hobbled a middle-aged Chinese woman, similarly laden with fish and cabbage. *This must be Hsi-chen's mother,* thought Robbie, *probably the housekeeper or cook at the mission.* She was striking in appearance, lovely like her daughter, with clear, unwrinkled skin, hardly revealing her age other than with a bit of gray in her black hair and in the air of maturity and practiced grace she wore. She walked with effort; her tiny crippled feet, which had been footbound when she was a child, moved along beneath a skirt similar in style to Hsi-chen's.

As the two set down their burdens, Wallace stood and extended a hand in their direction.

"I believe, Mr. Taggart and Mr. Drew," he said, "that these are the only two remaining members of our mission family that you have not met. My daughter, Hsi-chen, and my wife, Shan-fei[1]." His voice had softened as he spoke, and his tone held an unmistakable depth of love and respect.

Incredible! thought Robbie. The austere, implacable doctor married to a Chinese woman—a footbound one at that! If he was as intolerant a man as Robbie had already labeled him, this was certainly an incongruous way of showing it! But perhaps there was a certain consistency here. Wallace boldly spoke his mind and tolerated nothing less from others. If he indeed loved a Chinese woman, would such a man not marry her, mindless of cultural and social prejudices and obstacles, with the same single-minded boldness with which he expressed his opinions?

Hsi-chen and Shan-fei served the meal, waiting even on Miss Trumbull. But it seemed to Robbie that they acted more the part of hostesses than domestic servants. It was not until everyone else's initial needs had been met that mother and daughter took their places and joined into the conversation. As the meal progressed it became clear that Shan-fei herself, like her husband, also commanded a great deal of esteem from the others. Oddly enough, the tone for this respect seemed to originate with Wallace himself. His wife responded in kind,

1. Pronounced *Shan-fay.*

affording him all manner of submission and admiration. A strong sense
of equality came through in their relation to each other. The wife was
gentle, soft-spoken, and demurring, yet displayed none of the stereo-
typed attributes of the subjugated female so expected among Chinese
women. Robbie would later learn that this demeanor of confidence
she displayed had blossomed only after years of the husband's patient
efforts to draw it out of her. Shan-fei was not intimidated by her stern
husband because she knew that he loved her even above himself. She
thus held him in even higher regard than would have been possible
had she seen only that side of him which Robbie at this moment was
capable of seeing.

After the meal was laid out before them, Robbie lifted his fork to
begin. Midway to the rice on his plate, he stopped. No one else had
yet moved a hand. Sheepishly Robbie replaced his fork as Wallace said,
"Let us give thanks," and then proceeded to ask the Lord's blessing on
the meal, adding a prayer for the recovery of "our two guests, Moses
and Jonah." When Robbie opened his eyes, no one (except for the Vicar,
who directed a subtle glance in his direction) took the least notice of
his *faux pas*.

As the simple meal began, the conversation was soon monopolized by
Miss Trumbull, Coombs, and Wallace as they gave one another reports
of their day's activity. It appeared that the mission served five surrounding villages within a ten-mile radius. The clinic and dispensary attended
to the greatest number of residents, but the Sunday congregation often
numbered as many as seventy-five. Twenty children were a regular part
of the school, small by comparison to many. But in a poor, agricultural
village such a Wukiang, often children could not be spared for the relative luxury of an education.

"I went out as far as Takung today," said Coombs, midway through
the meal.

"That's past our territory," replied Wallace. "Father Froelich does not
appreciate our proselytizing his people."

"I know," said Coombs apologetically. "But there is an old gentleman
there who likes to receive our literature. He's not a Catholic, and I saw no
harm in supplying him. But unfortunately, there was another problem."

"What happened, Thomas?" asked Wallace, concerned.

"It had nothing to do with Froelich's people, I'm sure. By the look of
the ruffians, they were probably salt smugglers, or the like . . ."

He paused, seeming none too anxious to finish his account.

"Go on," said Wallace. "Were you hurt?"

"No, thank the Lord! But there were four or five of them, and they nearly capsized my boat—would have, too, if some decent Chinese chaps hadn't come along and rousted them off."

"You were alone?" asked Wallace pointedly.

Coombs nodded.

"We've discussed this before, Thomas," he continued pointedly. "You simply must not go so far out into the countryside by yourself. There are too many dangers." Wallace frowned and his jaw muscles tightened as he added with an intense quiver in his voice, "Especially *now*, Thomas. You know the situation."

"Yes, sir. I know that. But, Dr. Wallace, I came here to *assist*. How can I be of any use if someone must hold my hand all the time? There's too much to do here to spare someone for a nursemaid also."

"Indeed," sighed Wallace. "'The harvest truly is plenteous, but the laborers are few . . .' But, Thomas, while we must be diligent to pray to the Lord of the harvest to send forth laborers into His harvest, we do not wish the laborers He has already given us to be one fewer as the result of some calamity which might befall you. You are still new to us. In due time you will be able to shoulder your fair share of the burden. In the meantime, let us mingle a bit of practicality with our zeal."

The rebuke was gentle, even fatherly. Yet there remained an unyielding aspect to the doctor's voice, a tone of finality, and a resolution in his eyes that allowed no further argument on the subject.

The reprimand was well taken by Coombs, for he humbly nodded, then said, "Yes, sir, I will do my best." It was clear he meant it.

Wallace then turned toward Robbie and the Vicar. Both men unconsciously sank an inch or two in their chairs, perhaps fearing they were about to be pressed into service.

"You see, Mr. Taggart, Mr. Drew, the work of God's mission here in China is a mammoth task," he said. "Over four hundred million people, with souls crying out in their poverty for the Lord Jesus Christ, yet barely a thousand laborers now answering that cry. But we are by no means daunted. God is working wondrously in China! The labors of my colleague and brother, Dr. Hudson Taylor, of the China Inland Mission, have been instrumental in getting the Gospel into *all* the provinces. And there are now resident missionaries in most. Imagine!"

For a moment Wallace's measured voice nearly trembled in its enthusiasm. "God has taken a seeming impossibility and made it very, very possible. But as everywhere, there are thugs and hoodlums and resisters, and, yes, even good people who are simply slow in accepting the truths of God. Yet I doubt that any of us would choose another place on the face of the earth to be."

"Amen to that!" put in Coombs, unconsciously having been caught up in his mentor's inspired speech.

"But I suppose you gentlemen," Wallace went on, "are quite anxious to be elsewhere—back to your homes, no doubt?"

Such a question was a difficult one for either Robbie or the Vicar to answer. But it was Elliot who ventured one. "We are traveling men," he said vaguely. "Thus *home* is a rather nebulous term for us."

"It does not trouble you to be separated from shipmates and friends?"

Now it was Robbie's turn, and he answered in a deeply earnest voice. "It appears that all our shipmates were lost at sea—and that troubles us *very* greatly. As for our other friends, we are well used to being separated from them for long periods."

"Then you may consider tarrying with us a while?" asked Wallace. "Certainly for a couple of weeks, maybe more, until your bodies have completely recovered from their ordeals."

Drew quickly began his attempt to steer clear of any potentially awkward encumbrances. "I must, speaking for myself, get to Shanghai as quickly as possible."

Robbie attempted to follow his lead. "There is some . . . ah—business . . . that may detain me in China before I seek work on a return voyage."

"Business?" queried Wallace.

"I believe he is referring to the state of our ship's skipper," added Drew, "whom we have reason to believe may still be alive. We would be remiss in our loyalty if we did not do what lay in our power to locate him. We think he may be in trouble of some kind."

"That's it," agreed Robbie quickly. "Of course I would like to find some way to repay you for your kindness before I go. I have no money, however. Everything we had went down with our ship."

"We are not accustomed to accepting payment for our services," said the doctor, then paused thoughtfully. "However, if it would ease your mind, there is always work to be done here at the mission. As I said, the laborers are few."

"I'm afraid preaching is not quite in my line."

Wallace gave one of his subdued smiles. "I had in mind some desperately needed repairs on our buildings. Thomas and I have sorely neglected them for the more important call of our other duties."

"That sounds . . . well, a possibility," said Robbie, trying not to commit himself. Whatever he did, he didn't relish the thought of spending much time in the presence of the doctor. It shouldn't be too difficult to avoid him, he thought. He probably spent all his free time in his study preparing sermons or reading the Bible or something. Besides, a few days here would give him time to think things through and decide what to do next. With no money, and stuck in the middle of China, things would no doubt be a bit rough until he'd arranged for a spot on another ship. But whatever he did, he had to settle his mind about Pike. He'd never be able to rest until he knew for certain whether the old skipper had double-crossed them or not.

Robbie glanced in Drew's direction, curious as to his response to Wallace's suggestion.

The Vicar merely raised his eyebrows, as if to say he would be insane to consider staying in this place even for another day, much less a week. Robbie might be a friend, but no church was going to get its claws into Elliot Drew one second longer than was necessary!

Later, as Robbie and Drew walked back to their beds at the hospital building, the Vicar said, "I know these people saved our lives, Robbie. But we've got to get out of here! That doctor is a fanatic. I've met men like him before!"

Robbie laughed. "You're not worried about me, are you, Elliot?"

"I've been that path, my friend. And it's not for you!"

"So you'll keep me on the straight and narrow, is that right? Or should I say *from* the straight and narrow!"

Drew saw no humor in the interchange. The religious atmosphere was already stifling him.

"Don't worry. Finding Pike is the first order of business. Then, depending on whether we need to rescue him or turn him in, the next will be finding a ship bound for home."

For a brief instant, as Robbie's uncertainty about Pike surfaced again in his mind, his eyes narrowed and uncharacteristically hardened. When they turned into the building, he was already thinking of what he might have to do in order to locate the old skipper. For Robbie had no intention of turning into a white swan . . . or anything else, for that matter.

33

An Unexpected Witness

The searing heat burned Robbie's bare back as he crouched upon the hospital's roof. His hand clasped a hammer, while several nails were clenched between his teeth.

After several days of inactivity and relative confinement, he had finally managed to convince Wallace that his strength had returned sufficiently to lend a hand with some project around the place. But he had hardly anticipated this! Nor how taxing it would be to his system. But he would not flinch, even in the face of exhaustion.

Wallace had set him about the most pressing task at hand. With the rainy season almost upon them, every roof in the compound required immediate attention. From the makeshift patches that had been attempted in so many places, Robbie guessed that buckets had been in constant use the previous year.

This was now the third day of the job. The Vicar had joined in yesterday, and, with him now cutting shingles on the ground, while Robbie installed them above, they were attempting, section by section, to give the hospital building substantially a new roof. They were nearly finished, and Robbie was thankful that at least they were able to use wooden shingles instead of the stone materials used on most of the other village dwellings.

Robbie's path had not frequently crossed the doctor's the past few days, for which he was also thankful. Wallace was up every morning before dawn and spent much of his time during the day away from the compound. He did hold a clinic at the hospital twice a week, during which he saw a steady stream of villagers—the mission served some five thousand people in the surrounding area. And if only seventy-five attended church services, the rest made up for their absence on Sunday by coming in droves to avail themselves of the medical facilities. What Wallace did during the remainder of his time, Robbie could only guess.

Coombs usually accompanied Wallace, and Miss Trumbull kept mostly to her school. It was the women Robbie and Elliot saw most and they usually lunched with the three of them.

Robbie pounded in the last of his nails, straightened his back, and called down to Drew that he needed more supplies. But Elliot was behind in his cutting and had no more shingles ready. Robbie therefore descended the ladder, grabbed his shirt from the rail where he had tossed it, and, wiping it across his sweaty brow, strode over to where Elliot was furiously sawing a new length of wood before he could split the shingles.

"You're going to kill yourself in this heat at that pace, Vicar!" said Robbie.

"No doubt I'll die of thirst first. How much longer do you intend to keep us in this workhouse of righteousness?"

"I'm still trying to decide just what to do," replied Robbie. "But I doubt you'll go thirsty with all this water around."

"*Water* was not exactly what I had in mind. Now that we're not onboard the *Tiger*, surely you would have no objections."

Robbie chuckled. "I doubt you'll find so much as an ounce of sacramental wine around here."

"I know," was Drew's dour reply. "Imagine a good Scotsman stumbling into such a teetotaling nightmare?" As he spoke his arm slowed noticeably.

"Here, let me have a go at it," said Robbie, stepping up, taking the saw, and nudging the Vicar aside. Elliot conceded without an argument, dragged his exhausted frame to a nearby shade tree, and dropped down against its trunk.

Just as Robbie set his foot to the framing board in which the log rested in order to brace it against the action of the saw, Hsi-chen approached slowly from the house. Though the heat had obviously affected her too, and her skin was abnormally pale, she yet moved with an unaffected grace. Her movements were never hurried, yet there was purpose in her steps. When she smiled, Robbie found himself smiling in return, glad to see her as a respite in his work.

He had by now had two brief encounters with villagers, and the Chinese-Occidental barriers were very much evident, in more ways than language alone. But Hsi-chen spoke and laughed with him in an easy manner. Undoubtedly under Wallace's hand she had been well educated in Western ways. Although she still retained an Oriental charm, the cultural distinctions were not nearly so strong as he had seen in the villagers, nor even her mother Shan-fei.

"I have brought you some refreshment," she said, and now Robbie realized she was carrying a tray, which he had not noticed as she approached. "Goat's milk is not a luxury," she went on, "but it is cool and will quench your thirst."

"Ah, just what we were wanting," said Robbie, with a mischievous wink in Elliot's direction. "That was thoughtful of you," he added more seriously.

"You have worked hard—well beyond any debt you might owe us. I see the hospital roof is nearly completed."

"It should be before day's end," answered Robbie. "Then we'll begin on the residence."

"I think my father will prefer the church receive the next repairs."

"The living quarters get far more use. I haven't seen a soul enter the chapel building since I've been here."

"I know it does not sound logical, Mr. Taggart, but you see, we are here to serve the villagers. God has called all of us, especially my father and his colleagues, to meet the needs of the Chinese, sacrificing our own comforts to do so. How could we teach them to worship our God in a broken-down building while we ourselves lived in comfort?"

Robbie thought that even with a sound roof, the mission's living quarters could hardly be considered comfortable by any stretch. But when he spoke again, his tone was diplomatic.

"I thought such exterior signs did not matter to God."

"Perhaps not. Indeed, He cares more for what goes on inside them than for the exterior repair of our buildings, just as He is more concerned for the condition of our hearts than the look of our physical bodies. But the Chinese are less understanding. They look at the mission and say, 'See the foreigners! They live in such splendor while the house of their God is in shambles. Their God must not be worth much to them.' Besides, my father could not tolerate sitting in a dry house while his congregation stood in puddles."

She paused and smiled at the thought. "So you see, Mr. Taggart, it would be best for the church to be your next project. But you must ask my father."

Robbie merely nodded, wondering again about the man who put such stock in his religious notions.

"I think perhaps my father disturbs you, Mr. Taggart."

Robbie was taken by surprise, first by the girl's insight and then by her boldness to voice it. Hsi-chen gave a soft, subdued chuckle at his reaction. Then she motioned toward the shade tree to which Elliot had returned and under which he was now sound asleep. "Would you care to sit in the shade and finish your drink?" she asked.

Robbie nodded, and they strolled to the tree, seating themselves on the grass in as cool a spot as could be found.

Robbie took a drink of his milk, then tried to respond to Hsi-chen's comment. "I think we—that is, your father and I—are from two different worlds. I doubt that we would ever find much mutual ground. He thinks I am a heathen, and I think he is . . . well, somewhat fanatical in his approach. Mind you, I don't mean that disrespectfully. I am deeply indebted to him and I sense that he is a good man who means well. But I guess we just have different ideas about life and of how to approach things."

"Would it surprise you to learn that my father would not take offense at being called a fanatic?" asked Hsi-chen. "In fact, he would probably count it high praise to be considered thus where his God is concerned. What is so wrong with giving your all in a worthy cause, even in a cause worth dying for?"

"All fanatics think their causes are worthy," rejoined Robbie, "to the exclusion of all else. They have no tolerance for other ideas. They think everyone ought to conform to their way of thinking."

"Without such zealots as my father, China would still be in darkness, untouched by the quickening Word of God."

"But China was a grand and glorious civilization," argued Robbie, "when your father's ancestors were still carrying clubs and wearing animal skins. What right have we from the West to impose our ideas on them? I should think you, as Chinese, would be able to see the value and achievement of your native culture."

"I love my country, and its culture," answered Hsi-chen quietly, yet as she spoke her dark, almond-shaped eyes danced, for she was excited with the stimulating turn of the conversation. "*Culture* is not the issue here, Mr. Taggart. There are those who come to China in the name of Christ who *do* make it so, and it is most unfortunate. But no matter how civilized or uncivilized a people are, however noble or good, every man has an emptiness that must be filled by Christ. The question is not culture, but *truth*. Truth has no cultural boundaries. Those who make culture the substance of their Christianity, and try to convert my people not only to Christ but also to Western ways, they are wrong. Yet the truth of the gospel, the truth that Jesus Christ came to earth to proclaim, is universal and is a truth for *all* peoples of the world. And there are things in our culture that directly oppose the ways of God, which deny that truth and that gospel, and that therefore we as Chinese must yield if we are to be conformed to the image of Christ."

"Ancestor worship?" suggested Robbie.

"Fealty and reverence toward ancestors is a noble attribute," answered Hsi-chen. "It is intrinsically wrapped up in who we Chinese are, and in our underlying philosophy of life. No wonder that when its foundations are so shaken by this 'new' Way, whose God alone is worthy of worship, it should cause such furor. I have often pondered this—that Christ should require the laying down of the most elemental facet of Chinese life."

"Then it *is* a cultural battle."

"I still do not think so. Honoring one's father and mother is the fifth commandment—God's own law requires it. Yet the act has been taken by my people and used as a substitute for *real* worship of the true God. I think the Lord would say, 'Revere your ancestors. It is good to hold them in high honor and esteem. But reserve your *worship* for the Creator of all ancestors, all parents, all families, all peoples of the earth!' It is too bad that this issue has brought such conflict and caused God's messengers in China to appear unyielding and intolerant. What God requires would never destroy a society, but would in fact make it stronger. I could not love God so much if I thought it could. Placing the true God at the center of a society would only strengthen it and make it even more beautiful."

"I've never thought of it that way," said Robbie, amazed at this young woman's insight. "But the Chinese are a religious people. Who's to say Christianity should be imposed on them by outsiders? What about Buddhism or Taoism? How can people like your father make a judgment that the religions of all the rest of the world are wrong and only the Christianity of the West is the truth. It still sounds to me like a position founded in Western egotism."

"You forget, Mr. Taggart, that Christianity is not a 'Western' religion at all. Jesus was born in the Middle East. Christianity has its roots as much in the East as it does in the West. However, that is not the point. What matters, again, is truth. If Christianity is *true*, then does not that truth affect all mankind? My father would not necessarily say that all the other religions of the world are *wrong* in every way. He would simply say that they are not complete. Many peoples of many times have sought after God. And therefore many religions exist which reflect these yearnings of man's heart after the Infinite. But Jesus came directly from God, as God's *Son*, to show all men the *full* truth. Jesus is the fullest revelation of God. Therefore, once the truth about Jesus is known, all other religions become obsolete. They are partial revelations, containing some truth, but also error at many points. Only in Christianity is the fullness of God's truth made known."

"You present your argument like a seasoned graduate of the Cambridge School of Divinity!" said Robbie.

Hsi-chen laughed at Robbie's amusing comparison, but also at her own zeal in the direction the conversation had taken. "Now you must think we are all fanatics! But maybe that isn't so bad."

"No . . . perhaps it isn't," he said, smiling. "I may have been making a harsh judgment."

"There is one more thing I must say; then you may decide about your judgment."

Robbie's brow took on a puzzled look at her words, listening intently as she continued.

"We have spoken of the place of God in cultures and societies, and I am certain these are of great concern to Him. But it is the *individual* that is God's greatest concern, His greatest love. Jesus died not for cultures, but for each individual person—for *you*, Mr. Taggart, and for me, not Occidental or Oriental. For your sleeping friend there, for the people of this village, for all your friends and loved ones back home—for *everyone*! That is what God's love means. That is the gospel! *That* is the message of Christianity—it is why so many have sacrificed so much to come here to China."

Robbie looked away and said nothing. For the first time he felt uncomfortable with this girl in whom he had supposed he'd found a kind of ally. It was one thing to debate theological issues, but quite another to be confronted personally. Unconsciously he cooled toward her, not realizing that even his arguments about Western incursions into Chinese culture had been a mere defense, a way of keeping the heart of the conversation at arm's length.

He drained off the remainder of his milk with a finality that said more than merely that their conversation was over. He set the cup on the empty tray and rose from the cool spot. He found himself perturbed, though he wasn't sure if it was directed more at her or at himself. He was saved from having to ponder this further, however, and from having to make an awkward parting.

At that moment a Chinese man, middle-aged but running with the vigor of a youth, hurried into the compound.

"Tai-fu!" he shouted. "Ma-shang! Ma-shang!"

Hsi-chen sprang quickly to her feet and ran toward the obviously distraught man. There followed a lively exchange in Chinese; then Hsi-chen turned to Robbie.

"Chang Hsu-yu needs my father," she said. "His wife . . . is ill." She hesitated over the words, a look of apprehension in her eyes. "I must see what I can do until he returns."

"What can I do?"

She appeared both relieved and hesitant at his words. "I—I don't know—" she began, but seemed not to know what course to take.

"I'll go with you," said Robbie. He sensed trouble, though he could hardly imagine any danger present in the village he had thus far observed.

Hsi-chen consented, and while she gathered a few things from the dispensary, Robbie informed Elliot of their plans. Then they hurried away after the frenzied villager.

34

In the House of Chang Hsu-yu

When they reached the perimeter of the village, they turned northward along the bank of the smaller of the two streams, which Hsi-chen called Chai-chiang, or simply Narrow River. The other was K'uan-chiang, Broad River. The two rivers provided the chief thoroughfares within the village, and at this time of day several small junks were traveling upon the muddy water.

In about ten minutes at their hurried pace, the three came to a second bridge similar to the one located near the mission. It was congested with mid-morning bustle, largely as a result of the shopping and market activity that congregated about both ends of it.

As they stepped upon the bridge to cross, several of the passing villagers seemed to Robbie to give Chang, who was several paces ahead, noticeable looks of derision. These same abusive stares were directed at Hsi-chen when she and Robbie passed.

"T'i-mien!" said several, in tones clearly derogatory.

Robbie turned to Hsi-chen to ask what it meant. He had somehow imagined that this girl would have been held in high regard among the villagers. But as he opened his mouth to speak he could see on her face such a taut, solemn expression that he thought better of it. He sensed that to intrude at that moment would likely cause her measured grace to crumble.

He had been to the village but once previously, but had not before noticed such open hostility. What could be the cause? And Hsi-chen's reaction was particularly puzzling, for he had not seen such a tension on her face since the first day they had met.

Stepping off the bridge, they again turned north. Passing three houses, which in fact were more like hovels or shacks, they came to the home of Chang Hsu-yu.

The poverty about the place was evident, though perhaps no more so than in many of the surrounding huts, and was made to look even more dismal by the dank, hard-packed earth that fronted the house, without foliage of any kind, and comprised the entire floor of the inside of it. As they came nearer they saw that several baskets and tools were strewn haphazardly about, laundry hung on a line to the side, and an even poorer shack stood behind the house which Robbie later learned contained the family's meager silk farm. There was no glass in the windows, only shutters, which now hung wide open to let what breeze there was into the house. Two of these hung askew, partially broken or wrenched off their hinges. The front door also stood open, and a young boy in the doorway, standing silently with a finger in his mouth, gazed with childish puzzlement at the urgently approaching trio.

Chang rushed past the child into the house, followed by Hsi-chen, and then by Robbie. He gaped at what he saw. The inside had been made a shambles by something clearly other than mere poverty. The scene reminded him of the morning after a brawl in a dockside pub. Two homemade chairs lay in pieces beside a coarse table. Cooking utensils were scattered all about the floor; rice and flour had been strewn about, and Robbie felt the grains crushing beneath his shoes. A chest had been turned on its side, and its contents spilled out from the open lid onto the ground. Robbie stepped forward to help the young girl who was struggling to right the heavy wooden box. She started, then shyly stepped back while he turned it back to an upright position, then she took up a broom and quietly began attempting to clean the mess on the floor.

In the meantime Hsi-chen had hastened to a large brick bed, perhaps the most prominent feature in the one-room house. Here, in the *k'ang*, the entire family slept at night, often ate, and might spend many cold winter days, warmed by the stove nestled under the bed structure. There was but one figure on the bed now, slight and feeble in appearance, nearly swallowed up in the huge expanse on which she lay. Chang knelt at her side, grasping a thin, gnarled hand in his, while his silent lips showed obvious anxiety. Hsi-chen sat down on the edge of the bed and began wiping a cloth across the woman's damp brow. She spoke softly to the woman in Chinese. Chang's wife replied weakly but with a faint smile. Hsi-chen proceeded to dress the two or three cuts and abrasions on the woman's face, then laid her hand on the clasped hands of husband and wife, bowed her head, and murmured a few words.

Robbie shuffled awkwardly, realizing they were praying together, feeling rather like an intruder, as if he had unknowingly stumbled into a holy place. He understood not a word of what Hsi-chen spoke, but could sense its deep reverence; there was a fervor of conviction in the words no matter how softly spoken.

After only a minute or two, she rose to her feet, gave the patient a parting affectionate pat on the shoulder, though the poor woman seemed to have dozed off by this time, then drew Chang aside and spoke in low tones with him for a moment before turning her attention once again to Robbie.

"Do you wonder what happened here?" she asked.

"Perhaps it is none of my business," Robbie replied.

"Only if you wish it not to be. But you are already, in the eyes of the villagers, associated with the mission, and it may be that you ought to know."

"Have they been burglarized?" he asked. "It's hard to believe they could have anything worth stealing."

"That is true," she said. "And they have not been robbed. This was an act of vandalism, done by the villagers, their own neighbors."

"But why?"

"It is soon time for the transplanting of the young rice plants from the nurseries to the fields. And there is a local observance that has been traditional for years which is thought to bless this process. The villagers are expected to pay a tithe to the temple during this festival. But Chang Hsu-yu and his family are Christians and have refused to do so."

She paused and swept a hand around the room. "This is what has become of their courageous stand. You see, however much the gospel has come to China, the cultural and religious barriers are still enormous."

"Their own neighbors would do this to them!"

"The sense of *belonging* is deeply woven into the Chinese nature and culture. It is seen in strong family bonds, in the worship of ancestors, and it extends to the entire village life. If one thread of this fine fabric breaks, it is not surprising that the others would fear for the stability of the whole piece of cloth. That fear drives these people—honest, hard-working people—to do whatever they perceive must be done to protect the old ways."

"What harm would it do for him just to pay the tithe?" asked Robbie. "It hardly seems worth . . . well, that," he said, nodding toward the bed where the sick woman lay.

"Render unto Caesar the things that are Caesar's?" mused Hsi-chen thoughtfully.

"Exactly!"

"It is a difficult question," she replied, not evasively, but forthrightly. "We must speak of it again. Until then, you might simply consider the second part of that verse. But now there is work to be done."

While they had been talking, the old man had gone outside the house and had begun attempting to set the shutters back in place. Because of his small stature, he was having difficulty with the top hinge. Therefore, while Hsi-chen helped the girl restore order inside, Robbie offered his assistance to Chang, who smiled gratefully.

Chang handed an old hammer to Robbie, then shouldered the heavy shutter, pressing it against the wall with tough, work-worn hands, while Robbie reached up and hammered it back into place. When it was finished they moved to the next, and on around the house, working harmoniously together, mostly in silence, with occasionally Chang giving some kind of direction in Chinese, which he accompanied with sufficient gestures to make Robbie grasp his meaning. Robbie found an elemental form of exhilaration in the physical labor that seemed altogether oblivious to nationality or language. They worked for about three quarters of an hour on the shutters, and then moved to several other tasks about the place; Chang seemed extremely grateful for Robbie's help.

Normally Chang would have been out in the rice fields with his sons, but since his wife's injury he had limited himself to the house. This was his only outward sign of concern for her. Displaying the seemingly typical Oriental stoicism, Chang did not appear excessively anxious about the morning's turmoil, nor did he display any taste for retribution against his neighbors. Robbie found himself admiring the man's control and pleasant disposition. What effect Chang's time of prayer with Hsi-chen might have had in this he did not stop to inquire of himself.

It was well into the afternoon when Robbie and Hsi-chen took their leave. Before they departed, Chang Hsu bowed deeply to Robbie.

"Tō hsieh!" he said. "Ch'ing wen, hsien-sheng kuei hsing?"

"He says, *many thanks*," interpreted Hsi-chen, "and he would like to know your honorable name."

"I am Robbie Taggart, Mr. Hsu-yu," Robbie replied respectfully, holding out his hand. Then, thinking better of himself, he bowed instead, in the same way as Chang had done, though perhaps a bit more stiffly.

At Robbie's introduction, Hsi-chen and Chang smiled at one another as if responding to some private joke. Robbie frowned, puzzled.

"I've said something wrong?" he asked.

"I am sorry," said Hsi-chen. "I did not mean to make light of you. But even with the very little English Chang has, even he has detected your error."

"What have I done?" said Robbie with an apologetic grin. He did not mind joining in the humor, even if it was at his own expense.

"I have been amiss in explaining the complexities of Chinese names to you," answered Hsi-chen. "You see, in China the names are backwards from your way. *Chang* is the surname and *Hsu-yu* is the given name, even though Chang comes first. So the full name is Chang Hsu-yu. The surname is usually one syllable and the given name two. To address him, you would say Mr. Chang, or in Chinese, Chang hsien-sheng."

"That's simple enough," replied Robbie enthusiastically. "I'm sure I'll remember it next time."

"No one will mind if you do not. I'm sure if the tables were reversed, you would not mind being called Mr. Robbie."

Robbie laughed and Hsi-chen joined him. After a questioning pause, Chang laughed also, though he knew not why, other than that it felt good to release some of the tensions of the day.

Robbie and Hsi-chen were crossing the bridge to the mission when he tried to phrase what had been puzzling him for the last couple of hours.

"Chang Hsu-yu is a good man," he said. "Why do such things happen to him?"

"It is too bad," replied Hsi-chen. "And I do not have an easy answer for you, Mr. Taggart. Life is not always easy or pleasant for those who choose God's way. But his faith sustains him. Could you not see?"

"Yes. I suppose I did see a strength in him."

"That was Christ's strength. Mr. Taggart. I am sure Chang would want you to know that."

"And that is why he stands and takes the treatment from the other villagers without any thought of—"

"Reprisals, Mr. Taggart?" she queried with just the slightest edge in her lovely voice.

"Well, it seems that the incident ought to at least be reported to the authorities."

"These sorts of things are common, Mr. Taggart, among Chinese converts. It is one of the things they have to accept about the life of faith. My father strongly encourages his converts to avoid involving the law in these matters. Besides, the law, so to speak, in these rural regions, is almost nonexistent. This is all just one more factor in what is involved in bringing Christianity to my people, as is conflict between the missions and local Buddhist priests, and even sometimes with vengeful tribal leaders."

"But what are the poor people your father's converts supposed to do, just stand idly by while poor, sick, old women are struck down?" His tone again revealed his annoyance with the stern mission director.

They were now on the bridge, and Robbie paused a moment and gazed out on the water as if the peaceful sight might calm him. But he couldn't help but feel that men such as Wallace were doing a disservice to poor people like Chang. When he moved again, it was at an accelerated pace. Hsi-chen hurried to keep up with him.

"I know this must be difficult to comprehend," she replied after a few moments, a bit breathlessly. "But there are many reasons for it. There are some missionaries who see their efforts as political and social. The gospel they preach is less a gospel of Jesus than it is a gospel of conformity to Western ways. These will even use the might of their foreign powers, whether it be Britain or America or the Netherlands or Germany, to intercede on behalf of their converts and to bolster the power of their missions. But this just increases hostility toward the foreigners in my country and especially toward missionaries because they are the most visible foreigners. But that has never been my father's way. He does not see his calling as a legal or a political or a social or even a cultural one."

"What then?"

"My father's mission is a spiritual calling. There is something greater, deeper here at work to him than the surface events, be they bad or good."

"But how can he turn his back when things like this happen?"

"He will not turn his back, Mr. Taggart, I assure you. Would you like to know what he will do?"

Robbie nodded, but not without a hint of skepticism in his look.

"After he learns what has happened, he will no doubt spend several hours in prayer—"

She paused a moment to note Robbie's reaction, which was merely facial, but seemed to say, *I thought as much!* She began again with her own emphasis.

"*Then* he will go to the homes of each of those involved—both the victims *and* the antagonists, if they will receive him, and minister the love of Jesus to them."

"And no doubt get himself roughed up also!"

"Do you think that matters to him, Mr. Taggart?"

But before Robbie could answer, Hsi-chen stopped, grasping the wooden rail on her left, her face suddenly pale.

"Hsi-chen, what is it?" exclaimed Robbie, reaching out to steady her.

She brought a trembling hand to her face, tried to smile, and then said, "Nothing . . . only too much excitement, I think."

She pushed away from the rail, determined to continue on by herself. Then her knees buckled and she would surely have fallen had not Robbie's strong arms been ready to catch her. He lifted her slight body and carried her quickly the rest of the way back to the mission.

35

A Family Matter

Hsi-chen lay staring up at the rough ceiling of her father's dispensary. For the moment she was reflecting that only a few days earlier there had been a hole the size of an apple in the very spot where her gaze rested. Now, thanks to the new guests, it was sound again and would withstand the rains for many years to come.

Many years to come. . . . The thought of the distant future was sobering indeed, and took her mind off the hospital's new roof.

Behind her Hsi-chen heard the door creak and she was glad to have her thoughts wrenched from the direction they had begun to take. She turned her head and saw her father approaching. His face wore a deeply pensive look, striking for one whose face always seemed absorbed in thought. His look drew tiny lines of anxiety to the corner of her eyes. But she tried to shake the worry away, breathed a silent prayer, and smiled to her father, now acting in the capacity of her doctor as well.

"You need not mask your anxiety, Hsi-chen," he said. "I share your thoughts with you, and I know your feelings are coupled with faith."

"I pray always that I will be able to leave this in God's hands."

"He will honor your prayers."

"But I am still frightened."

Wallace reached out and took his daughter's hand. It was damp and cold in his strong, warm grip. She felt a security in his touch. She knew God had given her this man to be her father for just such a time. He had been all a father could ever be to a daughter, and yet at this moment she knew she needed his strength and his faith in God perhaps more than ever before.

Wallace prayed silently over his daughter for several minutes, then released her hand, stroked her silky hair, smiled, and began his examination.

When he was finished some six or seven minutes later, he spent several moments rearranging his instruments, apparently absorbed intently on that task. Hsi-chen sat up on the table and waited patiently. She knew her father's attention was not engrossed in the tidiness of his instrument tray, so she quietly gave him the time he needed to think, to draw his medical conclusions, and perhaps to collect his turbulent parental emotions.

At length he laced his fingers together and brought his hands to his chin, which he tapped thoughtfully as he spoke, keeping his voice, even then, professional. Indeed, perhaps even more professional than ordinarily, for *he* had emotions to mask as well as his daughter.

"Nothing has changed since the tests we made last month, my dear," he said. "To know anything for certain, we will have to send more blood to Shanghai. But perhaps it is a good sign. The longer we can keep it at bay—"

"I feel well," Hsi-chen said, eager hope imprinted on her features. "Perhaps I just became faint from the sun. It may be unrelated."

"Perhaps. We may always hope that is true. I know so little about this. If only more was known—" He stopped short, his voice catching on his rising emotion.

"Oh, Fu-ch'in, Father," she said, beginning to weep softly. "I so want to be brave."

Wallace wrapped his arms around her and stroked her hair, murmuring gentle words in her ear in her native tongue, as he had often done when she was a child and knew not a word of English.

"Always remember, dear child," said Wallace in a tender voice, still holding his daughter, "we have our God, and He is mighty—to heal, to renew strength, to give courage to accept the path laid before us. He will never fail you, Hsi-chen."

She nodded bravely, her eyes alight with faith even as Wallace wiped the tears away.

"Now," he continued in a lighter tone, "there are two very concerned people outside."

"Two?"

"Your mother, of course, and Mr. Taggart."

"Mr. Taggart? That is kind of him."

Wallace hesitated a moment, as if this were a new consideration where their guest was concerned, then said, thoughtfully, "Yes . . . I suppose it is."

"I do not think you like Mr. Taggart, Fu-ch'in."

"I believe Mr. Taggart is a man easily liked," replied Wallace, "but he does trouble me. It is apparent that he possesses a great deal to give to others. But because he refuses to reach beyond the shallow surface of life, I fear he may not come to realize the potential God intended for him."

"I see, Fu-ch'in. But he is not lost yet. Do not forget your own prayers for him when he came to us. I think perhaps he is on the verge of an awakening, like a bud ready to blossom."

Wallace smiled. "God has given you a wonderful spirit, dear Hsi-chen." His voice trembled slightly as he spoke, perhaps thinking of the special gift he had been allowed to have that might be all too soon taken away.

"I'm sure you are right. But who can tell what the Father in heaven may have to put our Mr. Taggart through in order for him to awaken to his own awakening. We must keep praying diligently for him."

"I have been, Father."

"I know, my child. And I thank you for reminding me of my own necessity."

Wallace turned and walked toward the door, but before he opened it, his adopted daughter called out to him,

"Fu-ch'in, I love you!"

He inhaled deeply, as if to gather strength for the smile that followed. "Your name was rightly given Hsi-chen—*Joy that is true*. Now rest, while I call your mother."

After a few minutes Shan-fei came in, leaning on her husband's arm.

She did not often venture far from the residence, and when she did so, it was always on her husband's arm, for her feet did not permit much adventuring. Wallace drew a chair for his wife up to the bed where Hsi-chen now sat, dressed and eager to return to her routine. Wallace did not miss the impatient look on his daughter's face.

"I have several calls I must make," he said. "Hsi-chen, you will stay in bed the remainder of the day."

"But I promised Chang that I would come back this evening."

"I will take care of that," he replied, now wearing his more stern countenance. "*You* must remain in bed."

When he had gone, Shan-fei turned to Hsi-chen with more pleading in her voice. "You must do as your Fu-ch'in says." Her motherly concern was evident even beneath her reserved demeanor. "He knows what is best. Perhaps you will do even more than he says—you will rest *many* days. It would be good for your body."

"Mama, we have spoken of this before. I will not become an invalid. That is why I want no one but you and Father to know of my illness. Can it be so wrong of me to want to live a normal life?"

"I understand, dear one," answered the mother sorrowfully. "Have I not myself lived the life of an invalid? But God gives grace."

"I know. But you had no choice. I do, and I want to invest what days I have in service, in living, not merely waiting—until God tells me I must stop."

"Will you hear God's voice in this matter, child?"

"Pray for me, Mama, that I will."

The older woman caressed her daughter's cheek and nodded her head. The lovely, flawless face showed lines of worry, hinting at the woman's true age. Her eyes wept, though no tears flowed, for her only daughter whom she loved. The years had cloaked her, too, with a kind of strength perhaps only a woman can know, though it came not from herself, but from the One whom she trusted, and whom she had given up so much to serve many years ago.

36

The Vicar's Fall

Robbie accepted Hsi-chen's explanation that the excitement and tensions of the day had simply taxed her strength. He had no reason to believe otherwise.

And in a strict manner of speaking, the exertion of the day *had* in all probability brought on this renewed manifestation of her trouble. After a day's rest indoors, she said, she would be fine. Perhaps that was stretching the truth about to its limit, but she could not be entirely certain such would not be the case. Even her father had said little was known of the thing.

The next two days were fine ones for Robbie. Hsi-chen's time was spent entirely in the compound, and on several occasions she walked out to visit Robbie and Elliot as they continued their work on the buildings. Though Drew settled more and more silently into himself in the midst of the stressful and awkward circumstances, Robbie found his budding friendship with the missionary's adopted daughter to be a pleasant experience indeed. With light conversation, interspersed with a good deal of laughter, she acquainted him with the culture of her homeland, salting her words with a regular but subtle sharing of her Christian faith.

One afternoon they fell to discussing the complex Chinese tongue. "It is a tonal language," she said. "One word can take on many different meanings, depending on the intonation of voice that is used."

"Could one like me learn it?" asked Robbie, more hypothetically than with any intention of seriously taking up the subject.

"Of course. But my father says it is a hard language to learn. I cannot say, because I grew up knowing it. Learning English was difficult enough. But there are so many different dialects here that even the Chinese become confused sometimes. Yet the written language has remained uniform for thousands of years. Chinese from different regions may not be able to understand a single *verbal* word spoken by one another, but they are able to communicate quite well in writing."

"It's not so different from Britain," offered Robbie. "Why, if you heard a Scots' burr and a Cockney twang, you'd probably understand neither one. And you'd have no doubt they were speaking different languages. But your written characters seem as confusing as the spoken tongue."

"The writing of Chinese is both an art and a skill," said Hsi-chen, "not easily mastered. There are many thousands of characters, as opposed to your simple twenty-six. Each possesses a beauty both in appearance and in content."

She paused a moment, stooped to the ground and picked up a twig that had fallen from the camphor tree, and made a sketch in the dry earth. "This," she continued as Robbie watched and listened, fascinated, "is the character for *righteous*. That word is often used here at the mission. Yet I still remember my father's reaction when he realized what an understanding the Chinese had of the concept long before any Westerner stepped on our soil. See," she traced the twig around one part of the character, then another, "this first part stands for *lamb*, and the other for *I*—it is as if from the beginning God were preparing these people to meet Christ personally, the *Lamb* of God who cleanses each one (the *I*) in order to make us righteous through Him. My father laughed aloud when this truth dawned upon him."

Robbie glanced up, and knew from the twinkle in her eye and from his own personal experience, that this was no everyday response on the part of Isaiah Wallace.

"So you see," she concluded, "the characters do a great deal more than spell words. They create pictures that add to the words' meanings."

For a man like Robbie, for whom no hidden motives lay beneath the surface, it was impossible to live in the presence of such a gentle and sincere faith without feeling somehow moved. Was this religion truly reserved for women, as he had once mentioned—for the Jamies and Hsi-chens of the world? What about Wallace, Drew, Coombs? The Vicar was an embittered coward, Wallace he didn't much like, and he couldn't tell about Coombs yet.

Women were weaker, he reasoned. It was only natural for them to turn to religion. But why should a man accept the kind of dependency religion seemed to require? Could a man truly be a man—*all* a man—and be religious at the same time?

Yes, questions raised themselves in Robbie's mind. But he avoided the answers perhaps even more determinedly than he might have before. At the same time, he could not help being drawn to Hsi-chen as he had been to Jamie. And it was not for her mystical Oriental beauty, nor for her wit that occasionally revealed itself beneath the reserved grace that was always about her, but for some deeper inner quality which might have been labeled peace, but which was even more than that, though he had no name for it. "The indwelling spirit of Christ" was not a reality with which Robbie was familiar, so he could not give Hsi-chen's serene strength of character its true name. He could only admire it from afar. And wonder, as he had with Jamie, whence it came. He had not got so far as to begin to desire it for himself in his conscious mind. But his subconscious was busily at work.

The day after his conversation with Hsi-chen, Robbie spent the afternoon cutting shingles for the chapel roof. Rain was expected, and word was about that they could be in for quite a drenching. Robbie saw Wallace approaching and inwardly braced himself. The doctor had remained close by all day, whether because of his daughter's fainting spell or the trouble at the village, Robbie didn't know. But the man's presence unnerved him. Had he analyzed his feelings, he would have found them completely irrational. For Wallace was, if anything, gracious, benevolent, kind, and certainly sincere—even if sometimes a little cold—in his faith. But in Robbie's present mood, the man annoyed him.

Wallace stopped and stood silently observing Robbie's labors a moment before speaking. Robbie took the look as critical, even though the first words out of Wallace's mouth were entirely positive.

"The work is going well, Mr. Taggart," said the doctor in an even, noncommittal tone. "We are all most appreciative of yours and Mr. Drew's assistance."

"Let's just hope we get this roof finished before the blasted rain comes," replied Robbie bluntly, hardly looking up.

"The Lord sends rain in its season, Mr. Taggart," replied Wallace in the same measured voice. "Thus we thank Him always for it, and trust our activities to His good will."

Robbie mumbled something the doctor did not hear in reply, venturing no further word on the subject. Pretending that he needed to refresh his supply of wood, he then excused himself.

Had such a harmless statement come from Hsi-chen's lips, he would likely have thought the words innocent enough, even sweet to his ears. But from Wallace it sounded like a rebuke. Why should it bother him so? Was Robbie afraid of the raw spiritual power represented by the gospel as presented by Isaiah Wallace, a gospel he had always written off as a soft and effeminate religion pandered only by women and weaklings? Wallace made the gospel difficult to sidestep or explain away. He had such a habit of forcing every conversation back to its spiritual foundations. With both Jamie and Hsi-chen, it had been easy for Robbie to look at the power of their changed lives and dismiss its cause with his rationalizations. But Wallace made such a maneuver impossible.

If Robbie was having difficulty ignoring Wallace, however, the Vicar had nearly reached his emotional breaking point. Wallace—in the strength of his personality and his sacrificial dedication to a cause greater than himself—typified everything Elliot Drew was running from. But even more, he represented what Drew had desired to be in his youth.

In the years before his downfall, Drew had been well-enough acquainted with Christians from every spectrum of faith to be able to recognize a hypocrite when he saw one. Robbie may have been confused on that matter, but Drew knew that Wallace was no hollow or shallow man. Here was a man of substance, a man of God. He could feel the difference so acutely that his spiritual sensitivities cringed at the thought of his own weakness alongside one like Wallace. Each day was a growing ordeal for him. Had he been younger, perhaps he could still have turned himself around. But it was too late now. Too much water had slipped under the bridge. If only . . .

But no—it is too late for me, Drew thought. And seeing Wallace every day only amplified that fact all the more painfully in his distressed heart. Neither Wallace nor anyone else had to say a word for Elliot to suffer so. Their lives, their very presence, lived purely and fervently for the God he had long ago repudiated was enough. As the days progressed he said less and less, hoping desperately that they would leave him alone. But it was not an existence he could long endure. The tension within grew taut, his forced abstinence from alcohol only putting him all the more on edge. Robbie's friendly and steadying influence could not overcome the sense building inside him that he was trapped behind enemy lines, with no way of escape!

By Saturday he appeared ready to break like the tropical storm that was brewing. He and Robbie were working as usual when Wallace approached them.

"You should soon come to a place in your work where it can be temporarily suspended," he said.

"Why?" asked Robbie innocently. "We are almost done, and ought to finish by tomorrow afternoon."

"Tomorrow is Sunday, Mr. Taggart," replied Wallace.

Robbie had scarcely given the days of the week a thought. It had not even registered in his brain that since this was a mission, Sunday might possess a special significance. The Vicar, on the other hand, had been dreading its coming. He had not entered a church since that day so many years ago when he had walked out of his own parish. And he did not feel inclined to alter that trend now. What he would do to avoid the inevitable services that must come with the morning, he didn't know. He certainly did not want to confront these people with his failure; he was just as afraid of their mercy as he was their righteous indignation.

When Wallace left, they continued their work in silence. In an hour, no thanks to Elliot's distracted mind, they had gone as far as possible without tearing up a new section of the roof. So they packed up their tools and finished up for the day. By the time they returned to their room at the back of the hospital to wash up, Drew was so agitated he could hardly talk. His head was throbbing, and he knew he could not face tomorrow. Had Robbie thought about it, he would have recognized the symptoms at once, would have seen what was coming, and could possibly have done something to stop it. But his mind was elsewhere, and he had not observed Elliot's state.

But Drew could not stand it another minute. Robbie's uncommunicativeness only intensified his anguish. He had to have a drink! Even if he had to steal the money from someplace at the mission to get one. He would die if that gnawing thirst inside him was not quenched! Even as he thought the words, the spiritual parallel of "living waters" leaped into his tortured mind. Even in his misery he could not escape the words and phrases and dogmas of his past! He slammed down the cup of water he had been holding, drawing a puzzled stare from Robbie.

"I'm going for a walk!" He blurted the words out like an accusation.

"Not a bad idea," said Robbie. "I'll join you."

"No! I'm going alone!"

Robbie shrugged. "Have it your own way," he said, still sensing only the surface of the Vicar's turmoil, and thinking that a quiet walk might indeed be just what he needed.

The Vicar stalked from the room. Robbie did not bother to follow him with his eyes, or he might have seen Drew head for one of the other buildings, skulk behind it, then disappear inside. Ten minutes later, unobserved by anyone, the Vicar exited from the other side of the building, and hurried, half running, from the mission compound. He crossed the bridge, and in a few minutes was in the next village. He paid no attention to the stares he drew, nor worried about his inability to communicate. At the sort of place he sought, thirst was the universal language, and he would be able to find what he was after more easily with the stolen coins in his pocket than by any words from his tongue.

Robbie arrived for dinner early that evening. He had begun to grow anxious about Elliot's prolonged absence. He had hoped to find him already at the residence, but when he walked in he found he was the first to arrive other than the women who were in the kitchen preparing the meal. Hsi-chen invited him to make himself comfortable in the front room, replying to his question that she had seen nothing of his friend. Robbie idly chose a book from the shelf and took a seat. Ten minutes slowly ticked away before Coombs walked in. He and Robbie exchanged a few words, but the young missionary seemed quiet and subdued. Though he was not the ebullient sort, previously he had at least been friendly and congenial. On this occasion, however, he walked silently toward the books after initial pleasantries, pulled one out, sat down, and buried his face in it, brooding.

A few moments later Ying Nien entered, followed by Wallace. Out of respect for the doctor, the three younger men rose, and a polite exchange of greetings followed. Coombs behaved with deference toward his superior, but it was clear that a tension had entered their relationship on the part of Coombs; Wallace seemed his usual self.

Moments later Hsi-chen announced dinner, but Wallace turned to Robbie.

"Mr. Drew is absent," he said. "Shall we wait for him?"

"I don't think he'd want us to do that," answered Robbie.

The group moved to the table, where tonight Miss Trumbull and Shan-fei served, while Hsi-chen took a seat immediately to her father's left. When all were served, heads bowed, and Wallace began to pray.

"Our Heavenly Father," he began, "we thank you and we praise you for your rich bounty. We thank you again for the opportunity of giving our lives in service to the people of this land. We pray for the rich harvest that is spread out before us on this continent. Make us worthy servants, Lord. Give us eyes and ears to see and hear the needs to which we can minister. Give us hands of service to—"

His words were interrupted with a creak from the front door opening. Wallace paused only momentarily, then continued on. But Robbie instinctively glanced up.

There in the doorway stood the Vicar. From his disheveled appearance, his shirt hanging out over this trousers, his smudged face, and his glassed-over eyes, it was obvious to all that he had been drinking.

Robbie's first instinct was to jump from his seat and lead the Vicar from the room. But he hardly dared further to disrupt the doctor's prayer. Thus he remained seated. He soon regretted that decision.

Elliot shambled toward the table, and almost simultaneously with Wallace's *amen*, he bowed deeply, nearly toppling over in the process, and taking part of the table with him.

"Pardon me, Your Holiness," he said in a slurred voice. "It would appear that I have most rudely interrupted your prayer. I humbly beg your forgiveness." There was, however, no shred either of humility or of repentance in the Vicar's drunken tone.

Wallace's eyes grew noticeably darker, and he drew himself up in his chair, seeming to debate within himself over which of the two options— severity or mercy—was most called for in this situation. When at last he spoke, his normal measured calm prevailed, masking whatever emotions may have been hiding within.

"Mr. Drew," he said, "I can see that you are unprepared for the dinner hour. Perhaps you could do us the courtesy of allowing us to finish our meal while you gather yourself together. We will be sure to keep a portion warm for you."

"Are you asking me to leave, Guv'nor?"

"I think that would be best, at least until you can make yourself presentable to ladies and youngsters."

Robbie wondered briefly at the term, curious whether it applied only to Ying or to Coombs also, or perhaps even himself? For Coombs winced at the word. There was not time to ponder nuances, however, for Elliot was hardly deterred by the doctor's unmistakable request, notwithstanding the gentle words in which it was couched.

"Aha!" replied Drew, leering at his host. Sober he would never have ventured such a confrontation. But drunkenness had filled him with every kind of foolish bravado. "I knew I could expect no forgiveness from the likes of you! You're all the same—whited shep-sep-sepulchres!"

"And you thought to test us?" asked Wallace, ignoring Drew's difficulty with pronunciation.

"Test you, Gov! Ha! I don't have to *test* you—I know from experience—very intimate experience." As he spoke he drew out the word intimate, then went on with a dry laugh, which contained no humor, only a pitiful emptiness. "Ain't that right, Robbie? I know better than anyone. All about whited sepulchres! Ain't I speaking the truth, Robbie?"

"Come with me, Elliot," said Robbie, standing as he spoke. "Let's you and I get some fresh air." Robbie stepped toward Elliot and laid a hand on his arm, but Drew wrenched it away.

"Fresh air makes me sick!" he brawled. "There's too much of the stuff here—too much goodness . . . purity. It makes me sick, I tell you! To blazes with every one of you and your puny God, too! I don't need it!"

But before the Vicar's final words were out, Wallace jumped from his seat and peered at the man he was commanded to love, difficult though it may be. But there were limits his integrity could not violate. He turned toward his guest, his voice now filled with the fire of righteousness.

"You will not blaspheme the Lord in this house!" he said. His hands were rigid at his side, but he made no move toward the Vicar. "I ask you again, Mr. Drew, to leave this house until you are sober enough to behave with the respect due our Lord."

Robbie now took Elliot more forcefully in hand and propelled him from the room. He did not resist; perhaps the subdued anger in Wallace's voice had cooled his own drunken fervor. He allowed Robbie to lead him outside, but as they started to cross the dirt yard to the hospital, he pulled away, not violently this time, but with obvious disgust both at Robbie's intervention and at his own behavior.

"You just couldn't leave the stuff alone, could you?" said Robbie, angry at the scene Drew had caused. He had hoped that the week's abstinence—forced though it was—signaled the Vicar's turnaround.

"Leave me alone!" mumbled Elliot.

"I hoped you were going to face things this time!"

"You're just as self-righteous as the rest of them!"

"You know that's not true. And where did you get money for your binge anyway?"

"That's none of your concern, mate!" snapped Drew. "Why don't you just go back in to your pretty little Chinese doll and her high and mighty, overbearing father!"

"You forced Wallace to react as he did—you left him no choice," said Robbie, hardly noticing the incongruity of his defending the staunch missionary doctor.

"Bah! What do you know? How could you know? Before you know it, you're going to turn into one of them!"

"You're looney, Drew!" replied Robbie. But as they reached the door of their quarters, he turned and faced his companion. "You had better be ready to apologize to them tomorrow," he said. "They deserve that much. Whatever else you or I may think about them or what they're doing, they did help to save our lives."

The Vicar said nothing, pushing past Robbie into the small room, now almost completely dark as there was no lamp lit. He threw himself on his bed and, to all appearances, fell asleep immediately.

Later that night, when Robbie returned to his own bed, he was not so fortunate. He had gone back to dinner, and, though a bit strained, the conversation never did allude to the Vicar's disturbing scene. But Robbie could not help wondering what they thought of him. *What do I care?* he tried to tell himself. It did not matter one whit what any of them thought! But inside he could not help wanting them to know he was—was what? Sincere? A good person? Why did their opinion matter to him at all? And now, as he lay on his bed trying to find the sleep that would displace all these uncomfortable thoughts and emotions from his brain, all he could hope was that by tomorrow it would all blow over. The Vicar would apologize, and somehow the stern Wallace would find it within himself to demonstrate some Christian love and compassion— which, despite Hsi-chen's obvious admiration of her father, did not seem to Robbie to be his strongest character traits.

However, when Robbie awoke the following morning after a fitful night, he saw that Elliot's bed was empty. Even before he found the hastily scribbled note, his instincts told him that the Vicar was gone for good. The shame of his actions, mingled with a fear of facing their consequences—especially face-to-face with a man like Wallace—had forced him to run.

Robbie could not help wondering if this was how it had been that first time he ran away from his life as parish Vicar.

37

Sunday at the Mission

Robbie made no haste to dress or leave his room. He had not forgotten what day it was, and he could not help a certain sense of apprehension. He, too, was reluctant to face the mission folk again—though he knew he must. Running away was an act of cowardice, not of manliness. And Robbie Taggart was proud of facing his foes squarely.

He did, however, allow himself the luxury of prolonging the inevitable moment. He washed, dressed, then took a book he had borrowed and lay back down to try to read. Ying had not come to issue his usual 7:00 a.m. call to breakfast.

Organ music from across the compound suddenly jolted him to the present. It seemed too early for church, though he had no watch. *It'll look even worse*, he thought to himself, *if I miss their blasted service. I'd better face it.*

He rose with a sigh, resigning himself to the inevitable, and stepped outside. Dark clouds greeted him, and before he had reached the residence, rain had begun to fall. Stopping briefly at the chapel, he had seen no one present but Miss Trumbull practicing the organ, and therefore continued on to the house. He entered to find Wallace himself sitting in a rocking chair with an open book in his lap. The doctor glanced up slowly and looked deliberately at Robbie.

"Good morning, Mr. Taggart," he said.

"Good morning, sir."

"I am afraid you have missed breakfast, but my wife can warm something."

"Thank you, but she doesn't have to trouble herself," Robbie replied somewhat stiffly. "I haven't much of an appetite."

The pause that followed was finally broken by the doctor, speaking out on the subject which was on both of their minds.

"I hope Mr. Drew is better this morning," he said.

"He is gone."

"Gone?"

"Taken off for Shanghai, I believe."

"I am truly sorry to hear that."

What irritated Robbie most about the man's statement was its complete sincerity. How could he possibly fault the man? But this fact only annoyed him all the more.

"Are you?" he asked caustically.

"Do you blame me for your friend's departure?"

"He was thoughtless and inconsiderate in what he did," replied Robbie. "But I think a little compassion would not have done him harm."

Slowly Wallace closed his book and leveled his full attention on Robbie. "You believe I am a hard man, unacquainted with compassion, don't you, Mr. Taggart? Perhaps in a certain sense you are right, and if that is true God will deal with me accordingly. But true *compassion*, of the kind our Lord felt, shows itself differently, depending on a man's different needs. I sensed hostility in Mr. Drew from that first day. I knew there were hidden hurts in the man's soul as well. But I felt it my duty not to patronize him. He would have twisted that behavior, as he twisted my response yesterday. To truly put on the face of love, as our Lord did, requires many different responses. That is one of the first lessons a missionary must learn. In Mr. Drew's case I felt it was more compassionate to make him face the reality of what he was doing. There is something in the man's past, I suspect, which—if I read him correctly—would have made him bitterly resent any patronizing words. I had prayed that a firmer response would bring him to repentance. It seems he chose to run away instead—and for that I truly am sorry. I do care about the man. I do not believe in accidents, only divine appointments. God did not bring either you or Mr. Drew here to the mission for no reason."

"But with him you never tried the other way," said Robbie. "How can you say what would have happened? You don't even know him. How do you know that a gentler approach might not have kept him here?"

"I don't. I had to act on whatever measure of spiritual wisdom I may have been given at the time. If it was my flesh reacting, then God will reveal it to me. This is a matter I assure you I will take to Him in prayer."

"Prayer! That's a convenient way for *you* not to face up to your own shortcomings," rejoined Robbie.

Wallace smiled, seemed to ponder his response for a moment, then opened his mouth to speak.

"For an unbeliever, you are bold, Mr. Taggart. And not without a good deal of insight, too. Indeed, it is precisely my human failings and shortcomings that most often drive me to prayer. But you are wrong on one point. Prayer does not *keep* me from facing my shortcomings. On the contrary, it is only through prayer that I am able to conquer them. Or I should say, that the Lord is able to conquer them in me."

"So you consider me an unbeliever because I do not practice your religious ways?"

"Not at all. If you are an unbeliever, it is not because of anything to do with religious ways, but because of belief. *Do* you think you believe, Mr. Taggart?"

"I suppose that depends on what you mean by believe."

"What do *you* mean by it?"

"What someone thinks is true, I guess."

"So do you believe on that basis?"

"I think there is a God, if that is what you mean."

"And that qualifies you as a believer, a Christian?"

"Well, yes, doesn't it? Isn't that what a Christian is, someone who believes in God?"

"That's what most people think," replied Wallace. "But according to the Scriptures, *belief* is something altogether different."

"What is it, then?"

"It's lifestyle, Mr. Taggart, not just intellectual agreement with an idea, or a set of ideas. Millions of people *believe* certain things to be true. But it makes no difference in their lives. It's merely a mental assent to an idea or notion. But biblical 'belief' means something else completely. It involves trust. To *believe* in the true sense means to put your entire trust in it—completely. You believe in the seaworthiness of your ship by entrusting your life and future to it by going to sea on it. If you said, 'I believe that ship is worthy, but I refuse to sail on it,' your so-called belief would mean nothing. Without trust, mental assent is no belief at all."

"And so what does all that have to do with what Christians believe?"

"To be a Christian, a believer, in the true sense, means to place your trust in Jesus Christ, depending on Him for all of the decisions and goals and priorities and attitudes and values of your life. To depend on Him entirely. To give yourself wholly to Him. To become like Him. To live like Him. To model your life after His. To obey His commands and instructions. *That* is what it means to believe! Saying, 'I believe God exists,' but then to do nothing in response, for it to make no difference in how you live—that is not belief according to the Bible."

"And you can say that about yourself?" asked Robbie, not wanting to expose his own reaction.

"I can say that is my prayer, Mr. Taggart. The desire of my heart is to live like Jesus, to model my life after His, to trust Him, to give myself in service to those people to whom He has called me. So yes, I believe in that way. And that is why I do pray every day. And I pray for my own shortcomings and weaknesses. One cannot pray and try to hide from God at the same time. Sincere prayer exposes a man's whole heart to Him—that is why it should not be entered into lightly."

Another pause followed; then Wallace stood. "It is time for me to prepare for the service," he said. "I hope you will consider joining us."

Robbie made no reply, only stood silently while their eyes met briefly— in a kind of battle of wills, but also in a kind of reaching out to understand one another. Had Robbie been able to probe the other man's mind, he would have seen that even in those brief moments that mysterious and awesome thing was going on which they had just been talking about— prayer. Wallace was not praying on behalf of himself, but that the heart of his young guest would somehow be opened to the truth of the gospel, and that in due time he would indeed find that fully trusting belief in the Savior.

Robbie was the first to break eye contact, but it was the doctor who walked away. At the door he turned once more to Robbie.

"I am curious about something, Mr. Taggart," he said, "and of course you don't have to answer me if you don't wish. But it puzzles me why you have remained here instead of following your friend."

Robbie had pondered that dilemma himself. The moment he had seen Elliot's note and knew for certain he was gone, his first instinct had been to grab up his jacket and make every effort to catch the Vicar. But he had remained. And even he was not quite sure why, though there were a hundred flippant things he might say, one of which he now found himself using on Wallace.

"I don't like to leave a job half-finished," he answered with almost a defensive air in his tone. "Besides, it was a foolhardy thing for him to do. We have no money, don't know the language, don't know which way to go. We're trapped here, for a while at least. He'll probably end up back here before the day is out." Even as he spoke them, though everything he said was true enough, the reasons sounded lame. But how could he express deeper forces than he even realized were operating upon him? How could he say that which he did not understand, that something beyond himself was compelling him to remain at the mission, for reasons he would not become aware of for a long time still to come?

When Wallace had gone, Robbie too left the residence. The rain was coming in intermittent spurts now, but he didn't mind a little moisture. He walked slowly away from the buildings, and spent the next hour walking along the bank of the stream, taking in again the scene that had so impressed him that first day with its peace and serenity. But now that he had become more familiar with this village, he knew that here also there was strife, discord, poverty and sadness.

His gaze moved back along the little river in the direction from which he had come, and to the mission compound, less than two hundreds yards off to his right. There was more than met the eye there, too—more to be discovered and experienced. But the mystery was wrapped in no quaint package out of some picture-book, like the picturesque village. There in the mission compound it was bound up intrinsically in the persons of Hsi-chen and Wallace, even Coombs and the proper Miss Trumbull and the others. Something waiting to be discovered, something almost as appealing to his sense of adventure as a new voyage on the open sea.

A momentary thrill coursed through his veins at the thought, but it was immediately counterbalanced with a protective defense that said, *Be careful, Robbie Taggart! Whatever it is, it may be wonderful—but it might also be dangerous!*

As he approached the slender bridge once more, his attention was suddenly drawn to dozens of village folk who had begun making their way across to the mission. Whatever it was, that *something* was drawing them also, from centuries of tradition toward worshiping a God who was radically new to them, a God brought to them by Isaiah Wallace. What was it that made it so compelling to these people that they would risk everything to follow where Wallace was leading them?

Robbie stood and watched for some time while the steady but silent flow of Chinese men and women was gradually swallowed up within the walls of the small chapel building. Soon only a handful of latecomers were crossing the bridge, hurrying forward even as Miss Trumbull's organ music once again began to play. Robbie vaguely recognized the tune, and from deep within his subconscious came remnants of the words, "Praise God from whom all blessings flow . . ." He could remember no more. Only today the words were different altogether, and the tune a bit stilted. The congregation was trying to sing in Chinese. Hsi-chen had once mentioned that translating Western songs into their native tongue was difficult because the two languages were so diverse. Robbie now realized what she had meant.

He had wandered back into the compound almost before he knew it. He slowly walked to the camphor tree under which he and Hsi-chen had lately spent many hours discussing life and faith. Leaning against the tree he listened to the sounds coming from within the church, hardly questioning at first why he listened as an outsider, reluctant to enter this place of worship. Soon came a brief pause in the music; then the organ took up a song unfamiliar to Robbie. It was sung in English by only a few voices, probably the mission staff and perhaps one or two others.

"*Come, thou Fount of every blessing,*" they sang, "*tune my heart to sing thy grace; streams of mercy, never ceasing, call for songs of loudest praise.*"

He could hear Hsi-chen's and Wallace's voices harmonizing above the rest. One would have thought the two very distinctive sounds would have been discordant and grating. Yet the gentleness of the one and the deep austerity of the other seemed to blend together into a sound both fervent and appealing.

"O to grace how great a debtor daily I'm constrained to be! Let thy goodness, like a fetter, bind my wandering heart to thee. . . ."

Suddenly Robbie realized he had wandered away from the security of the tree and all at once found himself on the steps of the chapel. Almost against his will he felt like he was being drawn into the sanctuary. He had given no conscious thought to Wallace's invitation, and had not even debated within himself about whether he would attend the service.

"Prone to wander, Lord, I feel it. Prone to leave the God I love. Here's my heart, O take and seal it; seal it for thy courts above."

Robbie opened the doors just as the final strain of the organ music died away. He hadn't expected what he now saw. Crowded into that small building were what had to be over a hundred and fifty people. A few heads turned as he entered, but the majority remained bowed as Wallace delivered a prayer in Chinese. Robbie found a seat toward the rear of the chapel, on a wooden, backless bench next to an old gentleman he had never seen before. The remainder of the service was in Chinese, except for a song or two in English.

In the few times during the course of his life when occasion had demanded it, Robbie had had a difficult enough time sitting through a church service in English. But in Chinese the boredom was magnified even further, and his mind wandered over a good many distant settings. By the time it was over he had gotten over whatever "sentimentalism," as he called it, had possessed him to come in in the first place, and had regained what he considered his "good senses." He was intent on making a quick getaway before he was noticed. He had begun to feel it signaled a weakness to have come, an admission that they had something he might need. The thing was ridiculous, of course, and it wouldn't do to give Wallace the impression that any of that talk about "belief" had stirred anything in him.

He had nearly ducked safely out the door when suddenly Hsi-chen appeared like an apparition at his elbow.

"Mr. Taggart," she said pleasantly, seemingly unaware that she had interrupted him in the very process of making his escape, "I'm glad you joined us this morning."

"Well, it *is* Sunday," he answered airily. "What else would I do?" But before he went on he stopped himself suddenly. Why should he try to cover up who he was? If they were such righteous Christians, then they ought to be able to accept him as he was. "Actually," he went on after a moment's pause, "there are lots of things I might find to do on a Sunday, and going to church is usually not one of them."

"Then that makes me all the more glad that you chose to so honor our humble chapel," she answered earnestly. "It makes it even more meaningful. And as you have perhaps noticed, there would have been many disappointed villagers if you had stayed away."

"What do you mean?"

"Our numbers are not often so swelled as they were today," she explained. "Many new folk came, curious to see the English sailor who was saved out of the water."

"I doubt your father will be happy about that," said Robbie.

It was Wallace himself who answered, approaching from the other direction. "On the contrary, Mr. Taggart. I am deeply indebted to you; you have attracted many who might never have come through these doors otherwise. Today the gospel was spread to many new listeners, thanks to you! Already the name we first gave you, Moses, is being fulfilled!"

A hint of a smile tugged at the doctor's lips, and an ironic twinkle gleamed in his dark eyes.

"But why did they wait until today?" Robbie asked. "They could have, and did, see me many times around the mission."

"The Chinese are a decorous, formal people," replied Wallace. "Most had no official reason to come to the mission without an invitation. So they waited for the day when they knew an invitation was extended to one and all."

"Well then, I'm certainly glad I did not disappoint them!" laughed Robbie.

"Come," said Hsi-chen, "I will introduce you to some of my friends. That may help to bring them back for two or three more Sundays." She chuckled even as she spoke.

"Have I become one of your missionary band without even knowing it?" rejoined Robbie, keeping up the light banter.

"Oh no, Mr. Taggart," said Wallace. "It has not gone so far yet. Do not forget the import of our conversation this morning." His tone had taken on its more usual imposing intensity. "You will know for certain when you have become a missionary."

Robbie was delivered from any necessity of having to respond when Wallace was spirited away by Coombs and several Chinese men. At that point, true to her word, Hsi-chen took him by the arm and began to introduce him, in Chinese, to several of the village families who indeed counted it a great honor to be thus singled out. After he had gone through the process of bowing in greeting to one man, as an aside Hsi-chen told

Robbie that the man he had just met had been one of the participants in the attack on Chang's home.

"What happened? Why is he here now?" asked Robbie in surprise.

"My father paid him a visit," replied Hsi-chen, "and now he is here with his whole family."

"Whatever did your father say to him?"

"You will have to ask my father that," replied Hsi-chen.

Robbie had little intention of doing that, he told himself—though with the thought came the recollection that he had not intended to attend the service in the chapel that morning, either. There was, indeed, a strange atmosphere in this place. Almost involuntarily he found himself wondering what other new adventures might be in store for him—planned or unplanned.

There was at least one villager, however, who was not intimidated or impressed by the doctor's ways. Robbie saw him approach from the direction of the bridge—he had obviously not been to the church service. He wore an expression steeped in bitterness and anger.

He stalked up to where Wallace stood in conversation with several men, took a position some ten feet away, and then began waving his fist and shouting biting insults and accusations. A few of the Chinese men attempted to reason with him, but he would not relax his tirade.

At length he approached still closer, walking toward Wallace, looking as if he might physically attack him. Wallace unflinchingly held his ground, speaking in his calm, measured voice, trying to soothe the man. Finally, with the help of two of his friends, half pulling, half cajoling, the man was made to retreat, but he continued to yell angry threats over his shoulder at Wallace, even as he approached the bridge.

Robbie cast a questioning glance toward Hsi-chen, whose face was drawn with concern over the outburst.

"That is Mr. Li," she said. "He comes often on Sundays to express his disapproval of the mission."

To Robbie her comment seemed highly understated, but he could tell she was trying to be benevolent toward the troublemaker. "His heart is hard toward our Lord," she went on, "but maybe it will not always be so."

Robbie was left with more mixed feelings about this place and its director. One man came to worship who two days earlier was an enemy; another cast threats. Yet in a way these two were representative of his own reactions to the mission. He shook his head, wondering why it seemed impossible to simply ignore the place.

Later that afternoon, as the dinner meal was being cleared away from the table, Wallace broached a new subject. Coombs listened attentively, as he always did when Wallace spoke. Yet there still seemed to be a sense of defeat and resignation in his manner.

"Mr. Taggart," said Wallace, "I have a request to make of you." His voice was uncharacteristically hesitant, perhaps because he wondered if, after what had occurred with Drew, a request might be out of place. He continued, however, "Tomorrow morning I must go to Hangchow. It will require me to be absent from the mission for two days. Mr. Coombs will remain here, as there are several calls he wishes to make, and some of these may take him some distance from home—"

"I'll be happy to act as chaperone to the mission," put in Robbie almost jovially.

"That is kind of you, of course," responded Wallace, "but that has already been taken care of—Ying and one of Chang's sons have agreed to attend to the mission. I was hoping rather that you would accompany Mr. Coombs."

"Me . . . to do what?" replied Robbie, taken by surprise at the request. "I would think that one of your local converts would be better suited to the task."

"This is the busiest time of the rice cultivation season, and they cannot be spared from their fields. I think you will find it a gratifying experience."

Robbie hesitated, then glanced at the younger missionary. "Is this agreeable to you, Mr. Coombs?" Even as he asked the question, he wondered if this had been the cause of his silent mood lately.

But Coombs replied firmly, "I would be honored."

So it was settled. Of all things Robbie would never have expected to do, he would soon be attending an itinerant preacher on his rounds through the Chinese countryside!

38

The Young Missionary

The old run-down junk was certainly no *Sea Tiger*.

It was, in fact, no bigger than the clipper's long-boat, though it did have a small cabin in the center where the single mast was located with its bamboo sail. Robbie hadn't realized how much he missed the water until he felt the junk's deck beneath his feet. He fell to work with a will, familiarizing himself with the simple rigging, making ready the small sail for hoisting, and doing all the other tasks of a shipman's pride. No matter that this was a lazy little river scarcely 70 feet across that the locals called a stream. To have a deck beneath his feet again felt like coming home after a week in a desert.

He found himself whistling a merry tune, just like in the old days:

> You jolly sailors list to me,
> I've been a fortnight home from sea,
> Which time I've rambled night and day,
> To have a lark on the Highway.
> Listen you jovial sailors gay,
> To the rigs of Ratcliffe Highway.

He thought fleetingly of the *Sea Tiger*. How grand it had been when she ran "with a bone in her teeth," her sails swelled and the beams creaking with the strain!

He sighed, saddened to think of her now lying dead at the bottom of the China Sea. A twinge of anger rose in him at the memory of Pike, who had apparently betrayed her to that fate. He hadn't thought of the skipper in a long time. He wondered if thoughts of his father's old wooden-legged friend would continue to plague him, taking from him some of the pleasure of his essential love for the sea. Yet even as the memories came back, he recalled that the days aboard the *Tiger* had not been all sweet. No, the "old days" extended further back than that—so far, in fact, that he began to wonder if they had really ever existed at all.

A shout from Coombs, who was standing on the dock, jarred his thoughts back to the present.

"This is the last of the gear, Mr. Taggart," said the young man as he hoisted a bundle aboard.

Well, thought Robbie, *this little excursion promises to be about as eventful as a walk across Hyde Park.* Coombs' mood had remained withdrawn; he had said less than a dozen words it seemed since they had met at dawn. It was too bad. Otherwise there might have been promise of, if not an adventure, at least a diversion from the mission.

Coombs swung aboard, and immediately set about stowing away the gear. He paid Robbie little attention. Robbie stood with his foot propped up on the thwart of the junk, his arms folded, able to take an amused look at the situation. He had seldom encountered such a serious creature as this young man was turning out to be. His bearing could not have been more in contrast with Wallace's self-assured intensity. Coombs seemed more to harbor the intensity of a boy trying very hard to please, so hard that no room was left in his life for anything else.

For Coombs' part, he did indeed feel that he had a great deal to prove with this sojourn in China, and thus it was little surprise that he tried so hard to please and felt so frustrated from being kept, as he thought, out of the decision-making process. From an affluent Birmingham banking family, his parents were perplexed at his announcement at the age of fifteen that he had given his life to Christ. They hardly knew what the words meant, but it most certainly sounded like the sort of thing one should keep quiet about. They convinced themselves that the best course of action was to ignore his burst of religious fervor, certain the "spell" would soon pass. What was their mortification when, six months later, he further announced that he had been "called" to become a missionary to China.

Mr. and Mrs. Coombs had scheduled an examination by the family physician, and even contemplated locking their son in his room until the whole business was forgotten. His father had always entertained hopes of his athletically built son entering Cambridge and distinguishing himself on the rugby field, and later doing the same thing in his own bank, or perhaps in a law practice. But now the fool lad wanted to throw his life away. It was unthinkable! But Thomas was an only child, and his parents could not long rave against him. They did, however, make it clear that China was no place for a gentleman, which he would find out on his own soon enough, and come home with his tail between his legs. How much better, they reasoned, not to have to learn the hard way.

But young Coombs had been determined to follow what he perceived as the Lord's leading, since the moment it had come to him at a service in which Dr. Isaiah Wallace, visiting from China, was the main speaker. His call was a true one, and no less so because of Wallace's moving presentation. Coombs became determined to serve with the doctor, and to distinguish himself, as his father would have said—whether pleasing God, or validating his own existence in the eyes of his parents. At his tender age who could have told for certain?

Now he had been in China a mere six months, and the twenty-one-year-old missionary was working hard, perhaps to accomplish both goals. Not only did he have to prove himself to his parents, but he also had to make his hero and mentor, Isaiah Wallace, proud of him. The five years of missionary preparation, including an intensive course in Chinese, had not come easy for Thomas. His bent was indeed more toward the athletic than the scholarly, but at the same time he was determined to serve his God in the capacity to which he had been called, no matter what it took.

And it seemed he was now required to drag this sailor along with him as some kind of bodyguard! He was a grown man; how could he serve God if he were continually treated like a child? Yet nagging even more at Thomas's mind was the fear that Dr. Wallace seemed to have little faith in him, and might never feel confident to give him the chance he deserved. Six months seemed to young Thomas Coombs as an eternity, plenty of time to have become self-sufficient in his particular sphere of mission work. On occasion Wallace had remarked that he was coming along fine, but apparently the words held different connotations to each man.

When the doctor had told him of his plans to go to Hangchow, Coombs had exultantly thought that at last this would be *his moment* to prove himself on his own. But then almost on the heels of the announcement came the doctor's declaration that the trip upriver would have to be cancelled in favor of the business in Hangchow. Coombs had argued fervently, at least to the extent he dared with the great man, and did succeed in convincing him that the commitments upriver would be broken only at a severe cost. "We have shaken off the watchdogs that have been oppressing us," argued Coombs. "We cannot put this tour off any longer without seriously impairing our ministry." Then the notion of Mr. Taggart's involvement had come up.

"But he knows less than I of the country or the language!" argued Coombs. "What possible assistance can he provide?"

"He can handle the junk," returned Wallace.

Coombs actually thought he was trying to be amusing.

"I can manage the boat well enough," he said.

"'Pride goeth before a fall,' Thomas," admonished the doctor.

"Sir, I don't mean to be prideful, but I long for more responsibility. I feel that with God's help I can handle it."

"In time, Thomas, I have no doubt that you will," answered the doctor, "but you must have patience. The ways of God take time, not the least of which is our inward preparation for His work in and through us. You must trust the schedule I have set for you."

"Then let me hire a villager," pleaded Coombs. It was especially degrading to be told that Taggart had to accompany him, for it was obvious that his only function was to act as a nursemaid.

"I believe Taggart will be more suitable," replied Wallace; then, rubbing his chin thoughtfully, he added, "and I have other reasons for wanting Mr. Taggart to go along with you."

"May I inquire as to what those reasons might be?" asked Coombs, not a little timorously.

"For his own sake, Thomas. I believe this opportunity has been ordained by our Lord, for I do not think Mr. Taggart would agree to join us on one of our expeditions of ministry unless he was needed. And I think he will gain a great deal from seeing the gospel spread in this manner. So, Thomas, look upon this as a mutually beneficial excursion. The Chinese are not our only mission field, you know. God sent Mr. Taggart to us for a purpose. And we must be prayerfully faithful to sharing the truths of God with him as well."

39

Through the Waterways

Coombs had resigned himself to the doctor's orders and had tried to take a positive attitude, but thus far had been too stubborn to offer much friendship in Robbie's direction. He now picked up the last bundle on deck to stow it in the cabin. Out of the corner of his eye he saw Robbie watching him. Suddenly he felt both guilty and foolish for his actions and his self-centered attitude. He was supposed to be a witness for Christ to this man who was, to all appearances, unsaved. Yet what kind of an impression must he be making?

Coming back out of the cabin, he cleared his throat as if that were his personal signal to take a new approach to the day.

"I believe we're ready to cast off, Mr. Taggart," he said. "Are you willing to handle the vessel?"

Robbie smiled. This was just what he had been waiting for. Quickly he loosed the rope from the dock pilings and pushed off into the current. A gentle southeast breeze helped guide them up Chai-chiang, the Little Stream, for some distance. Eventually they would meet one of the many canals that crisscrossed the region, and from there they would make their way to one of the tributaries of the Yangtze.

Once the yard was hauled to get the best from the breeze, Robbie stretched himself out and, with one hand on the tiller, lay back to enjoy himself. After all, the scenery was new and marvelous, and with the pagoda roofs and straw-hatted Orientals along the shore, he could easily imagine that he had escaped to another world—as indeed he had. He tried to forget the mission and imagine that all he needed to do was think about having a good time, in a world where his only care was deciding which tune to sing next. He might even be able to forget the glum missionary sitting opposite him.

Actually, Coombs was gradually doing much better. At that moment he was searching in his mind for some pleasant conversation to pursue with his new companion, even if he had to rely on facts he had learned from a textbook to make a beginning.

"You will soon see the Grand Canal," he finally said, his tone congenial. "It was built in 608, during the Sui Dynasty."

"Why did they build it?" asked Robbie.

"Contemporaries of the emperor, Yang-ti, accused him of merely trying to indulge his own comfort so he could travel more easily from the northern capital at Peking to the southern in Hangchow. Not to mention for the purpose of bleeding off southern tax grain to feed the imperial capital and army."

"I should think it would have been a rather useful bit of architecture," commented Robbie, glad for the apparent improvement in the missionary's disposition.

"Well," answered Coombs, "most of his critics were Confucian scholars, and there is perhaps nothing more alien to the Confucian way than progress. We still encounter that mind-set. But I suppose they had a point, when you compare the canal's usefulness with its cost. It was all done by forced labor. Hundreds of thousands of workers were brought in—at one point there were a million laborers. Even women were conscripted when the number of men fell short. But despite the critics of the time, the canal does remain one of the primary transportation and communication routes in the country."

"You seem to know a lot about this country," said Robbie. "You speak the language quite well, too, though I didn't think you had been here that long."

"I hardly do the language justice," answered Coombs, "and half the time it seems I unknowingly insult a native because I have used the wrong intonation. When I first arrived, I thought my four years of study had been for nothing."

"Four years! Why, you must have been a boy when you started."

"I was fifteen when I received God's call to come to China."

"Hmm," mused Robbie. "That was the age when I struck out on my own."

"That's when you went to sea?"

"No, I didn't discover the sea until I was eighteen—late in life. Most of the blokes my age had already been at sea half their lives. It's not that unusual to find boys of ten or twelve aboard ship."

"You must have had an exciting life."

Robbie scratched his head thoughtfully, as a rather novel idea occurred to him. "Your own life hasn't been dull either, I'll warrant," he said, then paused.

Since he had first encountered these folk at the mission, he had thought of them only as religious people—conservative and uninteresting for the most part. Now it suddenly dawned on him that perhaps they were different than the characters of his mental stereotype. The spirit of adventure must run high in persons like these who were willing to risk everything, even their lives, for a cause in which they believed in a far-off land—as high as for any sailor. They had broken away from the normal patterns and steered their own personal course for exotic lands, fraught with dangers and uncertainty and sacrifice. All at once Robbie looked across to Thomas Coombs in a new light. He too was an adventurer!

"And what does your family think about your chosen profession?" he asked at length.

Coombs laughed. It was one of the more abandoned laughs Robbie had yet heard from the serious young man. "They think I've gone absolutely insane!" he replied. "Though I think it is more the *missionary* part that troubles them than me being an adventurer in China. Had I come here as a diplomat or a merchant, I'm sure they would have been quite proud."

"They don't follow your beliefs?"

"It is difficult to judge one's own parents," answered Coombs, knitting his brow together as he considered how best to answer the question. "I suppose one might say that they believe similarly, but with a different intensity. They think I have gotten quite carried away. They see belief as something to hold in your head, so to speak, but not to ever do anything about. But perhaps that is your opinion also. That seems to rather be the norm in today's world."

The breeze had been gradually shifting to the port, and as Coombs posed his query, Robbie had to jump up and reset the yard. While he hauled at the lines he thought about the young man's words. He had indeed thought that very thing on a number of occasions. He wondered if the present occasion called upon him to be so honest with his companion, notwithstanding the growing sense of camaraderie that seemed to be developing between the two who were such strangers to one another only an hour before. But why not be open and honest, thought Robbie to himself? Such a practice had never failed him before.

"As a matter of fact," said Robbie, settling back into his place by the tiller as if there had been no interruption to their conversation, "I have thought that. Though perhaps not in strictly the same sense. I suppose people who try to push their religion off onto others rub me the wrong way."

"We are not *pushing* anything, Mr. Taggart," replied Coombs. "We are merely following the Great Commission issued by our Lord Jesus Christ himself, to go into all the world and preach the gospel. The response of another—any man or woman: Chinese or Englishman, banker or sailor, rich or poor—is something which rests entirely with that man in his own heart. We are merely proclaimers, not arm-twisters. The choice whether to follow Jesus in belief rests with each individual alone."

"But you must admit that many in your position *do* try to stuff it down anyone's throat who'll listen," said Robbie, a bit taken aback by Coombs's sudden burst of enthusiasm.

"I suppose you're right. And if you didn't know me and my own motives, you might accuse me of the same thing," replied Coombs. "But you see, Mr. Taggart, I have found Life! I have discovered something greater than my mother and father or anyone else was able to give me. What kind of man would I be if I kept the way to that Life to myself?"

"I never thought of it like that," said Robbie. He could see how this young man's parents might have questioned his sanity. And yet at this very moment, there was something very, very sane in his countenance, especially in his eyes. They were neither wild nor crazed. They were sincere and earnest, to the point of being compelling. Robbie said nothing, but looked away, pretending to be occupied with the tiller.

The conversation did not again approach that probing theme. A somewhat tricky stretch of water absorbed their attention for a time, and after that the talk focused on more mundane topics. By midday they had traveled in excess of fifteen miles upon various waterways. On and off they had met with much traffic and activity on their course, but now they merged with a quieter, backwater stream where a village soon came into view. Coombs announced that they should make for the stone moorings and make their craft fast there. While Robbie maneuvered the junk to the dock, Coombs began filling two rucksacks with supplies—mainly books, tracts, and food.

Their plan was to spend the remainder of the day traveling through this particular area of four or five small villages. They would then spend the night on the junk and cast off early in the morning, sailing upstream into another district. After a second night on the junk, they would sail for home. When Robbie asked about the territoriality of other missions, Coombs explained that these were areas that fell under no other mission jurisdiction and without any particular church connection. The established missions with an interest in such evangelism usually took it in turns to reach these backwater areas and to see that they received periodic Christian contact.

Robbie and Coombs each loaded up their packs with as many books and supplies as they could manage and climbed onto dry land. Then followed one of the most unique experiences in Robbie's life, even as adventurous as it had been.

Even before they reached the center of the village, they had begun to attract a considerable following of locals. And indeed they made a curious sight—two Occidental men of imposing stature, one dressed in black Oriental garb, the other wearing navy blue canvas trousers and the white shirt of a Western sailor. But Robbie soon realized that it was not merely the oddity of their appearance that had attracted the folk. The moment Coombs handed out his first tract, word spread that a missionary had come with reading material. Robbie could not help being astonished at the response.

"The Chinese are eager to learn new ideas," said Coombs when a lull came in the greetings and questions of the villagers.

"What about the riots and violence against missionaries? I thought you would be encountering opposition everywhere, like back in the village at the mission."

"It depends on the area, and the particular mood of the time. And it also depends a great deal on how much the local priests decide to stir things up against us," answered Coombs. "But things have calmed considerably in the last two or three years. Even at their height, those actions were not aimed only at Christianity. Take the trouble in Wukiang, for example. It was stirred up only because temple funds were threatened by Chang's refusal to pay. Violence against missionaries usually springs up more as an expression of anti-foreignism than any resistance to the gospel itself. And this occurs only because the Chinese have suffered so at the hands of foreign powers."

"Then why do they take it out against the missionaries?"

"Because missionaries happen to be here, ambassadors, so to speak, of those foreign countries. But the villagers, like these, are unbelievably open and receptive to the gospel itself when we can isolate it from all the larger issues that are more political. The Chinese react mostly against us when their political or economic stability is threatened. Otherwise they are extremely tolerant."

"But I thought they were closed to any attempt to impose religion on them from the outside?"

"Did you know that Buddhism, the second largest faith after Confucianism, is a transplant from India? Yes, it had built-in similarities to the long-established religions of China, but Christianity has many of those also—ethics and virtue, and even the most basic of all religious ideas, the concept of God, is familiar to them, though the various religions disagree as to what God's character and personality are like. The great Chinese leader, Kublai Khan himself, who lived in the 13th century, asked Marco Polo to take an invitation to the Pope asking him to send teachers of science and religion to China. So you see, historically, there has been an openness of this culture to new ideas."

"Are you saying that if Christianity had come by another route, and things had been slightly different, it might have been totally absorbed into the culture?"

"Perhaps not completely into the culture, but at least more peaceably accepted. There are facets of the Christian faith that *are* foreign to Chinese ways, and must remain so in order for Christianity to retain its purity. The faith expounded by the Apostles and set forth in the New Testament cannot be altered in order to suit a different culture. There are essential aspects of it on which we must remain unyielding. That is what separates it from the other mere religions of the world."

"Why do you say *mere* religions?" asked Robbie.

"Because all the other religions of the world are incomplete. They are mere religious systems. But at their core they do not have the one thing that Christianity has, the one ingredient that makes all the difference, the one thing that makes it *true* in the face of all other insufficient attempts to know God and discover the essential meaning of life."

"And what is that?"

"Jesus, Mr. Taggart. Jesus Christ—God himself come to earth to reveal to men the truth, and the way to know Him, Jesus—the true man. God defined and manhood defined—in the same being. No other religion has Jesus. So you see, no other religion can possibly possess the ultimate truth about God."

Robbie was silent for a moment. It had been some time since he had thought about the meaning of manhood. Now here was an unexpected twist—the idea of Jesus being the ultimate, the perfect man. It was certainly not something he had ever considered before. To Robbie Taggart, the Jesus of the Bible had always seemed rather an effeminate sop.

"And that's why we call the gospel 'good news,'" Coombs went on. "And that's why we feel such an urgency to proclaim it. Not to cram our particular *system* down anyone else's throat, but because of the wonderful news that we can *know* God personally and intimately through Jesus!"

Still thoughtful, at length Robbie said in a sincerely probing voice, "But it seems there is still an intolerance in it toward their religions. If you think you have the truth and they do not, how can you expect them to be open to what you have to say in return?"

"There is no particular virtue in tolerance for its own sake. Only a fool is open and tolerant to a false idea. The question is not tolerance, on either side of the issue. The question is truth. The things Jesus said, the claims Jesus made, the life Jesus lived—they are either true or they are not. And if they are true, we are fools to turn our backs on them. At the point of the truth of Jesus' words, the truth of His character, the truth of His resurrection, and the compelling truth of His claim upon our own lives—at that point culture and religion and tolerance and education all fade into meaninglessness. That's when the truth of Jesus Christ comes to bear upon every man, in the quietness of his own heart. And that is where the response must be made."

By now they had reached the center of the village. It was just as well that their conversation came to an end, for Robbie had heard enough to keep his mind busy for some time. Coombs paused in front of the local teashop, which stood at the intersection of the village's only two streets, actually little more than widened dirt paths. Then he turned to the crowd of about fifty people who had gathered around him.

For the next hour the verbal exchange was entirely in Chinese, so Robbie had no idea of exactly what was being said. But an understanding of the words themselves was hardly necessary to enable him to see that the young man Coombs was pouring out his heart in love and compassion and earnest belief to these people who had come to hear him. Coombs was a different man now, as Robbie had begun to see on the boat. Even while fumbling over the alien tongue, his voice was laced with passion. The villagers listened attentively, respectfully, with rapt attention riveted upon the young preacher, as if they had never heard such words before. And such was very likely the case for many of them.

For Robbie, who had grown up surrounded by nominal "Christian" society, the hungry looks on the faces about him was nothing short of astonishing. Here were people genuinely listening to "news"—good news. Suddenly the faith of his fathers took on a new dimension in Robbie's mind. Listening as through the ears of these Chinese men and women, something new and vital and alive for the first time seemed to penetrate Robbie's consciousness. Robbie found himself listening as he had never listened before—though he understood not a word. He listened instead with his eyes, and with a curiously softer heart than had ever opened itself to the gospel message before. When he came to himself some time later, he was shaken, realizing for the first time how absorbed he had been in the young missionary's bold street preaching.

His thoughts were jolted out of their reverie by a sudden clamor toward the back of the crowd. The people parted, and three men came to the front where Robbie and Coombs, who had stopped speaking, were standing. Between two larger men, walking very slowly and with occasional assistance from his companions, came the one for whom the crowd had obviously parted. Old and extremely brittle in appearance, his back was humped, which thrust his wrinkled face forward, causing his long, thin, white beard to swing freely down and away from his body. One look at his ancient visage gave the word *venerable* new meaning for all time.

Coombs stepped forward and bowed graciously to the man. "*Ni hao, lao-fu,* greetings, old father," he said.

The old man returned his bow, as best he could, and in reply spoke to Coombs at some length. His tone was not angry, but firm. In an odd sort of way he reminded Robbie of Wallace, and as with the doctor, Coombs seemed to defer to the man. He answered in an apologetic tone, bows were exchanged once more; then the old man, appearing satisfied, turned and made his way again back through the villagers, who immediately began to disperse.

Left alone on the street. Robbie turned to Coombs to ask what had just happened.

"That man was the village elder," replied Coombs. "He said we must move on because we are disrupting the rice cultivation. He was most courteous and invited us to return in the evening."

"What will we do until then?"

"There are other villages to be visited."

"Won't you encounter the same thing?"

"We won't know until we've tried."

They returned to the junk, loaded up with more supplies and reading material, then set off on foot. For the remainder of the day they visited another four small villages, though none proved as friendly as the first. In one a small gang of hoodlums heckled Coombs ruthlessly, finally inciting the crowd to such an extent that the missionary was forced to make a hasty exit.

"T'i-mien! T'i-mien!" kept being shouted at their backs until they were well outside the limits of the last of the town's huts.

"What were they yelling?" asked Robbie, recalling the word from his own experience in Wukiang when he had accompanied Hsi-chen to Chang's home.

"Haughty," answered Coombs. "It has become a byword for Western missionaries among those who are not so eager to hear our message."

"But from what you said before, and from the response at the first village where everyone seemed so eager to hear what you had to say, I thought the Chinese were open to the good news, as you put it."

"Many are. But the Chinese are no different than people everywhere. It's the same in Britain. There are those who are open to the truth; there are others who are not. Just because something may be true does not mean everyone is eager to hear it. Many are comfortable with their present lives. Truth in spiritual things is of no interest to them."

Robbie was silent. He realized Coombs' words could be applied to him. He had never made the truth a priority in his life. He had merely gone about with life as it had come. But his reply was not such a personal one. Suddenly he did not feel like exposing any more of his innermost self.

"But those young thugs seemed intent on more mischief than would have been likely if they just disagreed with your message," Robbie said.

"You're probably right. There are those in positions of power who are threatened by our presence. They could have been sent to incite the people against us."

"Sent? By whom?"

"There are many who would rid their land of us if they could."

"Who?"

"Priests of the old order. They can be a ruthless lot, despite all their supposed mellow and gentle ways. And then there are the ancient noble Chinese families who can sometimes be violent, often led by warriors like the samurai in Japan. And of course since the ancient days of the Mongol tribes, China has been famous for its independent warlords. There are still those who maintain their hold on their own private little medieval empires."

"Warlords! In this modern day?"

"Oh yes, Mr. Taggart. And believe me, you don't want to get mixed up with them!"

40

An Inauspicious Ending

The small gang followed the pair of foreigners the rest of the day from village to village, doing their best to stir up trouble. They succeeded in making the visits tense and unpleasant.

When they returned in the evening to the site of their landing, Coombs had hoped to end the day with the same sense of success with which it had begun. But the five or six troublemakers turned up there also, and serious trouble was only averted when the town council stepped in and kicked out the whole lot—Coombs and Robbie included.

Dejected and downcast, Coombs silently led the way back to the junk. Robbie attempted to cheer him with a few amusing sea stories, but to no avail, and by the time they had fallen asleep on the hard mats in the boat's tiny cabin, Robbie was nearly as dispirited as his companion.

They awoke suddenly just before dawn to the sound of a driving rain against the cabin's thin walls. A puddle had formed at Robbie's feet. He hardly knew whether to laugh or cry at the ridiculousness of their circumstances. But the rain only added to Coombs' morose mood.

"At least it will keep those troublemakers away," said Robbie, trying to look on the bright side.

Coombs, however, found it hard to muster up much thankfulness after a night in a damp bed, with rain dripping through in several places, and nothing to look forward to but a cold and cheerless breakfast. Robbie thought fleetingly of the fine new roof at the hospital, and sighed at the irony of being trapped in such straits during the first real rain since his arrival, when they could have been warm and dry back at the mission. He found himself thinking that this was even worse than his being stranded in the sea, where at least he was *completely* wet and *completely* cold, not teased with occasional hints of dryness and warmth.

Shortly before noon the rain mercifully stopped, and the whole land was soon bathed once more in warmth. Quickly cheered, as was his nature, Robbie was quite willing to forget the setbacks of the previous day. Whistling, he set about getting the junk ready to cast off.

The sunshine did little to lift Coombs' spirits. It became all the worse when he went back into the cabin to have a few moments of prayer alone, and there fell asleep. He was embarrassed and flustered when Robbie had to wake him to tell him they were ready to cast off.

"What direction?" Robbie asked as he loosened the rope from its mooring.

"Up river," answered Coombs, determined but hardly enthusiastic.

What was left of the day they spent visiting another cluster of six villages with varying degrees of success. At least the young ruffians had not seen fit to dog their activities and they were not bothered again on that front all day.

They spent a passable night on the junk, but by morning were both quite ready to embark for home. They had retraced their steps but three or four miles downstream when the rain began once again, this time accompanied by what appeared to be growing winds and rougher water. Such a little squall would have been nothing for the kind of ships Robbie was accustomed to. But for a shallow-hulled junk made of lightweight wood, every extra bit of turbulence tossed them around and made maneuverability difficult. Coombs halfheartedly suggested docking, but they were both too anxious to get back to the mission to give up easily, and Robbie was confident they could make it.

However, several miles from the first village at which they had stopped, the canal spilled into a river down which they had to travel half a mile before veering off into another much smaller stream. Already swollen from the two days of rain, the river was moving much too swiftly for their safety, and a cross-wind struck them the moment its current caught the small junk.

Unprepared for the rapid change of direction, Robbie had the sail in exactly the wrong position for the sudden alteration of the wind, now coming in strong gusts. The junk swept down a trough of water, then up the other side, its bow extending out of the water just as a fierce blast of wind caught the sail that Robbie was frantically trying to haul around to the right direction. Without warning, both Robbie and Coombs were thrown into the frenzied current. When Robbie's head surfaced, all he could see was the capsized old junk being carried out of reach toward the rocky shore. In minutes she washed to pieces. Coombs surfaced about ten feet away and they swam to the near shore and dragged themselves out. Nothing was said for a moment or two; then Robbie began to chuckle. A good old-fashioned Taggart laugh followed, which even succeeded in bringing a smile to the face of Coombs.

"Well, at least the rain won't bother us anymore!" laughed Robbie. "Come on, Coombs. Let's be off!" he said, rising, and extending his hand to his young companion. "I hope you know where we are and which way to go!"

They walked for about an hour, crossed the river by bridge, struck out down the smaller stream, and then set about trying to hail one of the few junks brave enough to be passing in such weather. They had no success, and thus continued to walk, hoping eventually to catch a ride on some river conveyance. The rain stopped in another thirty minutes, and suddenly Coombs spotted a large junk, a two-masted craft, as it appeared around the far bend in the stream.

"It looks like the mail packet," he said with rising hope. "It'll put in at the next village. If we can beat it there, maybe they'll take us on."

They began to run, their soaking clothes and shoes inhibiting them, and raced the two miles to the village, making it, footsore and exhausted, well ahead of the packet. But just as they reached the first of the outlying huts, from behind one of them stepped several young men in their late teens and blocked their path.

"Shih shen-mo?" asked Coombs in a tight voice when the ringleader stepped forward in the pathway.

Robbie could not understand a word of the brief conversation, but he recognized the hoodlums from two days earlier and could easily discern from their angry tone that they meant the two Westerners no good.

"T'a hen ch'un!" called the leader back to his companion, and they all roared with laughter. They approached, confident and cocky, outnumbering the strangers five to two.

"Please," pleaded Coombs in Chinese, "we wish no trouble. Let us pass."

"You make trouble everywhere, foreign pig!" spat the leader, and in the next instant all his followers spat at Coombs.

Coombs jumped back, took a handkerchief from his pocket, and tried in vain to wipe his face in the midst of the continued mocking laughter of the Chinese youths.

"Please, let us pass," tried Coombs again, his voice taking on a note of desperation as he saw the mail packet pulling up to the dock less than a hundred and fifty yards farther down the path. "We must get to the packet." Such an admission was a mistake if he hoped for any mercy.

"They do not carry foreign devils!"

Coombs was determined, however, and did not want to miss their only chance of a ride back to the mission. The day had already been one of the worst he had faced since coming to China and he was not willing to give in to another setback. He took a firm step forward and attempted to step between the leader of the small gang and one of his companions. But they laid their hands on his shirt and shoved him rudely away. He stumbled backwards, falling into the muddy path.

"Ha, ha! Wai-chu!" mocked several of the rowdies.

Robbie had understood nothing of what he had heard to that point, but now he had *seen* enough. He knew Coombs would continue to take such abuse without fighting back, just as Chang had been expected to do when attacked by his neighbors. But Robbie Taggart didn't have to take anything. His reserve of self-control had already been taxed to its limit with the previous encounters with these miscreants. Now they had crossed the line and would have to answer to him!

He took two quick strides toward the leader, who still stood in the center of the group, grabbed his shirt before he had the chance to react and threw him mercilessly back into his companions.

"See how tough you are, you little cur, with someone who'll fight back!" shouted Robbie.

With the help of his friends, the antagonist was back on his feet in an instant, and leaped bodily toward Robbie. But he was soon to learn, even with the help of all four of his friends, that this was no meek and mild missionary they were tangling with. Robbie knew how to handle himself in a street brawl as well as he could handle a ship—whether five to one or ten to one. He blocked the first attack but was immediately jumped upon from behind. A sharp backward thrust of his elbow slowed this attack, and Robbie was able to jump free in time to spin around just as the next was upon him. With his hands free, however, this new assailant was the next instant on the ground unconscious, the imprint of Robbie's fist on his jaw.

Robbie spun around again to see the ringleader back on his feet, a look of hatred in his eyes. He came toward Robbie screaming, leaped into the air, and attempted to jab Robbie's midsection with a punishing kick. Robbie deftly stepped to one side, grabbed the outstretched leg in midair, gave it a sharp twist, and sent the attacker sprawling to the ground on his back. From the corner of his eye Robbie saw that he was no longer alone in the fight. Coombs had joined in prying one of the Chinese youths from Robbie's neck, giving him a smashing blow to the midsection. Though Coombs had never been in a fight before in his life, his instincts served him well.

If the Chinese hoodlums had originally thought that sheer numbers would protect them, they had never taken on either Robbie Taggart or a powerfully built young missionary who had been rained on, heckled, and shipwrecked to his limit. After another two minutes, four young Chinese troublemakers lay on the ground, and the fifth was running as fast as he could toward the village, wanting nothing more to do with these wild barbarians.

"Very good, Coombs!" exclaimed Robbie. "You handle yourself very well in a fight. Thank you for saving my hide!"

Coombs collapsed on the ground, and Robbie walked over to him, gave him a slap on the back, laughed and sat down beside him. "I haven't had so much fun since my first day on the *Sea Tiger*!" said Robbie. "Where'd you ever learn to use your fists like that?"

"I don't know," said Coombs, smiling. "To tell you the truth, it's the first time I've ever found them necessary."

"Well, remind me to have you on my side the next time!" laughed Robbie. "What do you say we still try to make that junk?"

Coombs jumped to his feet. He had almost forgotten. He looked up and saw the boat was still there. The two were soon running toward it as quickly as their bruised, tired, and sore legs would carry them. Even as he went, however, Coombs' exultation over their victory faded as the full implications of what he had done began to dawn on him. Though their journey was shortened considerably by the decision of the reluctant captain of the mail packet to sell them passage back to Wukiang, and though Robbie remained in boisterously high spirits, Coombs said hardly another word throughout the remainder of the day.

It was after sunset when the two travelers crossed the bridge and walked with limping gait into the mission compound. Though they had attempted to wash from their faces the more obvious evidence of their row with the young Chinese gang, their bruises, a couple of black eyes, and their torn clothing could not be hidden.

Predictably, the first person they met was Isaiah Wallace.

41

Flight of the Phoenix

Robbie sat silent, wondering what could come next. The three of them were alone in the front room of the residence. The atmosphere was heavy with reproof.

"Now tell me exactly what happened, Thomas?" said Wallace, his tone reminiscent of the stern but benevolent schoolmaster.

Hsi-chen had prepared tea for them and then departed. As he sat there, though Wallace had directed all his attention to Coombs thus far, Robbie could not help but feel like a naughty schoolboy caught by the headmaster in the midst of some mischief. He didn't like the feeling.

As Coombs recounted the story of their travels from village to village, and of their being hounded by the small gang of hoodlums, it was clear from his tone that he was making a great effort to be solemn and dutifully humble. When he came to the end, however, the initial exhilaration he had felt during the row could not help from creeping into his tone.

He ended his report just short of admitting, "We knocked the tar out of them!" Yet he hardly had to *say* the words. No matter how he tried to subdue it, the thrill of victory could be discerned in his voice.

Wallace sat silent a long while once the report was concluded, apparently turning everything over in his analytical mind. In truth, he was trying to decide the best way to proceed, both for the benefit of his protégé's growth as a Christian, and for the benefit of the ears of the young unbeliever who had unwittingly been caught up in the mission's affairs. Achieving a successful result on both fronts would be difficult, if not impossible. Yet his chief responsibility had to remain with Coombs, and with the integrity of their mission in China. He would have to speak God's truth, and pray that somehow it would have a beneficial impact on Mr. Taggart, though he had little doubt it would alienate him initially.

At length Wallace took a deep breath, looked toward Coombs intently, with eyes which would have, to his daughter, revealed his deep love for the young man, but which to Robbie's undiscerning spirit seemed cold and critical. When he spoke, it was in his usual tone, a tone which Robbie took for one of reproach. He could not feel the pain and compassion that lay beneath the words of the experienced missionary who had given his life for a people Robbie did not yet know, understand, or love.

"Did you *enjoy* your experience, Thomas?"

"Of course not," the young man answered quickly. "Well, not the harassing that went on. Sharing with the people in the first village was fulfilling, and—"

"I mean the fight, Thomas."

"No, that is . . . I had never been in a fight before, sir. It was rather . . . it made me feel different, unusual."

"It made you feel good?"

"I don't know . . . it was—well, after them hounding us the day before and keeping us from being able to get out the gospel message, it was . . . Well, they were asking for it, sir! They would not have left us alone otherwise."

Wallace was silent, thinking again.

"What *is* the gospel message, Thomas?" he said at length.

"That God is love."

"And who does God love?"

"All men," answered Coombs a little sheepishly.

"Do you understand why we are in China, lad?"

Coombs licked his lips nervously. "Yes, sir . . . to spread the gospel."

"That is correct," said the doctor. "And is it not, as you said, a gospel of love and peace?"

Coombs nodded.

"Would our Lord have raised His hand against His oppressors?"

Coombs shook his head.

"Did He not say, 'Love your enemies,' and 'Resist not evil: but whosoever shall smite thee on thy right cheek, turn to him the other also'?"

"Yes, sir," answered Coombs humbly, then added in one last lame attempt at self-defense, "But they gave us no chance—there were *five* of them!"

"There were hundreds who came out against our Lord, Thomas. Do you remember His trial, how He refused to speak a word in His own behalf? Do you remember what He said when Peter drew his sword and tried to defend Him? He would have no earthly defense, no defense that went counter to the gospel of love and peace. He refused to physically defend himself, to the very point of death. And He is our example."

Wallace set down his teacup and stood, then walked slowly and deliberately to a window where he gazed out for some time before speaking again. Robbie found himself wondering if he was deliberating on what punishment to mete out to this errant pupil. But when he turned back to the two other men, he wore not the look of an executioner but rather that of a father, a tender look, but also very sad.

"Dear Thomas," he said, "did you think your Lord was powerless to protect you even against five enemies? Yes, you taught some hoodlums a lesson. But to whose name did you bring glory—to your Lord's, who himself was led as a lamb to the slaughter? Had you once remembered to call upon His name, what a mighty work He might have done!"

Coombs bowed his head contritely. "I never prayed even once, sir. I am sorry."

Robbie had listened to the progression of the conversation in silence. But at last he could take no more. How wrong it seemed that Coombs should be made to feel ashamed of his actions! By now Robbie was growing so heated inside that he scarcely noticed the comforting hand Wallace laid on the younger man's shoulder. And what did it matter if the anticipated punishment did not fall as Robbie had expected? It was enough that poor young Coombs was being made to feel like a villain simply for defending himself, and defending Robbie too, for that matter.

"Listen here, Dr. Wallace," Robbie finally said boldly, "you're being unfair to Coombs. What did you expect him to do, act the part of a coward and leave me to battle those thugs alone?"

Wallace turned toward Robbie as if only just noticing him. "There are many ways for a man to exhibit his courage, Mr. Taggart."

"Well, sitting and praying while another man is beaten to a pulp doesn't sound like one of them to me," rejoined Robbie sarcastically.

Wallace raised an eyebrow and might have been about speak, but it was Coombs who replied instead.

"Mr. Taggart," he said, "God could have interceded for *both* of us if only I would have given Him the chance, if only I would have asked."

"And now you feel ashamed for acting like a man!" said Robbie, shaking his head in frustration. "I don't understand you people!"

"No, I don't suppose you do, Mr. Taggart," said Wallace without rebuke, yet with an intensity Robbie found extremely uncomfortable. "To truly act like a man, as you put it, means to act like the world's only *true* man would have acted. And that is with compassion, especially toward those who would do us harm."

"That's just it! You turn everything around with all your religious jargon and make it into nonsense! There is no way I could understand you!"

"The Apostle Paul makes it clear that without a heart open to the things of the Spirit, there can be no understanding. Jesus himself talked about the mystery of the kingdom of God being hidden from those who did not choose to understand. You see, Mr. Taggart, it is not our words or our attitudes toward things that are in themselves difficult for you to understand. The understanding comes by choice, by opening your heart and mind toward God and the ways of God. Anyone who *wants* to understand and *seeks* God's wisdom, *will* understand. God promises enlightenment to those who seek Him."

"And so, because I don't understand, I do not have a heart open to God; is that what you're saying?"

"Only you can answer that, Mr. Taggart. Only you know how open your heart is."

"But it's clear enough what *you* think! You've considered me an outsider since the day I came, trying to preach your doctrines at me—both of you! Well I *don't* understand, and I don't think I ever will!"

Robbie stood, and with a finality in his voice which came from the decision that he found himself making only at that very moment, said, "I don't belong here. That is clear. I don't know why I waited so long. I think it is best I leave before my welcome wears out completely."

"I would hope you might reconsider, Mr. Taggart," said Wallace. "You are almost part of the family by now."

"No, I have to go. I must find a ship and get my life back where it belongs, on the sea. I will leave tonight."

"I would not do that. Don't make a hasty decision. What we have said here in no way should make you feel we think any the less of you."

"I thank you for your kindness, but I think it is for the best."

"It would be well for you to wait until morning—the roads may not be safe to travel at night."

"I appreciate your concern," Robbie replied, "but I can take care of myself. Goodbye to both of you. I hope it goes well for you."

They shook hands, rather stiffly on Robbie's part; then he left the room. Once outside he lingered a moment in the open yard. He had no belongings to pack. He was free to go at once.

Yet he hesitated. And he knew very well the reason.

He did not want to leave without saying goodbye to Hsi-chen. Yet it would be awkward to seek her out. He'd probably in the end have to go back inside and ask Wallace where to find her, and that he could not do. The whole thing would just be too awkward.

He wandered indecisively toward the camphor tree where they had spent so much time, then ran his hand along the trunk, as if that might somehow symbolize the farewell he could not verbalize.

She came up quietly behind him, but her unexpected presence did not startle him, perhaps because he had hoped she would miraculously appear out of his thoughts, which were centered on her.

"My father says you are leaving," she said quietly.

"Yes. It's time I move on." *How much does she know about what happened with Coombs, and the fight?* he wondered. Well, it didn't matter. He would have had to leave the mission sooner or later anyway.

"I want to give you something," she said. "Would you please wait a moment?"

"You don't have to do that."

"Please . . . only a moment."

He nodded in consent.

She left as quietly as she had come, and was gone about ten minutes. This time he watched her as she returned. Even at a distance she was lovely, her fragile figure framed in the soft moonlight, her sensitive face glowing as if it were the source of the light reflected around her. Something inside him ached at the thought of never seeing her again. But he quickly told himself that, yes, she was pretty, and yes, there had grown to be a certain bond between them. But there were many pretty girls the world over, and it would not do to become attached to one so different from him. It had not worked with Jamie. It would not work with Hsi-chen. But even as the thought surfaced in his consciousness, he knew, if vaguely, that the differences troubling him were not the obvious ones of race, but rather the ones related to her faith, the faith of her father, the faith—as much as he had always thought of himself as a "good and God-fearing man"—he could not understand.

"I'm sorry it took me so long," she said when she reached him. "But I thought you might need some provisions for your journey." She held out a rucksack, which he took with thanks.

"But I wanted you to have something else," she went on, "something so that you would remember us here at the mission."

"I doubt that I will soon forget—any of you."

"Take this small gift anyway. I want you to have it." She held out a small black New Testament. "It is not an expensive book. But I hope you will find pleasure in it. And meaning, too. And I hope with it you can remember the friendship you had with a humble Chinese girl in Wukiang."

"Thank you, Hsi-chen," Robbie said, not without obvious emotion in his voice. He took the book and stared at it silently for some time before he could speak. "I won't forget you, Hsi-chen; your friendship is something I will carry with me wherever I go."

"Neither will I forget you, Robbie Taggart. But I will remember you not only as Moses, as my father first named you, but also as *Feng-huang*, the Phoenix."

"Why is that?"

"Because it is a special bird in my culture, endowed with all that is noble and lovely, powerful and mysterious. Like the phoenix, you have touched our lives, Robbie Taggart, in a special way. I do not think it will be very much the same here after you have flown away."

"Sure it will," said Robbie lightly, mastering his own sadness. "And who's to say the phoenix would not return?"

"I think not, Feng-huang," she answered. "You must always be moving on—it is who you are, I think. The wind sweeps you from a place you have enjoyed, but it carries you to new, perhaps more wonderful places. You are sad, but you are happy too. You are, I think, what they call in your culture a rover. Maybe someday the time may come when to go away will bring more sadness than you can bear, and it will bring you no more joy to wander. But I do not think that day is yet. I pray that time will only come to you when the joy in staying surpasses any other joys you have known along the way."

When she had finished they stood silently. There was suddenly so much Robbie wished he could say to her. But he realized the time had passed for all that. He was leaving. The decision had been made. And no matter how much bravado he tried to present, he would not be coming back. He did not fit in here. And as much as it made him ache inside to think he would never see Hsi-chen again, he knew he did not fit with her, either.

Joy and sadness—he had known the conflicting emotions all his life. But even he did not realize in this moment that the sadness indeed was outweighing the anticipated happiness of being footloose again and free. It was becoming harder and harder to "move on," to say his goodbyes.

"I must be going," he said at length. "I only wish I had a gift for you."

"*You* have been a gift . . . and I will cherish that as long as I live. Tsai chien, goodbye, Feng-huang."

"I never say final goodbyes," said Robbie, taking her hand and kissing it lightly. "There is a saying in my country that I prefer, 'Happy to meet, sorry to part; happy to meet again!'"

He slung the strap of the rucksack over his shoulder, turned, and walked swiftly away. But before he had gone ten steps, Hsi-chen called out to him,

"God be with you, Robbie!"

He continued walking turning only briefly back with a smile and a wave. He tried to say something in return, but to speak now would be dangerous, for there were tears in his eyes and a strange tugging at his throat. An unfamiliar heaviness tugged at his heart and legs, but he kept walking. *Soon I will light upon a new place*, he told himself. *I'll forget all about Wukiang and what I am leaving behind there*—or so he tried to tell himself many times before he reached the bridge over the K'uan-chiang.

42

The Lieutenant and the Warlord

Pien Yi-tuo sat on his horse proudly as he hurried through the city streets. He enjoyed the feeling of prestige and distinction of being able to look down on the dirty peasants that crowded about him. He relished being in a position to sneer at the coolies who broke their backs in service to the foreign devils. Pien served a worthy master, a great man from an old and honorable Shanghai family. Well, perhaps it was not such an honorable family, but it was old. And who needed honor when you had wealth and power?

At least Pien's master was able to recognize a talented servant, and rewarded him accordingly. There were few others in his master's private little domain who rode such a fine horse or were given such high responsibility. Pien was proud of his position of service to the master.

Suddenly a cart crossing the road in front of him jerked to a stop. The old man pulling the cart had stumbled and fallen, and might well have been run over by the continued motion of his own cart had not the press of people impaired it. He was a slight man, probably in his late sixties, and hardly seemed able to the task of managing such a heavy vehicle.

Pien's horse reared, and except for the fact that his horsemanship matched the quality of his mount, he would no doubt have been thrown into the street himself.

"Get out of the road, you imbecile!" shouted Pien.

"I will try, honorable sir," said the old man as he struggled back to his feet.

"My horse was nearly injured!"

"Your humble servant is most sorry, sir." The old man grabbed the cart handles and limped away, favoring his right leg where a large bruise was already beginning to form.

"Bah!" growled Pien, urging his horse forward again. "Worthless coolie!"

He soon turned down a narrow side street. The crowd immediately thinned and the loud din of voices quieted. Pien, however, would have preferred to remain on the noisy main thoroughfare. Here there were not as many to be impressed with his equipage and to send up looks of fearful envy to him from the street. But more than that, he got all the quiet he needed in his master's quarters in the hilly country in the outlands. It was not often they came to Shanghai during the summer.

Within five minutes Pien had reached his destination. He reigned his mount to a stop before an ornate iron gate. He struck the small gong by the gate for the attendant—it was locked from the inside as a necessary precaution. Within moments an elderly Chinese man shuffled forward and peered out through the bars.

"Open up you buffoon!" barked Pien. "Or is your eyesight so bad you cannot even recognize your master's lieutenant?"

"A thousand pardons, Master Pien!" replied the old man, in a tone not nearly as subservient as he would have reserved for the master himself.

The man unlatched the gate, opening it while bowing decorously. Pien dismounted and, handing the reins to the servant, stepped brusquely past him into a small garden no less lovely because Pien stalked through it as if it were a grimy battlefield. Dwarf cherry trees lined a gravel path that led to the main building of the house, itself much larger as one drew near than it appeared from the tiny gate in the wall that surrounded garden and house alike. He opened the front door and was immediately greeted by another servant, whom he told to inform his master that he had arrived.

After another brief pause, this second servant returned to usher Pien through a small maze of corridors, and finally through a bamboo curtain into an elaborately furnished and darkened room. Pien nodded his head in approval of this finely appointed city-dwelling which he had not seen until now, especially in contrast with the more rustic one in the country. But then one could easily become soft and flabby if one languished too long in such finery, and that would never do for him—or for his master. Ancient porcelain, silk, and velvet were acceptable for a few days, but not to grow accustomed to.

Pien made his way with great reserve and dignity up the center of the tiled floor toward an enclosure that was separated from the rest of the room with a beaded partition, almost as if it were the throne room of a grand palace—indeed, not an altogether inappropriate comparison.

The servant leading him parted the beads, and Pien stepped into the enclosure, bowing deeply even as the servant departed.

"My lord," he said, with respect as deep as his bow.

"Pien Yi-tuo," said a man seated on a plush divan against the far wall of the enclosure, "I have grown weary waiting for your return." The man shifted in his seat and reached toward a bowl of fruit that sat on a low table before him. Even beneath the heavily embroidered silk robe he wore, his imposing muscular bulk was clearly evident.

"The delay was unavoidable, my lord," replied Pien. "I beg your forgiveness if I have caused you undue grief, Master Wang."

Wang K'ung-wu nodded his head and chortled deep within his fleshy throat. It was the kind of laugh that could have been taken a thousand ways—to an enemy it would have struck fear, to a friend benevolence, if such a man as Wang had any true friends. To Pien it signified a bit of both, but to Wang himself it simply meant that this servant was becoming a little too vaunted with his own importance to think, much less say, that his absence could cause anything even close to grief. It was not healthy—either to the master *or* the servant—to have a lieutenant who became too confident of his own importance.

Wang rubbed his manchu beard, which partially hid a deep scar that ran along the right side of his face, and wondered if the time had not come to bring Pien Yi-tuo down a few pegs. But first to the business at hand.

"I sent you to gather a report on the situation in Wukiang many days ago," said Wang. "Perhaps you lost your way, or found other interests besides the doing of my bidding."

"Oh no, my lord," replied Pien with due humility. "I felt it prudent to tarry until I had a complete report for you."

Wang snorted his doubt of the veracity of his lieutenant's excuse. Then plucking a peach from the bowl, he brought it to his long crooked nose, sniffing the ripe fruit like a true connoisseur.

"So . . . what is this report you bring?" Wang's tone made it clear that it had better be to the master's liking.

"All things were arranged as you ordered," said Pien. "Your men remained only on the outskirts, using eyes and ears rather than any show of force. But—"

Pien stopped short and took a sharp breath, for as he spoke the last word Wang cocked an eyebrow toward his underling. It was a glance that spoke volumes without need of words. *I accept no lame excuses*, said the large man's eyes. *What you say next is at your own peril.*

Pien took up his tale again, in a voice noticeably more strained. "The missionary did a most unexpected thing."

"What do you mean?" bellowed Wang.

"From what we had learned of the man," continued Pien, "he is an independent sort, calling upon the courts on behalf of his converts only in extreme cases, and *never* calling in the assistance of his own country. It was logical to assume—"

"Assume! Why, you idiot! Never *assume* anything. Have I taught you nothing? Now go on with your cursed tale!"

Pien cleared his throat, making a thin, high-pitched sound as he tried to gather his courage to continue. "The missionary confronted one of our men. We never imagined he would do such a thing."

"That is your problem—you have no imagination." Wang leaned forward with a menacing look in his eye. "Now come to the point—and quickly! Or I will cut out your tongue, for all the good it is to you."

Pien shrank back visibly, and would probably have fled had he not firmly believed a worse fate would await him for that.

"He told our man," answered the intimidated lieutenant, "that he had composed a letter to the British legate in Hangchow to the effect that the district of Christ's China Mission was being harangued by local bandits, and that the mission requested the peacekeeping presence of a Royal gunboat on the coast."

"Do not tell me you believed him!"

"*Your man,*"—Pien pointedly emphasized the words to hopefully remind his master that he was himself merely a humble message bearer—"felt the missionary was in dead earnest."

"What did the fool do?"

"He withdrew, my lord."

Wang cursed loudly, threatening and ordering every manner of instant death to the cowering idiot when he got his hands on him. Then, calming and stroking his beard as if for its soothing effect, he turned his attentions once more to the groveling coward before him.

"And the woman?"

"With my own eyes, I beheld a face I had not seen for thirteen years," replied Pien. "But no matter how many years pass, it is not a face a man would soon forget . . ."

Wang stirred portentously on the divan, and Pien hurried on, deciding his master was in no mood for flowery speeches. "It was indeed the face of the daughter of Tien Chih-lin!"

His final words fell not with the triumph with which he had hoped to deliver them, but instead rather timorously, as he unconsciously stepped back from his volatile master.

At the sound of that name, Wang's terrible presence faltered, and the peach he still held nearly slipped from his grasp. But his composure slackened only a moment. Immediately he regained the foreboding look of evil intent, which so accurately reflected his inner nature. Pien, preoccupied with his own possible peril, did not even notice his master's momentary lapse.

"Tien's daughter . . ." he said slowly, rubbing his beard. "Then the stories we heard *are* true! And you are certain?"

"Would I be so foolish to bring this report if I were other than certain? And how could I not be? I also was there thirteen years ago, and was she not the pearl of Shanghai in her youth? Is her family not in the council of the Empress dowager herself? A man does not so easily forget."

"What! Am I a spineless fool who pines away thirteen years after a woman?" cried Wang. "Is that what you insinuate, you worthless dog!"

"No, no, my lord," Pien said hastily. "I meant no such thing. Ha! Women are nothing—dirt beneath a man's foot. Especially a man such as yourself. I only said that such fairness is not soon forgotten by *any* man—especially one weak of mind like your servant."

"No," said Wang slowly, in as pensive a tone as Pien had ever heard from his lips, "a man does not forget."

"This is good news I bring, yes?" asked Pien, with an ingratiating grin showing a mouth only half full of teeth.

"You resurrect a ghost and call it *good*?" returned Wang grimly.

Pien's grin faded.

"But there is more," Pien went on with forced hopefulness in his voice. "I saw also the daughter of fair Shan-fei."

"Ah, yes, the daughter?" repeated Wang.

"Grown to a woman and even more beautiful than her mother. A woman whose loveliness surpasses anything I have laid eyes on."

"Why do you tell me this?"

"You are a man. Is it not a thing you would want to know?"

Wang turned the peach over slowly and deliberately in his hand. Then he raised it to his lips and took a thoughtful bite into its soft, juicy flesh. The lovely Shan-fei, whom he had lost, not once but twice, had a daughter even more beautiful than she. It was only fitting—divine providence no doubt—that since he had been denied the mother in her youth, he ought to have the mother's seed while it was yet merely a bud.

But this was more than mere providence. It was divine justice! He deserved Shan-fei's daughter!

Wang leaned back in the divan, fingering the end of his beard as these thoughts tumbled through his mind.

He remembered the first time he had seen Shan-fei. They were young then. Of course it was unseemly to look upon a potential bridal candidate, but he hadn't cared. His own family was not without a certain amount of power as well—not the same kind as Tien's, but power gave a man privileges even among an old and venerable family like the Tien's. Yet his father's marriage offer was turned down, and that lovely jewel married another—one beneath her station, Wang had always thought. Before the refusal Wang had boasted to his friends of his good fortune. And when he found himself rejected, the loss of face was a bitter pill to swallow. But that did not trouble him as much as losing Shan-fei herself. As much as a man like Wang was capable of, he had thought that he loved her.

Ten years later when she was suddenly widowed, she was just as beautiful, and Wang wanted her no less. He would never admit to having pined away for her during those years, though he had never married. There had of course been a steady retinue of concubines among his servants. But when he finally produced heirs to carry on his ancestral name, he wanted them to be of a worthy lineage—not children of servants and slaves, but from a family like Tien's.

In the ten years of her marriage, however, he had not exactly engaged in the sorts of enterprises that invited offers from the fine families of Shanghai. Nevertheless, he viewed Shan-fei's suddenly renewed freedom as a gift from heaven. And now the hard, proud Tien was gone to his grave. He would only have her in-laws, her dead husband's parents, to deal with. Surely they would not be stupid enough to reject him. Moreover, Shan-fei was a widow now, and one who had borne no sons to carry on her husband's life stream. She would have to accept a marriage beneath her former status, for she was not the young flower she had once been. Despite all this, Wang had to pay an exorbitant price for her—only to lose her once more. And on the eve of their wedding! To be spurned twice—the gall of the remembrance stung his memory like burning acid!

He would admit it to no man, but yes, the great Wang K'ung Wu had continued to rage inside for his lost love, though it was not but a smoldering fire. But whether he burned for love or revenge it would be hard to say. No doubt both. Yes he had loved her. But she had made him lose face twice, and the last was the most degrading of all.

All these years he had thought her dead, having committed suicide rather than marry him. Everyone thought she had done just that, she and her daughter. Though the bodies had never been found, the fact had been universally accepted.

But the rumor he had heard just two months ago had proved true! Pien's own eyes confirmed it.

She was alive! And by the gods, he would not lose her a *third* time!

"They remain there—at this *mission*?" he asked at length. The word *mission* was uttered with deep revulsion and hatred for any who would stand in his way. "They have not tried to escape?"

"No, my lord," answered Pien. "The men have been watchful and have seen no signs of such."

"That is supposed to appease me?" sneered Wang. "The incompetent clods!"

"I do not think the women will readily leave," added Pien. "The report is that she is married to the missionary."

"As long as the young girl is free . . ."

When Wang had first received news of the possibility that the daughter of the great Tien lived, he had entertained rash thoughts of sweeping through the village with his horde of bandits and carrying off both women. He had done no less on other occasions. But his rationality soon regained control of his instincts. One could not deal thus with subjects of the British crown. At least not without considering all the possible implications. He would rather find another way if possible. One had to use subtlety.

"My lord," said Pien, "I do not think it would be a difficult thing for you to take her. I doubt even this missionary would dare stand against your might."

Wang folded his thick arms and leaned back, his evil face softening slightly as he savored the anticipated pleasure of the granddaughter of the haughty Tien begging for his favors.

The room was silent a moment more; then Wang spoke again. "Is this the extent of your report?" he asked gruffly, wanting to have done with this simpleton now that he had more important matters to consider.

"There is . . . just one more thing, my lord," began Pien hesitantly.

"By all the gods!" yelled Wang, "you are a veritable fountain of gossip! What is it? Then be gone with you!"

"There are two visitors at the mission—"

"What do I care about that?"

"Perhaps they could be used to your advantage," Pien suggested.

"I am the one to decide that! Who are these cursed visitors?"

"British sailors, my lord—from the vessel, *Sea Tiger*."

"The *Sea Tiger*, you say?"

"Yes, my lord."

"Hmm," mused Wang, rubbing his beard again. The man was right; there were definite possibilities here. But inherent dangers also. It would require wisdom and cunning, and not a little shrewdly applied deceit— talents of which Wang had ample supply.

"Prepare my things for departure," he ordered Pien, then pondered a moment further. No, he would not go begging for this woman. But it was time he got himself closer to the fire, as it were. "And send that fool of a one-legged sea captain to me!" he added as an afterthought, at last dismissing Pien with a wave of his hand.

Pien backed out of the enclosure, bowing slightly and keeping his beady eyes fixed on the bulky man in front of him. His action came not so much out of trying to assume an attitude of respect, but because in his master's erratic mood, it would be most foolish to turn one's back on him.

43

The Sailor and the Monk

Robbie stretched and rubbed the sleep from his eyes.

He hadn't intended to sleep so soundly nor so long. But he had walked several hours that night, and when he paused on the roadside for a rest, still exhausted from the day's activities with Coombs, he had fallen into a deep sleep. Only the sunlight, combined with the early-morning clamor of farmers on their way out to their rice fields, finally woke him.

He judged he had walked eight or ten miles, and, from everything he had been able to gather about the lay of the land from his time at the mission, was generally confident that he was on the road toward Shanghai. Now that it was daylight and the possibility of seeking river travel presented itself, he began to think about looking out for a junk going his way. Yet his lack of money was a serious hindrance. And did he even know his final destination for certain? He was headed in the direction of Shanghai, the logical place to go to find a berth on some ship. But was that what he really wanted? *What else?* he asked himself. What else could a sailor like him hope to do? The very fact that he questioned it at all was absurd! Of course he had to find a ship! That was his life.

He sat down once more in the lee of the bamboo grove where he had spent the night and opened his rucksack in search of breakfast. But the first thing his eyes fell upon was Hsi-chen's New Testament.

Robbie sighed deeply. He had not been able to get her face or her hauntingly dear words out of his mind. She had even intruded upon his sleep, coming into his dreams as a ministering angel, as he had first perceived her that night in the hospital while he lay unconscious from his ordeal at sea. Many times as he had walked along that dusky road leading away from Wukiang, he had entertained the idea of returning to the mission. The thought of never seeing Hsi-chen again weighed like a millstone upon his heart.

The idea was ridiculous! How could he think he loved her? She was simply a sweet girl who had become his friend, and whose enchanting Oriental face had bewitched him in his sleep. She was like Jamie, who had become his friend. That was it, of course! He could not be so foolish as to confuse friendship and love again. *Love* was something else. Love was . . .

He shook his head, trying to get such bewildering thoughts to leave him. It was not time to philosophize now. He had said his goodbyes, and that was that. He would forget soon enough. He might return someday, who could tell? But now he was off, and it felt good to be moving again, to have his feet under him, his destination unknown, his freedom secure! He was a traveler, after all, an adventurer, and this was the life for him!

He broke off a chunk of bread from the loaf Hsi-chen had packed and munched on it with an exaggerated vigor. With water from a nearby stream he washed down his breakfast, then resumed his journey.

He tried to muster up his enthusiasm for what new adventure lay in store for him by whistling a tune, but it was dry and stilted. A pall hung over his mood, which he could not shake. A bird winged overhead, and immediately the thought of the phoenix, *feng-huang*, returned to him. And with the thought came the bittersweet memory of Hsi-chen's gentle, lovely voice.

But suddenly a different connotation of the poem she had quoted flooded him. This was no noble creature who magically touched lives and left blessings scattered after it. Rather it was an animal that came to a place, took all it could from those who dwelled there, and then left them to their own "regrets" with no thought but for itself, no thought but for the satisfaction of its *own* needs, its *own* wants.

A parasite! That's what the phoenix was. Never giving, always taking, always in search of his own pleasure—giving no thought for the sadness he left in his wake.

Now a great regret seizes upon my mind—
If only I had my home in a different place!

But what could he do? He surely could not stay in a place just to make someone else happy! That would be no good for either of them. Anyway, Hsi-chen understood. She knew he must move.

Yet all at once Robbie was not sure *he* understood. He was always moving, leaving, going. But did his leaving the mission really have anything to do with his wandering spirit? That certainly made it easier to carry out when the time came. But was there something else? Yes—he had been uncomfortable there, out of place. Wallace's way of doing things was not only alien to Robbie, it was distasteful. There was only so much intolerance and self-righteous religiosity he could put up with, especially from a man like Wallace, who could talk easily about so-called loving behavior. He expected perfection from a youngster like Coombs, while he himself presented nothing but a harsh, domineering character to the world. Now that Wallace was on his mind, Robbie was glad he was out of that place!

He wondered just what Wallace would have done in the same situation he and Coombs had found themselves. He could talk about loving his enemies, but when had he ever done so?

As he thought about Wallace, Robbie forced himself to see only the negative. His worldly vision could probe no deeper than the mere surface, and had no capacity to perceive the spirit of man—Wallace's or his own. To have allowed himself to see more would have been to admit a serious flaw in the reasoning to which he had become accustomed. And it would have indicated an error in his decision to leave the mission.

Without realizing it on the conscious level, Robbie was confused. Something undeniably drew him to the mission. Was it merely the person of Hsi-chen? Yet something repelled him as well, just as strongly. Was that only the person of Wallace? How could he be both so drawn that he longed to turn around and go back, and yet afraid to do so?

Afraid. Was that really it? Then it *was* more than Wallace himself pushing him away! When had he felt this way before?

With the question, Robbie's mind suddenly filled with the stinging memory of the face of the child in Calcutta. He would never be able to forget those huge eyes that pierced his very soul! He had been oddly afraid of her also, and when the guardian had urged him to visit the orphanage, he had resisted—perhaps too strongly. What was it that had frightened him then?

This was no good, he told himself! He had to get rid of the plague of such self-defeating thoughts. He had to inject some realism into this introspective mood, and despite what the Vicar said as they struggled near death in the China Sea, he *didn't* want to get used to that particular emotion. *'Tis best to forget this line of thinking altogether!*

His strides gradually became long and quicker. If he could do it no other way, he would physically beat these ideas from his mind. Suddenly his resolve to get to Shanghai became all the more intensified. What he needed was to get aboard a ship! A place where he belonged, a place he understood, with men who spoke his language, liked what he liked, laughed at what he laughed at! And this time there would be no Pike or Vicar to muddle things up. It would be grand—just like the old days!

It hardly took thirty minutes at his rapid pace, in the pervading heat of the late morning, before Robbie was nearly exhausted. Still he pushed himself, mile after mile—always thinking how far he was now from the mission, never thinking how close he might be to Shanghai. Once or twice he paused for a rest, but each time his stop was brief because of the unwanted thoughts that continually tried to push themselves into his brain.

By late afternoon he could go no farther. His legs ached, and his head throbbed from the constant, unrelenting sun. Wearily he pushed on to the next village, which was about a half a mile distant, hoping there might somehow provide a respite in his journey.

It was very much like Wukiang, though perhaps a bit larger. If only he could find a roadside inn to stay in for the night! In his fatigued brain he did not find himself troubled by his financial straits nearly so much as by his inability to communicate. If he could just make himself understood, he reasoned, there would be some way he'd be able to wrangle a meal and a bed.

As the narrow road widened toward the center of the village, Robbie tried to stop several passers-by, but none understood a word of English. The women looked frightened of him and hastened away without even pausing to listen. In all his travels, he had never been so far from a port of call. He had thus never before experienced the feeling of being utterly alone, completely stranded and helpless in an altogether foreign place. The feeling was now strong, and not altogether comforting. He was isolated, utterly alone. He wondered how Elliot had made it.

Robbie hailed a man pushing a vegetable cart.

"I am looking for a place to stay," he said, gesturing with every manner of hand and facial motion to embellish his words and hopefully give them meaning.

The farmer gave him a suspicious, not altogether friendly look, mumbled something unintelligible in Chinese and hurried on.

Every person Robbie tried offered a similar response. Even if this little place had something resembling an inn, which he had not seen, it would do him little good if he wasn't able to communicate some kind of barter for a room. Money, he had learned long ago, was the universal language. But he had none of it to flash around to encourage a more willing response.

With every step Robbie's legs grew weaker. He had covered more than thirty-five miles in the last twenty hours, and the strain was now taking its toll, even on one as strong as Robbie Taggart. He had all but resigned himself to another night alongside the road, but at this point even the steps required to get out of the village and to some deserted spot seemed more than he wanted to think of.

At last he reached the outskirts of town. In the distance, and off the path fifty or so yards, he spied a long flight of steps leading up a slight hill to a temple of some kind at the top. It wouldn't hurt to rest there a moment before he continued on his way.

Robbie turned off the road, took the path to the right, and climbed the steps part of the way to a point where they were shaded by the walls of the temple. There he sank down with a grateful sigh. It was hardly a surprise that he began to doze off. Twice he jerked himself awake, but each time it proved more difficult to rouse himself, and at length sleep completely won control.

He did not waken again until night had fallen. Some three hours had passed. Suddenly he jerked up with a start. Two men stood hovering over him; one had a hand near his rucksack. In the bewilderment of a sleep-excited brain, Robbie jerked it away and tried to stand.

"Get out of here, you thieves!" he yelled, despite the fact that they couldn't understand him. "You've come to the wrong man for that!"

Robbie's form had been imposing enough asleep on the temple steps. But awake it was far more than the two thieves wanted to tangle with in a fight. They turned on their heels and fled down the steps. Robbie rubbed his hands through his hair and shook the remainder of sleep from his brain; he was about to get up and continue his journey when a voice from above stopped him.

"If you would like a proper rest, hsien-sheng, sir," said a man standing near the temple door, "you may enter this humble dwelling."

"You speak English!" exclaimed Robbie with wonder as he spun around, almost as if he had encountered some magical being.

"Only very poorly, I am afraid," returned the man. He bowed deeply, and Robbie could see atop his shaven head rows of scars, from some ordination rite he supposed. It was apparent, from this and from his dark flowing robes, that this must be a temple priest. "Come," he added in a welcoming but subdued tone.

Robbie hesitated. A temple, even a pagan one, was not exactly the sort of place where he would have chosen to spend the night. But the thought of a bed away from the elements, perhaps a bite or two of food, and the possibility of someone to aid him in this foreign land—it was all too much to pass up.

Therefore he followed the man up the remainder of the temple steps and through the massive door, actually but a gate in the high wall surrounding the buildings. They passed through a large courtyard, which was the focal point of the temple complex, around which were situated the several smaller buildings comprising the whole. Even in the dark shadows of evening, Robbie could tell that the courtyard was lovely and peaceful and well groomed by the sweet fragrance of cherry and lotus blossoms carried on a gentle breeze that rustled the leaves of several dwarfed, well-sculpted trees. He was led to the left of the courtyard, down an open corridor that skirted the garden, and finally to a room no larger than a sitting room. Sparsely furnished, it had only a long low table in its center. There was not even a rug or mat on the hard, stone floor.

"I will bring you something to eat," said the priest, and before Robbie could protest or offer a word of thanks, the priest disappeared behind a curtained doorway.

Robbie walked idly around the room while he waited, although there was little to arrest his attention. In a few minutes the man returned carrying a tray that he set on the table, motioning for Robbie to sit. The floor was hard and cold, but Robbie had eaten meals under worse circumstances. He lowered himself to the table, where he had some difficulty arranging his long legs before he could turn his attention to the meal, which consisted of rice, dried fruit, bread, and tea.

"We live very simply here," the priest explained. "And, of course, we are vegetarians."

"This is wonderful," replied Robbie enthusiastically. "I am most grateful. I have no money, and don't know how long my provisions would have lasted. I am more than willing to work in return for your hospitality."

"The aim of hospitality is not the seeking of payment," replied his host. "Now eat, and if you would like, we can talk. My name is Hui K'o. I am a humble priest of Buddha."

"And I am Robbie Taggart, British sailor."

"You are very far from the sea."

Robbie launched into a brief account of how he came to be in inland China.

"So, you come from the mission at Wukiang," said Hui K'o thought-fully.

"You've heard of it?"

"I have had some dealings with them."

"I'm surprised. I would have thought it was much farther away than that. I've been traveling hard since last night."

"You were on foot?" asked the priest.

Robbie nodded.

"That explains it. By water your journey would have taken less than half a day, with the right winds and currents. In the morning I can direct you to a boat for your return trip."

"Oh, I'm not going back." The words were spoken quickly, defen-sively, and Robbie regretted them immediately. "That is, I'm bound for Shanghai," he added.

"You have come out of your way for Shanghai," said Hui K'o in a simple voice that seemed to hold deeper meaning than was apparent on the surface.

The priest poured tea into two porcelain cups, then, setting down the teapot, folded his hands together and thoughtfully tapped his lips. At length he spoke. "You were not happy at the mission?"

From anyone else the question would have seemed out of place, even impertinent. But it was only fitting that this Chinese sage, not one to be satisfied with trivial small talk, should thrust directly to the heart of a conversation. It did not escape Robbie's attention that this priest of Buddha was not unlike the austere missionary doctor in this respect.

"It has nothing to do with happiness," answered Robbie. "I simply didn't fit in there. I'm a sailor and they were missionaries. I guess that's all there was to it."

"And sailors do not need spiritual things?"

"Maybe they do. I don't know. Let's just say I didn't get along with this particular missionary."

"Ah, yes," said Hui K'o. "I had occasion to meet the Doctor Wallace some time ago."

"Oh?"

"I had a young pupil who became ill. He was near death when I finally knew my own skill would not avail him. So in desperation I sought the doctor's assistance."

Hui K'o paused for a brief moment, as if the conjuring of the memory had taken him somewhat by surprise. Then he went on.

"The doctor sat with the boy for two days, using his medical skill and his prayer, and in two days the boy was not only on the way to recovery, but he had also espoused the doctor's Christianity."

"He took away your student?"

"It is so, and I admit it with humility." The priest bowed his scarred head a moment. "When the doctor was about to leave here," he went on, "I thanked him for coming to my aid and for helping the boy, for I cared about the child deeply no matter that he rejected my teachings. The doctor looked upon me in a manner I will not soon forget."

Robbie nodded that he was fully acquainted with that look of Wallace's eyes.

"He said to me," Hui K'o continued, "he said I was amiss in thanking him, when I should have known well that it was not his own skills but those of the Almighty God that had given life back to my pupil. He said that I should be giving thanks to the Lord God instead, and turning my heart over to Him, as had the young man, Ying."

"Ying Nien?" interrupted Robbie.

"Yes," answered Hui K'o. "The doctor said to me, 'Your pupil has ended his search for perfection in Him who alone is perfect. Is the pupil wiser than the teacher?' I answered that I had been a seeker all my life, and bore the scars of my search—"

Here Hui K'o raised his arms as he must have done with Wallace, and as his wide sleeves fell away, Robbie saw scars in various shapes branded into each of his forearms. In the same action he also bowed his disfigured head.

"But it is not easy to give up a quest on which you have spent your life," he continued. "Should I forsake my journey to Nirvana even in light of the Christian God, who heals and claims the hearts of Buddha's pupils? He said to me, 'Has the *seeking* after enlightenment become more important than the enlightenment itself?'" Hui K'o sighed. "It is so, perhaps. The man is wiser than many of my religion would give him credit for being."

"It hardly seems appropriate for him to come here, take your student, and then preach at you like that. He can be so unreasonable!"

"I did not see him as unreasonable," said the priest. "I have taken the

Bodhisattva's vow, and by it have sworn to forego entering Nirvana until every other being has come to the place of realizing it for himself. The unity of humankind is important in my religion. I think it is similar for Dr. Wallace, so in his mind he is being expedient rather than unreasonable."

"Well, I question if he's going about it in the right way," parried Robbie.

"What is the right way? For every person the methods will vary. But as it is essentially his mission, he has to proceed in his own manner, whether it would perhaps be different than what you or I might do. But you seem hostile to the mission," added Hui K'o. "I have seldom seen even the Chinese react so."

"It's not hostility so much as—" Robbie stopped, searching for an answer he knew would not be there. "Well, I don't know. Wallace's methods just don't appeal to me."

"You make me think of two great potters, Chia-tao and Shang-yin, who set out each to create a gift for the Emperor. Now when Chia-tao removed his bowl from the kiln, it was lopsided and spoiled. In a fit of rage, the great artist kicked at the oven, cursing it as the cause of his failure. But his friend who was nearby said, 'But the kiln has never spoiled your work before.' Then Chia-tao struck out at his wheel, blaming it for the imperfections of his work. His friend said again, 'That wheel is the finest in the land, my friend, and with it you have made a name for yourself as a renowned potter!' Then Chia-tao cursed the inferior quality of his clay. At that his friend merely sat and silently shook his head.

"Shang-yin also made his bowl, and it too came from the oven flawed. But he displayed the true greatness of his spirit, which in the end made of him a better potter than Chia-tao, by sitting down to study his bowl. For long hours he meditated on the imperfections that had shown themselves in his first attempt, turning it every way so that he could see all that he had neglected to take into account before. At length, when he was ready to begin again, he set a new lump of clay on the wheel. And this time when the bowl was completed, it was perfect, and delighted the Emperor.

"It is a wise man, my young sailing friend, who contemplates failures and imperfections and flaws, and looks for the cause within himself rather than trying to pass blame elsewhere. For looking inside oneself is the beginning of the road to wisdom."

Robbie remained silent at the conclusion of Hui K'o's parable. The words had perhaps struck even more deeply than the priest intended.

From the moment he had set foot in the mission, he had been laying the blame for his turmoil on them—their intolerance, their fanaticism, their unreasonableness. Before fate had landed him at the mission he had laid blame on Pike, the Vicar, and old Barclay.

Now he wondered—were all these people and circumstances present in his life in order to point out some weakness, some flaw within himself? Had he always run away in order to avoid seeing what he was supposed to see?

What about the times recently when hints, and sometimes more than hints, of fear had come over him? What had kept him from going with the child and the lady in Calcutta? And when he had been struggling for life in the water, what frightened him most of all had been the fear itself. And that very morning when the thought of returning to the mission had come to him, had he truly been *afraid*? It was unthinkable!

His fears had always been vague and undefined. Had he all along been afraid—like the potter Chia-tao—of having to face up to his own weaknesses, or even admitting he had them? Yet how should that surprise him? To admit weakness, one had also to admit helplessness. And what man wanted to do that?

Weak . . . helpless—could that really be the person he was? *Men* were strong! *Men* could take care of themselves! *Men* were not religious weaklings propped up on all sides by crutches of dogma!

Yet . . . yet he could no longer deny that he *had* indeed known fear, he *had* known the isolation of being alone, he *had* known the emptiness that he had always denied to Jamie. He bowed his head, rubbing his face with his hands.

"I sense, Robbie Taggart, that you also are a seeker," said the priest.

"I've always been pretty content," said Robbie in automatic response. He did not feel compelled to add that recently just the opposite had been the case.

"That is indeed a sad thing," answered Hui K'o to Robbie's surprise. "Only those who seek have hope of finding enlightenment. Those who seek nothing . . . find nothing in the end."

44

Man of Faith

Robbie had never run away from a fight before in his life. He had always stood up to his foes.

Of course, his foes had always been easily identifiable. Now it seemed the enemies were inside his own self.

How could he run from these? And if he did so, how would he be any better than the Vicar, forever running, never facing up to himself?

Such were the thoughts that had plagued his mind in the simple monk's chamber where he had passed the night. It was morning now, and he must decide what to do.

But he already knew the answer.

It was as clear as Hui K'o's story about the two potters. He had to confront these gnawing fears, and he knew instinctively that he must do so at the mission. There he must do battle. The fight might be with himself, or it might be with Wallace. That hardly mattered. He had to face those fears that had forced him from the mission—face them like a man.

If Hui K'o was disappointed at losing another potential convert to the mission, he did not show it. He gladly arranged a river conveyance for Robbie and bade him a fond farewell. Perhaps he sensed that what this young man was looking for would not be found in a Buddhist temple. Perhaps, too, he was recalling the expression of joy and contentment in young Ying Nien's face as he left the temple to join the mission. Such joy was not often found in this world of sorrows. So how could he, a seeker after enlightenment, stand against him?

Robbie's return trip to the mission proved not nearly so arduous as had been his departure. Though the river voyage took longer than the half day the priest had predicted, and required another night on the water due to their afternoon start, Robbie arrived the next day several hours before sunset. He left the junk a mile or two north of Wukiang. He had had the entire boat trip to reason out his actions and intentions, but now that he had actually arrived, he was suddenly unsure of himself all over again.

Perhaps this had been a foolish notion after all. He was no philosopher like the priest Hui K'o, content to spend his energies searching the mysteries of life. He had always been a doer, not a thinker. He did not relish the idea of having to battle with inner conflicts. Searching heart and soul was something he had always left to people like Jamie, the Vicar, Wallace. And he especially did not relish a battle of wills and emotions and ideas with Wallace. He could never match wits with the intense, fanatical missionary.

He could not deny that the thought of seeing Hsi-chen again quickened his pace. Yet the dread of having to confront her father overpowered even that. Perhaps what he dreaded most was that unrelenting gaze, with a righteous finger pointed out in front of it, and his penetrating voice shouting, "I was right about you, sinner that you are! The time has come for you to repent!"

But was he merely *hoping* Wallace would react in such a manner in order to give him further fuel for his own indignation? When had he actually *seen* the doctor treat anyone so? Vaguely he recalled the man's reaction to his errant young disciple. He could have been vindictive and self-righteous. But that had not been his response. He *had* been unyielding. But there had been something else in his demeanor at the moment too, something Robbie had not allowed himself to see until now—almost a kind of tenderness toward the young man!

Robbie walked along the dirt road, casting a gaze out toward the rice fields that lay to his left and right. He absently observed the workers until his attention was suddenly arrested by the activities in a particular field just ahead of him. On first glance the workers appeared no different than any of the other Chinese villagers. Each wore a wide, round straw hat to keep off the beating sun. But all at once Robbie realized that one of the two workers he was looking at was none other than Isaiah Wallace himself. The doctor's pant legs were rolled up to his knees as he waded ankle-deep in the muddy field. From the back, he was hardly distinguishable from the Chinese, except for his height, and he was wielding the hoe like an expert.

The scene was enough to give Robbie a severe jolt. He had certainly never before pictured Wallace as the type to sweat for hours in a hot rice field. Though now he recalled noting the doctor's calloused hands on the first occasion they had met. But Robbie was equally taken aback when he at last realized that the second man in the field was the same who had accosted Wallace after the church service.

How could it be—the two men working side by side together? Such a short time ago the Chinese villager had been filled with such hate and threats against the mission, and even now his face appeared etched with hard lines that came from more than his present toil. Was he accepting the help of this "wai-chu" in his field out of necessity, but despising himself for having to stoop so low? What had transpired, wondered Robbie, to have forced this unlikely pair together in common cause in this muddy rice field?

As Robbie continued on, he could not avoid approaching the spot where the two were hard at work. As he drew alongside the man's field, Wallace paused in his work to remove a handkerchief from his pocket and blot it across his sweaty brow. Glancing around at nothing in particular as he did, he saw Robbie walking toward them on the path.

Immediately his lips turned up in a smile, almost as if he had been expecting to see him on the road at that very moment. Yet along with it came a brightening of his face that Robbie could take no other way than as the cheerful and heartfelt greeting Wallace intended.

Robbie waved a hand in reply—unable for the moment to conjure up a return smile. If he'd had the chance, he probably would have run for cover in order to avoid the awkward interview he had been dreading. But instead, he walked to the boundary of the field, a small irrigation ditch, and there paused, silent, not knowing what to say.

"Good afternoon, Mr. Taggart," said Wallace, approaching him with outstretched hand. "It is *good* to see you again!"

The words were spoken with such true sincerity that Robbie remained speechless. Wallace's words had always been sincere. That was one thing Robbie had never denied. But now all at once a new dimension had been added to his tone, which his previously blind eyes had failed to see, but which he could no longer avoid. There *was* a sincerity to the man that went deeper than his words. As much as Robbie had argued to the contrary before, here was a man standing before him who did more than merely talk about his faith. And how many other fields had he thus labored in? It was obvious he did not handle that hoe like a novice. How many other sick pupils of pagan religions did he travel a day to visit? How many other helpless sailors had he harbored beneath his roof? The man's actions did indeed back up his words.

"I hope—" Robbie began, but his voice was dry and he had to swallow before he could continue. "That is . . . I'm sorry to have left like I did. I was wrong." He hadn't intended to apologize. He had not even realized until the moment the words were out of his mouth that he had any need to apologize.

Wallace laid his tool in the dirt and walked over to Robbie. He placed a hand on Robbie's shoulder. "I must help Li," he said. "His father fell ill yesterday and he is alone to work his field. But I accept your words as I know you mean them. Though I want you to know that on my part you have no need to require my forgiveness. My heart has always been open to you. Go on to the mission, and we'll talk later if you wish. Your room is waiting for you, just as you left it."

Robbie nodded, and turned to go. He was unable to say anything further.

"Lad," added Wallace gently, "do not be afraid for having come back. Perfect love casts out all fear, and you have nothing to fear from any of us."

Robbie did not recoil at the words as he once might have. He hesitated, half turned toward Wallace and glanced at him momentarily, nodded again in acknowledgment of his words, then continued on toward the mission.

45

Questions and Answers

Robbie crossed the bridge and saw Hsi-chen sweeping the church steps in the distance. He paused, unnoticed, and watched her motions, as he had her father. How could he not have seen through into Wallace's true nature, just from beholding the kind of person *she* was? His eyes had been closed to so many things!

At last he continued on, almost involuntarily breaking into a run.

"Hsi-chen!" he called, and suddenly it seemed easy to smile.

Her head jerked up and turned toward him at the sound of his voice. Gladness quickly replaced the initial expression of surprise on her face. She dropped the broom from her hands and lightly descended the steps running to him. Before either realized what had happened he had lifted her light frame off the ground, planting a tender kiss on her forehead.

Suddenly they both seemed to come to themselves. She colored slightly.

Robbie set her down and stepped awkwardly back. Then without warning Hsi-chen broke into a musical laugh.

"Robbie Taggart!" she said. "I have prayed for you, but I did not think my prayers would be answered with your return!"

"You can never tell about Feng-huang!" he said, laughing now himself. But quickly he sobered. He knew he could not leave the explanation for his return at that. "I had to come back," he said, his own blue eyes now filling with intensity. "I left because I was running away, and I finally realized I could not do that and continue to respect myself. There's a lot I need to explain."

"Only as you wish, Robbie," Hsi-chen replied. "Come, we can walk and talk, if you would like."

"Yes. I would like to do that more than anything."

As they walked along the stream in the quiet afternoon, Robbie began by telling her of his encounter with her father in the rice field a short time earlier. "I could hardly believe what I saw," he said, "and yet at the same time it should have come as no surprise to me. But I still wonder what could have happened to bring two men, seemingly bitter enemies, together in that way."

"Bitter enemies, not really," answered Hsi-chen. "On Li's part, perhaps that has been true. But my father has long prayed earnestly for that man, and for an opportunity to serve him. Poor Li! He has had a difficult time lately. Several months ago his two oldest sons became Christians, here at the mission. Li blamed my father for tearing his family apart—his bitterness has been simmering since then. Last month both sons were drowned in a boating accident on the Yangtze, and this only intensified his hatred. Finally, the evening of your departure, Li's father became seriously ill. Even then it was a neighbor who sought my father, for Li himself would have let his own father die before his pride would have allowed him to come to the mission asking for help. My father did what he could for the old man, and old Li still lives, but he is past his good years and will soon die, I am afraid. The work was hard enough for Li with just his father to help, but left alone in the midst of transplanting the young rice, it was overwhelming. So yesterday morning my father took up his own hoe and went to Li's field. The poor man screamed and yelled to my father to get out. But my father climbed over the irrigation ditch and walked to the far end of the field and began to work. Li could do nothing to stop him short of striking him down. So he merely took up his labor on the opposite side."

"They were bound to meet eventually," observed Robbie, feeling not altogether unlike this Li fellow.

Hsi-chen smiled. "It was so. When they drew near to one another yesterday afternoon, no words were spoken, but at least Li allowed my father to continue to work in peace. Today they have been working side-by-side, though Li has still said nothing. My father is most anxious to be able to speak to him. Poor Li dreads it. He is in a most awkward position of seeing my father's compassion toward him, but being too proud to acknowledge it."

"Why did not the other villagers pitch in and give him a hand?"

"They are sorry for Li," replied Hsi-chen, "but he has alienated most of his neighbors, especially after the incident with Chang. Li was responsible for that whole attack, and even the handful of his companions had not intended for anyone to be hurt. Even the villagers who are opposed to the mission would never stoop to violence, and are in fact appalled by it."

They walked on in silence for some time. Then Robbie paused and turned to Hsi-chen. "I realized now that I've been wrong about many things," he said. "But I still don't know what to think of your father."

"What you think about my father is not so important, perhaps," she replied. "He is but a man and does what good he can. He makes mistakes like everyone, and will continue to do so. He is but a tool, and yet a tool greatly used by our Lord. I think it is not the tool, but the Master Builder upon whom you must base your understanding, Robbie. Do you know whom I mean?"

"I suppose I do," answered Robbie with a perplexed crease in his brow. "It has to come down to what I think of God himself, doesn't it?"

"Yes. It always comes down to that for all men and all women in the end. That is really the only question in life there is."

"Hsi-chen, I don't know what I think. I'm not sure I *want* to think anything. I'm not even certain I *can*. I've just never been the type to go in for . . . you know, for religion."

"With the religions of my people, it *is* perhaps a matter of religion. But Christianity is not a matter of religion. It is a life with a God who is personal and who is love. That's what is so different about the Christian way, Robbie Taggart. The man Jesus makes everything different, Robbie. Different and new."

Robbie kicked at the dirt. Again the confusion washed over him. And the questions! Why did God require him to make a choice? Wasn't it enough just to believe and let it go at that? He was no heathen. He was trying to live a decent life. Wasn't that good enough?

"God will show you the answer," said Hsi-chen quietly. "He is the God of peace, not confusion, He carries the answer to your frustrations in His heart."

Later that evening Robbie sat at the table for dinner with the mission "family." It was a different sort of dinner than any previous had been. Now Robbie sat among these people not as a fighter, or a rescued sailor, or a temporary worker at the compound. Instead, he was a seeker. No one had to say anything about the change. Yet something in the air told him everyone was aware of the difference—including him.

For the first time since the shipwreck and his seemingly accidental landing at this most unusual of places, his vision was clear. Now he saw each of these people in a new and different light. No longer did they appear to him as weaklings unable to face life, hiding behind their religion, cowering under the thumb of the authoritarian figure of Dr. Isaiah Wallace.

Coombs, for example, was no weakling. He had proven that the day of the fight. But he had *chosen* instead to serve a God of peace and love. He could have had dozens of other occupations, perhaps with more glory or riches. But he had *chosen* this life!

Prim and proper Miss Trumbull was not a stoic and unfeeling school-marm. Now he could see her as a courageous woman who had sacrificed her Victorian nature and whatever fineries might have been hers to enjoy in the drawing rooms of England to serve her God in a backward foreign land with no luxuries to look forward to.

And Wallace himself . . . he loved these people just as the God he served loved them. Yes, he expressed that love differently than Jamie had. But it was there, and it was real, and Robbie could no longer ignore it.

But what now?

What would be required of Robbie Taggart, Highland sailor, adventurer, wanderer? Where had his journey across the oceans of the world led him? Had he been led here, on some sort of holy pilgrimage, without even realizing it? Of all the places he could have landed, why here?

Was he now to give up everything he had known, everything he held dear in life, to do as these people did? Was he to serve the God these people so nobly espoused? Yet Hsi-chen had already answered that question for him. He could not accept a God only because of the people, the tools, He used. They might alert him to God's presence, and they might help him to understand God's character. But in the end, this God had to become real . . . to *him*—He had to become a personal God, as Jamie had always said.

When dinner was over, Robbie found himself alone in the sitting room with Wallace. One by one each of the others had gravitated away, perhaps sensing the need for the two men to talk together.

Robbie thought back to the first time they had been alone in that room. How indignant he had been at the man's righteousness—*self-righteousness*, he had thought then. Now Robbie sat quietly sipping a cup of tea, wondering what the good doctor was thinking. For a long time they sat, Robbie thinking that Wallace would begin at any moment, not knowing if he relished such a private interchange. But when at length it began to appear that Wallace did not intend to initiate any conversation, Robbie sucked in his breath and decided to plunge in with a question that had been nagging him all afternoon since their meeting in the field.

"I've been wondering, Dr. Wallace," said Robbie, "this afternoon when we met in the field, why did you tell me not to be afraid? How did you know?"

"I did not know," answered Wallace. "I only guessed—from experience. It is a fearful thing to come into the presence of the living God. I sensed that you were struggling with Him even as we spoke."

"Why should I be fearful? I thought He was a God of love."

"He is. But until you *know* that, know *Him* in an intimate and personal way, it is not so easy to stand before Him, or even to think about the possibility of casting aside your reservations to claim this Lord as your own Friend and Companion and Redeemer."

"Yes, I have been afraid—and I have wondered," said Robbie, simply but thoughtfully. "But something inside keeps telling me that it's only when you're weak or in trouble that you should need God. I've always prided myself on being a man, on being strong, on being able to take care of myself. Isn't that what it means to be a man?"

"In the kingdom of man, yes. But in God's kingdom things are often just the opposite from what they seem to our earthbound eyes. All men, all women need God, whether they be weak or strong. You are drawn to Him because there is an emptiness within you that will always be hungrily searching, even unconsciously, until it is filled with the Spirit of Jesus Christ, God's Son. You *can* take care of yourself, Mr. Taggart, feed yourself, fight for yourself, think for yourself. You are a very self-reliant man. But the one thing you cannot do for yourself is satisfy that hunger within you, which is in all men, that hunger after something more than the world can give you, that hunger after the person of the God who made you. It will always be there, aching to be satisfied, until you turn to Him. It is the same struggle that all men and all women must face sooner or later in their lives. In God's providence, your time seems to have come now."

Robbie was silent, staring vacantly into his cup of tea. He had many things to think about, things that had come to him unsought, but which now he could not escape.

"Do you think you will be less of a man in confessing your need for God?"

"I suppose I have thought that," answered Robbie earnestly. "I suppose that is the basis for my reluctance, for my fighting so hard against what Jamie used to tell me, and what you and Hsi-chen have been telling me now. I have always looked upon religious people as somehow . . . I don't know—lacking in something. Lacking in self-confidence, lacking in that strength to take care of themselves. I always thought religion was all right for women, of course, and old people—"

He stopped abruptly and looked almost sheepishly toward Wallace. "I'm sorry. I didn't mean—"

"Think nothing of it, my boy!" laughed the doctor. "I'm not offended in the least! Believe me, I've been called many things worse than *old*!"

Robbie smiled.

"Please go on," said Wallace. "I truly am interested in what you're thinking."

"I suppose I always thought that there must be something wrong with a man if he had to use God as a crutch. You must know what I mean—men like the Vicar—I mean Drew."

"The Vicar?"

"He used to be a clergyman. But he was so filled with turmoil inside him that now he's nothing but a drunkard and a coward."

"Hmm," mused Wallace thoughtfully.

"And other so-called religious men I've run across. They've all seemed to be . . . well, if you'll forgive me, mollycoddles—if you know what I mean."

The doctor laughed again. "Weaklings, not quite men in the full sense of the word, is that it? Not the sort of men you'd go to the pub with and have a good time?"

"That's it! And I couldn't stand to become one myself, or even to be looked upon as one. I can't help it—I've got a certain pride about who I am. I'm not sure I want to let go of that."

"That's the great fallacy, Mr. Taggart," said Wallace, "that we have to let go of our beings when we come empty-handed to the Lord. True, there is a moment, like a brief moment of death, when we must give it up, lay it on His altar and say, '*I give my whole self up to you, Lord God.*' And yet that moment of death to the old is also a moment of birth—of birth into the new life. We leave behind the kingdom of man, and are born into the kingdom of God. And that moment *is* sometimes a frightening one. There is a relinquishing of all that has come before, of all we have wrongly thought about God, of all that pride we have built up around ourselves. All that must be laid down. But at the same time there *is* a wonderful new birth. And out of that birth emerges a new perspective on life, new goals, new attitudes, new priorities, and a new and more complete personhood. Out of that new birth comes your *true* self—even greater and stronger and more vital than what you *thought* your old self was. Because now it is not a self-reliant existence; instead, it is God-reliant. The moment of death is brief, and it is followed by receiving back so much more than you laid down. We lay down little bits of twigs and straw, thinking them so valuable; and yet the moment we do, we are given gold and silver in return."

"You make it sound both wonderful and easy," said Robbie almost sarcastically. "But from where I stand you might as well ask me to jump over the moon."

"Wonderful? Yes, though not without its own kind of hardships. But easy? No. I realize that it is an awesome change to confront in one's life. I am afraid I cannot assuage your fears with words, Mr. Taggart. There is only one thing that in the end will dispel them . . ."

He let his words trail away as he rose and went to the bookshelf. There he drew out a Bible. He leafed through the pages a moment, then stopped and read: "'And we have known and believed the love that God hath to us. God is love; and he that dwelleth in love dwelleth in God, and God in him. Herein is our love made perfect, that we may have boldness in the day of judgment: because as he is, so are we in this world. There is no fear in love; but perfect love casteth out fear: because fear hath torment. He that feareth is not made perfect in love.'"

"You said that this afternoon," said Robbie, "that perfect love casts out fear. What did you mean?"

"When you discover that Love, you will find the end to your fears. But no one can *talk* it into you. *You*, on your own, must come face-to-face with the reality of God's love through His Son Jesus. Only when you see Him for who He truly is will you be capable of understanding fully what I am saying. Then you will be able to perceive what the scripture means by having boldness. Then you will see that it is only a *true* man who can face Christ and admit his need—not because you are weak any more than all men are weak in light of Christ's strength, but because you have seen the reality of His person, and know you are nothing without Him. Contrary to the world's view, it is the coward who shrinks from that admission, and it is in fact the true sign of manliness to make it."

Robbie sagged back in his chair. He had never heard such truths before, even from Jamie. He sat in silence a long time. Wallace seemed not in the least bothered by the lapse in the conversation. He remained standing by the bookcase reading further in the Bible as if their talk had ended. Perhaps for him it had; he knew it would accomplish little to attempt to talk Robbie into a faith. Robbie felt constrained to speak, but for the moment he had nothing to say.

He was, for the moment, spared from having to give the matter further thought when Hsi-chen came quietly into the room.

"Fu-ch'in," she said, "forgive me if I interrupt you."

"Come in, my dear," said Wallace, holding out his hand to her. "What is troubling you?" Her face was etched in tension, the same look Robbie had seen about her when Chang had come into the mission that day seeking the doctor.

She approached her father and took his outstretched hand as if for very life. "A man has come to the mission," she said, "from one of our villages upriver." Seeming to gather strength as she spoke, she continued on. " A small group of bandits came through their village last night. They were fearsome, he said, though they did no harm other than getting drunk and stealing some food. But one let it slip that they were on their way to the mission—on their way *here!*"

"This frightens you, Hsi-chen?"

"I know God will care for us, but . . . I am frightened, yes. Fu-ch'in, they are with—" She paused, as if the name caught in her throat. At last she forced out the rest, "Their leader is Wang K'ung-wu!"

It seemed impossible, but for a brief moment even Wallace appeared daunted by the mention of the name. Robbie also started forward where he sat, for there was something familiar about the words, though he could think of no reason there should be. As he searched his mind, suddenly the words of a pirate aboard the ill-fated *Sea Tiger* leaped back into his memory.

"I would not miss watching you squirm before Wang K'ung-wu . . ."

What can it mean? Robbie wondered. *What could be the possible connection between some friend of the pirates and the mission?* Was he, Robbie, somehow the reason for their coming?

But the look that passed between Wallace and his daughter said something else. Wallace was hardly the type to be frightened over mere bandits. They could take or destroy what they would about the mission compound. That was always a danger inherent in missionary work, and he had accepted it long ago.

But the danger they feared was much worse than that.

46

Tale From the Past

Robbie and Hsi-chen were walking again outside, only now it was under a star-studded evening sky. A light breeze wafted over them from the river, relieving some of the stifling heat of the day.

"What can the fellow Wang want here?" asked Robbie, perplexed. "I heard his name mentioned by the pirates who sank my ship, as if he was even worse than that lot."

"Wang is a very powerful man in this area," replied Hsi-chen, "perhaps in all East China. But his power comes not by government sanction, although the very weakness of the central government makes it possible for men like Wang to wield their will over the land. They rule by force, instilling fear in the folk of the country. Because here we are closer to Hangchow, our villages have been relatively free from their terrible sway. Such bandits prefer to concentrate their activities in the outlands where they are not near the scrutiny of the legal authorities, such as they are. We had been free from them until several days before your arrival here."

"I was afraid I might have somehow drawn them here."

Hsi-chen sighed, then turned to face him. "No, Robbie, it is not you they seek."

"Then who? What could they possibly want here?" Robbie's eyes reflected the depth of concern that had begun to form in his heart for this tiny piece of the world, previously so unknown to him, where he found refuge in the midst of his soul's turmoil.

"I am afraid you will hardly believe me when I tell you, for it is the last person you could imagine being drawn into such an evil drama."

"I don't understand," replied Robbie, puzzled.

"They seek my mother."

"Impossible!" exclaimed Robbie. "What for?"

"You once asked me how I came to Wukiang," answered Hsi-chen. "I said it was a long story. But in the story is contained the answer to your question. That same day you also told me you loved stories. But this will not be a pleasant one to hear."

"Don't tell me what I shouldn't know," said Robbie. "But if there is any way I could help, I would like to know."

As Hsi-chen began to speak, Robbie listened attentively. But as she had warned, the story was tragic, despite its seemingly happy ending. Hsi-chen's voice often broke as she spoke, catching on the emotion which lay in her heart as she related the events that had befallen her mother, Shan-fei.

The story was of a girl, the daughter of an old and wealthy merchant family. The power of the House of Tien dated back nearly as far as the great Manchu dynasty itself. Tien Shan-fei lived as a princess, no matter that she had no royal blood in her delicate veins. Indulged and pampered in every way by her parents, by the age of fifteen—two or three years beyond what was considered the best age for such things—she had still not been promised in marriage. Other families might have begun to worry about their daughter making a good match at such a late age, but the parents of Shan-fei harbored no such concern. She was sought after by the best families, not only for her beauty, but for the promising family connections she would offer. Yet because marriage for a Chinese maiden meant separation from her family, sometimes forever, Shan-fei's parents were loathe to encourage the inevitable. In poor peasant families, girls were a drain on the meager budget, and as they reached a certain age were usually married off by necessity. Such was not the case for the Tiens. Yet they could not keep their beloved daughter indefinitely.

As the girl turned sixteen, therefore, offers had to be considered. The most insistent came from the family of Wang—it was almost unseemly how persistent they could be. Wang was a relatively new name among Shanghai's cultured families, though their wealth was real enough. Rumor had it, however, that the old man's fortune had been gained in most disreputable enterprises. Moreover, the son, the marriage candidate, was reputed to be wild and unmanageable.

Shan-fei, however, chanced one day to see young K'ung-wu and was much taken with him, for he was handsome and manly. As contrary as it was for one in her position to meet a potential marriage candidate, much less have any say in the decision of her parents, Shan-fei had never been forced to submit to most of the expectations of culture. Thus, she used her favor in her parents' eyes as an advantage to press for a match with Wang K'ung-wu. Her father wavered, unfortunately raising the hopes of the headstrong K'ung-wu. In the end, however, they stood firm against this family whose reputation they shunned, and a match was agreed upon instead with the family of Chu Tun-ru. Shan-fei's desire for young Wang, springing as it did more from girlish fancy than true passion, waned, and she conceded to the choice of her father. And when she married a year later, she found her new husband to be a kind and considerate mate.

Her new mother-in-law, however, proved to be the fatal flaw in what might have been a good marriage. Discord between mother and daughter-in-law was not only culturally accepted, oftentimes a mother-in-law lost face if she treated the wife of her son too tenderly or with respect. Simply bred herself, old Mrs. Chu carried such a custom to the extreme, resenting the Tien clan. She was pleased enough for her son to have married into the wealthy family, but felt it was her duty to rectify the life of ease that the spoiled daughter of Tien had enjoyed throughout her young life—for the sake of her son, of course. She did not want to see him subjugated to this spoiled young girl.

Thus, an abrupt end came to Shan-fei's idyllic lifestyle. The fortune of Chu had come upon hard times, and though they managed to maintain the appearance of wealth, the household itself was run very strictly. Shan-fei often received the brunt of the difficulties. She was given only cast-off clothing to wear and often served in place of slaves; only her bound feet kept her from the most rigorous labor. But it was not the physical hardships that troubled the young girl most, but rather the older woman's biting tongue, accompanied by her constant attempts to sow discord between Shan-fei and her husband. Though he had to be careful not to offend his mother, had it not been for his diplomatic mediation, life would quickly have become intolerable for Shan-fei.

When after ten years of marriage Tun-ru died, Shan-fei thought she would die too. Returning to her parents was simply not possible; she was now owned by the family of her husband. Most Chinese widows do not remarry, and suicide is sometimes a solution to such a desperate situation. But the thought of leaving her young daughter to the heartless wiles of Mrs. Chu dispelled suicide as a possible escape for Shan-fei. Remarriage seemed the only way out.

Wang's intercession, however, was no longer desirable to Shan-fei. His reputation through the years had followed his father's in ruthlessness, and to one of Shan-fei's delicate sensibilities, such a man had no appeal.

The Chu's, however, did not see beyond his money. How could a troublesome daughter-in-law compare with the price Wang was offering? Especially a daughter-in-law who had born no sons!

Shan-fei's father, old Tien, meanwhile, had gone the way of his ancestors, and Shan-fei did not want to burden her aged and ailing mother with her troubles. She was too proud to call upon her brothers, now holding the reins of family power. By rights, they might have demanded redress for her mistreatment by her in-laws, but such cases were usually too tragic and unpleasant even to consider. And the Chu name also belonged to her dead husband, and she had cared for and respected him and could not now bring dishonor to him.

Silent endurance of her fate seemed the only answer. Perhaps Wang would prove an acceptable husband despite his reputation in matters of business. Could not men hard in the marketplace be tender at home? It was a feeble hope, but Shan-fei clung desperately to it as the day of her wedding appointed by her father-in-law approached. By chance, however, she learned a terrifying fact that immediately crushed even the small thread of hope she had possessed.

Wang had carefully kept from sight his disdain of children. Sons of his own he might tolerate, but girls, either his or anyone else's—they were useless. He kept this fact quiet for fear of losing Shan-fei, and would no doubt have shot on sight the person who divulged the information. Yet now it came to Shan-fei's notice that Wang had already signed a marriage contract for her daughter, Hsi-chen, with one of his soldiers, and would no doubt rid himself of this excess baggage the moment she matured—perhaps even sooner. The marriage of Hsi-chen was to be expected one day; Shan-fei knew that well enough. But never to one of Wang's ruthless bandits! For all she knew, the man could be one of his paid assassins!

Shan-fei then knew that she could submit neither herself nor her daughter to such men. She had but one option left—she must run away.

Taking into her confidence an old servant she had brought with her to the House of Chu, they together began to devise a plan for her to escape from the clutches of Wang.

"I must go someplace where they will never think of looking," said Shan-fei. "Perhaps Peking. I can easily lose myself in such a large city."

"You are known there," said the old woman. "And even rags could not conceal your noble lineage." Besides these words she spoke, the woman, who had been faithful to the House of Tien all her life, could not bear the thought of innocent Shan-fei and her precious daughter alone and helpless in the cruel city.

Then she rubbed her wrinkled old lips thoughtfully. "I must tell you a secret, dear Shan-fei," she said at length, rather cryptically. "I meant not to deceive you. But I must be careful what I say. There are those who would take my life if they knew, and it was difficult for me to speak openly of this. But you see . . . I am a Christian."

Shan-fei raised her eyebrows at this startling disclosure, shrinking back a moment from the tender old lady.

"Why do you tell me this now?" asked Shan-fei.

"There is a place where they would not think to seek you, and where you will be treated with kindness," replied the old servant.

"A church?"

"Not in Shanghai. Even that would be too dangerous. But a missionary from a station some ninety miles from here comes to the church in Shanghai occasionally to visit. At his mission, I believe you would find refuge."

"A mission?" mused Shan-fei, the uncertainty clear in her voice. "But I have heard things—"

"All lies!" exclaimed the woman, for a brief moment forgetting her station as a servant. "None of them are true. I have heard the stories, too. But you must believe me, you will find nothing but compassion and understanding there."

Shan-fei argued no further. She trusted her servant. And the idea seemed assuredly the most promising they had had thus far. Alongside the thought of becoming Wang's wife, even an unknown mission did not sound so fearsome.

Over the next several days, Shan-fei made as if to willingly submit to the discretion of Chu for her forthcoming wedding. When the night came for her escape, not a soul in the house suspected a thing. Travel in her crippled condition was difficult, but the servant had arranged everything with Christian friends. She accompanied her far enough to see her safely aboard the junk that would take mother and daughter the first half of the way. Then she hastened back, crept in the way they had left, did what she could to make the final ruse of apparent suicide believable, climbed back into her bed, where she slept the rest of the night through, praying even in her dreams for the safety of her beloved Shan-fei.

Thus, Shan-fei and her daughter came to Christ's China Mission in the country village of Wukiang. There, indeed, they discovered the compassion her faithful servant had promised. There too they found a home and a new family, and a new life in the Christ for whom the mission was named.

And as the wise old woman had predicted, no one gave even a thought to searching for the missing daughter of Tien there. For thirteen years they lived in peace and anonymity. And best of all, they lived in a deep happiness that Shan-fei had feared she would never know again.

"But Wang has now found my mother," said Hsi-chen, as she finished the story, her sad voice tinged with anxiety.

"She is married now," said Robbie. "What can he do?"

"A man like Wang takes what he wants. But it may not be that he would take her at all. He may only be seeking . . . revenge."

"After thirteen years?"

"It is difficult to imagine, I know," replied Hsi-chen. "But when darkness rules a man's inner being, evil thoughts and designs are given full freedom to grow and fester and blossom, and length of years only perpetuates the evil."

Robbie slowly shook his head. It was odd that one such as Hsi-chen had more wisdom in such matters than he, worldly-wise man that he had always thought himself to be.

"What will you do?" he asked.

"My father already has tried to intimidate them by threatening to call in the British."

Robbie raised an eyebrow, for he knew Wallace disdained the use of political or military power. Then Hsi-chen added, "It was only—how do you say it?—a bluff. But no matter; it only frightened them away for a while, and now Wang himself is coming."

"Well," insisted Robbie, "Dr. Wallace would be totally within his rights to call in the British Navy. He certainly doesn't intend to sit by while this blackguard steals away his own wife! Turning the other cheek can only be carried so far!"

"He will not resort to violence, Robbie. You should know that by now. God will intercede for us."

"God!" exclaimed Robbie with frustration. "Do you expect a thunderbolt from heaven or something? Believe me, Wang will laugh in your face if you start to beseech heavenly powers."

"Do not scorn the power of God, Robbie." For a moment Hsi-chen's eyes flashed and her voice took on a tone very reminiscent of her father's.

"I can't believe in such miracles," persisted Robbie, though he could not help being a bit stunned by this gentle girl's change of demeanor. "A man has to fight his own battles," he went on. "He has to protect those he loves and cares for. A coward waits for the intercession of another."

"I will forgive you for your unbelieving words, Robbie," she said tightly. "I know they come because you are concerned, and because you cannot understand my father or men like him who are willing to be seen as fools to demonstrate the greatest kind of courage of all—trusting in God. Bravery as the world defines it means nothing to him if it interferes with doing the will of God. I think you know by now that my father is no coward."

Her voice had been so stern, so intense, her eyes so dark, that Robbie suddenly felt very much alone. Hsi-chen had begun to mean more to him than he dared imagine. Even to think of losing her friendship caused a painful void within him.

He stopped in their slow walk across the compound. Turning toward her, he grabbed her hands impulsively in his.

"Hsi-chen . . . I'm sorry! I don't want you to be angry with me. Your friendship means so much to me."

"Dear Robbie, I am not angry. But you must understand how hard it is to have a friend such as you have become, who cannot grasp the things that are the most important to me." She paused and closed her eyes. Yes, she also dared not think what this man was coming to mean to her. But her reasons were far different than his.

"Please," he said earnestly, "help me to understand."

"How I want to, Robbie Taggart. But this understanding must come from your heart. And *I* cannot change your heart." She glanced down at their hands, still clasped together as if both were desperately afraid to let go. "The very center of my life is not the center of yours. Yet how can I feel so close to you when we are so far apart?"

"I wish I could make myself change—make myself believe the way you do."

"I would not want you to believe for *my* sake."

"I suppose I could not," answered Robbie dismally, "no matter how much I wanted to. Even *I* know that would be no belief at all."

"I will pray for you," said Hsi-chen.

Their hands fell apart. As sincerely as she had meant them, Hsi-chen felt an emptiness in her last words. She wanted them to represent a statement of her faith, but she could not help thinking they seemed but a hollow phrase to Robbie. But whatever they had sounded like, she *would* pray for him, and pray diligently. And the Lord would answer and would, in His time, give Robbie the understanding he sought.

They turned in silence and walked slowly back to the residence, each feeling more than they could put into words. Whatever lack of understanding existed, at the same time both deeply sensed something wonderful within, though they were reticent to give it its true and fearsome name. Robbie was afraid of the commitment *love* might require of him. Hsi-chen was afraid that, even if they were one day of kindred spirits, she had no right to ask love from anyone to whom she could not promise her life in return.

47

Interlude

The next day found Robbie once more atop the residence roof at his seemingly permanent occupation. He was especially thankful for his labors today, for they prevented him from saying and doing and thinking things best ignored for the present.

That morning he had attempted to reason with Wallace over his passivity. He had even made the mistake of suggesting that he be allowed to go to Hangchow to purchase some rifles. But Wallace had risen up ominously from the chair in which he had been seated. With his eyes dark and a deadly finality ringing in his voice, he quoted as if he were a fiery prophet of old:

"'The angel of the Lord encampeth round about them that fear him, and delivereth them.' There will be no weapons on *this* compound, Mr. Taggart!"

Robbie threw up his hands and without another word marched from the room and to his present labors.

Was Wallace merely naive to the reality of the approaching danger? Or did he truly believe his words?

Robbie knew the answer, but would never understand it. Yet he had to admire the man. Despite his statement to Hsi-chen, he *did* see the doctor's courage, foolhardy though it might prove to be. He thought back to his first day at the mission. It had taken courage for Wallace to meet with that man he had seen in the distance, if these bandits and their warlord leader were in fact as evil as Hsi-chen seemed to think.

Could Wallace's God indeed be capable of delivering them?

It was the first time Robbie had, from sincerity, asked himself such a question. Wallace was not the kind of man to spend the energies of his life frivolously.

All at once it seemed to Robbie that this God they were speaking of might actually be more than his own narrow attitudes had given Him credit for being. Could He indeed be the axis upon which the universe turned—the *Almighty*? Not merely a crutch, a hollow system of belief for the weak, but the source and foundation of everything? "The life stream," as the Chinese would say? Or, as Wallace had once declared, "The One who alone is worthy"?

Robbie noticed that his heart was pounding. He was sweating. If all that were true, then Wallace's God would not be One to be lightly denied, certainly not one to turn your back on. *If it were true . . .*

Again, seemingly for the hundredth time, Robbie searched his mind for an answer. "Could it be," he asked himself again, "could it be *true*?"

But no answer came. All he could think was that if someone he loved were in danger, he would have to act! He could not take the stand Wallace had taken. Yet . . . *if* it were true, then his puny attempts to right the scales of justice would prove pretty inconsequential alongside anything a truly almighty God might himself do.

If God truly *was* almighty, Robbie would have to acknowledge Him. What other choice would there be? He would *want* to acknowledge Him. If he could just be assured that it was all true, it might be possible for him to give his life for Him, as had Wallace and Coombs.

Without realizing it, Robbie had taken a giant step in his journey toward faith. Admitting to the possibility that truth was being revealed to him was halfway toward the recognition of that truth.

But still he held back. Even the revelation of an all-powerful God was not enough to convince him. For having recognized the possible claim on his life by an *almighty* God, he still needed to confront the personal and *loving* God. Both facets of God's character were necessary to complete the picture and win Robbie's seeking heart to Him. He must meet not only the God of power but also the loving God of relationship, who gave His Son that Robbie Taggart himself might live.

Yet these few steps closer were momentous ones for Robbie, for they signaled giant steps of beginning. Even as he pounded the next nail into the roof, he sensed that he had embarked upon a voyage of discovery such as he had never before taken, fraught with more hidden dangers, and more hidden treasures too perhaps, than any sea voyage of his life. He was no longer merely being carried along by events, but in his heart he was purposefully striking out for himself. For the first time, he *wanted* to know the truth, whatever he discovered in the process! He must find answers to the questions of life. He knew that now. He could no longer shrug the questions off. And he no longer wanted to.

Perhaps part of the reason for his new honesty with himself was his desire to find common ground with Hsi-chen. But even that was only a small part of it. For the most compelling question still lay in Isaiah Wallace himself. Wallace was not physically powerful as many men Robbie had known, nor as strong as he himself was. Yet within his character in some unseen, inner reservoir of being, the man possessed a might and fortitude that Robbie had seldom witnessed in other men, himself included. It was a sobering revelation, for Robbie had always considered himself tough enough. Yet Wallace, in some ways a giant of a man beside Robbie, possessed a masculinity that revealed itself in none of the ways it should have. It was all turned upside-down in Robbie's mind! He *had* to find out why! And he knew it was intrinsically connected with the God this man served.

Unconsciously his eyes wandered over the compound spread out below him, seeking out Hsi-chen. He did not want to move from his perch. But even as he wrestled with the questions filling his mind, part of him wanted to share the search with her. For somehow he knew that she was wrestling with him—maybe even *for* him.

She was helping her father in the clinic. A long line of village folk shuffled about in front of the hospital door, waiting to be seen by the doctor. Occasionally Hsi-chen stepped outside to assess the prospective patients as to the immediacy of their needs. She was there now, speaking to an elderly lady. In a moment she placed her arm around the woman's bent and crippled back and gently led her inside out of the heat.

The simple act sent a rush of emotion through Robbie. He shed no tears, but a peculiar tightness gripped his chest. He knew just what her voice would sound like to the old woman. The soft, high-pitched, musical tone, speaking so tenderly, as if to a child. What a mother she would make! The small gesture made by sweet Hsi-chen toward a frail old woman gave him a further glimpse of godly compassion. Yet with it came still another question: he too had always tried to be a good, compassionate man. So had many others. That did not make them Christians as Wallace or Hsi-chen would describe that belief. What was the difference between being good and believing? Certainly God's people did not have exclusive interest on being good. And further-more, what about so-called Christians who *weren't* as compassionate as nonbelievers?

Two hours later, when he had come back down to the ground to cut more shingles, Hsi-chen approached Robbie from the hospital. All the patients for the day had finally been attended to. She wore the same easy warmth that he had grown accustomed to, and he returned her smile.

"You work hard, Robbie the sailor," she said.

"I never minded a bit of work," he replied. "It helps keep the head clear, if nothing else."

"And your head needs clearing?"

He laughed outright. "Need you ask? Never before in my life has my head been in such a muddled mess!" He paused. "But it's starting to clear *a muckle wee bit*, as we say in Scotland. Or so I think, just before some new dilemma comes over me."

"I am glad."

"But I do have a question for you."

"Let us sit again in the shade of the camphor tree," she said. He rose and followed her. "Now," she said at length, "ask what you will. But I may not be worthy to answer."

"Tell me, if compassion is a trait that comes from God, how can an unbeliever exhibit that virtue? I've known many good men who were not believers."

"That is a large question," replied Hsi-chen slowly, pausing in thought. "There is no simple answer," she went on after a minute or two, "but consider perhaps a story like one Jesus told. When seed is scattered upon the earth, some of it falls into the furrow that has been prepared for it. But some is carried off by the wind and falls on a field for which it was not intended. But there it grows, as all seeds must. When it grows and matures, it can yield good fruit. But just think how much more splendid it would have been had its soil received all the proper care!"

"Do you mean that Christians are more compassionate than unbelievers?"

"That is not exactly what I mean, for unfortunately it is not always so. But if the seed were getting its nourishment from the very fountain of love, would it not flourish all the more? It is true there are some believers who have not tapped into this fountain, and some also who are trying but must give more time for their fruit to show. All love is but a shadow of God's character. There is no other answer I can think of for your question. All men are made in the image of their Maker, whether they know it or acknowledge it or not. And in all men, the love of that Maker cannot help but spill out from time to time, whether or not they are planted in the furrow He intended for them."

"It must be a pretty powerful love to touch even those who don't know Him," mused Robbie. "A woman once said to me, 'Even a sailor can be used of God.'"

"It is true," replied Hsi-chen, smiling. Sobering somewhat, she added, "It is powerful, Robbie, for how do you think unbelievers come to Him and become believers? They are touched by the love of God, a love that shows itself to men and women in millions of different ways. It is the only way to meet Him. I have seen many worthy Chinese intellectuals try to reason their way to a state of higher consciousness. But if they are to continue their quest where it is meant to lead, in the end it must come to the point of discovering *His* love personally in each of their hearts."

"Why does He love us as He does?"

"He is God, that is all. He made us. He created us to be like Him, to enjoy relationship and fellowship with Him. It is His nature to love."

Robbie did not reply. Another moment he sat, then jumped up and began pacing about, agitated once more.

"I think perhaps I said something to confuse you," said Hsi-chen.

"It's all still so hard to understand."

"Do you have the New Testament I gave you?"

"Of course."

"Perhaps if you read there, it might help you," she suggested. "It is sometimes difficult for me to put into words what in my heart cries out to be said."

"Oh no, Hsi-chen, that's not so!" Robbie exclaimed, coming near to her once more and dropping down beside her. "You've expressed it beautifully! But even if you hadn't spoken a thing, I would have been able to see all you've said in the way you act, the way you were just now with the people from the village, and so many other times. Who you *are* speaks louder than anything you've said!"

"That is the finest thing anyone has ever told me, Robbie."

"I mean it, Hsi-chen. To me you're a wonderful person!"

The words slipped out unchecked in his exuberance, and the moment they did they seemed to hang in the air. Robbie could not grab them back even if he had wanted to.

He took her hands in his. "You *are* wonderful," he repeated the words, this time softly, but with even greater fervor. But he saw unexpected tears rising in her eyes.

"What is it, Hsi-chen?" he asked gently.

"Think nothing of my emotion," she answered. "I do not know what it means." She slipped her hands from his and stood. "I must go now."

He watched her walk away. She moved not with her usual fluid grace, but now with uncertainty, despite her hurried pace. Robbie knew he had said more than he should have, more than he had planned to. But the words had come so naturally.

He, too, did not know what any of it meant. Was it possible that here, in this strange and foreign land, he could be falling in love—and with someone so intrinsically different from him in every way? He did not want to consider it.

Yet there were feelings within him he could not deny. Just as there were truths regarding Hsi-chen's God he could no longer deny either.

48

Evil Schemes

Nestled in the hills surrounding the valley where Wukiang lay, sat an ancient abandoned monastery. Over a century earlier, Taoist monks had lived out their secluded, priestly lives within its stone walls. But when a plague swept through the place more than half the residents had been killed. The remainder of the order soon disbanded, and since that time none dared inhabit the picturesque spot where it was generally believed "bad Karma" dwelt.

But for the past week and a half this once holy site had been occupied again, this time by an evil breed of men who scoffed at spirituality of any kind. Wang's handful of soldiers, using it as a barracks while performing their surveillance of the mission only a few miles away, were not intimidated by the ghost stories that had long been associated with the place. The day before Wang K'ung-wu himself had arrived, with his lieutenant Pien, and a very much degenerated Benjamin Pike.

If the sea captain had ever possessed any redeeming qualities, surely they were wiped away with his act of betrayal. When he had watched his dear *Sea Tiger* sink and his crew struggling futilely in the water, he might have experienced a small twinge of remorse, especially as he saw Robbie swallowed up by a seemingly fatal comber. But Pike was a survivor of the worst kind. He kept telling himself that the ship was doomed with or without him. He did not exactly betray his crewmen. The pirates were going to do what they were going to do regardless. He might as well save himself if he could. It would make no difference to the others, and as far as Robbie was concerned, hadn't he hoped for just such an accident all along?

Pike could not live with guilt. He had no use for it. Yet he had to live, to survive, at all costs. So he squashed out that last remnant of humanity left within his sick and twisted mind. He forced from his brain the memory of his men going down with the ship. It would do no good to remember now. All life for him had to be focused on one goal—Benjamin Pike. First he had had to concentrate his efforts merely on staying alive. But as his position in his new surroundings became firmer, he began to think how he might get the better of these dirty foreigners.

He had been very fortunate when the pirate Chou brought him before Wang. For all Pike knew he might lose his head. But his bluff on Chou had worked, for it turned out that the warlord hated the pirate's cocky arrogance even more than Pike's pitiful countenance. Moreover, he could see some usefulness in having a white barbarian, hated though they were, in his counsel.

It had been with profound shock that Pike had learned that Robbie Taggart was still alive.

"He's a bloody wraith!" screamed the old captain. "Ye can't kill the blag'ard!"

He pounded his fist against the table and then tore at his greasy, matted hair like a madman, suddenly bent on a new goal other than staying alive—destroying Robbie Taggart, who all his life had given him no peace.

But that had been a week ago, and he had kept his thoughts to himself. Now he sat in close council with Wang and Pien. Why Wang included him was a mystery Pike never bothered to consider in-depth. Vaunted with self-importance, Pike did not stop to consider that in reality he was still but a prisoner, ever at the mercy of Wang's twisted will and violent temper.

At the moment Pien was in the midst of a report gleaned recently by Wukiang's spies.

"There have been no signs of gunboats, my lord," said Pien in his ingratiating though cautious manner, speaking in Chinese, "nor of any other British presence. Wallace did travel to Hangchow a few days ago."

"Speak in English!" ordered Wang, "so our esteemed guest can understand." He cast a deprecating look in Pike's direction that contradicted his verbal compliment.

"And why did those fools I so freely call soldiers not prevent him?" shouted Wang, shifting uncomfortably on the hard monastic floor, inwardly cursing those monks for their simple and stoic ways.

"It was believed you would not want an incident with a British subject."

Slowly Wang shook his head. Someday he would rid himself of the whole pack of fools, and get rid of the British from his territory too! But the time had not come yet. In the meantime he'd have to show caution.

"And the girl . . . what is her name?" asked Wang.

"Hsi-chen, my lord."

"Is she legally adopted by this missionary?"

"No, my lord."

"How can you be certain?"

"I sent a man to Hangchow—I thought you might want to know." Pien could not refrain from a satisfied smirk at his own ingenuity.

Wang made no comment on his lieutenant's foresight. He only rubbed his beard and mused, "So, the little lotus blossom is not technically under the British protectorate . . . ?"

"As a Christian convert, my lord, she might call upon the government, and with Wallace's support would very possibly receive help," suggested Pien.

"Bah! The British government is not quick to come to the aid of converts! Too many of those Chinese betrayers have only espoused their

Western religion for the protection the powerful governments can give them! But I think those times are past."

Wang leaned back against the wall, and, folding his hands before him, paused in thought. But it was only a reflex action. He knew what he must do; there was no need to deliberate over it.

Pien cleared his throat timorously. He had one more piece of information to deliver. But how he wished he could have forgotten about it. He feared Wang's reaction. Yet even more he feared for his life if his master discovered that he had withheld it.

"It may be, my lord," said Pien, "that swift action will be required in this matter."

Wang sat forward, glaring. "What can you mean? Speak quickly, you fool!"

"It appears as if the girl and the British sailor"—here Pike perked up—"are becoming intimate."

"Intimate?" asked Wang. "How do you think so?"

"They have been seen frequently together. Often alone."

"Ha, ha!" barked Pike, breaking at last his silent observation of the council.

"What do you know of this?" demanded Wang, turning his menacing gaze on the sea captain.

"Only that if there's a pretty lass about," answered Pike with just a touch of admiration mingled with his sarcasm, "Robbie Taggart'll win her heart!"

"What do I care?" shouted Wang, though inwardly galled that a cursed foreign devil should dare tamper with *his* prize. "Let him have her heart! It will do him little good when I have the rest."

Now it was Pike's turn to become pensive. Expert manipulator of situations that he was, he had immediately taken note, as Wang spoke, of a small crack in the warlord's redoubtable armor. The shrill, almost desperate quality of his outburst had told cunning Benjamin Pike more even than Wang realized about himself. To the egomaniac Chinese overlord, it was the final insult that the woman he wanted might have pledged her loyalties to another—a white man at that! Working upon him were thirteen years of shame at the hands of the girl's mother.

It took Pike but a moment to see how this realization could work to his advantage and help him see the fulfillment of his own cherished plan for revenge.

"Of course, of course," mumbled Pike as if the whole matter was of no concern to him. "What do a woman's affections mean to a man like you?"

"Love and affection are foolish Western notions," said Wang. "They mean nothing in China when a man wants a woman."

"And a good custom it is too," agreed Pike. "Who wants a woman's love, her loyalty, eh? You'll get what ye really want from the woman—and it don't bother ye none if ye gots to hold a gun on her fer it. Ha, ha!" Pike laughed, leering at his captor, hoping he didn't cross the line of the madman's tolerance. "A man like yersel' gets what he wants an' who cares that she silently curses ye all the while, right, mate?"

Wang suddenly lurched at Pike, grabbing the front of his shirt. "What are you trying to say, you foul pig?" he screamed. Pike had indeed taken his little game right to the edge of safety and was dangerously close to imperiling his life.

Pike did not wince at the insult. He had sunk too low years ago to be bothered by verbal abuse, especially when he sensed himself gaining the upper hand in a life-and-death game of mouse chasing cat. "I wasn't gettin' at nuthin', guv," answered Pike nonchalantly.

"You are saying I am a man who must use violence to win a woman!"

"It don't matter to you, now does it?"

"No it doesn't!" yelled Wang.

"That's good," returned Pike calmly. "So ye'd have no interest in learning jist how ye might win this little lotus flower, win her *completely*."

In a mighty fit of wrath, still holding Pike's shirt, Wang slammed the skipper's body against the stone wall. "Speak your mind, imbecile!" shouted Wang, his mouth but an inch from Pike's. The jolt had winded Pike, and, coughing and sputtering, it was a while before he could regain his previous composure. "Speak!" repeated Wang, "or you will die where you stand, you groveling fool!"

Pike opened his mouth. His voice was noticeably weaker, but he had come too far to falter now. Despite the warlord's portentous bluster, he knew Wang was in the palm of his hand.

"You know how women are, Lord Wang," said Pike. "They like to be made o'er, they do. An' the best attention ye can give a woman is fer two men to fight o'er her affections, if ye take my meaning. They love it—and it makes them love all the more the man what wins."

Wang loosened his deadly hold on Pike, allowing the skipper to collapse on the floor. He turned and paced about the room, rubbing his beard all the while. Finally he turned back to Pike.

"Tell me what you have to say."

Pike pulled himself up as straight as his degenerated figure could go, and spoke with a casual tone, though triumph glistened in his yellowed eyes.

"I figured ye was plannin' on kidnappin' the little lady," he said. "Ye might jist go ahead as planned. Ye'll win her in the end, but she might need a bit o' proddin' at first. Then, sure as my names's Ben Pike, Robbie'll come to try to rescue her."

"He will come alone?"

"Now's the Vicar's gone, he don't have no one but those missionaries—none of them Chinamen are going to help a white man get one of their women. And even so, he ain't never goin' to raise anything to match yer crowd here. So once he gets here, ye challenge him to a fight to the death, fer the hand of the woman. 'Course ye'll win, ain't that so?"

"It is so, you white pig!"

"There ye go!" laughed Pike. "She'll see that ye was willing to risk yer life for her, an' she'll fall madly in love with ye."

Wang stopped his pacing. The dirty sea captain's plan was simple enough, and was not without merit. Though why shouldn't he simply take the girl and go? Why wait around for something to go wrong? What did he care, after all, if the daughter of Shan-fei loved him?

"And if she should see the qualities you speak of in the sailor instead?" he asked at length.

"He'll be too dead to matter to her anymore. A living hero means more to a woman than a dead one."

"And this sailor . . . what skill has he?"

"He is a tough one, I gots to admit that," replied Pike. "But nothing compared to yer lordship. He don't know nothin' about weapons—take swords, for instance. Now with guns, he might get lucky. But with swords, it's skill pure and simple. And he ain't got none."

"Tell me this, sea captain: is your sailor stupid enough to walk in here where he knows that—however remote his chances—if he *should* win, he will be instantly killed?"

"Robbie's a headstrong lad," said Pike, running a hand over his four-day growth of beard. "But if he hesitates, ye're a smart fellow. Ye can figure something out."

"You may go, pig!" ordered Wang. "Get your wretched, stinking self away from me!"

Pike grabbed his crutch, and, partly leaning on it, partly bracing himself against the wall, he hobbled from the room, not once looking back over his shoulder, neither worrying about an unexpected rear attack from the warlord. Wang needed him. He'd be safe for a while, and by then he'd have figured out some other safeguard. Nothing would deter him from his prime goal—self-preservation. Especially now that the destruction of Robbie Taggart was within his grasp.

He grinned to himself as he limped along the deserted corridor to his own little cubicle. The true beauty of the plan he had just laid before Wang was that Pike himself would not have to lift a finger against Taggart.

Not that he was squeamish. He could do it if he had to. But he would just as soon have someone else handle the actual deed.

Perhaps, after all, there was a small, misplaced shred of humanity left in Benjamin Pike. Enough at least to make him afraid of forever seeing the face of his best friend's son in his dreams, if he *had* to be the one to strike him down. He remembered too vividly that first time . . .

He had been in one of his hateful fits on the *Macao*. Robbie was just a kid, and the apple of the captain's eye. How his favor with the officers had galled Pike, himself nothing but a grimy sea cook with no hope of advancement. One night he sneaked up into the rigging, nearly killing himself with that fool peg leg of his. But he had made it to the top, and had fixed the ropes so that no one would be able to make that climb again and survive. He made sure it was Robbie who took that line the next day—it hadn't been hard to do; Robbie loved nothing more than going aloft.

A pang of guilt—he'd had some feelings left back then—suddenly struck him, and he nearly cried out a warning at the last moment. But in silence he watched the lad fall to the deck, saved from a certain death only by a turn of the wind. The gust had forced his descending body against the other rigging that had remained secure. It had been weeks before Pike could get the vision of that falling body from his mind.

"He's inhuman!" cried Pike, his voice echoing against the stone walls of the monastery. "More lives than a bleedin' cat!"

Robbie had survived, though badly injured. Yet the incident still haunted Pike, and he'd rather not risk repeating it.

Better to let that fool Wang do the deed. Let him have the nightmares!

49

Fools Rush In

Hsi-chen made her way slowly across the mission compound from the hospital.

It was dark now, and the last of the evening patients had gone home hours ago. Her father had been called to the village to see to the state of a pregnant woman, while she had remained to put the dispensary in order for the following day.

As she walked, she hoped to see Robbie returning across the bridge. He had gone with a villager to gather more wood for his shingles. He should not have been so long, but he must come soon.

She ran a hand across her perspiring forehead. There was not even a hint of breeze to dull the oppressive heat of the mei-yu season. The *plum rain* was good for the rice, but insufferable for humans, though somehow they managed to survive the few weeks it lasted. This year, however, Hsi-chen seemed to feel it more than ever before. Her body sagged as if all vitality had been sapped from it by the heat and her plaguing illness.

"Dear Lord," she silently prayed, "please give me more time. But . . . help me to be strong, and to say not my will but *yours* be done."

Her prayer reminded her how unreasonable it was for her to seek Robbie out. She was being unfair to him and causing herself unnecessary pain by thinking there was any possibility of . . .

She did not complete the thought. On this evening she simply wanted to see him, for his own sake. She wanted to look upon those eyes, the color of the sea he loved, sensitive, laughing eyes. She wanted to see his smile, so easy, so unabashed, so filled with the very thing she felt at the moment she lacked—life.

She chided herself for her vain thoughts. She possessed eternal life. And that was enough.

"Oh, Father!" she prayed again, "make it enough!"

But Hsi-chen was young. All the faith in the universe could not keep her from loving life and desiring more of it. Neither could it keep her from sorrow at the prospect of parting from this world, a world which the Spirit of her Lord had given her such an appreciation for. Her heavenly

Father would not condemn her for this; He too had suffered great anguish of heart at His parting from the world of men.

Yet she had to admit that it had not been so difficult before Robbie Taggart came along.

Dear Robbie . . . whose vibrant energy she had felt even that first day when he lay unconscious in the hospital.

Oh, what a man of God you will make! she thought with a smile. *Why do you struggle so against the life that is pressing toward you?*

She knew, however, that the harder fought the battle, the more glorious would be the victory in the end. And Hsi-chen harbored not the slightest doubt that there would be ultimate victory yet in Robbie Taggart's life.

Hearing a sound behind the chapel building, Hsi-chen paused.

It sounded soft, like the whimpering of an injured animal, or perhaps a small child. The children did sometimes play there. But it was so late! Could one of them have been hurt and somehow got left behind?

The servant spirit of the Chinese maiden prodded her toward the sound, giving no heed to the dangers the night might hold. In her longing after ministration, she had innocently forgotten that the mission was under siege by a notorious band of strangers.

Robbie returned to the mission later than he'd expected. The farmer who had helped him with the wood invited him to stay for supper. Robbie consented, accepting the challenge of attempting to put to use some of the Chinese phrases Hsi-chen had been trying to teach him.

The evening had been an enjoyable one. Robbie had been able to lay aside his mental quandaries and enter into the hospitality of the village folk, though he could understand nothing of what was said. He left in a contented mood, glad to have another pocket of local friends to add to the many such encounters he had had all over the world.

When he crossed the bridge it was quite late. Yet he immediately noticed all the lamps in the residence burning brightly. Something must be amiss, he thought, for he had been at the mission long enough to familiarize himself with the habits of the place. There had never before been such activity at this hour, though an individual lamp occasionally burned past midnight in Wallace's study.

Therefore Robbie turned his steps toward the residence, not wanting to barge in where he was not wanted, but sensing trouble in the wind.

He opened the door and immediately perceived that he had stumbled into the middle of a tense and highly emotional prayer meeting. Coombs, Miss Trumbull, Shan-fei, Yien Nien, and Wallace were all kneeling in a circle, holding hands, with heads bowed. All heads shot up and turned in his direction at the sound of the door creaking open.

"Come in, please, Mr. Taggart," said Wallace. "Won't you join us?" Robbie could see from the man's eyes that evil omens were in the air. His voice was an empty shell, drained of fervor, clinging thinly to the hope that went against the instincts of his flesh.

"Where is Hsi-chen?" asked Robbie anxiously, slowly approaching the circle.

"She has been taken," replied Wallace.

"Taken!" exclaimed Robbie. "Taken ill? Taken . . . what do you mean?" His words spilled out in a rush of intensity and confusion.

Wallace tried to explain, though every word was a great effort. "Wang has apparently been here," he said, "and has kidnapped her. We believe it happened an hour or two ago."

"What! But here where . . . was she alone—did no one see anything?"

"She was alone. I was in the village. The others were here. We heard nothing. One of her sandals was found behind the chapel. There were signs of activity, perhaps a struggle, in the brush bordering the area."

"But I thought it was Shan-fei—?"

Hsi-chen's mother shook her head. "It was revenge he wanted more than anything," she said dismally. "He is an evil man!"

"What are you doing about it?" said Robbie, almost shouting. By now his tone was frantic, his eyes wild with fear. He wanted to scream and run all at once. He could barely control his emotions, much less his tongue. His agitated body cried out for action. "Why are you all sitting here! Why hasn't someone gone after her?" The accusation in his tone was felt by everyone in the room.

"We are doing the best possible thing we could do, Mr. Taggart," answered Coombs. "We are surrounding Hsi-chen with prayer. The power of the Lord is greater than an army of ten thousand."

"Prayer! And nothing else?"

"Wang will not harm her," said Wallace, holding out a piece of heavy paper. "This was left. It says he has taken her to be his wife."

"Wife! And you say he will not harm her!" yelled Robbie, his control breaking. "What kind of man are you! You're going to let this happen without a fight?"

"The fight is not ours, Mr. Taggart. The battle is the Lord's, and *He* will deliver her. We are praying for that deliverance. And in the meantime, I have sent one of the village men to Hangchow to notify the British legation—"

"Hangchow!" Robbie threw his hands in the air. "Do you have any idea what a man like Wang could do to her in just one night?" he exclaimed in disbelief. "How can you be so callous!"

"God will protect her, as He did Esther in the court of Ahasuerus."

"God! I don't believe what I am hearing! How can you recite fairy tales at a time like this? You can do what you will. I'm going after her!"

"Mr. Taggart!" warned Wallace, resuming some of his old tone. "Do not act foolishly. I know your heart is right. But your actions could do more harm than good."

"No more harm than sitting idly by and doing nothing!"

"There are other steps I have undertaken besides Hangchow. But we must wait upon the Lord for guidance at every move. Without Him both before us and behind us, we are certain of failure. In trust of Him, there is certain victory."

"You call this victory! You, with your pious words that prove empty to save your own daughter."

"Leave it in God's hands, Mr. Taggart."

"For a while, I almost thought I could believe in this God of yours," retorted Robbie. "But not if He requires me to sit still while someone I—"

He stopped short, flustered even in his anxiety at the word which nearly escaped from his lips. "I won't do it!" he yelled, spinning around and stalking from the room.

He did not even know where to go, but he'd find out. He had no weapon, but he'd get that too. He might find himself facing an army of cutthroats, but he didn't care. Even if he was slain trying, he had to make the attempt. He had to show them that what they were doing was wrong!

Hsi-chen had taught him the expression, *Where is . . . ?* He would try that. He could use her name, perhaps Wang's. He could pantomime *bandit.* Somehow he would make himself understood!

I must free her, he thought blindly. He shrank even at the thought of Hsi-chen in the presence of such men, much less being forced to—

He shuddered and forced the thought from him.

I've got to find her! I can't be too late! God, help me! he cried, half-aloud, before he even realized what he was saying.

Across the bridge Robbie ran, aimlessly, just to be moving. Suddenly he found himself at the door of the farmer with whom he had spent the evening. He managed to make himself understood, and a few minutes later left the way he had come, jamming the knife he had been given into his belt. Pounding on doors and making frantic signals and crying out in a most unintelligible form of gibberish, he made his way throughout the village, waking half the hardworking men and women of the fields, until at last he found what he suspected to be the information he needed.

Then, lightly touching the hilt of the farmer's blade for reassurance, he raced into the hills toward an ancient monastery.

50

Where Angels Fear to Tread

When Robbie caught sight of the imposing monastery, he slowed his frenzied pace.

Now that he was near his destination he knew he must pause and force his distraught mind to focus on practical considerations. All at once Wallace's words seemed more rational than they had earlier in the evening.

" . . . I know your heart is right, but your act could do more harm than good . . ."

He shoved Wallace from his mind. Prayer was not a weapon men like Wang understood or honored. Perhaps God had put Robbie at the mission for just this occasion. Hadn't God used force over and over in the Bible? This must be another such occasion where prayer had to be supplemented with strength. Maybe God had brought Robbie here so that there would be a man of action ready to intercede when the need arose.

He looked up at the ancient walls a hundred feet above where he stood. Part of the edifice was carved right into the rock of the mountain, giving it the appearance of a fortress rather than a place of contemplation and worship. *What a fitting contrast!* Robbie thought.

He stepped off the path he had been following. He could not walk right up to the temple gates! Instead, he climbed a more circuitous route, over rock and through brush, hoping to approach the compound unobserved. It was still dark, with an hour or two left before daylight. If he could just sneak into Wang's hideout, locate where they were holding Hsi-chen, he might be able to get her out and avoid any unnecessary violence.

Wang's lookouts, however, had been watching for and expecting Robbie. They had, in fact, known of his approach even as he left the village.

When he reached the south wall, Robbie began to assess it for breaches. There had to be another entrance other than the front gates. Slowly he began to walk along the length of the wall. He had not reached its end before three stout figures jumped from the undercover of darkness and laid hold violently on him. With a sudden horrible ache, Robbie knew the truth of Wallace's words. His madcap flight had been a foolish gesture of knight-against-dragon. But this was no fairy tale. The dragon's lair would no doubt be his tomb.

Struggling uselessly, he was half carried, half dragged inside the fortress-monastery, then forcefully thrown down in the center of the courtyard at the foot of a statue of some deity he did not recognize, nor care to.

Before he could look up, a searing and shrill laugh, devoid of all humor, rent the night air. It was a familiar sound he had never expected to hear again.

Robbie's eyes moved in the direction of the sound. Benjamin Pike!

"Oh, laddie," said the broken-down old sea captain, "how I wish I didn't know ye so well! But ye showed up jist like clockwork!"

All the questions that came to Robbie's mind didn't seem so important just then. Pike was here, that was all that mattered, no doubt in league with these scoundrels. He quickly surveyed his immediate surroundings. It was not unlike the Buddhist temple where he had passed the night several days ago, only this was larger and built on two levels. Glancing up toward the long balcony that skirted the second level, he spied some ten or twelve of Wang's soldiers heavily armed, positioned along its length. Robbie had imagined Wang's forces to be larger—as in truth they were, for only a small portion had been dispatched from his main headquarters farther inland. But even though there were fewer than twenty men altogether, the chance of escape seemed hopeless.

Robbie brought his attention back to Pike just as two more men left one of the buildings and approached him. Without having laid eyes on the man, he instinctively knew Wang at first sight.

Robbie pulled himself to his feet, and his three captors fell away. Pike and Pien took their positions on either side of Wang, and the warlord eyed his enemy up and down with a derisive glint in his narrow eyes.

"So this is all the barbarians could spare to rescue their little flower! Ha, ha!"

"You won't get away with this, Wang!" retorted Robbie. But his empty words of challenge were met only with mockery for his fool's hope of rescue.

"But you see, I *have* gotten away with it, as you say!" Wang laughed again, then turning coldly sober, motioned to one of his men.

The next moment another door opened, and two more men emerged, bearing Hsi-chen roughly between them. She appeared pale, even in the lantern-lit darkness, and fragile. But she walked proudly, bearing a strength within her that even these ruthless villains could not daunt.

"What of your feeble rescue attempt now, Wai-chu?" spat Wang.

"Let her go!" begged Robbie.

"Even now you think you may convince me to release my prize, perhaps this time by pleading rather than violence."

Wang rubbed his beard.

"Hmm," he mused, "what would the maiden think of her brave barbarian, watching him grovel in the dirt before me, begging for his life?"

"Any coward could make a man grovel, with a dozen guns pointed at him," returned Robbie defiantly.

"Ha! I will kill you for such insolence!" shouted Wang.

A nudge from Pike, who cleared his throat meaningfully, seemed to bring the warlord back to his senses. He stopped to reconsider his strategy.

"We will soon see who is the coward," growled Wang. "And my sweet lotus blossom herself will see who is the true man, and to him she will give her loyalties." He paused, then issued Robbie a challenge: "You want little Hsi-chen, barbarian? Then fight for her!"

Robbie cocked his head toward the armed listeners. "What kind of fool do you take me for? How can I expect a fair fight from you, much less your living up to your bargain?"

Even as he spoke, Robbie began to hope that all was not lost yet. For some reason Wang wanted to toy with him. That was fine; it gave Robbie the edge, for Wang was a proud man. And Robbie well remembered the proverb, "Pride goes before a fall."

"You stinking, filthy pig!" screamed Wang. "As if I needed those clumsy buffoons to crush a worm such as you into the dirt!"

He waved an arm at his soldiers and shouted out an order in Chinese. It was instantly obeyed, as with a clatter and shuffle, all weapons were lowered. With a sudden sweep of his arm, Wang pulled his cutlass from its scabbard. Robbie's original captors retreated, as did Pien and Pike, to the walls—well away from the center of the makeshift arena—the courtyard of an ancient monastery.

Robbie jumped back, drawing the fisher's knife in readiness.

Sword against knife. Though it was a hefty blade of some twelve inches, it was hardly an equitable match. Yet Robbie was swift and daring, and driven by a desperate need to win. But he could not keep from being solely on the defensive, as Wang approached, an evil glint of blood in his thin eyes.

With amusement showing on his face, Wang came on, thrusting a few tentative strokes toward Robbie, playfully rather than seriously. Robbie dodged, blocking them with his short weapon as best he could. This was a form of defense utterly foreign to one who had grown up knowing how to use his fists. Yet, as instinct had served Coombs on the riverbank, it also came to Robbie's aid now. What he lacked in experience with blades, he made up for in savvy, a quality of character with which Wang was scantily endowed.

Suddenly Wang lunged at Robbie's midsection with his cutlass. Robbie quickly sidestepped the maneuver, though the sword caught the edge of his shirt, slitting a clean gash through it. Another blow came on its heels. Lurching to the other direction, Robbie's foot caught on a broken stone in the floor and he tripped, falling to the ground. Hsi-chen screamed as with a mighty thrust Wang leaped toward his downed foe. But Robbie rolled to his left, avoiding the near-fatal blow by the merest of inches. While Wang recovered himself from the miscalculation, Robbie jumped back to his feet, and prepared himself for the next attack.

Robbie steered off with his knife the volley that followed, managing to keep his feet. All was silent except the clang-clanging of steel on steel, mingled with the dusty shuffling of booted feet on the stone floor. With each renewed approach by Wang, Robbie parried the blows with increasing skill. The dark worked to Wang's advantage, for his blade was difficult to see as it sliced through the air. The longer the battle went, the more Robbie's chances improved, but he could not keep Wang's blade from penetrating dangerously toward him. By the time the first hints of the dawn began to show gray in the sky to the east, his shirt was smeared with blood from several damaging gashes, and across one thigh ran a six-inch bloody impression of Wang's deadly weapon. All it would take would be one split-second lapse in his concentration, and he would be dead. Wang was waiting for that moment to come with cunning expectation.

Robbie had managed to inflict only minor damage to Wang. The big man handled his sword with great skill, and kept his presence of mind despite his great bulk. As light began to bathe the compound, both men were bruised, Robbie badly cut, and each panting from the exertion that had by now gone on more than twenty minutes. However, the time factor was more seriously telling on Wang, some twenty years Robbie's elder. The Chinese's experience served him well, but the white barbarian with nothing more than a knife was a wild man—as the decrepit sea captain had once said.

All at once, without warning, as if divining the enemy's thoughts, Robbie charged, taking the offensive and lunging fiercely at the warlord. The change took Wang, lulled momentarily into a slackening of concentration, by complete surprise. Each had been watching the other's eyes, but Robbie's gaze probed more deeply into his opponent's psyche. Almost without realizing it, Wang retreated a step, and in the confusion, lowered his guard for the merest fraction of an instant. Robbie's swift thrust sliced a deep gash in Wang's cheek. The bandit reacted with a crazed attack in reprisal. But his frenzy was ill-timed and only played into Robbie's hand. As he pressed his sword forward, leaning toward his foe, Robbie was in perfect position to step aside and grab deftly at his arm. Gripping it with all his might, he twisted it with a sharp sideways motion. The sword fell with a clanging echo to the stone below. Robbie wrenched Wang to the ground almost in the same motion, and the next instant had his knee rested on the warlord's chest with the sharp point of the fisher's knife pressed against the warlord's throat.

The fight was over.

Throughout the fight Robbie had not given so much as a moment's attention to Wang's henchmen surrounding him. But now suddenly he heard a clatter all about him as hands were quickly laid to their weapons.

"Tell them to keep those guns out of sight, Wang!" ordered Robbie through gasping breaths. "And tell your two over here to let the girl go."

Wang squirmed as if to test both the man's sincerity and his strength. But in reply Robbie pressed the knife painfully against its target. The tip broke the skin and a trickle of blood began to flow.

"I have nothing to lose, Wang! Do as I say or you're a dead man!"

Wang shouted the order in Chinese and again it was obeyed. Hsi-chen was released and she ran toward Robbie. Violently he shook his head as she approached. "Go!" he yelled. "Run . . . get out of here—now!"

She hesitated but a moment, then obeyed, ran across the courtyard to the gates, flinging them wide, then ran from the temple down the path.

Robbie eased the pressure of his knee against Wang, drew the knife back, and slowly pulled the adversary to his feet. With the knife still held dangerously in place, and with his left arm around his shoulder gripping Wang to the front of his own body, Robbie backed toward the open gate, using the girth of his enemy as a shield against some foolish bandit who might want to raise his position in this den of thieves by killing the interloper.

When Pike saw that again Robbie had eluded the fate he had planned for him, the last and final bond of his sanity and human control broke. As Robbie began his retreat toward the gate with Wang, steadily eyeing the men on the second level, Pike inched his way toward where the sword had fallen several feet from him. Slowly he retrieved it, then began cautiously working his way around the outside of the courtyard in the opposite direction, remaining all the while out of Robbie's direct line of vision.

At the gate Robbie paused. He could take the big man no farther; that would only tempt disaster. Wang's men still had not moved from their positions, and thus Robbie would have several moments after he released Wang before they could either shoot or make pursuit. He only hoped Hsi-chen had kept running and was well away from this hideous place! There should have been time for her to get halfway down the mountain by now.

He backed several paces outside the gate, not realizing who was waiting for him there. With a great heave he shoved Wang forward, taking no pleasure in seeing the mighty bandit crumble to his knees, and turned to dash away.

But as he did he saw the narrow path blocked by Pike, wildly brandishing the blood-stained cutlass in the air.

"Get out of my way, Ben! My fight's not with you."

"Ye've ne'er understood, have ye, laddie?" said Pike with menace in his evil tone. "Ye've never understood what the fight was about!"

"I don't know what you're talking about, Ben. Just get out of my way! I'm coming through!"

Knowing that to pause even a few more seconds would mean certain death, Robbie charged down the hill, doing his best to ward off Pike by waving the knife he still held in his right hand.

He did his best to twist his way around to the right of Pike, having no intention of trying to do him harm, only trying to get past him so he could flee down the path ahead of Wang's men.

But Pike stood his ground, heedless of the knife, heedless of death, heedless of former friendships, thoroughly given over to the madness which had come over him. Clutching the razor-sharp saber in both hands, almost as if the weight were too much for him, he sliced it through the air wildly, his hysterical eyes gleaming with the delirious and maniacal fire of crazed revenge.

Robbie ran by him unscathed, then, with the words, "Ye son o' an evil man!" Pike made a final, desperate sweeping gash with the fateful weapon toward Robbie's retreating form.

As he reached full stride, Robbie's swinging arms were extended from his body. The final blow of the saber found its mark just above the wrist of the left hand.

Every nerve of Robbie's body exploded in pain. With a terrifying scream of tormented anguish, he looked to see blood pouring from where his left hand had once been.

"Oh, God!" he screamed, even as his legs continued involuntarily to carry him down the hill. "God, what has happened to me?"

Behind him he was unaware of Wang's voice from just inside the compound, "After him, you fools! Get him!"

"I got him!" yelled Pike, his demented eyes still glowing with sickening dread at his awful deed. "Ha, ha! Got him better'n killing him! Let him go! Let him see what it's been like all these years! Taking away Robbie Taggart's strength's better'n putting a bullet in his heart! Let him go, if the blag'ard don't bleed to death first! Ha, ha, ha!" A stream of barking laughter rolled from his twisted lips even as the sword fell from his hand.

Down the path Robbie stumbled, his legs weakening, his brain growing faint, his face white with shock and loss of blood. He could not tell whether he had gone but a few steps farther or a great distance. All gradually slipped into slow and heavy motion, sounds faded from his ears, all about him seemed to be seering light, until finally the pain and shock overwhelmed him.

The light dimmed, his consciousness faded, and Robbie collapsed into utter blackness.

Part IV

Awakening

51

Changes

Great clouds moved across the western sky, glowing around the edges with red and orange and amber as they reflected the setting sun. A storm was making its way inland from the coast. Possibly the tail end of a typhoon. It would hit by tomorrow and release a torrent of rain over Wukiang.

Rain was good for the newly planted rice. But not a few of the farmers, shaking their heads in concern at the rolling clouds, were already busily testing the soundness of their drainage systems, a maze of ditches designed to carry off the expected surplus.

Robbie marveled at the perennial quality of the lives of these Chinese country folk. Watching them from atop a little hill about a mile from the village, it was not difficult for him to believe that their revered ancestor had weeded their rice and watched the skies with the same concern. For hundreds, even thousands of years, day in, day out, they walked to their fields and went about their labors—the same fields, the same dirt, the same rice, all underneath the same storm-laden sky. A baby might be born, an old man die, a son leave home. But all these passing incidents were but threads of a slightly different texture woven into the huge, unchanging fabric of life.

How odd it was, Robbie thought, that he should be reclining on the grassy hillock, thus musing upon the unchangeableness of life. Why should the daily routines of these people so impress him now—not only impress him, but deeply stir him with a kind of envy?

For young Robbie Taggart—sailor, adventurer, soldier of fortune—all life had been dramatic change. New ports, new people, new journeys, new assignments—he had grown accustomed to a life where his footsteps never retraced the same ground twice. Yet even in his life as a wanderer, as he now reflected on it, he could see that there had been a perennial aspect to it too. Perhaps he was not so different from these farmers as one might have thought at first glance. Even the diversity of his life had contained a certain predictability, a certain unchangeableness.

But everything was different for Robbie now.

Almost against his will, his eyes wandered to the empty end of his sleeve. He shuddered, as he always did, wondering if he would ever get used to it, hating it, wanting desperately to ignore it. But how could you ignore such a horrible reminder that you were different, maimed, grotesque in the eyes of others—that life would never again be the same?

When he first learned his fate, he only wanted to die; and that attitude remained even after the days of weakness, delirium, loss of blood and nausea subsided and his strength returned. Why couldn't Coombs have just left him on the mountain road where he and Hsi-chen had found him, rather than trying to stop the bleeding long enough to load him into the rickety old cart? He was already unconscious; if they hadn't found him, he'd have died a painless death, if not from loss of blood, then from Wang's sword through his heart. In either case, the pain for Robbie would have been over.

But they had found him, had somehow managed to get him loaded before Wang's men arrived, and kept him alive long enough to lay him out on Wallace's operating table, where the doctor had saved his life. At first he had cursed the doctor for sending Coombs to follow him, for rescuing him from the jaws of death. Dr. Wallace had calmly told him that he was experiencing a natural reaction and that soon he would come to accept his loss. He bore not a trace of self-righteousness, only tenderness and understanding and compassion—which at first had made his words and his presence all the more impossible to tolerate. Robbie had been in a hateful mood and wanted an excuse to despise Wallace all over again. But the good doctor had given him none.

Since then three weeks had somehow inched past. But still the gnawing ache remained. Not the weird pain, as if his fingers still throbbed, of the itch that his right hand unconsciously sought to scratch only to find nothing there—phantom feelings, Wallace had called them. No, the ache that plagued him was of a deeper, an even more frightening quality.

For a man in love with life, it was sheer terror wondering if he could go on another day. Every morning he had to face his unendurable fate all over again, asking himself over and over: could he survive another twenty-four hours?

He had survived. His presence here on the hill was witness to that. And though he dreaded tomorrow, he knew it would come also. Each day would come, one upon the other, just as it did in continuing cycle for these Chinese peasants. It was a fact he had to face—and accept.

He had to ignore that cursed voice that kept telling him he was no longer a man. When that voice came, he could only focus on what he *wasn't*, what he no longer could do. The voice told him that people would stare at him the rest of his life as a freak, as an incomplete human being. The voice told him he would never sail again, or if he did, it would only be as a result of the courtesy of some compassionate skipper. The voice told him he could no longer carry his own weight, no longer protect himself, no longer fight for what he believed in.

But was his entire existence wrapped up in one hand?

He tried to shake the probing question from his mind. Over by one of the streams, a tributary of the K'uan-chiang, an unskilled boatman was having difficulty with the small bamboo sail of his junk. The wind had picked up considerably in its effort to usher in the storm, and the young sailor had not trimmed his sail in time. It was now stubbornly refusing to obey his inexperienced hands—his *two* hands.

Wherever he looked, Robbie could not shake off the sudden new quandaries of his life. One way or another, sooner or later, he was going to have to look them squarely in the eye and deal with them. He had begun to realize that. Yet still he put it off.

Wallace told him he did not have to face his future alone. There was a God, a *Lord* if he would make him that, who was very near, who was listening to the cries of his heart, who was waiting with outstretched arms to welcome him into a future of purpose and wholeness.

But what did "wholeness" mean to one like Robbie? How could he now lean on God to support his own faltering being without admitting that he was *not* whole, that he now *needed* the crutch of a Savior, something he had always prided himself that he didn't need?

He had to smile at the question. It was not, however, one of Robbie's open, infectious grins. They came seldom these days. This upward twisting of his lips more resembled one of the Vicar's bitter, sarcastic smirks. The reason for this rare attempt at mirth was his growing familiarity with the subject of dependence. Miss Trumbull or Shan-fei (Hsi-chen had the good sense to defer to others in these tasks) had to cut his meat and spread the butter over his bread for him. Thomas or Ying had to tie his shoes, and Wallace was still struggling to teach him to button his own shirt with only one set of fingers.

Dependence . . . ha! Why should he quibble over such a thing any-more? He needed people now—he was helpless! So why not need a God, a Savior, too? Why not admit it—proud though he had once been? He *needed* a crutch now!

When several weeks ago he had been thinking so much about what being a Christian might mean, he had still conceived of it primarily as a mental process. He had heard Wallace tell him that belief meant to trust fully. Yet still he envisioned his own potential coming to faith on his own terms—as active and vibrant. Now it seemed, he must come crawling to God, helpless, weak, with nothing but half a body to offer.

"Oh, God!" he cried out to the stormy heavens, "what am I to do?"

Then as if in answer to his unintentional prayer, voices from the past weeks flooded into his thoughts. Wallace and Coombs and Hsi-chen had poured their lives and knowledge into him—and their prayers too, though he had not seen that aspect of it. By their words they had given him the key to all his questions, though it was only now, with hindsight clarified by his present suffering, that slowly the pieces of the eternal puzzle began to fit together in his anguished heart.

Wallace's words had been clear, though Robbie had tried to discount it because of the doctor's demeanor. But Wallace had given him the answer to his most basic question.

"To be a believer, a Christian, in the true sense, means to place your trust in Jesus Christ, depending on Him for all of the decisions and goals and priorities and attitudes and values of your life. To depend on Him entirely. To give yourself wholly to Him. To become like Him. To live like Him. To model your life after His. To obey His commands and instructions . . ."

Was dependence on Him the only way to follow God? Again the question nagged at him. How could he trust this Jesus so much as to forsake what had always been essential to who he was as a person?

In response Hsi-chen's gentle voice came back out of the past to remind him that it was precisely his personhood—his, and his alone!—that Jesus came to give himself for, to fulfill, to make whole. *"Jesus came from God, as God's Son, to show men the truth. Jesus died for each individual person—for you, Mr. Taggart, and for me—for everyone. That is what God's love means. That is the gospel."*

Still Robbie resisted. Still he held back from admitting that he needed the kind of wholeness God had to give him. Still he tried to excuse his reluctance by imagining it was the loss of his hand which had suddenly made him less than whole and more in need of a Savior. But it was not the loss of his hand. Robbie, like all men since Adam, had *always* been less than whole and in need of the Savior. He was only now beginning to see it. He had had to lose a hand in order to enable God to focus his eyes on the true nature of his need.

But at last, by degrees, his eyes were opening and his spirit was struggling to awaken. Even as he wrestled with question after question, he recalled Wallace's words: "*Understanding comes by choice, by opening your heart and mind toward God and the ways of God. Anyone who wants to understand and seeks God's wisdom will understand. God promises enlightenment to those who seek Him.*"

"Is that it?" he asked himself. "Is that the answer, God? Have I been so confused about all these things because down deep I haven't really *wanted* to understand? Have I resisted your truth?"

Robbie pensively looked down over the valley spread out below him.

"God . . . God," he said at length, very softly but audibly, "I *do* want to understand. I *do* want to know the truth, and I want to live the truth. Please . . . help me. Show me the truth."

Still God continued to answer the quiet and sincere search of Robbie's heart with voices from his past. Coombs had said, "*Christianity has the one ingredient that makes all the difference, the one thing that makes it true in the face of all other insufficient attempts to know God and discover the essential meaning of life.*" And Hsi-chen had simply said, "*There is really only one question in life. It comes down to the Master Builder, to a life with a God who is personal and who is love. That's what is so different about the Christian way, Robbie Taggart. The man Jesus makes everything different. Different and new.*"

The man Jesus . . .

What was it about this man who lived so long ago that made all the difference?

Coombs had called Him *the true man . . . manhood defined*. Robbie remembered how shocked he had been at the words. Jesus—that person whom so many took for a meek, soft-spoken weakling—is in reality the essence of what *true* manhood is all about! It was such an explosively new thought. How could it be? All his life Robbie had been seeking his manhood by being stronger and wiser and tougher and more vigorous than anyone else. By being a man's man! Wasn't that the essence of the seafaring life—outwitting one's companions, the ship, the elements, the sea itself, and coming out on top, with one's own strength? Robbie had been proud of his strength!

Now was it all to be reversed? Was masculinity none of those things at all?

Jesus, the true man . . . manhood defined. It was revolutionary! He had laid everything down, even His life. He had laid down strength of muscle. He had laid down position, fame, honor. He had been spit on, then executed. He had not lifted a finger to defend himself, uttered not a word in His own defense. Yet was this *true* manhood? The very opposite to what he had always thought! Was this *true* strength—strength, not of might, but of character; strength of value and purpose, not of wit or brawn; eternal strength, not temporary gain?

Robbie pondered the life and person of Jesus more personally and sincerely than he ever had. He reflected on all he had read in Hsi-chen's little black New Testament about the man. And gradually as he thought, the power of the life of Jesus began to steal over him. Here was indeed a life of strength, a life that had turned the world upside down by the very might of its central character. Here was a story where in a humiliating death was born the ultimate victory, where in laying down one's life is one given more life, where in giving one receives, where the last are in fact first, where gain comes from serving. In the life of Jesus, indeed, all the world's values *had* been turned upside down. What Robbie had all along been searching for as the ultimate requirements of manhood were in fact just the opposite.

The manhood he had so long been seeking—*true* manhood—sprang from another source.

For Robbie Taggart, his existence had always been wrapped up in his physical self, and in his self-sufficiency. To lay down what he had always held dear, to utter a simple expression of need, went cross-grain to all he had been.

A scripture Wallace had read him two days ago came back to mind. *"My strength is made perfect in weakness."* He was beginning to see a little of what it might mean. Yet what a bitter pill it was to have to admit that he, Robbie Taggart, was *weak*! Not just from the loss of a hand. That was weakness as the world judged it. But he was weak in every way—as a *man*, he had *always* been weak, inside, in his heart, but only now were his eyes opening to that fact. What an agony it was to accept that reality! He was *not* strong—not strong as Jesus was strong. He had no strength of compassion, no strength to lay down his life, no strength of eternal purpose. His whole life had been focused on a form of supposed manliness that was in truth no manliness at all! Never before had he seen or acknowledged his need of anything, of anyone.

Now, it was all at once abundantly clear to him. Robbie Taggart was a man in need!

He sat watching the farmers gather up their tools at day's end, remembering a similar scene from weeks earlier, a field, like these he was gazing upon now, where two men had toiled—one a farmer, the other a missionary, a man of God.

Robbie recalled his initial surprise at seeing Wallace thus engaged in backbreaking physical labor. He had seemed so out of his element. But did it not take more of a man to give assistance to his enemy than to wield an awkward Chinese hoe? *Any* man could be taught to hoe a field. But what a different kind of strength it took to lay down hostilities and embrace an enemy as a brother! Wallace had not praised Coombs for what Robbie had considered his courage in battling their foes, but what praise he would have received for returning love for their evil! Everything was backwards now! It might, in fact, take more courage—in the *new* sense—to admit his need before God and to relinquish his desire to stand on his own than to stumble through life in the power of his own strength.

The first drops of rain brushed Robbie's face: the storm would come earlier than expected. Robbie hoped the farmers were prepared. The winds and rains would strike the coast with wild fury, torrential rainfall and hundred-mile-an-hour gusts. By the time the storm reached Wukiang it would have abated to about half its original power. It would still be formidable, but the farmers would be ready, for they met with such weather from the heavens every year and knew how to prepare themselves for it. If only he had been as prepared for the violent blast that had touched his life. He had always thought himself immune from such things—tragedy is far away when one's life consists of a happy-go-lucky grin, a gust of wind off the sea, and a merry jig in an earthy pub.

At length the rain forced Robbie to his feet. He sighed deeply, then had to pause a moment to steady himself before walking on down the hill. It served as a reminder of his weakness, of the fact that things would never be the same again.

52

The Hillside Again

It was dark when Robbie reached the mission compound. His clothing was wet through from the rain that had steadily increased as he had descended from his pensive hilltop perch.

Passing the camphor tree, his eyes fell on the old, beat-up stump where he had worked so many days cutting shingles for the missing roofs. He hadn't finished the job; he was sure Hsi-chen was already placing pails in key positions around the residence to catch the drips.

Nor would he finish it. How could he now? He was incapacitated. He might be able to wield a hammer, but who would hold the nail? How would he climb up the ladder? How would he be able to cut more shingles? The nagging practical questions brought on by life with only one hand only heightened what he had known all along: he *wasn't* a complete man now! He had lost that most visible symbol of manhood—his capacity to do things for himself!

Robbie stopped. Someone had left the hammer out. He stooped to pick it up. After a moment he hefted it in his hand, then brought it down with a great dull thud against the stump.

He threw his face up into the black sky and let the rain wash over it, unable even to say the words that always led the torrent of questions: *Why did it happen to me?*

He did not say it, perhaps because he was finally beginning to realize the bitter answer: because he would not have listened in any other way. The Voice from heaven had been calling a long time, but he had closed his ears. He had refused, pretending such voices were only for other people. But the Heart behind the Voice was not one to give up so easily. Wallace had told him that God loved Robbie too much to let him escape. He loved Robbie so much He allowed this in order to get Robbie's attention, to get him to look up, to get him to the place where he was able to accept that love. *Ha!* Robbie had thought. *He took my hand because He loves me! That has got to be a divine joke of cruel magnitude!*

Perhaps Wallace had been right. Was it possible—incredible though such a notion would have been to the old, happy-go-lucky, independent

Robbie Taggart. Incredible . . . but just possibly true. *Could* God love him that much? So much that no price was too small, that any sacrifice—even his hand—was worth waking Robbie up to that love?

Maybe it wasn't so much of a sacrifice, really. God had—so the story goes—lost a Son, *given* His Son, because His love was so great. Jesus had laid down, not a hand, not an arm, not a piece of himself, but His very *life*! He had died a cruel and unjust death because of that Love. He had willingly sacrificed himself to make that love come alive in the hearts of men.

Maybe the loss of an arm wasn't so great—if it did indeed awaken that love within him.

He knew what Wallace would say. *"One day, Robert, you're going to give God thanks for allowing this to happen. Whenever you think of it you're going to praise Him, because that's how He showed you the depths of His love. That's how He made real to you just how great was Jesus' love."*

Would that day ever come when he would count it a privilege to share in a tiny way in the sufferings of Jesus—for the sake of being opened more fully to His Father's great love.

Slowly he walked to his room adjacent to the hospital, and clumsily changing his wet clothes, he lay down on his bed. He knew he had missed the dinner hour. He had intentionally done so. During that afternoon he had begun to feel so close, so on the verge . . . of something, of a breakthrough, that he feared the distractions of people and food and talk might push it out of his reach. He stretched himself out, wishing he could sleep, but doubting he would. He lay for many hours, turning many things over and over in his mind, before finally dozing off a few hours before dawn.

When he awoke it was still raining. Robbie remained in his room reading the New Testament Hsi-chen had given him. During the days of his recuperation from his near-fatal wound, he had spent most of his time studying that little book and had read it completely through twice, though so much still remained a mystery to him.

Occasionally he had asked questions of the mission folk. But during his recovery Robbie had been unusually taciturn, withdrawn, speaking little despite the frequent visits from everyone. And still he felt more comfortable alone, wandering over the fields and hills when the weather permitted, or keeping to his room. The others seemed to respect this need for solitude and had made few demands on him.

The light knock he now heard on his door was a rare intrusion. He closed his book, rose from the bed, and opened it. There stood Wallace.

"We missed you last night—and this morning," he said simply. "I was concerned."

"I'm fine."

"You are still recovering from a serious drain to your system. As your doctor, I need to make sure you get adequate nourishment."

"I just haven't felt very social."

"I understand. Solitude is sometimes as healing as a meal." Robbie knew Wallace did understand. It was clear from his tone, and in the depth of his eyes. Robbie had come to see the doctor in a new light. For the first time he was able to see through what he had taken for surface harshness, into the spirit of the man. "Please," continued the missionary, "may I conduct a brief examination—as a precaution?"

Robbie nodded in reply and sat on the edge of the bed. Wallace opened a leather bag and withdrew a thermometer and stethoscope. He pressed the stethoscope against his patient's chest and listened for several moments while he placed the thermometer in his mouth.

Several moments of necessary silence passed; then Wallace removed the thermometer and peered at it.

"Well, everything seems in order," he said. "I'll have to redress the bandage on your arm, probably tomorrow."

Robbie nodded. It was the most distasteful part of his recovery.

Wallace packed up his instruments, but before leaving laid a fatherly hand on Robbie's shoulder.

"All of us here at the mission will respect your desire for solitude," he said. "But I want you to know that when the time for solitary musings comes to an end, my heart and my ears are open to you. A man often needs to verbalize his feelings to another man. The Word of God says, 'Where no counsel is, the people fall: but in the multitude of counselors there is safety.' Christ himself often sought out solitary places, yet the core of His ministry remained with people. This is a lengthy way of saying that you must not shun completely the fellowship of your companions here at the mission. You need not feel constrained to come to me—Thomas, or my daughter, or any of the others will happily receive you as well."

"I'll remember that. I appreciate it Doctor."

It rained persistently all that day and into the evening. By the following morning the clouds had begun to break up and the storm had degenerated into a damp, dank heat. The moment the hot, misting rain ceased that afternoon Robbie was back out-of-doors. Though he did so by choice, he was not essentially cut out for musing alone in a tiny room for days on end. The wind, the sky, the trees, the hills, the air, the smells of the fields—all called to his spirit, saying, "Come to me, let me teach you and heal you and refresh your spirit!"

He breathed in a deep draught of the stifling afternoon air, and it tingled through his body. It made him feel richly alive. He looked up to see Hsi-chen approaching him with a small tray of food.

How he wanted to talk to her—*really* talk, as they used to. She had been most respectful of his solitude. She had been shy and reticent around him, and at first he had imagined the cause to be his lost hand. He feared that he repelled her. But now he realized that such could never be the case with Hsi-chen. Instead it had been *he* who had backed off in their relationship, and she was merely waiting, biding her time until he was again able to open up to her.

The very moment Robbie had dashed off to rescue her from Wang, he knew it was more than friendship that had spurred on his irrational attempt. *He loved her.* He knew that now. Though the very words ached within him, they were true. But he could not face such emotions at present. Perhaps when everything else was resolved . . .

It took every bit of power within him to exercise restraint on this present occasion, to smile in that friendly but detached manner, to exchange those few meaningless words of gratitude. How he wanted to pour out his heart to her, to *give* his heart to her, to take her in his arms and hold her. Yet that unguarded thought caused him to cast an involuntary glance at his empty cuff, and suddenly all he wanted to do was get away.

He took the tray back into his room after their brief meeting, though her sweet presence still lingered with him.

He could not eat now. Once he had given her time to return to the residence, he again exited the hospital building, this time walking toward the village. He reached the bridge of the Chai-chiang when he saw Wallace returning from talking to a shopkeeper. Instinctively, Robbie's initial reaction was to turn on his heels and head back in the other direction.

Suddenly Wallace's words of the previous morning came back to him. The pounding of his heart told him that perhaps he was running from people now, not merely seeking helpful solitude. Maybe the moment had come. Maybe it was now time to look beyond himself for a resolution. And if that were so, Robbie knew it was to Wallace he must go, because it was Wallace all along whom he had most feared. In a symbolic sense, this is where it began, and perhaps it might now end with the missionary as well.

So Robbie walked deliberately forward. The doctor smiled in greeting, seeming to know the younger man's thoughts without anything needing to be said. On the village side of the river they met. Wallace threw a strong, gentle arm around Robbie's shoulder, and they headed slowly upstream along a secluded path that skirted the edge of the village.

When they returned an hour later, the doctor's face was alive with the glow of love. For Isaiah Wallace's intensity was not limited to preaching or service or exhortation, but it also extended to the greatest gift of all. Robbie's face was serious with determination and purpose and apparent decision. His talk with Wallace was one he would never forget, and now he knew what he must do.

When they parted, it was with a firm handshake and a penetrating look each into the other man's eyes. At last they each understood one another fully. It was a bond that would never be broken.

Wallace crossed the bridge back to the compound. Robbie turned in the opposite direction and again sought the hillside. It was a lonely spot, rarely visited by the villagers and well away from any traveled thorough-fares, and in a short time had come to symbolize for Robbie the solitude of his soul. Solitude, yes. But perhaps even more, it was coming to stand for a decision he was about to make. Upward he trudged, with a strong and purposeful step, like the old Robbie might have used. But this was not the old Robbie. This was a Robbie Taggart on the verge of becoming a new man. And with that change all things would indeed be made new.

Today the sky held no ominous portents. It was a clear slate today, a haze of blue and white, tinged all over with pink. By coincidence it was nearly the same time of day as it had been two days ago, and the farmers were packing away their tools into their carts; some were already trudging along the paths toward the village, others led an ox or a cow.

For the first time in weeks, Robbie felt at peace. His peace stemmed from the fact that he now knew what had to be done. Moreover, he was resolved to do it. He was eager to do it, as he had never been before. Yet there remained a fear mingled with his anticipation.

"Perfect love casts out all fear . . ."

The words echoed in his mind, and at last he knew what they meant. There was no need to fear a God who had laid down His own life for man. It went even beyond that. For what God had done through Jesus He had done *just for him—for Robbie Taggart*. Not only for heroic, manly, exuberant, strong Robbie, but also the helpless, empty, confused, maimed and sometimes embittered person he had recently become. At last he knew that God looked only upon a man's heart, and had sacrificed the life of His Son Jesus to clean the stains that were *there*—in the heart! That's where manhood existed, where all true personhood began—in a heart made one with its Creator! It was there, in his heart, that Robbie could now enter into lasting fellowship with this God of love, and thus become, for the first time, *truly* a man.

Robbie had reached the top of the hill now, and stopped. Tears crept into his eyes. For the first time since he was a young boy, he did not try to check them or hurriedly dash them away. Today he let the tears flow, for they were the cleansing tears of a broken and contrite and humble heart. Feeling the hot drops running down his cheek was a feeling he could not remember ever having before. For the first time, he took them, not as a sign of his weakness, but of his dawning manhood in God. How could Jesus, he wondered, in the garden of Gethsemane, have wept tears of blood? How could any but the strongest of men have been moved to such depth?

"God," he thought to himself, "make me a man in the image of your Son. And give me the strength to do what I know I must do."

For though Robbie's were tears of joy and release, there was also pain in them. For still he had to make a sacrifice of his own. All that he had always thought important he now had to lay at Christ's feet.

Robbie sighed deeply. Why should it be so hard to do? Jesus had given up everything for him. He had only crumbs to offer in return. Yet it took an agony of will to yield even that small crumb, because it meant to relinquish all he was as a person. And if the promise was that he would receive an even greater personhood in return, it was not something his present vision could see clearly. It was something he had to trust God for in faith, risking humiliation before himself and others. And that was not an easy thing for any man.

Quietly Robbie sank to his knees on the wet earth. He covered his face with his hand. Tears continued to run between his fingers.

"God," he whispered, trembling as he spoke the words aloud. For a moment he could not go on, then at last in a hoarse whisper continued, "God . . . I *do* need you!"

He paused, then said again, louder this time, "*Father!—I need you!*"

Now Robbie wept in earnest, tears streaming down his face. He had never before acknowledged deep personal need before anyone. Now he had done so before his Maker. And in so doing, at once it was as if a tremendous burden was lifted from his sobbing shoulders, even as a knife stabbed through his heart, putting to death a part of his very being.

"Oh, God," he sobbed, "God . . . God! Help me! Jesus . . . I give myself to you! Make me . . . *your* man! Make me the man *you* want me to be!"

The words seemed to reverberate all around him, down the hillside and over the rice fields and mulberry groves below, even to the heavens, where they were received with triumphant joy. But Robbie no longer cared who heard his cries, in the world of angels or the world of men. For he was a new man. Slowly he rose to his feet and lifted his arms into the air. He looked at his whole right hand, and at the stub of his left wrist. "Thank you," he said quietly. "Thank you, Lord! Thank you for loving me . . . and for doing what you had to do to show me your love!"

Heavenly rejoicing seemed to flood over his being for Robbie Taggart was a wanderer no more.

53

Letter From Afar

It was on days like this that Jamie thought most poignantly of her dear Donachie.

Snow had fallen during the night, covering the sooty Aberdeen streets in white purity. The city was suddenly clean and fresh and sparkling. But Jamie's mind could not keep from straying to her beloved mountain. There, in February, the snow would be piled so thick and clean that she wondered that there was a rocky mountain under it at all. Oh yes, the bitter cold kept her imprisoned indoors most of the time. But how much more deeply she appreciated spring as a result!

She would, of course, thrill at the coming of spring to Aberdeen. In those northern climates of Scotland, April brings with it enormous quantities of hope and optimism: there is still warmth somewhere in the world, and it is on the way! The city would shine then, and Jamie had learned through the years that the sea had its merits, too. She could just catch a glimpse of it from the dayroom of her Cornhill home where she now sat. Today the waters of the chilly North Sea were slate blue; she could almost feel the cold emanating from its surface.

She glanced at the clock on the mantle. It was almost noon; the baby would be waking soon. Perhaps, if she bundled him up well, and put two or three extra layers on Andrew, they could play in the snow a bit after lunch.

She returned her attention to the household accounts with renewed resolve at the anticipation of the afternoon's outing. Life was comfortable for Jamie these days, though she never lost sight of those years in the ancient stone cottage on Donachie, or even the dim, cramped room she had occupied in Sadie Malone's place.

Her new baby was a joy, as Andrew, at seven, continued to be also. Edward made a good living as a partner in an Aberdeen law firm. Their staff of servants was small, consisting only of the two who had come with them from Aviemere, Janel the parlor maid, and their loyal housekeeper, Dora Campbell. But Jamie's own serving spirit made it quite difficult, if not impossible, for others to wait on her. Therefore the three women shared most of the household duties, and the staff had become friends and fellow-workers rather than servants.

From time to time there *were* indeed more employees in the house, but they were usually folk to whom Jamie opened up her home because of *their* need rather than hers. During the previous Christmas Season there had at one time been fully ten persons employed at the same time. Edward had laughed that Jamie even bothered calling them employees at all, for there was precious little for them to do in the small household. But despite his amusement over his wife's propensity for taking in waifs, he enjoyed having some small part in this life of service.

Neither Jamie nor Edward gave a great deal of thought to Aviemere. Their life was too full to pine over the past. As Jamie had once testified to Robbie, God had taken nothing away that He did not replace tenfold. Derek Graystone still controlled the estate, though there had been word that he had again rejoined his regiment, losing interest in the agrarian life. He had asked, through the family lawyer, for even he had not the nerve to ask Edward to his face, that Edward return. But of course Edward Graystone did not need Aviemere any more, and politely declined the offer. Only by specific direction from the Lord could he ever return there again.

All at once Jamie realized her thoughts had strayed once more.

The accounts *must* be done, she told herself, though this task was one of her least pleasurable duties as manager of the home. Dora had made it clear that she would willingly undertake the job, but Jamie felt it was a good discipline for her to continue with it. She had only to remind herself to give thanks to God for her ability to do such things at all, for it was not that many years ago when she could not even write her own name, much less run a household and family.

Just as she lowered her gaze once more to the papers before her, determining to continue on, Dora entered the room.

"I don't want to interrupt, my lady," she said, "but the mail just arrived, and I was sure you would like to have it."

"You're not interrupting at all," Jamie replied. Then she added with a grin, "I'm only doing the accounts."

Dora's eyes twinkled and her lips broke into a smile. She knew only too well her mistress's plight. She handed the small stack of letters to Jamie and departed.

Jamie shuffled through the envelopes, expecting nothing to detain her from the job at hand. It was not often the mail brought anything of great interest—all the return addresses seemed to be from people she knew in Aberdeen.

But wait—what was this? This strange looking letter had Chinese symbols on—

Robbie!, Jamie exclaimed, seeing for the first time the name on the reverse.

Dear Robbie . . . what can this mean? Jamie's sudden joy turned quickly to anxiety. Robbie had never in his life written her before. What could be wrong? She breathed a hasty prayer, then tore open the envelope.

Dear Jamie and family,

You must wonder why I should break my long and unthought-ful silence just now. How I wish I could be there with you to see you and to share face-to-face all that is on my heart. But I will have to resort to this method I have used all too seldom in my travels.

Shall I begin by saying that your prayers for me have been answered? For I know you have faithfully held me up to your Lord . . . who is my Lord now also. Yes, dear Jamie, as difficult as it may be to believe—and I can hardly believe it myself—I have at last laid down my wandering spirit and put myself in the hands of our God. You were so right in everything you said to me—why did I resist so? But how I thank you for never giving up on me! Yet God has his time for everything, and I suppose he had to wait until I was willing to sit still long enough to hear his voice. That time for me came when I was forced to admit my great need for him, and it took a severe accident for that to happen. I am in good health now, though I lost my left hand about an inch above the wrist. It is hard at times, I must be honest. But I am learning every day that the grace of God is sufficient for what I count my own weakness. And every day I try to give him thanks, for the loss of a hand is surely a small price to pay for true *life!*

There is more—if that is not enough.

God directed me to a small village in China, and here, I believe, my itching feet will at last find rest! I am at the Wukiang station of Christ's China Mission. Of all places for God to lead a poor heathen sailor! Of all places for that sailor to find renewal, respite, and love! I do not know when you will receive this letter; it is fall as I write—late September—though it will no doubt be mid-winter in my bonnie Scotland before you receive it.

I hope you are sitting down, Jamie! I am planning to be married soon! I never thought I'd find a woman to match you. But I have, and I will not let her get away from me. She is Chinese, the adopted daughter of the director of the mission, with whom I am now working. Hsi-chen is so much like you, and yet so different also. God has made you both unique—my sister and my wife to be! I tremble at the sound of the word wife, but not in the way I used to. Now it is with awe that I should have such a gift, and wonder that I should have for so long shied away from it. I am somewhat intimidated at the responsibility which will now be mine—for a wife, perhaps a family, and even for the work of the mission. Can you believe it is the footloose sailor Robbie Taggart writing these words? I hope one day you and Hsi-chen can meet, but . . . that must be in God's hands.

We do not know what he has in store for us, but we are content with the present, and trust him for the future. Perhaps I should be clear, for even as I tell myself I am protecting you from sorrow on my behalf, I think the truth is that I am only trying to protect myself. You see, Hsi-chin has a rare illness which her father, a doctor, fears may one day prove terminal. We live, not knowing how long we may have together. But God has filled our lives to overflowing, so how can we live with regrets over a future that has not even happened?

I do have many questions about trying to live as a Christian. For so many years I measured my worth as a man by how others saw me on the outside and what people thought of me. Breaking those habits and learning to see true worth by the stature of one's heart toward God and toward one's fellowman, that is no easy task! Thank God a true giant of the faith and compassionate servant of Christ's, Dr. Isaiah Wallace, is here to encourage me. Not to mention the others at the mission, and Hsi-chen herself.

See how richly God has answered your prayers! And now you are in mine also.

Please give Lord Graystone my regards, and Andrew also. He is a special young lad, and I will always remember fondly that day we spent together in London.

I must close now, for the mail packet will be casting off soon. Please continue to pray for me as I seek God's direction for my life, and as I become more and more a part of the work here at the mission.

I have never written a letter this long in my life!

My love to you, dear Jamie, and to your family!

Robbie Taggart

As Jamie read the final words, she sat back and closed her tear-filled eyes, trying to allow all Robbie had said to sink in through her quiet prayers of thanksgiving. She could not feel sorry that such pain had to befall him. For he was now where she had long prayed he would one day be. And he was happy and content; what else could matter?

In the years she had been praying for Robbie, she had always harbored a quiet sense that he was one whom the Lord intended to use in a great way. Some Christians had been called to simple walks of faith, as Jamie herself had—to touch, however profoundly, a small circle of those immediately around them. But others were set apart to influence multitudes, nations, armies, as had the Apostle Paul.

Jamie could not guess what God intended for Robbie Taggart, but she somehow knew he would do great things.

She had begun to fold the letter and replace it in the travel-stained envelope when the dayroom door flew open and a small figure bounded in. Jamie smiled and held out her arms to young Andrew, now seven, who skipped to her.

"Mother!" he exclaimed, "did you look outside? It's snowing again!"

Jamie had completely forgotten about the weather. She turned toward the window to behold a fresh snowfall descending on the city of gray granite.

Sensing his mother's change of mood, the boy turned pensive. "What's wrong, Mother? You look sad." His sensitivity toward others mingled with his own tendency toward introspection made it occasionally difficult to remember that he was just seven.

"No, dear, I'm not sad," answered Jamie. "These are tears of joy you see in my eyes."

"What's happened?" he asked; crying for joy was still a difficult concept even for Andrew to grasp.

"Look," said Jamie, holding up the letter. "It's from Robbie Taggart."

"Really, Mother? From Uncle Robbie? Did he ask about me?"

"Yes, he did," laughed Jamie.

"You must tell him I still have his hat."

"I will. In fact, we can *both* write him a letter right away. He is very far away from us, in a place called China."

"Will he ever come to visit us again?"

"I don't know. Let's pray that he does."

Andrew frowned. "Well, if he doesn't, I'll go visit him," he said firmly. "I'll wear his hat and sail a ship to see him!"

There was a deeply earnest quality in the boy's words. As much as Jamie would ordinarily have been amused over the announcement, she somehow sensed that the statement might be more prophetic than she was yet prepared for. Ever since the two had met a year before, Andrew had never ceased asking about Robbie. At the same time he had developed an obsession with ships. Jamie constantly found him buried in picture books of the sea and ships and faraway places, and when his own books failed him, he begged Edward and Jamie to read to him out of whatever adult books they could find. At first it had seemed only childish fancy. But the longer it had continued the more there grew to be something in his look when he spoke of the sea that brought motherly anxiety to Jamie's heart. As much as she loved Robbie, she could not help hoping that Andrew would not follow in his footsteps—at least at such a tender age. Yet he was in God's hands, and there was no better protection, wherever in the world his feet might one day go.

She gave Andrew an extra hug, sighed, then rose from her now-forgotten accounts.

"Let's see about lunch," she said, "and I will tell you all about Uncle Robbie's letter. Then we can go out into the snow."

Jamie took his hand and they left the dayroom, her momentary heaviness of spirit lifting almost immediately as she began to tell her son of the joyful intercession of God on behalf of their dear friend.

54

Expectation

A chill November wind swept over the mission compound as evening made its approach. Hugging his jacket close to his body, Robbie continued to pace back and forth before the front door of the residence. He had always heard of men behaving in this peculiarly nervous manner before the birth of their firstborn, but he had never imagined himself in such a position. And now here he was—the anxious, fidgety father-to-be, unable to relax even for a moment.

Yet how could he sit still when one of the greatest events of his life was occurring behind that closed door? Pacing was the only way to relieve the pent-up emotions. Even Shan-fei's tea had not helped.

He wanted to burst into the room and yell at his father-in-law not to take so long! But he knew Isaiah would only look up benevolently, and in a loving but patronizing tone say, "These things have their own timing, Robert. Babies come when they are ready, and when the Creator is ready to let them go."

It had been two hours since the heaviest stage of Hsi-chen's labor had begun, and that following almost fifteen hours of moderate pains. How much could her weakened body endure?

"Dear Father! Protect her!" he cried.

The words were hardly necessary, for Robbie knew the Lord's strong arms were ever around his dear wife. If only he could communicate that truth to his pounding heart.

A child was the last thing Robbie ever expected to have during his days of adventuring. And it certainly had been far from his mind that day more than a year ago when he had asked Hsi-chen to become his wife, especially when she had revealed the sad secret in her life.

So many things had changed so suddenly for Robbie!

His mind wandered back to that day, filled as it had been simultaneously with great joy and deep sorrow. They had walked up to the little hillside where he had made his final commitment to God. It had been no idle stroll or surprise destination. He had planned their steps exactly. All day he had been rehearsing in his mind that very moment, and knew the words must be spoken in that spot. A gentle breeze had been making its way over the hilltop, but it had nevertheless been dry and warm, for the summer monsoon still clung tenuously to the river delta.

"I will never come here without being reminded of how loving and merciful our God is—to *all* men," he had said, gazing out over the rice fields, now being harvested by the village folk. "But there are many things besides which also stir that knowledge within me."

"When one knows God," Hsi-chen replied, "it is impossible to look upon any of His creation and not be aware of His goodness."

"Yes," agreed Robbie. "I see it also when I look at you, over and over. How wonderful it was of God to have allowed me to find you." He gazed into her lovely eyes, then continued. "So often I wonder if I am worthy even to know you. Then I realize all over again that I am not worthy of any of His gifts. But it is that awareness which enables me to come to you now with what I must say—with what cries out from my heart to be said."

He paused, and took her hands in his one large, warm hand. "Hsi-chen . . . I love you!"

She opened her mouth to speak, but he stopped her with a quick shake of the head. "Please," he said, "let me finish before you protest. I haven't much to offer, though I know God is able to make up for what I lack. And I know my life has not been a stable one, and I don't even know how much of that I can change. But for once I am willing to lay all that in God's hands, if you are. For I love you and want to marry you!"

He ended abruptly, with a sharp breath and a look of anxiety on his brow, for he did not see a look of reciprocal joy on Hsi-chen's face that he had hoped for. Was he doomed never to find happiness in love?

"Oh, Robbie!" Hsi-chen finally answered in a voice filled with emotion. "I have been so selfish and unfair to you!"

"What are you talking about! You have never been selfish to me! You are incapable of such things," Robbie declared. "It's my own fault. I thought only of myself—I wanted so desperately to believe that you loved me also—"

"But I do, Robbie!"

"Then what can be worrying you so? If you are afraid of *Feng-huang's* wandering—?"

"It is not that."

Hsi-chen released her hands from his and walked a few paces from him, as if she would already begin breaking the bonds that held them. At last she spoke. "I have selfishly withheld something from you, Robbie.

I wanted so many times to tell you. But I knew when I did it must mean the end of any love we might have been able to have. So I put it off, and put it off still further, until now, when I fear I shall break *both* of our hearts."

"I don't understand."

"Robbie, I . . . I have—my body is not well, Robbie . . ."

But that had not mattered to Robbie. God had brought them together, whether it might last a year or ten years or fifty. And could not the God who brought such dramatic change to a sailor's life also heal Hsi-chen's body? And yet, as much as Robbie hoped their love might last for fifty years, in the days of bliss following their marriage, he had come more and more often before the Lord to pray for strength to accept the loss he knew must come.

He had to write Jamie again, Robbie thought. The time flew by so quickly. It had already been more than a year since his first letter, and he had had her reply months ago. What he wouldn't give to see her face when she read that Robbie Taggart was a father!

The thought of fatherhood brought Robbie quickly back to the present. He glanced toward the door. If only he could be spared from having to bid Hsi-chen farewell today! A lump rose in his throat and tears to his eyes. "I'm not ready, Father. Please, give us more time," he murmured.

When he looked up again Robbie saw old Chang approaching. He gathered in his emotions in time to greet the man with a smile.

"We hear little Hsi-chen's confinement is come," said the old man in broken English. He and Robbie had been working together to teach one another their respective languages.

"Well spoken, my friend!" said Robbie. "I wish my Chinese was progressing as well as your English."

"You have others occupy your mind," said Chang with a knowing grin. "And Chinese difficult to learn." Now he held out his hands, and Robbie saw that he held a package. "We bring gift for new little one. If son, may he bring delight to old age. If daughter, may she bring years of joy."

"*To hsieh, to hsieh,*" Robbie replied with a bow. "Many thanks, dear friend."

"My wife make," said Chang, pointing toward the package. "Need not open now. You be lucky man, and will find many blessings in firstborn!"

Robbie could not keep still the surge of emotion that rose in him. He threw his arm around the old man and embraced him. Then they parted, the old Chinese even more reticent than Robbie to display his innermost feelings.

But his words lingered in Robbie's ears. *"You . . . will find many blessings in firstborn."*

Yes, Robbie was sure he would. Though fatherhood was an experience, a gift he never thought he'd have, he now looked forward to it with great anticipation. Eleven months ago, when Hsi-chen had first approached him about the subject, he had vehemently shaken his head. He would do nothing, he said, which might increase the danger to her life. His words had been harsh and he had refused to hear another mention of the subject. Yet her downcast eyes and quiet spirit over the following days caused him to repent of his hasty judgment. Yet had not Wallace counseled him about the dangers of childbirth before their marriage, as much as physician as a concerned father? How could Robbie even dream of putting in risk this dear gift God had given him?

It was not many nights later that Hsi-chen had broached the subject once more.

"I know I must leave this world soon, my dear," she had told him.

Again Robbie tried to shake off her words. She had been looking so well lately, with high color and a healthy glow about her cheeks. He had begun to convince himself that this whole business of her illness must be a mistake. He did not want to be reminded otherwise.

"Please listen to me, dear Robbie," she implored. "I have spent many hours in prayer about this. I do not think it is wrong of me to want to leave a part of myself behind when I go. It would only be different if I knew that you did not want—"

"You know that is not it," he answered quickly. "But I want you more than any child."

"From the beginning you knew that you could not have me always," she said gently.

Robbie hung his head. "I know," he whispered at length. "But I have never given up hoping."

"I have but one reservation," she went on. "I would not want to cause you to be tied to a child . . . after I am gone. With nothing to tie you to this place, you may again—"

He raised his hand to interrupt her, but no words would come. He turned away.

Did Hsi-chen hold a latent fear that when she was gone from him, his roving feet might once more call to him? Did she think that he was still afraid of lasting ties?

Was he? No, he had put his past as well as his future in God's hands, even before he had asked Hsi-chen to be his wife. God had directed his steps thus far, and he need not fear the future.

Finally he turned his face to hers. "Oh, my dear," he said passionately, "haven't you known? Don't you yet feel it? I ceased being a wanderer on that hillside months ago—I am now a white swan! I have come here to stay. I want to have a family now. No matter what God calls me to do, our child would never be anything but a further reminder of His love—and our love, yours and mine! I would count it the greatest honor of my life, other than being your husband, to hold in trust this most precious of all gifts—your child."

"Oh, Robbie, you make me so happy!"

"You are sure it is what you want?"

"I am so sure," she answered. "And though my father will not say so, I sense that having a child will do nothing to accelerate what is coming anyway. I believe God will allow me enough time for this one last earthly joy."

Robbie drew Hsi-chen to him, kissing her tenderly. It seemed impossible that he should have discovered such a treasure!

As her final request became a reality, he tried not to think that they must soon part. Yet as the months of her pregnancy progressed through the following spring and summer, that truth became all the more painfully evident. Every day Robbie said goodbye to her in his heart, though his mind continued to struggle with what he still tried to convince himself might never happen. Something would happen, he kept telling himself—a miracle, a breakthrough of some kind.

55

Fulfillment

Robbie's thoughts jerked back to the present as the residence door swung open.

He ran forward as Wallace stepped outside and closed the door softly behind him. *How worn and spent he looks*, thought Robbie, momentarily forgetting his own anxiety in concern for the missionary. He was Hsi-chen's father, "if not by blood, then in every other way," as Hsi-chen herself had once said. His agony must be equally as profound as Robbie's; Wallace and Shan-fei would also need comfort. Yet as close as they had grown through the past year, it was still difficult for Robbie to think of this mighty man of God in need. He had been such a strength to Robbie, helping him learn to cope with the loss of the use of one hand, and even more helping him in his growth as a new Christian.

Robbie could not even count all the conversations they had had, many lasting into the early hours of the morning. Any remaining reservations he held toward Wallace fell completely away. He came to see him with spiritual eyes, and the man he had once feared gradually had become a friend—even a father to him. Many times he and Wallace and Coombs were seen trekking about the countryside together, visiting church members in the five surrounding villages, calling on the sick, handing out tracts and booklets in the Chinese language. Before Wallace had said anything, Robbie had sensed there was more involved in these activities than was perhaps visible on the surface.

Finally one day Wallace had clarified his feelings.

"I have been praying for you, lad," he said.

"Thank you, Isaiah," Robbie had answered. "You know I need prayer. Changing a lifetime of habits doesn't come easy for me."

"That is true for each one of us. I know there are many things about trying to live as a Christian that may run counter to how you were used to thinking in the past. Yet you have been giving the Lord every opportunity to remake your thought patterns and your attitudes. I must say you have earned my respect. Rarely have I seen one grow so rapidly in new faith. But I have had a specific intent in my prayers of late."

Robbie cocked a curious eyebrow. "You know Thomas is preparing to join Dr. Taylor's China Inland Mission," Wallace continued, "where he feels he will have greater opportunity to fulfill the call God has lately laid on his heart to bring the gospel further inland, perhaps even as far as Tibet."

Robbie smiled. He had known all along that Thomas Coombs was an adventurer at heart.

"And thus," Wallace continued, "I have been praying for God's direction on your life."

"As a replacement for Thomas here at the mission?" said Robbie. The thought was not a novel one; it had crossed his mind previously.

"The work we have done thus far together seems to come naturally for you," said Wallace. "You enjoy talking with people. When your Chinese tongue becomes more skilled, I perceive that the villagers will flock to hear your story. And I am certain there will be a place here for you . . . even when Hsi-chen is gone."

He paused, and both men were silent, as they usually were when faced with the reality of what her loss would mean.

"I am honored that you would feel that way," answered Robbie at length. "You know I am praying about my future, too."

"But you must hear God's leading, Robert."

"I know that," replied Robbie thoughtfully.

In the weeks which followed their conversation, Robbie had prayed even more urgently. Yet no specific answer had come, unless he could count his deepening involvement in the life of the mission as a subtle direction from above. This involvement came to be expressed through more than itinerant preaching and visitation, however. By degrees Robbie's heart began to be bound up not only with the mission itself, but also in the Chinese people it served, such as Chang, and the old rabble-rouser Li—himself very close, Robbie thought, to embracing the faith he had once so despised. In addition, lately Robbie had been drawn into friendship with a young man, a new convert by the name of Shen Kuo-hwa, whose wife had recently died in childbirth. Despite their vast cultural differences and the barriers of language, they had immediately developed a bond with one another. They had been able to encourage each other in their first steps as Christians, Robbie passing on much wisdom he had gained from Wallace. And they were also able to strengthen one another as men—Kuo-hwa from his recent loss, and Robbie in his anticipated grief. When Robbie one day all at once realized that he and Kuo-hwa were friends, in the most profound and spiritual sense of the word, he knew he had taken a great step forward. Wallace had once said to him that one of the great flaws in the character of many foreign missionaries was that, though they spread the gospel, they tended to keep to themselves. Very few actually became intimate friends with their converts, for it often took years to discover any common ground. Yet such a knitting of minds and hearts had occurred between Robbie and Kuo-hwa within a matter of months.

What does it all mean? Robbie frequently wondered to himself. He told Hsi-chen that he had become a swan. And he had meant it. But did this mean that China was in fact to be his final abode? Would he ever sail the sea again? Would he ever see his beloved homeland of Scotland?

When he had said the words to her, he had not really considered such questions. He only knew that he no longer had the desire to roam with never a thought of destination. But could he be content here? That was a question he couldn't yet answer. He desired the will of God above all things. But the question always remained—what *was* God's will? For him to remain in China? Or something else?

Well . . . that was not a question he had to receive an answer to now. He was about to become a father! And that was sufficient to occupy any man's mind for the present, and a good deal beyond!

As Wallace drew near, Robbie could see that he wore a look of anxiety. But at last the doctor's lips broke into a smile—a weary one to be sure, but a smile nonetheless. Robbie needed no more encouragement in order for his pent-up emotions to suddenly break forth. He ran forward to Wallace and threw his arms around him. Both men stood in that manly embrace for some moments before either could speak. It was Wallace who managed the first words.

"God be praised!" he said quietly.

"Hsi-chen . . . ?" Robbie forced the words past that hard lump in his throat.

" . . . is fine," said Wallace. "God is strengthening her as she knew He would. But . . ."

Here he paused while gathering his own strength. "You must be prepared when you see her, Robert," he went on. "This has taken a great toll on her body."

"Will she . . . recover?"

"That is in God's hands, my son." Wallace paused again, but this time he let another smile invade his features. "But you have not asked about your new baby! You have a daughter—a tiny thing; she weighs only five and a half pounds. But she is healthy!"

Robbie closed his eyes, though the words of thanksgiving could not seem to form to express the depth of gratitude he felt. He had hoped for a daughter, who might somehow carry forth the spirit of the mother. But he had reserved the expression of his prayers solely for Hsi-chen. In his compassion, God had seen fit to grant this small hope.

"Go into your family," urged the doctor to Robbie, who still stood speechless in front of him.

Robbie turned and ran up the steps into the residence and to Hsi-chen's room.

In the doorway he stopped short. Though Wallace had tried to prepare him for what he might see, and, if his words were not sufficient, the last months of his wife's pregnancy in which she had declined tremendously should have done so. Yet even with these warnings, the sight of Hsi-chen's face stunned him. Her normal pallor had turned ashen, her sensitive eyes were sunken and ringed with dark circles.

Suddenly for the first time Robbie found himself facing the graphic appearance of approaching death. He was too shocked to move, or even speak, only thankful that Hsi-chen had not heard him approach and that her eyes were closed and she could not see his reaction. At length Shan-fei's soft voice brought him again to himself.

"Come in, Robbie," was all she said. But it was enough. He walked the rest of the way into the room, a broad smile of love cast upon his wife, who opened her eyes and turned her head toward him.

"I hear there is a new little Taggart screaming her lungs out," he said as buoyantly as he could.

Hsi-chen held out a hand. Robbie took it in his, successfully hiding the inward wince that passed through him at how cold and clammy hers felt. His attention was immediately diverted to the small bundle nestled in the crook of Hsi-chen's arm. He could not help thinking that she was not much to look at. The baby's skin was splotched and ruddy, wrinkled almost like a prune. Her only distinctive feature was a thick thatch of black hair atop her tiny head.

Robbie's immediate reaction was that this unseemly creature could not possibly be worth the price he was paying for her. With the thought he remembered the interpretation he had heard of the Chinese word for daughter—*she-pen huo,* "goods on which one loses." Yet almost as quickly these initial thoughts were swallowed up in the smile of joy he could see in Hsi-chen's weary eyes, and he chided himself for his hardness.

He bent down and kissed his wife. "She is lovely," he said.

Hsi-chen smiled in reply, as if she had read his thoughts but did not mind because she knew his *heart* too well, to be concerned. Robbie would love his daughter with the fullness with which he loved all of life; she knew that.

"I have thought of her Chinese name," said Hsi-chen, "but you must approve."

"I'm sure I will."

"It is Chi-Yueh, which means *to record a covenant.* She is the symbol of our covenant, Robbie, and the covenant of love God has poured out on us. But she must also have a Western name, for that is part of who she is also."

She paused, clearly taxed by her speech.

"And what shall that be?" Robbie asked when he saw she had caught her breath.

"I have thought of nothing yet. We must continue to pray." She motioned him to the other side of the bed where the baby lay. "You must hold her, Robbie."

"I'll just watch," he said lamely. In all his thoughts of fatherhood, holding his own infant child had never occurred to him. He had thought of talking with her, playing with her, but *holding* her on the day of her birth? He recoiled at the thought, suddenly aware of his missing hand. How could he possibly pick up such a delicate creature in his rough, muscular arms?

"Robbie . . ." Hsi-chen's eyes saddened as she spoke, "you must learn to hold her. She will need her father's arms around her more than ever when I am gone."

"Hsi-chen . . . please!" implored Robbie, but the sob he had tried so hard to repress broke from his lips and tears began to stream from his eyes. "Oh, Hsi-chen, I don't think I can face life without you!"

"Come, my love," she said quietly. "She will comfort you."

Though Robbie wondered how even God himself could comfort him at this moment, he obeyed Hsi-chen's request, mostly because he could not bear to refuse her anything. Nearly stumbling for his tears, his body trembling, he moved closer to the child. Then he paused, not sure how to proceed. Shan-fei, who had been sitting in a chair beside her daughter's bed, now stood and lifted the baby from her mother's arms. The grandmother gently laid the child in the crook of Robbie's right arm.

The moment Robbie touched his child, all her newborn ugliness fell instantly away. Hsi-chen must have suspected that such a thing would happen. As Robbie gazed into her now opened eyes, he beheld only beauty. Very clearly Hsi-chen could be seen in the tiny face, which made Robbie happiest of all. But he could at the same time distinguish hints of himself, and in that moment, his daughter became a real person to him, a fragile tiny human being whose price was beyond reckoning.

"Dear Father," he said through his tears, "you do all things well!"

Was it right for a baby to mean so much, to represent so deeply the love of its parents? Even as he asked himself the question, Robbie knew it was impossible for this child to do otherwise. For in her small form she represented both deep loss and great gain—joy and sadness. Robbie knew, as he gazed down upon her peaceful form, that this would always make her special. She would not only be the image of her mother to remind Robbie of the woman he had loved. She would at the same time grow to become her own unique person, a precious child of God, a little covenant not only in the personal sense for Robbie and Hsi-chen, but on the larger scale between the Lord and His people. She would bridge the gap between cultures, and between faith and unbelief.

"Ruth," said Robbie suddenly, and the word seemed not of his own volition.

"It is good," affirmed Hsi-chen, then added, reciting the scriptures: *"Entreat me not to leave thee, or return from following after thee: for wither thou goest, I will go; and where thou lodgest, I will lodge: thy people shall be my people, and thy God my God: Where thou diest, will I die, and there will I be buried: the Lord do so to me, and more also, if aught but death part thee and me."*

56

The Call on a Man's Heart

The days and weeks following the birth passed slowly. Robbie was thankful for that blessing. They were days of joy, despite the cloud which hung about the compound as a result of Hsi-chen's failing health. Watching Ruth take on new characteristics each day brought her parents a great shared joy, and helped them not to think about what soon must happen.

As Wallace had been subtly training Robbie in the work of the mission, Shan-fei and Hsi-chen, with some worthy pointers from Miss Trumbull, began to instruct him in a kind of parenthood most fathers never have to learn. Of course Robbie would not be altogether alone; Shan-fei would be there to help, and would joyfully care for Ruth when her father was about the work of the mission. But Robbie had determined that the brunt of responsibility for the child would rest with him. How this would work out in reality, Robbie did not know, for mission life could be demanding at times. But God knew, and for the present that was sufficient.

These days he remained close to the mission. With increasing one-

handed dexterity, he finished the roofs on several of the smaller out-
buildings that he had not had time for, amid scoldings from the older
women that his hammering would wake the baby. But Hsi-chen was
not troubled, and neither apparently was Ruth, who slept soundly and
awoke contented.

There had been no further trouble from Wang. It had been rumored
that his defeat and loss of face caused him to lose influence with many
of his followers. Whether he was in fact merely laying low until his forces
could be regrouped, or whether he had given up his designs against the
mission altogether, who could tell. In the meantime, Robbie was not concerned, although thoughts of Pike did occasionally flit through his mind.

Winter gradually closed in upon the community. This was a slow
time for the villagers. The rice had been harvested and the winter crop
of wheat was in. But the more industrious always found use for their
idle time. As Robbie walked one day back to the mission along the river
from Kuo-hwa's house, he saw several of the village fishers out in their
boats. For them, the winter was a busy season when they would sail to
a nearby lake, and in teams of three or four boats form a circle and fish
with nets and hooks strung from the boats. *Perhaps I'll join them next
season,* thought Robbie. *It would be a good way to get to know these
men and tell them about the Lord while working side-by-side. Not to
mention an opportunity to set foot aboard a boat again!*

As he reached the bridge leading to the mission, Wallace, who was
coming toward him, waved and called out.

"I'm off on a call, Robert," he said. "Why don't you join me?"

Robbie's eyes strayed to the mission, specifically to the residence.
Perceiving his thoughts, Wallace added, "It's not far, only in the next
village. We should be back before long. I only just now checked on Hsi-
chen. She is well and about to have a bit of a nap."

"In that case, I'll tag along!" said Robbie cheerfully. "What is it you
have to do?"

"I'm going to try to see an old woman who is desperately ill."

"Try?"

"Women are not usually allowed to see doctors. Up until recently it
was even unusual for a doctor to be allowed to feel a woman's pulse—and
that only through a curtain! The Chinese are incredibly backward when
it comes to their view of women. We of the West have a great deal to
learn, but Chinese women can be treated so abysmally at times."

"What makes you think you will be allowed to see this woman?"

"Through the years I've cultivated a relationship with her family. One of her sons comes to our services. Everything takes time here Robert. But if you invest the time in these people, the rewards can be tremendous."

Thirty minutes' hard walk brought them to Lungsi, a village some two or three miles from the mission. It was similar to Wukiang in most ways, except that it was set back from the water and elevated on a small hill. They approached the house prayerfully, made their presence known, then waited. In another minute or two Wallace was shown inside; Robbie was told to wait outside. Five minutes later Wallace reappeared. They did not speak again until they were well away from the house.

"The poor woman is at death's door," said Wallace at length. "A bad heart. But at least they allowed me to see her."

"Is there anything you can do?" asked Robbie.

"Not really—at least for her heart. I did the one truly valuable thing I *can* do for her: I prayed for her soul."

"They allowed that?"

"I sensed a desperation in the atmosphere of the home. All her relatives were gathered about, expecting her to die, no doubt. I believe they were open to help from any quarter, even the foreign God. And they know the son knows me well enough. So I just bowed my head and began to pray, and no one tried to stop me. Perhaps they think that I am safe enough, so my God must be also."

"It's lucky you have your medical training."

"Luck has nothing whatever to do with it, my boy. I sought my medical training specifically so I would have a service to offer these people hand-in-hand with the gospel. It has gotten me into many places where others without that calling have failed."

All of a sudden a sharp cry tore through the quiet streets of the village. Instinctively Wallace and Robbie dashed off in the direction of the sound, which seemed to be coming from a house near the end of the street. Robbie was the first to arrive, and rapped breathlessly on the door. Inside he could still hear a child's voice screaming in agony. In a moment the door swung open.

"What is wrong?" asked Robbie; "can we help?" His Chinese, however, was unintelligible, for the middle-aged woman who stood there merely scowled blankly back at him in reply.

Wallace ran up to Robbie's side, adding, "I am a doctor. If someone is ill—"; but he stopped short as he glimpsed a clearer view of the inside of the house.

Robbie peered beyond him and saw a child, a girl of about five, sitting on top of a table, her legs extended out in front of her, with long strands of loose bandage hanging about them. Tears streamed down the pale pathetic face, her screams now reduced to choking sobs.

"As you can see," replied the woman, "we need no help." It was then that Robbie noticed that the woman's own eyes were reddened and her cheeks damp also.

"Yes, I see," replied Wallace. Then, turning to Robbie, he said, "Let's be on our way; we are not needed here."

"But—" Robbie began to protest, but Wallace shook his head and nudged his son-in-law down the step.

When the door was closed and they were several strides away, Robbie turned to Wallace.

"Her feet were being bound, Isaiah!" he said, as if a description were necessary for the experienced missionary who had seen the cruel procedure dozens of times. "We could have stopped it."

"Do you not yet perceive what our purpose is here, Robert?" asked the doctor.

"I only know that child was being tortured," Robbie replied heatedly. "If the mother herself was crying over the hateful task, that is just all the worse. She was doing it even though her own instincts tell her it is wrong. I don't understand how you can let it continue."

"What would you have me do? Forcibly tear the child from her mother? And to what avail? Tomorrow she would have been submitted again to the process, and I would no doubt have a riot against the mission on my hands for trying to interfere with the local customs."

The two walked on as Wallace continued. "The practice has been with the Chinese for nearly a thousand years. The Manchus tried to forbid it when they came into power, but the people strongly protested. Small feet on a Chinese woman is looked upon as a sign of beauty and culture. The mothers who inflict this pain on their daughters firmly believe they are doing the best for them."

"So we should turn our backs on it?" queried Robbie, his old nature rising at the thought of such injustice going forever unpunished.

"We are not here to change the Chinese culture. We've discussed before what the consequences of that can be."

Wallace paused, then stopped walking and turned one of his intense looks of deep meaning and concern on Robbie. "If I could pass anything on to you, son, it would be this one vision, this single purpose: we are here to change *hearts*, Robert! *Hearts!* Not customs, not practices, not superficial behavior. That is what I would want for you to see. Look beyond the externals, both the detestable *and* the beautiful, and let the eyes of your spirit gaze into the hearts of those around you. That was the perspective Jesus always had. When a man or woman truly yields the *heart* to the Lord, the rest will follow in time. New attitudes and behavior, those are for the Lord to transform, not for us to worry about. If we can help people to set Christ on the throne of their hearts, *that* is what will ultimately cause the undesirable in their nature to fall away—not the might of righteous indignation, but rather the silent witness of the Holy Spirit deep in their being."

Wallace paused a moment, then added, "To be sure there may occasionally be a time and place for godly indignation." And as he said the words a smile tugged at his lips, for he must have known that Robbie was at that moment puzzling over the times when he had seen that very quality manifested in the doctor himself. "But more often than not, even old missionaries can be overly impetuous in their zeal."

"I'm afraid I'll never have the wisdom to know when to be impetuous and when to use restraint," said Robbie. "Though I'm pretty certain which side will most often win out. I've always been known for jumping in the thick of the fray and asking questions later. I'm a born sailor, remember?"

Wallace laughed.

"Why, if you hadn't been there just now, I probably would have stormed in and done something stupid," said Robbie, sighing heavily.

Wallace laid a hand on the younger man's shoulder. "I pray for you, lad. Your life is bound up in my own now, and nothing is happening between us that is not of God's design. I know God will give you the wisdom you need when you need it."

"I hope so, Isaiah," said Robbie with a depth of earnestness in his voice. "I believe God does want me to remain here in China. I don't know why He should want me. I'm hardly worthy of a calling as noble as yours. I've been nothing but a rowdy sailor all my life who didn't have the foggiest notion of what it really meant to be a man. I still don't feel I fit in either at the mission or with the ways of the Chinese. Yet my heart is here. God has changed *my* heart. So perhaps the external baggage and old ways of Robbie Taggart, sailor, will fall away from me also, so that the Lord can make me worthy to be called Robbie Taggart, missionary of God."

"God bless you, son—!" Wallace stopped, forcing himself to swallow hard before trying to continue, tears spilling from the corners of his eyes. "God be praised! How I have prayed that the Lord would work this in your heart. You have so much to offer this work, and I believe God will turn even the things you or I may deem undesirable into assets for Him.

Your energy, your exuberance, even your impetuous nature—God can use them all mightily."

Robbie felt as if he ought to reply, but could find no words that seemed appropriate.

"We once named you Moses," Wallace continued. "But then I had no idea how truly fitting the name was. He protested even to the face of God himself, calling himself unworthy. Yet God used him to deliver an entire nation. He will use you, Robert. I believe it! It is my humble desire to be granted the honor of pouring what little wisdom He may have given me into you as you grow, toward that end of God's call upon your life."

Wallace stopped, his eyes penetrating deeply into Robbie's own. Robbie felt the older man's gaze boring straight into his heart, probing depths that even he himself did not know existed. Then slowly, almost methodically, Wallace extended his arm. The two men clasped hands, each gripping and shaking the other's firmly in a grasp full of love and mutual vision. Dropping hands, as if by common accord, in the middle of that village street, both men opened wide their arms and embraced— father and son, teacher and pupil, mentor and disciple: spiritual brothers.

Somehow in that moment, Robbie felt as though a responsibility, a burden of leadership, was being transferred to him. Wallace would continue to carry the load for a time. But Robbie sensed that one day the burden would be his alone. He found himself awed, excited, and frightened all at once.

When he and Wallace silently resumed walking back toward the mission once more, Robbie did so with a noticeable trembling in his knees.

57

Whither Thou Diest

The days following his affirmation of commitment should have been wondrous and challenging for Robbie. But for a time he lost all sight of God's call on his life and the steadily growing commission he felt toward China.

Hsi-chen's health worsened. Robbie feared that she would not even make it to the holiday season. But Hsi-chen prayed earnestly that she would be allowed to see her daughter's first Christmas. The rest of the mission staff did their utmost to make the place festive, though none had the heart for it. Yet for Hsi-chen's sake they wore smiles, made and bought presents, and Robbie even found a tree that, when decorated, resembled an evergreen. It was Hsi-chen who continued to remind them all that, though the celebration was of Christ's birth, it was through His death that new life was given to the world. "Death is not the end," she said, "but only the beginning of new and even more wonderful life. When I am gone, remember me as dying *into* life, not dying from it."

A week before Christmas Hsi-chen was finally confined constantly to her bed. Most of the time she had not even the strength to hold her two-month-old baby—but she rejoiced that she had been allowed to live so long into Chi-Yueh's life. Though her face was pale, her eyes were alive with the life she would sense gradually stealing over her, the life of the world to which she was bound. For hours on end Robbie lay next to his wife, with the child nestled between them so Hsi-chen would not miss the nearness of her child and her husband for a single moment.

Christmas was celebrated around the bed. Much laughter, and many tears and prayers were exchanged, along with presents among the small group of missionaries. When the last of the simple packages had been opened, at Hsi-chen's leading, each person went around the room and gave all the others the "gift" of their personal prayer for each loved one. There was not a single dry eye in the room by the time Hsi-chen's turn came; for she had intentionally asked to be allowed to go last.

"To my mother," she said in a soft voice, "I give my prayer of thanksgiving to the Lord. She gave me life, and endured much that I might find new life here at the mission. May God's blessings always be yours, dear mother!"

Hsi-chen turned next toward Wallace, down whose face were by now streaming tears of sorrowful joy. "And to you, dear Fu-ch'in; had you been my real father I could never have loved you more. To you also I owe my undying thanks. You took us in like the Christ whose servant you are. You showed us the Master's love by the example of your life, and thus you led us into His kingdom. I will always thank my God upon every remembrance of you, Fu-ch'in. Because of you, I am not now afraid, because I am about to go to the Father of us all, and I know His love because of yours.

"Oh, Thomas," continued Hsi-chen, twisting her head slightly toward the other side of the bed where Coombs sat, "for you I pray for a rich life serving our Savior. Godspeed to you, Thomas, as you join Dr. Taylor. You have been a true help to my father here, and I know you will be an invaluable servant of Christ at the Inland Mission as well." Hsi-chen paused, took a breath, then went on.

"Ying, faithful friend of my father and this mission, you and I have nearly grown up side-by-side. But now the Lord has marked out different paths for us. Yours, I know, will be a significant one for the future of this work. God's best to you! Know always what a blessing your faithfulness has been, and will be, to my father.

"Dear Miss Trumbull, your servant heart has truly made our lives both richer and easier. I know my father and mother could not have made it through the years of ministry here without your support and help. I know that blessings of Christ are upon you for the practicality of your service to His little children."

Here Hsi-chen paused for several moments. No one dared interrupt, for each sensed that these were sacred moments, anointed by the Spirit to knit their hearts together for all time. At last she spoke:

"Dear Robbie Taggart, my friend, my husband, Feng-huang, father of my daughter, the swan sent by God from over the water to share life with me . . . dear Robbie, man that I love!"

Hsi-chen was weeping now, yet she struggled to continue. "Never in my dreams did I think the Lord would allow me to be loved by one so tender as you. Though our love has been brief, it has been more rich than anything I dreamed of ever having. Such a man you have become, Robbie. Such a man of God! In my flesh I never dared to hope that I might be allowed to live my life out with you. Yet in the Spirit I have known that God's best is not measured in hours or years. We will not be parted, my dear Robbie. The Lord's life will live on in both of us. Our love has been good; it will never die. My prayer for you is that you will never forget how much I love you, and that you will love and serve the Lord mightily all your days. I love you, dear Robbie . . . how I love you!"

Finally Hsi-chen took little Ruth in her arms. "My Chi-Yueh, little one whose life is a covenant of love, for you I pray that you will know all the goodness of life with God the Father of our Lord Jesus Christ. May you strengthen your father in my absence. Remind him of me, little one. Remind him of the love that will always bind the three of us together.

May you look out upon him through eyes that assure your father, through all the hardships of the life of faith, that he is loved by your mother, and by the Father of us all."

Hsi-chen then gazed around the room at the weeping faces of all her family. "I will miss you all," she said gently, through her tears, "though perhaps not as you will miss me, for I will be with our Lord. But I will be waiting for the day when He allows me to rejoice with you again in our new home."

The yuletide meal that followed was subdued, yet peaceful, resembling a quiet celebration of the Passover rather than a holiday feast. Much of the remainder of the day was spent in prayer. Hsi-chen had said her farewells and seemed prepared to go.

The following morning dawned with a bright sun shining in a pale winter's sky. The day would have been crisp and invigorating, but Robbie awoke with a heaviness upon him. Even before he came fully awake he noticed that Hsi-chen's breathing was shallow and strained. He turned sharply toward her and saw that she was already awake.

She smiled a weak greeting, then nodded her head as if in answer to his unspoken question.

"I'll get your father!" said Robbie in a ragged voice as he jumped out of bed.

"Please don't go, Robbie," she said, each word now an effort. "I am suddenly a little afraid."

Without hesitating, Robbie turned back to her, and taking her frail hand in his, bent down and kissed her cool lips. He had said goodbye to her a hundred times in his thoughts, but not one of them had prepared him for the real thing. He had wanted to be so strong for her, but he now knew that would be impossible. He only wanted to lay his head on her breast and weep.

"I am the phoenix now," she said. "I will miss you, my dear Robbie . . . but I had a dream last night, and I was away from you. Then there came a rich, warm light and it took me to it, Robbie, and I was not so very sad anymore. I have known for many years that heaven would be a joyous place. Now God has reaffirmed that belief. But it is still hard to leave—"

"My love . . . !" was all Robbie could utter, though there was so much he wanted to say—so many years worth of things he wanted to share with her. Now all he could do was dumbly grip her hand in his.

"How much I have wanted to do for you, how much I would give to you if I could," Hsi-chen went on.

"You have given me yourself, Hsi-chen . . . and Ruth," said Robbie. "What more could I ever want?"

At that moment the door opened quietly and Wallace and Shan-fei came softly into the room. Immediately they perceived what was happening by the stricken look on Robbie's face. He motioned them to her, then stepped back, and for several moments looked on as the daughter said her final goodbyes to her parents. Shan-fei's poised reserve broke down at last, and Hsi-chen spent a good while comforting and reassuring her mother.

Wallace wept freely as he spoke his final farewell. "My dear daughter, my true daughter. I have never ceased to be proud of you, and God has used you to touch my life in so many ways. I give praise to our Father that you will soon have the pleasure of seeing Him face to face!" His final words were spoken through such tears that an onlooker would have attributed to them anything but the praise he spoke of. But Hsi-chen understood what was in his heart, for she knew well what was awaiting her in the life that was about to break in upon her.

At last the two parents stepped back. Wallace lifted little Ruth from her cradle and laid her in her mother's arms. Hsi-chen kissed her for the last time, murmured some soft words in Chinese into her ear, then laid her down on the bed beside her.

"Robbie, hold me," she said in a bare whisper. "I am trembling."

Robbie eased his large frame onto the bed beside his wife and tenderly took her in his arms. "I love you, Hsi-chen . . . I love you!" he whispered.

"Oh, Robbie," she cried out, clutching her arms around him tightly, "Robbie . . . I love you."

Robbie glanced quickly down to where Ruth lay, then back to Hsi-chen as he opened his mouth to speak to her again. But as his glance fell upon her face, he knew from the peaceful closing of her eyes, even as her arms relaxed their hold on him, that she was gone. Yet about her face there seemed to linger a faint glow, as of a presence of angels come to take Hsi-chen to her new home.

Robbie lifted his head, still gazing at the peaceful face.

"Then it flies westward toward the K'un-lun Mountains . . ." he murmured. *"And who knows whether it will ever return? Now a great regret seizes upon my mind—if only I have my home in a different place!"*

For an instant, all Robbie's faith and hope fled him. He was suddenly alone! Desolate! He wanted only to run . . . to die, that he might be where his dear Hsi-chen was! What was there left for him in this world any longer? He had said many farewells in his life as a wanderer. But this was one too many!

All at once little Ruth stirred on the bed where she was still gently pressed between Robbie and the lifeless form of her mother.

The Spirit of God moved through the tiny child to remind Robbie that he was *not* alone. He had a heavenly Father and would never know true desolation again. And as they were one in the presence of God, Hsi-chen was as much his at this moment as she had been before.

Robbie picked up little Chi-Yueh deftly with one hand and held her close, looking at her tenderly through tear-filled eyes. Suddenly he knew that everything mattered. Now perhaps more than ever! Hsi-chen had left him with a high calling—fatherhood! He would fulfill that calling honorably through the loving direction and wisdom of his heavenly Father. His hope was *not* gone! He held a reflection of it now in his arms. For he had taken the reality of that hope, the Spirit of Jesus himself, into his heart some sixteen months earlier, on a small hill near that Chinese village that had become his home.

Part V

Return

58

A Man and His Daughter

A gentle breeze played against the sail of the old junk, pushing it steadily along the Chai-chiang.

A man who looked to be about forty was hitching the yard a few degrees astern to gain the best of the wind, but the eastward current of the stream itself was so strong now in May that he hardly needed the aid of the spring breezes. He seemed to be enjoying himself, however—the sort of man who would be fiddling with the sails even if the air was completely void of movement. A Westerner by the look of him, and oddly out of place on the traditional Chinese craft, the man's dark windblown hair was streaked with the beginnings of gray, and a lively smile of pure delight illuminated a face still boyishly handsome. He was clearly at home on the water, though the junk did not appear to be a vessel worthy of his skill.

As he looked over the starboard rail he noted they were drifting out of the current.

"A bit more to port," he called astern.

The child at the tiller had the whole of her small body pressed against the wooden mechanism, but the boat seemed reluctant to respond. An Oriental by the look of her face, the slant of her eyes, and her dark black straight hair, the girl yet contained characteristics of physique and manner that only Western blood would explain—of mixed parentage, no doubt; an uncommon thing in this region of China.

"I can't get her back, Papa," she answered in perfect English, notable not only for its lack of Chinese accent but also for the hint of Scottish brogue. The girl was indeed a puzzling mix.

The sailor smiled proudly at his daughter. *She is quite a helmswoman even at nine,* he thought, *even if she hasn't the strength to fight against this deceptively strongly currented river.*

With the rapid movement of skilled fingers, he deftly tied off the rope he had been working on, using only his right hand, then strode to the poop, where he added his strong arm to the process of steering the boat, and together they maneuvered the junk back into the center of the current.

"It was my fault," he said. "I didn't get the yard adjusted soon enough. You must be tired," he added. "I'll take the tiller for a while."

He sat down on the thwarts between his daughter and the mechanism, and placing his right hand on the tiller, he put his left arm around her. She snuggled up closer to him, giving not the least notice to the maimed arm that held her. She had grown up accustomed to it from birth, and for all she knew in her first years perhaps all men had but one hand. When several years later she learned how he had lost his left hand, it only raised her loving and devoted estimation of her brave father.

"How far are we from home, Papa?" asked Ruth, with just a touch of disappointment in her voice. A whole day alone with her father was wonderful, and though, not rare, it was still an experience she was not anxious to have end.

"Not far; perhaps a mile or two," answered Robbie. "As soon as we get around that next bend, you'll be able to see the mission off in the distance."

"Will Grandfather be pleased that we handed out all the tracts?"

"I'm sure he will be, and he will be especially pleased to hear what a diligent worker you are, my little missionary!"

They laughed together, and Robbie marveled again, as he had so many times in the past, at how Ruth's laughter reminded him of the girl's mother's—so musical and merry, yet deeply sincere. If there was any difference between them when they laughed, it was that it occurred more often in the girl, for Ruth was a lively child, energetic and ebullient, high-spirited like her father.

Robbie saw Hsi-chen so clearly in his daughter, particularly at moments like this, as her merriment quieted and she sat pensively gazing out upon the rippling water. Her silky black hair shone in the sunlight of the afternoon, her delicate Oriental features and her fluid grace clearly visible even at such a young age. The girl possessed an unusual capacity for quietude and reflection, often displaying a maturity beyond her years—noteworthy, perhaps, because of how smoothly this contemplative side of her nature intermingled with the vivacious side she had inherited from her father. Yet as seemingly opposite as the distinctive sets of attributes were at first glance, in this particular youngster they blended into a harmony as pleasantly as did the mixed heritage of her Scottish and Chinese blood. She had already committed her life to Christ. It still could bring tears of quiet fulfillment and joy to Robbie's eyes when he recalled that day a year and a half earlier when she had come to him.

"Papa," she had said, "I love the Lord and want to live my life for Him."

"Do you know that means your *whole* life, dear?" he had said.

"Yes, Papa. It doesn't seem like so very much when I think of all He has done for me," she answered.

Yes, she had inherited her mother's depth and spiritual sensitivities. Sometimes, Robbie thought, she had a deeper sense of what it meant to serve God than most adults. *She's further along the true road of life at nine than I was at twenty-nine!*

Yet despite all this, there were times when the differences from her mother seemed more pronounced than the likenesses. On the physical level, her Western heritage would have been especially evident to any discriminating Chinese. Her eyes were paler and rounder than Hsi-chen's, and she would undoubtedly grow to be taller than most of her Oriental ancestors; already she was nearly as tall as her grandmother Shan-fei, and her graceful figure was more willowy and agile. She was more apt to climb a tree than any village girl in Wukiang, and she often scandalized the sedate Chinese neighbors with her tomboyish behavior. *Like father, like daughter!* Robbie had said to himself more than once, and he could not have wished it otherwise. The balance of Shan-fei's faithful training in proper decorum for a Chinese girl, along with the occasional ring of Scots that rolled off her tongue, brought about such an enchanting interweaving of her diverse character traits that even the Chinese matrons smiled when the girl passed by. She was so delightful, despite all the cultural idiosyncrasies that clung to her, that they could not help following her growth with the keenest of interest.

As thankful as Robbie was for every reminder of Hsi-chen, he had not cared to artificially try to create a duplicate of his wife in his daughter. Therefore, he was in no way disappointed as these differences gradually revealed themselves. On the contrary, he relished them, praising God that she was a unique individual all her own, praying constantly for the wisdom to keep her so.

He had required a double portion of that wisdom in those early years, and still did for that matter. The grace of God and the love of his mission family had enabled him to bear his grief over the loss of Hsi-chen victoriously. His sorrow was no less painful but infinitely more endurable in that it was a grief shared universally by all. Occasionally self-pity had displaced the victory of his still-young walk of faith when a crying infant, who should have had her mother, felt like an awful burden for him to bear. Many times in the middle of changing a soiled diaper or during an all-night vigil walking a sick baby, he'd think fleetingly of the men who had wives to do such things.

Yet his had been the privilege to participate in joys that other fathers miss; he could not feel sorry for himself for long. That first smile had been showered all upon him, and when she took that first wobbly step, it had been into his arms that she had tumbled, giggling. Papa kissed the childish wounds, read the bedtime books, made her eat her vegetables, and told her stories about ships, about Scotland, about Jesus, and about her mother.

He had known more joy with Ruth than he had ever imagined possible on that black day when Hsi-chen had died. So many times since he had vividly recalled what she had once said to him: "I pray the day will come to you when the joy in staying surpasses any other joys you have known along the way."

It had surely happened. For even aboard one of those magnificent ships he so loved, he had never felt such a fulfillment and satisfaction that fatherhood brought him.

This trip up the river with his now-nine-year-old daughter had proved one of his greatest thrills, both as a father and as a missionary. It was the first time he had taken her such a long way from home. While she was young, he himself had not traveled much outside the close environs of the mission district. For short jaunts he was often seen in the neighborhood toting her on his back in a pack his friend Kuo-hwa had fashioned for her. But by the age of five or six, her presence began to become gradually disturbing to the villagers. Part of the cause may have been due to her mixed heritage, but a far more likely cause was the simple fact that she was a girl.

By this time Robbie had grown accustomed to Chinese ways sufficiently to take no offense at them, nor to think it his duty to change them. But he still found them insufferable at times, especially when the men of the village began to seem uncomfortable in his presence, and when the women looked with chagrin upon the daughter he loved. He knew that a Chinese child is treated not much more different in its early years than children the rest of the world over. But he still found it hard to accept the change that came, especially in the case of Chinese girls, at about age five. With the beginning of the process of foot binding, a whole new era of life began, founded in a strict enforcement of segregation between the sexes. The once-free child was taught utter submissiveness and reserve, was kept close to home, and was rigidly disciplined in the customs and practices of an ancient culture that had scarcely changed in a thousand years.

Ruth was an obvious incongruity and Robbie would have it no other way. Out of respect for the villagers, he began to take her along with him less frequently. But he refused to keep her housebound, which would have been like trying to keep a captured butterfly healthy in a box. So, though he and Shan-fei and Miss Trumbull all had a hand in the girl's education, during the remainder of the time she was allowed to run and roam and explore about the mission compound, and even along the near banks of the river. And by and by the local folk began to grow accustomed to the missionary's daughter, even gradually permitting a different standard for her, probably in much the same way the older villagers had years previously with Hsi-chen, whose somewhat different status allowed her more latitude in their cautious eyes.

This latest overnight trip to several new villages had shown Robbie that acceptance at home did not necessarily mean a like reception abroad. Yet despite the difficulties and awkwardness, it had been grand to share even a small portion of his ministry with her. He had sensed a vibrant potential growing within her and hoped that his instincts were true which told him that she had much to offer the work of God. There was no compunction in his mind about her being a woman, even in China, for he had already seen how effectively women such as Miss Trumbull and other female missionaries he had met since could contribute to the overall evangelizing effort. It remained to be seen whether Ruth's Oriental heritage would be an asset or a liability for her in her own land; overcoming deeply conservative Chinese attitudes toward women was difficult in any sphere, especially when it came to mission work where teaching and speaking were often involved. It was not unusual for activities accepted from a Western woman (they were barbarians, after all) to be looked upon with outrage from an Oriental.

The difficulties inherent in their peculiar position were never far from Robbie's mind, yet they were not burdensome or oppressive. God's purpose was evident in every aspect of their being here. If anything, Robbie was excited in the anticipation of seeing how that purpose would work itself out.

Suddenly Ruth jumped up from where she sat in the crook of her father's arm. "Look!" she exclaimed, pointing eastward, "there's the bend."

"Aye," replied Robbie. "We'll be home just in time for dinner."

Ruth leaned against the gunwale of the boat, and folding her arms in front of her, took on a pensive expression. When she finally spoke her words were earnest and well-considered.

"Thank you for letting me come with you, Papa," she said.

"It was a pleasure to have your company, dear. I'm only sorry for the bit of trouble we encountered."

"Will it mean I won't be able to go with you again?"

"I don't know," answered Robbie thoughtfully. "I'll discuss it with your grandfather. I *want* you to join me as often as possible, you do know that, don't you?"

"Oh yes, I do," she said.

"But your grandfather is still head of the mission and we must trust his wisdom."

"Papa, why do some people become so upset when they hear about Jesus?"

"There are many reasons, little Chi-Yueh. I did myself when I was trying so hard to hang on to my old life. I could not realize what glorious things God had ready for me. I was even a little afraid. Most people are afraid of new things, Ruth. Even when they are better than the old ways."

Robbie paused, then smiled as a pleasant memory came to him. "I stopped being afraid when the *love* of Jesus became a reality to me. Your mother helped me to see that—she had such a capacity to love and care for others."

"And Mother helped you to give your life to the Lord, didn't she?"

"Aye, she most certainly did!"

"I'm glad, Papa, for I don't think I should like it much if I couldn't talk to you about God."

Robbie said nothing for a moment, touching his chin in thought as he considered his daughter's statement. He had never thought of it in quite that way before. He continually acknowledged the gift Hsi-chen had left him in their daughter, but only now did he see that she had left Ruth a gift too—that of having a Christian father who could share the faith with her.

"I'm glad too, dear," he replied. He held out his hand to her. She came to him and he hugged her lovingly.

59

Stormy Waters

Isaiah Wallace paced back and forth in the front room of the mission residence. It was late. Everyone but he and Robbie had already retired.

Robbie sat in a rocking chair silently watching the doctor, waiting for his response to his report of the excursion upriver. The grim look of intense deliberation on Wallace's face had been unexpected, and Robbie wondered if the core of this reaction was the fact that Robbie had taken Ruth. Wallace had not been enthusiastic about the idea. But Robbie had followed his impulse rather than bow to his father-in-law's experience of three decades in China, and at last the older man had relented.

Now Wallace stopped and turned to the younger man. Robbie recalled a similar moment ten years ago when the young man at the receiving end of the doctor's remonstration had been Thomas Coombs. Robbie had been angry that day, for he had been able to perceive none of Isaiah Wallace's fatherly concern. This time, however, he had no difficulty discerning the doctor's love. It was clearly evident in his deep-set eyes, drooping with sadness, but alight with compassion.

"It makes no sense to dwell on what is past," he finally said decisively. "She wants to go with me next time."

"And what will you tell her?"

Robbie sighed. He had hoped the decision would not rest fully upon him. "I was afraid when the mob crowded around us," he answered. "Thank God their abuse was only verbal. But I cringe when I recall all the debaucheries they accused me of. Ruth understands Chinese as well as I; only her childish innocence protected her from grasping what it was all about. I would never willingly put her in that position again. Yet she hungers after service, and to be part of the work of the mission. How long can I keep her from it?"

"She is but a child."

"I have never pushed her," said Robbie defensively.

"I know." Isaiah's reply was gentle.

"In so many ways she grasps the truths of the faith more deeply than I do. There has been so much for the Lord to clean away in my life. With her, He has a fresh, clean soul to work with. But I would never have taken her along if I had known something like that was going to happen."

Wallace walked to a shelf and took down a sheet of paper, which he handed to Robbie.

"I'm afraid we are in for some stressful times," he said. "This handbill came into my possession this morning along with some very disquieting news. There have been riots in Wuhu—only a hundred miles from here, Robert! Apparently some Chinese Sisters of Charity were accused of bewitching children. They were arrested, the Catholic mission was burned, even the British consulate was placed in danger for a time. These handbills are believed to be a major source of the trouble."

Robbie looked at the paper in his hand. It was covered in Chinese characters that he had difficulty deciphering. The quality of the printing was also rather poor, as if many copies had been quickly produced. When he looked up once more at Wallace, his eyes were dark and his brow creased.

"Who would believe such nonsense?"

Yet even as he spoke, Robbie knew the answer to his own question. The people would believe what they wanted to believe, and where they might waver, the gentry and the literate, along with a good number of government officials, would use any method to convince them. They would never forget that the presence of Christian missionaries in China came as a result of the coercion of foreign powers. And the preceding decade had only served to lubricate the growing tensions and bitterness on the part of the hardest elements in Chinese society. As the European powers had carved up the continent of Africa, they were now greedily eyeing Asia. Already much of China's buffer empire had been lost: Burma, Indo-China, and Tibet among them. And while disputes continued to rage over Mongolia, Turkestan, and Korea, past experience told the Chinese not to hope for much. It was scarcely any wonder, thought Robbie to himself, that the situation was so unstable, and that various missionary movements were at the core of the trouble. What could many of the local peasants think but that the missionaries—grouping the good in with the bad—were simply agents of the imperialistic designs of the foreign European governments?

Robbie shook his head at the handbill. It accused the missionaries of using drugs to possess the minds of the Chinese, of aborting infants from their mothers' wombs, and even removing the eyes of the dead to make silver. Jesus himself was charged with all manner of debauchery and evil, and Christians were accused of worshiping a pig—no doubt a play on the word for Jesus, *Yeh-su*, which was similar to the word for hog. Such rumors had always circulated to a limited degree in areas penetrated by missions, but it seemed that they were now combining with current events to make them more readily accepted by an easily swayed public.

"We must brace ourselves for trouble," said Wallace.

"I had hoped the minor disturbances last year were isolated incidents. I thought the year 1890 was a fluke and this year would open a new era of peace."

"That," Wallace nodded toward the handbill, "indicates that there is possibly a central force behind what is happening. If not a single individual or movement, then certainly a coordinated effort among a few. We've always been a bit off the beaten track from the trouble areas. But I'm afraid we will not be so immune this time."

"We'll have to remain close to the mission," said Robbie, with resignation in his voice. Then he crumbled up the paper and tossed it across the room. "That's just what these people want!"

Wallace cocked an eyebrow. "You'll not do anything impulsive, will you, Robert?"

"I pray I've matured beyond that, but—"

Now it was Robbie's turn to jump up and pace the room impatiently. "I cannot help being frustrated when we are viewed so wrongly, when the truths of God are muddled up by political rivalries and intrigues and lies. I know that many of the missionaries have asked for this by dabbling in politics and by forgetting what you have always told me—that we are here to change hearts, not cultures. But it makes it no easier to bear. God's work is being compromised and stifled by all this."

"A little persecution never hurt the work of Christ before," said Wallace.

"Have you heard from Dr. Taylor? Has his work been affected?" asked Robbie.

"I have not had word from him for some time. So I don't know. But I'm sure we all will be affected by these increasing riots."

"I need to be reminded to pray more diligently for our brothers there."

"And so must I," agreed Wallace, then paused with a little shake of the head. "I was wrong before," he resumed in a moment, "to warn you about impulsiveness. I'm afraid I let my concern for Ruth cloud my perceptions, should anything happen to you. I do not worry about you, Robert. The Lord's mind is working in you. God has called us to proclaim His Word boldly, not to cower in our mission compound. I once told you, even risking the life of my own daughter, that the Lord would protect His people. Now I am forgetting my own advice. I am getting old, Robert, and my days of tramping in the wilderness are drawing to a close. But I should be working counter to the will of God if I should attempt to hold you back. I know how you long to take the gospel to the remote districts. I've seen your face light up when you hear reports from Thomas Coombs of the work being done in Hunan and Szechwan and other difficult regions."

"You are not holding me back, Isaiah," said Robbie, walking toward his father-in-law and placing a gentle hand on his mentor's stooped shoulder.

"Perhaps you should not let Ruth hold you back either, if it is to such a thing the Lord is truly leading you."

"The work here in Wukiang is established," said Robbie. "In the last two years we've had at least a dozen converts who have come into the faith by the word of their Chinese Christian neighbors, not by our preaching. By the grace of God we have been allowed to see the great-est goal any mission can dream of—establishing an ongoing witness among the local people. Lately I have thought more and more about the many places where this still needs to be done. Yet I've wondered if this may not simply be my wandering nature beginning to goad me once again. I would never forgive myself if anything were to happen to Ruth because of my own selfish motives. Fatherhood will be my great-est call—at least for another ten years. That is my chief responsibility, and I can do nothing that will stand in the way of my being all the Lord would have me be to her."

"I know you have committed this to our Father," said Wallace. "Wait for His answer, then trust Ruth into His care. I respect you, for I know in all these areas your heart's desire is to do nothing but what God would have you."

"Thank you. I will follow your counsel. In the meantime, what do we do about our present situation?"

"We must conduct ourselves in the usual manner. I see no cause for any immediate changes."

"What has been the reaction of the village folk to these handbills?"

"Apparently they've been circulating for some time, and no one has seen fit to mention anything until now. I believe most of the folk, even the non-Christians, realize the charges are ridiculous. They know us by this time, and that will hopefully count for much more in the end than these obviously trumped up and radical notions. There could be problems if outsiders come in. There are those in Wukiang, as you know, who could be stirred to trouble. We have seen such in the past. So you should know there is a possibility of such an occurrence. The man who passed through here from Wuhu made mention of a name that gravely concerns me. It was rumored that one of the spearheaders of the riots was none other than our old adversary, Wang K'ung-wu."

A sharp cold surge of forgotten emotion shot through Robbie at the sound of the name. All the years of healing suddenly seemed to flee from him, and he felt as though he could be consumed with hatred once more. In his mind's eye he saw helpless Hsi-chen in the rough cruel hands of the villainous soldiers, and felt the sickening agony of his severed hand. And for the hundredth time he asked himself how God might have been able to rescue Hsi-chen had he depended on *Him* instead of the strength he thought he had on his own. Was it possible he would not have had to lose his hand if he had been willing to trust God sooner?

But the question was a futile one. He had discussed that very thing with Wallace many times over the years, and the older man's wisdom had always been the same: "When we step outside God's will, in that moment God is able, as it were, to restructure His will to incorporate into it even our disobedient actions. In the end, even our acts of selfishness are taken up and miraculously made part of His best for us. There are no *what ifs?* with God, because He turns everything into the best for those who are trusting Him. What God would have done had you joined us in prayer instead of following Hsi-chen up the mountain, I do not know. He *would* have delivered her, of that I am certain. *How* is a moot question. But when you did go, He then used your going as His means for her deliverance, even though He also used it to bring you face to face with your own need, through the loss of your hand."

Robbie shook the memories from him, and closing his eyes, uttered a fervent prayer for peace in his heart, and for God's love to fill him for this evil man.

His flustered emotions finally calmed and he turned his attention to the many questions that filled his brain. If Wang had returned, what were his motives in instigating riots against the missionaries? Had he forgotten the old animosities, or was he still intent on seeking his promised revenge?

Robbie looked into the old missionary's solemn eyes. He clearly perceived that Isaiah considered his wife's former suitor still a threat, perhaps now more than ever. Yet whatever Wang's reasons for withholding, or postponing his vengeance, Robbie knew that God would somehow use them for His purposes.

He recalled Wallace's words to him of long ago: "*One day, Robbie, you're going to give God thanks for taking your hand. Whenever you think of it you're going to praise Him, because that's how He showed you the depths of His love."*

Silently Robbie prayed, "Oh, Lord, whatever this news does for us, give me strength to face it by your might not my own. And bring Isaiah's words to fulfillment in my heart, Lord. I do thank you for what has happened. Yet increase my thankfulness, Lord. And deepen still further my trust in you."

60

How the Mighty Have Fallen

The old building used to be one of Nanking's seamier opium dens. But the run-down structure had been boarded up a few years ago because the proprietor had fallen on to hard times and could no longer supply the opium that kept the place in business.

Pien flicked a cockroach off his frayed and worn pant leg and could not help reflecting on the days when he had proudly ridden fine stallions and reclined in rich apartments on silk cushions. Perhaps he ought to be thankful Wang still owned this rat-infested hovel or they'd likely have even worse accommodations.

He asked himself why he was still here at all, but the answer was easy. After that fiasco in Wukiang ten years ago, the British had wanted blood—one does not kidnap the adopted daughter of a missionary (curse that fellow who had tried to tell him the girl was not legally adopted!) and then seriously wound and maim a British subject, without incurring the mortal wrath of the pompous foreigners.

Most of Wang's army had fled after the incident, some out of fear of reprisal; but most had deserted simply because Wang had lost face in their sight. Pien surely would have been among them, but unfortunately his name was too closely associated with that of Wang. He had, as a result, known it would not be easy to escape the clutches of the authorities. Besides, a part of Pien truly did admire Wang's cunning, even after his shameful defeat, and knew that in the end he would triumph over his troubles. Thus, when Wang was caught and arrested, Pien had the misfortune to still be with the warlord. It was just lucky for him that the name Wang still carried some influence, and banishment instead of death had been the punishment meted out.

After ten years of an exile that was supposed to have been for a lifetime, the bandit had been able to bribe his way back into the country. The bribe had ruined him financially, but he swore over and over that it would be worth every ounce of silver and gold when the filthy British sailor had paid for Wang's lost honor.

Pien glanced over at his master where he slept on the tattered straw mat in the far corner of the room. Ah, pity that poor sailor when Wang gets his hands on him! The fallen warlord would show no mercy on him, even if he was now crippled and an unworthy adversary.

All at once a clatter behind the closed door caught Pien's attention. He tensed, grabbing his pistol at the same time.

"Who is it?" asked the former lieutenant sharply.

"It's me, you lubber!" came a gravelly, menacing voice. "Open the door!"

Another foreign devil! thought Pien disdainfully. And this one-legged seaman was the lowest of the lot! Why Wang kept him around, Pien could not guess. He supposed the two must find a certain camaraderie in their shared hatreds. The worst of it was that it had been Pike who had struck the decisive blow in the battle with Taggart. A coward he certainly wasn't, but in every other respect he was a miserable excuse for a human being!

Pien hitched his frame up from the rickety chair and shuffled toward the door. He unlatched the lock and Benjamin Pike unceremoniously pushed his way in. His cavernous, yellowed eyes glanced quickly around the room, finally resting on Wang's sleeping figure.

"What's he still sleeping for?" said Pike, dropping a cloth sack on the only table in the dingy room. "I thought we was going to be gone by nightfall?"

"We are!" shouted Wang, now stirring on his mat. "I want out of this place!" He flung the blanket off his husky frame, which gave little evidence of the hardships of the past ten years, and heaved himself to his feet. "And what has taken you so long?" he said, striding to the table and ripping open the sack.

"Don't ye shout at me, ye blag'ard!" retorted Pike. "Why'd ye send me out for supplies in the first place? I can't say a word in the stinkin' language, and I near ran headlong into a brigade of British soldiers."

"At the moment," replied Wang impatiently, "you are freer to roam about, even with your crude tongue and absurd leg! Now, what is this about soldiers?"

"What do ye think? They captured me and hung me from a gallows!" replied Pike with a smirk. "What ye see before ye is an angel of mercy! Ha, ha!"

"Shut up, you fool!" Wang reached a fleshy hand into the sack and pulled out a bottle. At least the idiot bought a good rice wine, he thought. The Shaohing vintage was the only Chinese brew that could pass the tongue without repulsion. He pulled the cork, and bringing the bottle to his lips, drank deeply.

"These troops," Wang continued, wiping a sleeve across his mouth; "you are certain you were not observed and followed?"

"O' course I am! They was too busy guarding them missions you ransacked and tried to burn."

"You make it sound as if I were solely responsible for the deed," mused the warlord. "As in Wuhu, I was but a part of a riotous mob, caught up in the righteous fervor for the rescue of my country from the evil foreigners."

"Jist don't let none o' them true patriots see that ye be sharing yer wine with one of them very devils ye say ye hate!" Pike grabbed the bottle from Wang and took a greedy swig.

"You insolent pig!" cursed Wang, as he wrenched the bottle away from Pike.

The violent action pitched the aging one-legged ex-sea captain off balance, and he tumbled to the grimy floor. The next instant his crutch was in his hand and he swung it violently at Wang.

"You yellow-skinned—" he yelled, but before he could finish, Wang caught the crutch and shoved it into Pike's face. When Pike recovered himself he was still screaming. "I'll kill you!" he shrieked, trying to climb back to his feet, but the warlord was in possession of the crutch now, and Pike was forced to crawl on his hands and knees to get at his adversary.

Laughing wickedly, Wang tossed the crutch across the room. Nothing gave him greater pleasure, now that his once-proud domain was reduced to these two slimy river-rats, than to see Pike helplessly dragging his crippled body across the floor to where his crutch lay. Yes, he had kept the old fool around like a cheap bauble on a chain. But his actions did not spring from love, that much was certain. His hatred of foreigners had not wavered, and in fact had only been fired all the more since his troubles began at that cursed monastery ten years ago. But even if he despised white men, he was not above using them to his advantage. He could even see a certain twisted form of his own brand of justice in the action.

Pien now delicately cleared his throat, hoping to restore some peace again to the premises. "What is there to eat?" he asked, peeking into the sack Pike had brought in.

In the meantime, Wang dropped his thick body into a chair, while Pike, having retrieved his crutch, limped to a bench that sat against the far wall, and sat there quietly, hunched over, sulking privately.

The two had fought in this manner for ten years, Wang treating Pike like yesterday's gruel, and Pike daily threatening to take Wang's life. Upon countless occasions Pike had limped out of whatever hovel they happened to be in, vowing never again to lay eyes on the fat, yellow moron. But the miserable sea captain had always returned, perhaps thinking, and rightly so, that his only hope of getting safely back into China was through Wang. And Wang had always received his enemy back into his company. They each possessed a common goal, an obsession: Pien believed they would keep company even with the devil, if that was what it took to see a final end to their common enemy, the sailor Taggart.

That goal would be reached soon enough, and none would be happier than Pien. He was a rational man, and this craziness was beginning to wear on him, not to mention the ridiculous accommodations! But things were looking up. Since Wang's return, he had been working to rebuild his strength and power. He had established a small band of cut-throats in the mountains, but after the fiasco in Wukiang had determined that he would have to use different methods in the future. Pien supposed his involvement of late in anti-foreign activities must have something to do with that. He was certainly being paid handsomely by that circle of wealthy noblemen to instigate trouble. And money was one thing Wang needed more than anything just now.

"Pien!" shouted Wang after a lengthy pause. "Prepare us a meal! And quickly! There is much to do before we leave."

Pien shuffled toward the stove, purposefully taking his time. He threw a couple sticks of wood in, then stirred around the nearly dead ashes, thinking that he had risked too much to continue to accept his servant status indefinitely. *It had better all change after this Wukiang business is concluded,* he thought bitterly. If it were up to him he would forget all about Wukiang and Taggart and the whole stupid lot of them. The insane obsession that drove both Pike and Wang could only breed trouble.

The lieutenant stirred the embers to life. He had begun to feel as if he were the only sane man around. It was good he kept sight of reality, for Wang was beginning to lose his grip. *If I keep my wits about me,* thought Pien selfishly, *I will be the likely candidate to take charge of things when Wang finally goes over the edge, however matters fall in Wukiang. Let Wang enjoy his petty revenge—he will end up with little else!*

While Pien was thus massaging his vast ego, Benjamin Pike had managed to recover at least a small portion of his lost dignity. He lifted his head and hatefully eyed Wang, who was at the moment absorbed in his rice wine and took no notice of the Britisher's evil stare. *The overconfident blackguard!* thought Pike, cursing silently. *As if I need him now that I'm safely in China again!*

But even Pike's degenerated mind could see that his wishful statement was far from true. Of course he still *did* need the lubbering fool! He couldn't speak the blasted language, and if he tried to get about alone he'd only draw attention to himself. But if that miserable rat tried to push him around again, he'd sooner try his luck outside. Nobody probably cared about him anymore—the British were no doubt long past caring about following his track. With a bit of a disguise and a change of name . . .

Then he glanced at his wooden stump. *How do ye disguise that?* he said to himself. *I'll do it some way, and I'll get Robbie on me own! What'd I need Wang for anyway? Although it would be nice to get 'em both! Ha, ha! That'd show the whole lot of 'em! I ain't no has-been!*

The old skipper's eyes glistened as he recalled something he had heard earlier on the streets.

"I forgots to tell ye somethin'," he barked in a sly tone.

Wang's head shot up. His eyes were dull and bleary; the wine was having its effect on his senses.

"I heard a fellow use your name," Pike continued in a matter-of-fact tone.

"What!" cried Wang. He had taken great pains to keep his identity carefully cloaked even from the men who were paying him. The name of Wang could not be associated with this present work, for it must not get back to Wukiang that he was afoot—not yet at least. They must suspect nothing. When he finally struck the mission, it must be believed to have been merely the act of riotous anti-foreign mobs. He would not be implicated this time—there would be no one after him, no banishments.

"How do you know this?" Wang demanded. "There are many with my name."

"I know enough of your cursed babble to know when the *once*-great bandit, Wang K'ung-wu, is mentioned—"

"Why you—" seethed Wang, rising ominously though unsteadily from his chair.

Now Pike laughed.

"An' I thought ye'd be glad to hear ye was still remembered after all these years!"

In two lumbering strides Wang reached Pike and had his hands at the smaller man's throat. "If you have betrayed me—" He let his tightening hands complete the threat for him.

"W—why would I do such a thing?" Pike squeaked. "If the great Wang is betrayed, I am betrayed."

Wang loosened his grip." What was said? Who spoke of me?"

"I only understood your name and the word *tsei*. Does that not mean robber?"

"Why were they speaking of me?" asked Wang, knowing he would get no answer from the ignorant seaman. He let go of Pike and returned to his wine.

Pike brushed at his crumpled shirt as if the worn and filthy fabric were fine linen. "If I'd known ye'd take on so, I wouldn't 'ave said nothin'." His triumphant eyes, however, said that he had thoroughly relished seeing the warlord caught so off his guard.

"If you lie, Pike—!"

"Well, ain't that gratitude! I should have kept me mouth shut! But then I figure we need each other—an' no matter how much you bluster an' shout, Wang, you can't deny you need me."

"Ha!" retorted Wang. "Why would I need the likes of a lizard like you? I think your demented mind has mistaken my benevolence."

"Oh, I ain't mistaken nothin'! You need me because it's me what's going to hand you Robbie Taggart on a platter. Only I can do it, and ye knows it!"

"Do I now . . . ? And just how do you intend on doing that?"

Pike leaned forward, rubbing his hands eagerly together. He suddenly forgot about all his animosity toward the warlord, as his prime objective refocused itself in his brain. Simply maiming the picture-perfect Robbie Taggart had only whetted Pike's thirst for revenge. Fanned by Wang's rancor, his hunger to once and for all do away with his nemesis had grown once more into a fevered obsession.

He had vaguely kept track of Robbie's activities over the years, and just the fact that he was still with the mission was proof enough that he had cast his lot with them. This came as hardly a surprise to Pike. He had always seen the younger sailor as a hopeless do-gooder.

Now it would be Taggart's undoing, and Pike nearly drooled with relish at the thought.

61

A Friend in Need

As the sun set behind the hills toward the west, Robbie and Ruth crossed the bridge leading toward home. They were coming from a visit with Kuo-hwa and several other church members.

Since the uprising in Wuhu, the spiritual climate around eastern China had steadily degenerated. Though most of the continued troubles were concentrated along the Yangtze valley, the plain of its delta had not gone untouched. Robbie and Wallace had redoubled their efforts to strengthen and unify the body of believers in the district against further testings of their faith. The village people had been genuinely frightened by the news that had begun to leak down from the regions closer to the great river. Missions in Nanking, Protestant and Catholic alike, had been broken into and burned. In Wusueh, two English missionaries had been murdered.

There had been a few minor flare-ups in the Wukiang district, but Wallace had taken a strong lead in being an example to his flock to pray for and demonstrate charity toward their oppressors. Thus far, such a nonviolent response to the trouble that occasionally arose had been successful; the troublemakers, usually so taken aback by the peaceful responses of their Christian neighbors, had dispersed peacefully without serious incident. Yet the situation remained tense, for though most villagers wanted no part of the trouble, there were still more than a few rabble-rousers who were caught up in the doings elsewhere, and still others with grievances whose volatile emotions could easily spark an incident.

"Look over there, Papa," said Ruth, stopping on the bridge and pointing toward a colorfully decorated small sampan gliding down the river. It was a "meeting boat," in which a groom carried his new bride to the home of her new family. The sight was comforting, for it indicated that the minds and hearts of the village folk were not totally preoccupied with the tumultuous political events of the last weeks and months. A wedding brought hope and joy, and Robbie felt an unrestrained smile rise to his lips. He and Ruth waved as the boat passed beneath them, watching until it turned into the smaller river and disappeared from sight.

"Ah, lass," said Robbie thoughtfully as they resumed their walk, "we must never lose sight of God's promises. 'We are troubled on every side, yet not distressed; we are perplexed, but not in despair; persecuted, but not forsaken; cast down, but not destroyed!' He is with us, little Chi-Yueh, we have no need to fear."

"I am not afraid, Papa."

"I cannot help being a wee bit afraid at times," replied Robbie, smiling to himself. He could still recall the days when it had not been so easy to make such an admission.

"Grandfather says that perfect love casts out all fear."

"So he does!" Robbie tossed back his head and laughed a free and easy laugh. "He is right, and he has told me those very words many times. We are indeed blessed, Ruth. Come, I'll race you to the mission!"

Still laughing, Robbie allowed his giggling daughter several paces lead before jogging after her.

"I'm about to catch you!" he shouted merrily, but in a concerted burst of effort, Ruth sprinted ahead, and Robbie found he had to work a good deal harder than expected in order to keep pace. *She is growing up,* he thought. *Soon she'll be able to win in a legitimate race!* He let her get to the compound yard first, where he planned to jog up breathlessly behind her, declaring her the fastest girl in Wukiang.

But before she reached the residence, Ruth stopped dead still in the middle of the yard. Intent on the race, Robbie nearly collided with her.

"'Tis no way to give me the lead!" he joked, catching his balance. But one look at her face showed him she was no longer laughing. Instead, an intense look of questioning had supplanted the earlier merriment.

"What is it, Ruth—?" Suddenly as he looked up, he saw the cause for the unexpected change in her countenance. The mission had a visitor, and she had been the first to notice him.

Before him was a sight Robbie had never expected to see again. Although now that he found himself standing face to face with

Benjamin Pike's withered and aging form, Robbie knew that another encounter with the man was inevitable sooner or later. His throat tightened, and instinctively he reached out and pulled Ruth protectively near to him. Every fiber within him screamed out for vengeance; even if he had wanted to, he could not control the sudden look of violence that spread across his face. Pike was quick to note it.

Leaning against the chapel door, he shook his head with mock dismay. "Robbie, lad," he said, "is that any way to greet a dear old friend?"

Robbie made no immediate reply, merely gaping ahead; how could Pike speak in his old tone as if nothing had ever happened?

"Surely," Pike went on, "ye can't be holding old mistakes against me after all these years."

Robbie swallowed hard. The words which finally came from his mouth were forced and terse. "What do you want with me?"

Robbie had often wondered what he would do if he ever saw Pike again. He had never let that line of thinking progress far enough to come to a conclusion. He had gradually come to consider Pike a part of the long-distant past, forgotten and gone forever. But now here he was facing his old skipper as if the years had been but the blink of an eye. Here he was, an unresolved agony from the past, and with sight of him, years of pent-up bitterness and unforgiveness rose up from within Robbie. Why had he come back now? What new horrors would he bring with him this time?

"Papa," came Ruth's voice as if from a fog, "he's hurt like you."

The sound of her voice struck him with a jolt—there was compassion in her tone. Did she expect him to pity the miscreant? *Dear God, you can't ask such a thing of me!*

"Blimey!" croaked Pike, with a gloat that must have been intended to have a fatherly appearance, "do me ears deceive me, or do ye gots yerself a young'un? A China doll at that, ye old sea dog!"

"Get out of here, Pike!" Robbie could take almost anything, but not to hear Pike's evil lips speak degradingly of his daughter, Hsi-chen's daughter. "We want nothing to do with you."

"Papa?" said Ruth, puzzled. She had never heard her father speak thus to anyone.

"Go into the house, Ruth," Robbie snapped. When she hesitated, he added sharply, "Quickly!"

She scurried away, but Robbie did not relax even when she was safely behind the closed door of the residence.

"I ain't got no other place to go," said Pike pitifully as soon as they were left alone. "I told myself, Robbie was ne'er one to hold a grudge, especially now as I heard ye gots religion. I says to myself, Robbie Taggart won't turn me out."

"Well, you're wrong! I can and I will!"

But even as Robbie spoke, words that he heard from the lips of his own daughter only a few moments earlier came tumbling like an accusation back into his agonized mind. "Perfect love . . ." *I cannot be expected to love him, God! That's asking too much!*

But a quiet voice within gently responded to his cry. "Just such as he I gave my life for. Do you think I love Benjamin Pike any less than I do your daughter Ruth . . . or you? Yes, Robbie, I *do* expect you to love—and forgive."

I can't! cried Robbie in silent misery.

Pike had in the meantime hobbled on his crutch down the chapel steps, and Robbie saw more clearly how pathetic the old sailor had become. His clothes were mere rags and hung pitifully from his emaciated body. His scant, greasy hair was now completely gray, and his bloodshot eyes were rheumy and dull. Under any other circumstances, his was a figure toward whom Robbie would have felt instant compassion and pity. But stubbornly he shook his head at the emotions raging through him.

In the midst of his turmoil he heard his name being called. He looked up and saw Wallace standing in the residence doorway.

"Robert," said the doctor, "your daughter tells me we have a visitor. He looks tired and no doubt hungry as well. He is welcome to join us for our evening meal."

Oh, Isaiah, you don't know what you are doing! thought Robbie to himself. *Surely you must know who this is, even if you have never laid eyes on the old captain. I've described him clearly enough to you.* Surely Hsi-chen's father could not have forgotten, no matter how many years had passed, that this was the man who had aided in kidnapping his daughter, and in nearly killing Robbie as well. How could he now invite him into their home? How could he even consider allowing him near Ruth? Robbie cast a questioning, resistant look in Wallace's direction.

"Robert, I have never turned away a seeking soul from this mission in all the years I have been here." The words were spoken in Wallace's stern intractable tone that clearly said he would not be moved in his decision.

Robbie stepped reluctantly aside.

"Thank ye, laddie," said Pike. "I swear to ye, I'm a reformed man—at least I wants to be. I jist needs the helpin' hand of an old friend, Robbie. I knew ye wouldn't let me down."

Following behind his old skipper, Robbie could not see the glint of triumph in Pike's eye as he followed Wallace inside.

62

God's Power Made Perfect In Weakness

Was it possible for a man such as Benjamin Pike to reform?

Over the next several days Robbie spent many hours pondering that very question. The man was such a study in affability—helping around the mission compound like a devoted slave, lavishing all with the most gracious of mannerisms and cordial *pleases* and *thank-yous*. He seemed hardly the same man Robbie had always known. Every chance he had, he plied Robbie and Wallace with religious questions and listened attentively to their answers.

Robbie had almost begun to repent of his own harsh reception of the man on that day he arrived.

Yet part of him still held back his complete acceptance of Pike's supposed reformation. There remained something in the old sailor's eyes that still didn't quite ring true, an occasional flash of cunning that might have been missed by one less wary.

So Robbie ate with the man, allowed him to sleep in the spare room in the hospital where he and the Vicar had once stayed before he himself had moved into the residence. And he even—though only in his presence—let Pike tell Ruth an occasional sea story or two.

Yet Robbie could never let himself lose sight of the man's past treachery. Something inside told him Pike was up to no good. For two days he was especially vigilant over Ruth. However, during that time Pike did not give him the slightest provocation or reason for mistrust. On the afternoon of the third day, suddenly Pike was nowhere to be seen. Robbie did not know whether to be afraid or relieved. At least with Pike nearby and visible, he had been able to monitor his activities—he didn't relish the idea of not knowing what the former friend of his father was up to.

But at dinnertime, there was Pike again, a toothless and lopsided smile spread across his hideous face.

"We missed you earlier," said Robbie tightly.

"Ye have every right to be put out with old Ben," said the seaman contritely. "It were jist downright thoughtless o' me to go off without leavin' a word. An' I would ne'er 'ave done such a thing 'cept ye an' the reverend was nowheres about, an' I didn't want to disturb the ladies."

It was a plausible enough excuse, for Robbie and Ruth had gone for a walk, and it was only on their return that they had discovered Pike gone.

"You are free to come and go as you please," said Robbie.

"Ye're a saint, Robbie! But I always told meself that Robbie Taggart was good as gold."

"So, Mr. Pike," put in Wallace, "you were perhaps exploring our little village?"

It wasn't like Wallace to make trivial small talk, but he had probably decided it was in everyone's best interests to be fully apprised of Pike's activities.

"Matter o' fact, yes, Reverend," answered Pike in a smooth tone. "An' a fine old place it is, too. Why, I wouldn't mind settlin' down here meself."

Wallace cleared his throat as he searched for some positive response to such a disquieting notion. "As God directs, Mr. Pike."

"I've been driftin' from place to place an' job to job, ain't had no place to rest my sea-weary bones all these ten years. Maybe I'll jist join yer little mission community here, Reverend."

Robbie said nothing. He had seen that wild glint flash through Pike's eyes again, even as he spoke to Wallace. Whether Wallace knew he was being lied to, Robbie could not tell. But what could he do, short of forcing Pike to leave? And that he could not do. If he was truly a servant of God, and if that God was a God of love—and Robbie knew beyond all question that He was—then he was compelled to respond in love toward all men. Thus far such a requirement had not been difficult for him. He was a man who naturally liked others. However, neither his natural nor his spiritual self had ever been called to such a test as this.

He had discussed this very thing with Wallace earlier that day.

"Isaiah," Robbie had said as they sat in the doctor's study, "I know I must somehow express the love of Christ to Pike. What if his only chance to hear the gospel is to come through me? What if the only love he may ever experience is what I offer him? Yet I can barely look at the man without all the old hatred and bitterness rising up within me. Much less love him with the love of Jesus! I thought I had fully accepted my injury. I thought I had truly come to the point of thankfulness in my heart. And yet the moment he showed up, all the old resentments came instantly back. Ten years I've been walking with the Lord, and yet suddenly it's like I'm a week-old Christian struggling with the most fundamental of things inside my heart. It's all I can do to keep the hate from consuming me!"

"The Lord has done a great work in your life, Robert," replied Wallace. "In ten years He has remade you in almost every way. You turned everything over to Him. You gave Him all your former attitudes and priorities. Everything except that one most crucial place deep inside you where dwelt the memory of Benjamin Pike and all he represented. He was a hanging thread. We all have them in our lives—the one hidden thing we don't even realize we are holding back from the Lord until that painful day when He finally reveals our own self to us all over again. Everyone has a Benjamin Pike. And now is your opportunity to give God thanks that he is providing you this chance to complete the circle of your growth in this area."

"Oh!" wailed Robbie, "if it were anything but this!"

"If it were anything but this, then it wouldn't be the supreme test of your commitment to walk in the way of our Lord."

"But he's the man who took my hand!" Robbie protested.

"What about Jesus? They took His life. And He forgave them. Dare we strive for anything less, Robert? We may yet be called on to give our lives, too. I found myself praying earlier today that God would prepare me, if that was in His plan for me. We never know what blessings and sacrifices the Lord has in store once we become completely His."

Robbie was silent, agonizing within his soul over his father-in-law's words. He knew they were words of truth.

"I think it is no accident that God has brought you to face Pike at this time," continued Wallace thoughtfully. "His timing in our lives is always perfect. He has strengthened you through the years in preparation for this supreme test of your spiritual strength and manhood. You are a man, Robert. A man after God's heart. A man I am proud to call my son, if not in blood, then certainly in every other way. It has been an honor in my life to know you, and to share these past ten years of ministry with you. You have blessed me, served me, and loved me. I could not be more proud of my daughter's choice of husband. But my time in China is nearly over. The time is coming—"

Robbie opened his mouth to protest, but Wallace cut him off.

"Please. Let me finish. I have something I want to say to you. I have lived a good life, Robert. I hope I can say with Paul that I have fought the good fight and run the good race. But I will be seventy in not so many years. I am old. And the Lord has been speaking to me about the end of my service to Him on this earth."

Tears streamed down Robbie's face as he listened, his heart thinking of Pike no longer but full of his great love for this man who had become his spiritual father.

"The time of earthly endings must come to all. Earthly endings and eternal beginnings. And as my time of ministry here draws to a close, it is my prayer that you will take up the work and continue to carry forth the banner of God's truth to these people you and I have grown to love so much. I want you to know that I believe God's hand is upon you to accomplish great things for His church in China as this century ends and the 20th century begins. It is you, Robert, to whom I entrust the work of my life."

"But you have many years left, Isaiah," said Robbie at last, through his tears.

"Perhaps that is true. But I feel the Lord is showing me otherwise. Only the Lord knows. His timing is always right. But we cannot tell what these coming days of persecution may bring. And I want you to be ready, Robert, whatever may come. God will call upon you to make decisions affecting many. But His hand will be upon you. That is why I feel so strongly that He has brought your old friend and adversary, Mr. Pike, back into your life now. He is preparing you, Robert, for deeper, and possibly even more painful things. He is taking you further along the road of sharing in both the sufferings and the victories of your Master."

Both men were silent for some minutes, each deep in his own thoughts.

"What does God want me to do?" Robbie finally asked.

"I think you know the answer to that, Robert."

Robbie ran a frustrated hand through his hair. "Yes, I suppose I do," he sighed. "But he's an evil, hateful man, and my flesh cannot love him."

"More evil than the men who put Jesus on the cross?"

"No," sighed Robbie again.

"It will take real courage to face the task God has put before you. It is no less than what His Son faced as He hung there."

"Courage?"

"Yes. Courage that only genuine men and women of God can summon. This will be the most difficult task you have ever faced in your life.

You have braved storms and angry seas and battles of fist against fist and brawn against brawn. But victory in the arena of the Spirit will take an altogether greater kind of strength. It will take the greatest courage and the greatest humility of all: the courage to forgive."

"You know, Isaiah," sighed Robbie, "I have always been more amply endowed with the other type."

"And now God is calling you again, as you have already done many times, to lay that fleshly strength of your old nature down, and exhibit courage on an altogether more profound level."

"I am so weak! Not only do I have only one hand, not only has my former physical strength been taken from me, I feel I have no emotional strength either."

"The power of God will be made perfect in weakness, Robert. So says the Word of God. For it is His strength you need only rely on—He will work the changes in your heart that will enable you to love. When we are strong, we can still rely on ourselves. That's why God strips away all our earthly pride and strength, so that we will finally learn what it means to depend on Him. And out of such dependence, in the end, true spiritual strength is born."

"That will be the only way it can possibly happen," replied Robbie, with more determination than assurance, "for Him to work the changes in me."

"Just keep your heart submissive to God's leading," added Wallace. "Make sure that when He shows you what is required, you don't rebel against it. It may be a heavy burden He gives you to bear."

Robbie smiled at these words, though he knew Wallace meant them more as a reminder than a rebuke. The old corner of his heart had been rebelling ever since Pike had made his appearance. Even after this talk with Wallace, though Robbie knew what God wanted him to do, seeing that old look in his former skipper's eyes made his rebellious nature more alive than ever. As much as his father-in-law's words were turning over in his subconscious mind and working themselves gradually deeper into his heart, he still found it nearly impossible to open himself to the man who had crippled him.

Robbie was saved from having to agonize over what to do much longer, however. For the next day Pike disappeared again, and this time did not return.

Two days after that, the trouble they had feared since Wuhu, a serious riot with ramifications throughout the entire region, erupted in Lungsi, a village only about three miles distant from the mission.

63

The Fanning of the Flames

As soon as the trouble broke out, Wallace went to Lungsi.

At the root of the disturbance, it seemed, was one of the mission's communicants who had, against Wallace's advice, taken an unbelieving neighbor to the authorities over the destruction of some property. Tempers had flared, and the Christian had been accused of being bewitched by the foreigners. This sentiment incited other anti-foreign, anti-Christian accusations, with several of the Christian members of the village attempting to defend their stand. Verbal sparring soon gave way to blows.

Wallace arrived in the midst of the mayhem. The elder of the village and his council had thus far had no success in dispersing the twenty or thirty members of the angry mob. Wallace's presence on the scene managed to quiet the crowd, especially in that he was able to encourage his own people to back off, despite taunts directed at him by several on the other side. The crowd shuffled off in various directions, but in no way did a sense of peace return to the community. Wallace helped restore order to the homes of his church members that had been vandalized during the row, then returned to the mission.

During the doctor's absence, Robbie had had his own share of problems in Wukiang. As darkness had enveloped the village, an unseen arsonist had set fire to Chang's home. Though no one was hurt, it took some time to quell the blaze, and then not until the small place had been destroyed. Robbie reached the mission with the homeless Chang family just as Wallace returned. Shan-fei and Miss Trumbull prepared beds for the family in the school, but they were still in the midst of this when old Li ran into the compound.

"Tai-fu, ching-kao!" he cried, pounding on the residence door.

Wallace swung the door open. The look on his face was tense, expectant of more trouble.

"Li hsien-sheng, what is it?"

"Tai-fu, you must believe me when I say I do not know how this began," said Li frantically. "I am not one of you, but I hate you no longer."

"I know that, Li. But what is the matter?"

"They are gathering outside the village," answered Li, his face panic-stricken. "Some are from Wukiang, some from Lungsi, and the other villages. Some I have never seen before. Evil men. They are very angry and are trying to stir the people into a riot. There is talk of burning the mission. They say you are a devil, that you charmed the people in Lungsi today into dispersing. Even one or two of your own members are among them, declaring that they were indeed bewitched by you. They all cry that the mission must be destroyed before all Chinese are defiled. They speak nothing but lies, but will not listen to reason."

"How many are there, Li?" asked Robbie, who had come up behind Wallace.

"Seventy-five, possibly a hundred when I left," replied Li. "But their numbers are growing. I will stay and help you."

"No, Li," said Wallace. "Thank you. But it is best you do not become involved in this way. Go to your home. God will protect us."

Wallace paused, then added, "There is perhaps one thing you can do."

"Whatever I am able."

"Could you shelter the Changs until this is all over, and my granddaughter also? The fewer at the mission right now, I believe, the better."

"I would be most happy to assist," answered Li. "But they must come quickly, for the crowd may come at any time."

Ying Nien, now a fully trained pastor himself, went with Li's party to help with arrangements there, while Wallace gathered the remaining mission family, including Robbie, Miss Trumbull, and Shan-fei, together in the sanctuary of the chapel.

"What are we going to do?" asked Robbie.

"We came to China that God might be glorified," answered Wallace. "Our buildings, even our lives, are infinitesimal in the heavenly scheme of things. We have all known the moment may come when we would be called to the ultimate sacrifice. Our only purpose is to bring glory to God, and to trust our lives into His care."

He paused, then reached out his two hands, taking his wife's hand in one of his, and laying the other on Robbie's left shoulder. They in turn reached out to take Miss Trumbull's hands, and following Wallace's lead, the small band sank to their knees on the chapel floor.

Wallace quietly cleared his throat, then began to sing in his deep baritone voice, a song they all knew as well as any scripture or liturgy. But suddenly the words, grown somewhat dull over the years with repetition, struck them with new and meaningful impact. "Praise God from whom all blessings flow . . ."

The others joined him with fervent voices, and though there were only four of them gathered together as one, the melodious tones carried out into the heavy night air.

On a fallow rice field a mile from the village, a few horses impatiently stamped in the soft dirt.

Wang peered through the darkness, then nodded his head with approval as he spied the torches bobbing up and down in the distance. By their elevation he gathered they had now reached the bridge, and by their numbers he guessed that his men had been successful in rousing a good number of the villagers. There must be a hundred or more crossing the river, he thought with wicked satisfaction. He could almost hear the creaking of the ancient timbers.

He turned to his companion. "You are certain they will not abandon the mission?"

"I tells you, guv'nor," replied a self-satisfied voice, "that mission is everything to the blokes. I done my job good. I knows what I'm talkin' about. They won't leave for nothin'."

"For nothing . . . ?"

"'Cept to help a friend, and I found out Taggart's got just such a friend, a Chinaman, no less—"

"Watch what you say, you scum of a sailor!" warned Wang.

"'Course there are Chinamen—that is, Chinese—and there are *Chinese*. And they ain't all as noble as yersel', Wang." The uneasy rider bowed with a mocking smirk on his face. "This one'll do fine fer what we wants."

"Taggart must be separated from the mission," said Wang. "Not only will that weaken the mission against our mob, but it will also make Taggart all the more vulnerable."

"He were alone ten years ago in the monastery," observed the other.

"I was too overconfident then. *This time* I will be prepared!"

"Let's jist hope so."

"You better hope you have done *your* job!"

Pike merely snorted his disdain for Wang's doubt. He knew he had done his part perfectly. During his short stay at the mission he had become fully apprised with the layout of the place, and had learned the names of those who might prove useful to them such as this Chinaman, Kuo-hwa. But the most important thing he had discovered was that Robbie had changed. Religion had made the lad gentle as a dove. Why, he had even overheard the Reverend and Robbie talking about loving their enemies, and not using fists to fight their battles.

The fools! Prayers and platitudes were Robbie's stock in trade now, and Pike was more confident than ever that when Wang went after him, he'd not so much as raise a finger, much less a fist, to defend himself. That might take some of the sport out of his death, it was true. But by now it was no longer a matter of enjoyment for either Pike or Wang—it was sheer, undefiled revenge.

Wang glanced about again, only this time in the opposite direction from the torches.

"Where the devil is Pien?" he asked angrily. "I told him exactly where to be tonight!"

"Probably off gettin' hissel' drunk. I don't know why ye keeps that dullard around."

"I'll kill him if he fails me tonight!"

"Ye should 'ave killed him long ago," muttered Pike. "I never did trust the blag'ard!"

64

The Passing of the Torch

Robbie could not fully understand the peace that had stolen over him as he and the other missionaries knelt in the tightly knit circle praising and worshiping God.

He knew it was against his nature to sit still when external circumstances and internal emotions cried out for action. Yet even as he heard the noise of the inflamed mob drawing near the mission, he realized the most potent action possible was the one he was now performing. As the four of them prayed, each knew this was no battle against flesh and blood, nor against mobs with torches and clubs and weapons. Rather it was against the Evil One himself—and only the name of Christ could prevail against such an enemy.

When the clamor of the mob finally reached the compound yard, Robbie's thoughts were dominated by Wallace's words: *"Our only purpose is to bring glory to God."* As each one of his beloved mission family lifted their heads, he saw on the faces of the other three what he felt within himself—a quiet peace at being given the opportunity to do what they had been called here to do—trust their lives into the care of their Father. They gave one another fervent embraces, intending encouragement, not knowing it was also a final goodbye to one of their number.

Then they rose as one body and moved to the chapel door.

Wallace flung it open as if he were welcoming the Sunday morning congregation. The entire mission yard was swarming with shouting, hostile people who also moved as one—as an angry and frenzied mob. Among the dozens of strangers from both near and far, Robbie could discern many faces he knew and with whom he had had many friendly encounters over the years. But they were hardly recognizable now that they were twisted and distorted with violence.

Conscious as never before of his role as shepherd of the scattered flock, Wallace stepped onto the porch. But if he had wanted to speak, his attempt would have been drowned in the cries of the crowd when they saw him.

"There he is!" screamed several. "The enemy of our people!"

"Please," said Wallace calmly, though he had to shout to be heard over the din. "I ask you to judge us by what you have *seen* these many years. You know we mean nothing but good for you. Go to your homes before harm is done that you will regret."

"You will not cast any more of your spells over us, you devil!"

"Destroy this wicked place!" cried many voices, almost in unison, as if their taunting shouts had been rehearsed.

"Destroy! Destroy!" The chant rose up like an incantation.

Suddenly, as if out of the darkness itself, a torch shot through the air, landing squarely on the residence roof. The shingles Robbie had once labored so long and hard to replace, leaped instantly into flame.

Miss Trumbull gasped. Robbie placed a comforting arm around her, realizing there was nothing he could do. The roof was too dry to halt the spread of the blaze. Everything she had, everything representing the work of her life, was in that building.

Breaking free from Robbie, she tried to make a dash across the compound to rescue what she could before flames engulfed the entire structure. But the mob would not let her go. Gently, Robbie led her back into the chapel as she wept softly. After a moment she calmed, looked up at Robbie, and returned his heartfelt smile. He knew that her initial shock had been supplanted with the assurance that her real treasures were not to be found in that building at all.

"It is only against God that you sin!" cried Wallace. "But He loves and forgives you, as we do also."

"Devil! Pig!" the taunters in the crowd shouted as if he had not spoken at all.

"Dear Father," prayed Wallace, his voice now soft as he spoke with his Lord for these people he had spent his life trying to serve. "These children of your making do not know what they are doing. They are caught up in an awful web of misunderstanding and fear. Show them the glory of your love—"

"Stop him!" shrieked a hysterical voice in the midst of his prayer. "He is attempting to cast another spell!"

The crowd surged forward.

As they did so, Robbie stepped up next to Wallace, as Shan-fei and Miss Trumbull retreated to a safer distance. He did not know for certain why he did so. He knew he could not raise a hand to stop them. But something inside him recalled the doctor's words of passing the leadership of the mission on to him. If this was how it was destined to end, then at least he wanted to share that burden of leadership for these few moments. If he was to die, he wanted it to be at the side of dear Hsi-chen's father.

"Stop!" yelled Robbie, but his voice was lost in the frenzied shrieks from the mob.

The crowd continued to surge forward. Robbie could see that those in front carried weapons—some crude clubs and farm implements, others brandishing knives about. He saw no guns, but there were too many people to be certain in the dark. He called back to the women to shut the door and stay inside, just as the first rioter reached the steps swinging a heavy stick. A stinging blow glanced off Robbie's shoulder. Instinctively he lurched toward the assailant. Out of the corner of his eye he saw Wallace dropping to his knees. The doctor was being attacked by a half dozen men, but he made no move except to protect his face with his arms against the flurry of fists pelting him.

Our only purpose is to bring glory to God.

Wallace's words rang in Robbie's mind, and with them other words often quoted by the older missionary: "He was led as a lamb to the slaughter . . ."

Robbie stepped back from his attacker, now joined by several others. Following his friend's lead, he fell to his knees and bowed his head murmuring praise and thanksgiving to God as the blows rained fiercely on his defenseless body.

Dragging the two men down the steps, the attackers continued their deadly assault. With sweat and blood seeping into his eyes, and pain dulling his consciousness, Robbie lost track of Wallace. He prayed for the doctor, for deliverance, for their persecutors.

All at once a new sound rose in the darkness, not the blood-thirsty cries of the mob, but shouts of a friendly sort. Arresting the attention of the rioters, a new group of locals, led by Chang and Li, entered the compound. With them were twenty-five or thirty others. The mob slackened their attack momentarily as they faced their challengers.

"Get away from here!" yelled Chang. "These people have done no harm. They are friends of our community!"

"No!" screamed a rioter, a man Robbie did not recognize. "He is the devil. He must be destroyed!"

Robbie stood and staggered a few steps toward Chang. *Where is Isaiah?* he thought, looking around groggily. But before he could make sense out of the scene before him, a fresh blow from the side of a farmer's hoe landed against the side of his head and sent him sprawling to the ground. Immediately he felt the warm rush of blood trickling down his neck from the gash on his ear. The light from the torches swirled around in the blackness as consciousness began to fade.

"Stand back from him!" he heard a voice yell. Moments later Robbie could feel Li's arm under his neck, supporting him. "They will not strike you again, Robbie Taggart, my friend," said Li. "To do so they will have to kill me first, and I think they will not do so."

At the same time, Chang had pushed his way frantically through the crowd until he located Wallace. He stooped down to his missionary friend, screaming at the frenzied mob to stand clear. In his hand he wielded a great club, and the fire in his eyes told those nearby he would bash in the head of any who tried to stop him.

Wallace lay prostrate on the ground, blood streaming from his nose and mouth. Broken and bleeding from a great gash across his left thigh gave ugly evidence to the violence that had gone further than any of the locals had intended. But the doctor who had helped tend so many of these very men's families and deliver their own sons and daughters felt no pain from his wounds. He had lapsed into unconsciousness several minutes before with a prayer of forgiveness on his lips.

In the momentary lull that followed Chang's action, most of the crowd stepped back. The weeping, prayerful voices of the mission's supporters, the groans from the injured, the crackling from the blazing residence behind them—all seemed to combine to bring them to their senses. And in the center lay Wallace, motionless, in Chang's arms.

Robbie struggled to his feet, surveyed the scene before him, then limped toward the still form of his mentor.

All at once, from out of the center of the crowd ran one of the strangers who had instigated the riot.

"The devil must die!" he shrieked like a madman. In his hand glistened the cold steel of a long knife.

"Dear God, no!" mumbled Robbie, stumbling toward his friend.

But it was too late. The crazed hireling shot into the open space at the center of the crowd before anyone could stop him, kicked Chang viciously aside before the kneeling farmer could protect himself, and plunged the knife into Wallace's heart.

"God, what has he done!" cried Robbie.

"You can't stop us!" declared the murderer, running back through the crowd, which, stunned by the sudden attack, parted and let him pass. "The devil is dead! All foreign devils must die!"

Then just as suddenly as he had come, the assassin disappeared into the blackness of night.

All was still. The blazing fire roared through the night. Some of the crowd silently ran back across the bridge to the village. Others now inched their way forward, crowding around Wallace's mutilated body. Several knelt to pray.

The horrifying end of their supposed enemy, the man most of the villagers had known as a friend, sobered the angry mob into scattered outbursts of grief and penitence. They had been roused to violence by foolish lies, but none had considered what the consequences might be. Now the shock of what they had done seared through them with excruciating suddenness, as if they had been standing in the midst of the fire raging behind them.

One by one a few continued to flee, each desperate to protect only himself.

Robbie staggered forward, weeping and speechless, crumpling to the ground beside Wallace's lifeless form.

Ying Nien, who had arrived with Chang and Li, came up next to Robbie, sobbing with Oriental abandon in passionate grief. He dropped to his knees beside the body of the man who, many years ago had led him to his Savior in a Buddhist monastery and who had been as a father to him. The two were joined by Chang and Li, both weeping as well. Robbie felt the hands of shared grief on his back and shoulder. He reached out in return, grasping first Li's hand, then Chang's, then reaching his left arm around Ying, and giving his brother and friend a compassionate hug.

They were alone now. Robbie knew that. Wallace's words had been prophetic. The mission, what was left of it, was now Robbie's to lead.

"How . . . how could they do this?" wept Ying. "It is they who deserve to die!"

"I loved him too, Nien," said Robbie. "But we must not give up on these people. Jesus did not deserve to die either. Our friend Isaiah has been honored to share martyrdom just like his Lord. He would want us to rejoice for him."

"I hate them too much to care anymore."

"Nien, Isaiah loved these people enough to die trying to reach them. His death is a reminder of Jesus' death. We will honor his death, and allow God to use it, by doing the same."

The words were difficult to say, for Robbie's flesh cried out for revenge too. But he had learned from Wallace long ago that the values of the kingdom of God were directly opposite those of the kingdom of man. And in God's kingdom, a mighty and valiant warrior had just been called home, giving cause for rejoicing in heaven. Even if he had to force the words out, he knew they were true. And if they were at the moment only a forced mental response in the midst of his terrible human grief, one day they would settle deeply into his heart, and become a calling to guide the rest of his life in the footsteps of both his Master and his mentor.

But with the world still swirling in disarray around him, Robbie could give little more thought to just what Dr. Wallace's death might mean to him. From their position inside the chapel, Shan-fei and Miss Trumbull had been spared seeing the cruel events of the past moments. Now Robbie looked up to see them slowly approaching. He stood, another heartbreaking task confronting him.

Robbie walked toward his mother-in-law, opening his arms to receive her just as she realized that the prostrate form around whom the men were kneeling was her husband. Scarcely uttering a sound, she fainted into his arms.

Yet even now the rush of events did not cease.

A young man came running into the yard. Robbie recognized him vaguely. From another village, he had come to the mission's services once or twice.

"Another mob has formed!" he panted, breathless. "Men on horses . . .

the people are stirred up again. They have gone wild and are burning the village . . . Kuo-hwa's house . . . he has been hurt."

For the first time Robbie realized that his friend had not been among the group of mission defenders. He did not stop to question this, nor why Kuo-hwa should have been singled out.

He gave Shan-fei into the care of Ying and Miss Trumbull, embraced the weeping Chang once more, gave Li one last pat on the shoulder and a sincere look of thanks, then sped away to help his friend.

65

Last Battle Against Old Enemies

From the bridge Robbie could see several small blazes scattered throughout the village.

Half the mission contingent had followed him on hearing the newcomer's report, and now, seeing for themselves the truth of the man's words, they all raced in various directions toward the fires. These were soon joined by additional villagers who had remained tightly shut up in their homes during the riot. Though they had wanted no involvement in the madness that had erupted, they could not now turn their backs on neighbors in need. Moreover, if the fires started in the homes of Christians blazed out of control and spread, the whole village would ultimately be endangered.

Instead of crossing the bridge, Robbie continued to his left. Kuo-hwa lived at the northern end of the village, across the far bridge. But as Robbie neared the area, he saw there were no fires here. The rioters had gone east from the mission, and had not reached this section of Wukiang.

Kuo-hwa's house appeared sound, but the air was uncannily quiet.

Robbie paused. He could sense a different kind of danger. The questions he had not had time to consider previously now began tumbling into his wary mind.

Kuo-hwa surely would have come to the defense of the mission if he had been able. Why had he been absent? And if his home was one of the few remaining untouched, why had his name been specifically mentioned?

Slowly he approached the darkened door of the little hut, knocking several times before hearing movement from within.

"Who is it?" came a small, tremulous voice from behind the closed door.

"It is Robbie Taggart."

The door opened a crack. The pale and ancient face of Kuo-hwa's mother appeared. Assuring herself it was indeed a friend, she opened the door more fully.

"There is so much trouble in the village," she said as an explanation for her caution. "I am alone and was afraid."

"I understand. Where is Kuo-hwa?"

"He went away with the other white man about an hour ago."

"The other white man?" queried Robbie, his stomach tightening in dreaded anticipation of the answer to his question.

"The man who said he was your friend."

"My friend?"

"He was here some days ago—the man with one leg. He took my son with him."

"*Took* him?" asked Robbie. "As a prisoner?"

"The man said you needed his help. My son went willingly, but in much anxiety."

"Do you know where?"

The old woman shook her head, but pointed north, in the direction of the rice fields.

Robbie turned in the direction she had indicated and ran off as quickly as his bruised legs would take him. Even as he did so his mind filled with the memory of a similar trap he had rushed into ten years before. Then he had dashed in foolishly to do battle against those who had dared to harm someone he loved. He had been armed and prepared to kill if necessary.

But his heart had changed since then. On this night, he knew only that he was powerless in his own strength to rescue his friend, but also that love and prayer were the only weapons necessary. He would not rush in to do battle against earthly powers, but prepared to give his life, if necessary, against the principalities of darkness. For he knew the armor of God was upon him. God would be his strength and his deliverance. His only calling was to follow the example of his Lord and lay down his life, if it came to that, for his friend.

Wallace had shown him the way tonight. In giving his life and spilling his own blood, he had demonstrated to Robbie the fullest example of God's power to deliver His people out of the bondage of fearing the hands of men.

No longer was Robbie Taggart afraid of what men could do to him. As he ran toward whatever destiny awaited him, Robbie felt as never before the power of peaceful forbearance in the face of physical persecution. He had looked death in the face this night, and at last he knew that it could not conquer him. It could not conquer anyone whose hope rested in the Lord of the universe.

He was compelled to continue on, drawn toward a necessary confrontation—a spiritual confrontation for which God had been preparing him for the last decade. He would face a battle, as much against emotions within himself as against any mortal enemy. It would be a battle where no physical power would avail him. An ache in his arm where his hand had once been reminded him of the futility of physical prowess and earthly might. Tonight he had received new wounds. A deep cut over his eye and the one on his ear still throbbed and bled, while many other bruises and cuts from the blows of the angry rioters made him conscious of his earthly body. Yet these wounds only served to focus his mind on the truth that the Spirit of God does not dwell in a tabernacle made with hands.

Our only purpose is to bring glory to God!

"Oh, God," Robbie prayed, "let me be worthy to follow in the footsteps of your servant! Strengthen me in the might of your Spirit, Lord, and strip me of all thoughts of power in myself."

As he ran, suddenly two figures rushed out of the darkness and grabbed him. Robbie neither struggled nor fought. He had expected them. He had known all along that he was the target, not Kuo-hwa. But God was with him. He *would* be delivered by the Lord's protective hand, even if that meant he was about to join Wallace in his homeward journey through death into life. God would be glorified!

They prodded him savagely across a field, shoving him, twisting his arm, knocking him with blows to the ground, taunting him and reviling him each step of the way, until they arrived at a small campfire that burned in the lee of a grove of mulberries. There in the dim, eerie, flickering light, he discerned Pike and Wang, both hunched down by the fire-like specters. Though many of his former attitudes had gone the way of the cross, Robbie half expected to feel the same surge of hatred he had experienced when he had first seen Pike on the chapel steps. Yet amazingly he now felt only a forlorn sense of compassion for these two pathetic men.

"I knows ye like a book, laddie! ha! ha!" laughed the old seaman. "Only I did expect more of a fight from you. Ha! ha!"

"Where is Kuo-hwa?"

Pike cocked his head. Following its direction, in the shadows a few feet away, Robbie saw his friend sitting, bound and gagged. In his eyes Robbie read Kuo-hwa's apology for so endangering him.

"Have no fear, Kuo-hwa," said Robbie. "God is with us."

"You will learn fear before this night is over," spoke Wang for the first time. "Tonight you will die, Robbie Taggart!"

"Do you expect that to trouble me, Wang?" asked Robbie, standing tall between the two captors who still held him. "I am only disturbed that I have been the cause for such hate and bitterness to so harden your hearts. But I am praying, for I still believe there is hope for you. And for you also, Ben."

"Don't do me no favors!" retorted Pike. "You always was too good. It used to weaken me. But it ain't going to work no more. You Taggarts have haunted me long enough!"

"What have I ever done to you, Ben?"

"Ye was born, that's what! An' ye're jist like him—"

"Enough of this!" shouted Wang, jumping to his feet. He pulled a pistol from his belt and strode menacingly up to Robbie. "How would you like to die, barbarian!"

"Any method you choose will have the same end—bringing me into the presence of my God."

"Bah!"

"But for your own sake, Wang, I implore you," said Robbie, "you will only be driving yourself further away from the only One who can help you if you stain your hands with more blood."

"Preach no more to me, you vermin!" shrieked Wang. He spat hatefully into Robbie's face. "If you are so willing to die, then let us make it a *slow* death." Wang smashed the butt of his pistol into Robbie's face. He staggered back, but his captors held him fast.

"That's it!" screamed Pike. "Mess up his pretty face!"

Wang leveled several more blows into Robbie's face and head with the back of his hand, to the gleeful encouragement of Pike. Then he rammed his fists three or four times into Robbie's stomach. As Robbie doubled over, his knees buckled beneath him, but Wang's two lackeys prevented him from falling to the ground. When Robbie at last was able to lift his head again, his eyes were closed.

"Dear God, forgive them," he gasped in a barely audible voice. "Reveal your love to them!"

Robbie's prayer only further incensed Wang. "You waste your breath with your prayers, you white fool!" he spat. "If you must pray, then do so for yourself—I am finished with you! Do you hear? Whatever you utter now will be the last words you ever say!"

Wang stepped back several paces and took aim with his pistol.

"Goodbye, laddie," called Pike. "I might be a little sorry ye had to end this way, but I'll have no peace till ye're dead and gone. I only wish I could have been the one to do ye in mysel'."

Wang cocked his gun, savoring the moment for which he had waited so long. But in the pause that followed, suddenly the camp seemed to erupt to life.

Robbie could only make out blurry images through his swollen eyes, but the figures on horseback were unmistakable as they tore through the little fireside gathering.

Robbie heard the expected shot from Wang's gun, but did not feel the sudden impact of the bullet. Knocked off balance by the sudden rush of a dozen horsemen, Wang's shot fired wildly, missing Robbie.

Robbie's captors let him go in order to dash for cover under the mulberries. He stood swaying, still on his feet, desperately trying to sharpen his senses in order to take in what was happening.

"What is the meaning of this?" cried Wang, peering into the darkness in an attempt to identify the intruders. "Pien . . . is that you? What are you trying to do, spoil everything, you fool!"

"That, my lord, is precisely what I intend to do!" returned the lieutenant triumphantly. "Your schemes will indeed be spoiled! I will no longer pay for your whims! And most of your army agrees with me. You are now speaking to the new commander. You may be my soldier if you—"

"You filthy vermin!" shouted Wang, swinging his pistol in the direction of his former servant. He fired before Pien could respond, but in the darkness Wang's aim was off, and the shot hit the man to Pien's left.

Pien raised his own rifle, but desperation had quickened Wang's reaction, and he instantly lunged to the right, leaping out of the perimeter of the glow of the fire. Surrounded by darkness and the mulberry trees, Wang deftly made his escape.

"After him!" ordered Pien.

Two of his men raced off, but already the sound of pounding hoofs could be heard as Wang sped away on one of his own mounts, which had been tied among the trees.

In the meantime, Pike had been stunned by the rapid reversal of events.

At first all he could grasp was that somehow Robbie had again eluded death. But Pien's shout brought him to his senses. Suddenly he realized his imminent danger. He too must escape!

Slowly he tried to hobble inconspicuously away, no easy trick with a wooden leg. However, Pien's wits were quicker.

"Not so fast, pig!" cried the new warlord, his rifle swinging around and taking direct aim at Pike's head.

"It's about time ye got rid of Wang," said Pike with a forced laugh. His voice was shaky as he recovered himself, but he had no hesitation about changing sides, especially with his head in the sights of Pien's weapon.

"Now it is your turn, wai-chu! And what pleasure it will give me!"

"No!" cried Robbie, leaping toward Pike, even as the words were still falling from Pien's mouth. Two shots rang out almost simultaneously.

One was from Pien's rifle. Robbie could not immediately tell whether it had found its mark. The other shot must have come from one of Pien's men, and as Robbie's body shielded Pike, he felt a sharp, searing pain as the bullet pierced his right leg. He braced himself for another volley of shots. But none came.

Instead, Pien's commanding voice barked an order Robbie never expected to hear.

"Cease your firing!"

Slowly and painfully Robbie turned and looked up toward the voice where its owner still sat atop his horse.

"That snake you have tried to protect," said Pien in answer to Robbie's questioning look, "is the only foreign blood I wish to have on my hands. I have no grievance against you. Move aside."

Robbie looked at Pike. He saw a widening circle of blood in the sea captain's abdomen where Pien's shot had found its mark. Barely conscious, Pike's face was contorted with agony, and something almost akin to shame.

"What'd ye do a fool thing like that for, laddie?" he asked weakly.

"Your life is of great value to God, Ben," answered Robbie, "and I could treat it with no less care."

"Ye're crazy," croaked Pike.

But Pien was becoming impatient. "You are free to go, Taggart. I will do everyone a great favor to eliminate this lizard."

"Leave him in God's hands, Pien," replied Robbie. "He will give him the justice and love due him."

"And rob me of my pleasure?"

"Then you will have to kill me also."

Pien snorted with disgust. "That snake is right. You are crazy! Have your way; he is half dead now anyway."

With a jerk at the reins of his horse, Pien swung around and rode away with his small contingent at his heels.

Turning his attention back toward Pike, Robbie ripped off his own shirt, wadded it up, and pressed it against the wound to stop the flow of blood.

"I hates you, Robbie Taggart!" cried Pike in response to Robbie's ministration. "Let me die. It's the only way I'll ever be rid of you."

As he had a hundred times before, Robbie puzzled over Pike's aversion to him. But there was no time to ponder now. Pike would die if he did not move quickly. All at once Robbie felt it of paramount importance to do everything possible to keep the old man alive.

66

Out of the Depths of the Past

Bracing himself painfully on his wounded leg, Robbie untied Kuo-hwa and sent him in search for a cart. When Kuo-hwa returned, they lifted the wounded seaman onto the vehicle and began to inch their way back toward the village.

By the time they reached the mission, Robbie was so numbed with pain that he could barely react to the horror that greeted him. The residence had burned completely to the ground, only the brick chimney remaining. The wall of the chapel facing the fire was badly charred, but by God's grace the building had not ignited.

He collapsed in front of the hospital, the only building untouched by the fire. The last thing he was aware of was Ruth's loving arms around him as she covered his face with kisses.

When he drifted back into consciousness an hour later, he lay in one of the crisp, clean hospital beds much as he had on that first day he had arrived at Christ's China Mission, and as on that day, his whole body ached. Only now the pain was intensified in his right leg. Unlike that first day, however, he would not hear Hsi-chen's sweet, comforting voice speaking to him out of the darkness. Nor would Isaiah Wallace's austere countenance greet him in the morning.

Dear God! he cried silently, *I need you now more than ever.*

As if in answer to his cry, Ruth bent over him, wiping a cool cloth across his brow. He took her hand in his and knew that God never brought His children sorrow without joy following it in return. He had heard the Chinese proverb that sorrow was the container into which one's joy was poured; the larger the container, the greater volume of joy it can hold. And as he felt his daughter's hand, he knew it was true.

"Papa," Ruth asked, tears filling her eyes, "you won't die, will you?"

"No, my dear."

He paused.

"Ruth," he went on, "do you know about your grandfather?"

She nodded, the tears escaping and running in two glistening rivulets down her cheeks.

"He is with our Lord now, little Chi-Yueh. We can rejoice."

"I know, Papa," she replied, then laid her head on his chest and wept.

They comforted each other for some minutes, but at length the present situation intruded back upon them. Ruth was the first to mention what had been at the back of Robbie's mind since he had regained consciousness.

"Papa," said the girl, "Mr. Pike is also dying."

"Dear child, I am so sorry you must see all this," said Robbie tenderly. "I must go to him. Will you help me up?"

Leaning on his daughter for support, Robbie limped to the neighboring bed where Pike lay. The wretched figure had never looked so pathetic, yet with nearly all the life drained out of it, his face seemed somehow less evil, more vulnerable. Sensing someone near, his eyes opened.

"Am I dreamin'," croaked the raspy voice, "or are ye hauntin' me even in the pit o' hell?"

"No, Ben," answered Robbie quietly, "we are still on this earth, and you are awake."

"I'm dyin'," Pike said flatly.

"I believe you are, Ben. Perhaps it is time you made a few things right."

Pike's eyes glazed over, then squeezed shut.

"None o' this would 'ave 'appened if ye'd been 'ere to help me, Hank!" he finally said, though with great effort. "Why'd ye run off an' leave me—I needed ye!"

"This isn't Hank, Ben. I'm Robbie, his son."

"Oh . . . you—" replied the weak voice bitterly. "'Tis yer fault . . . ye took him. He was me only friend."

"I took him, Ben?"

"He left the sea 'cause o' you. Left me, his friend! Left me alone . . . left me t' stump about the world on one leg, which would 'ave ne'er happened if it hadna been for yer bein' born!"

"But, Ben," said Robbie, "he left the sea before I was even born."

"An' if it hadna been for you, he'd 'ave stayed wi' me, an' I'd still 'ave me leg! But the justice o' the gods came back t' haunt the blag'ard! Ha! ha! Now it's you what has t' live wi'out a hand! Ha! ha! A leg fer a hand, isn't that what they say? An eye for an eye! Ha! ha!"

In disjointed pieces, some of which he was unable to put together until much later, over the course of the next two hours Robbie listened to a bitter, tragic account of how a man's whole life could be destroyed by a misplaced and groundless hatred.

Benjamin Pike and Hank Taggart had taken their first berth together on an *East Indiaman* bound for China. They were but children then, but even in those days Pike had exhibited erratic, antisocial, and sometimes violent behavior. Hank, from whom Robbie had inherited his good-natured friendliness, felt pity for the sometimes-surly lad who could get along with no one but him. Hank was a year or two older, and became to Pike as an older brother—probably the first, and only, taste he had ever had of true brotherly affection. For all Robbie could tell, his father had given Pike the only affection of *any* kind the poor man had ever known, for his entire family life before running away to the sea had been as twisted and cruel as he himself had later become.

Hank was able to moderate Pike's inflammatory temper, many times preventing a disgusted captain from throwing him off a ship. When people asked Hank why he associated with such a bum of the sea, he could find no ready answer, other than that Pike had no one else. There were times when Pike would even turn on Hank in a crazed fit. Such moments caused the older of the two young men to seriously consider a parting of the ways with his oft-demented friend. But when Pike came back full of apologies, Hank was always too kindhearted to turn him away. Despite Ben's idealistic illusions of one day taking his master's certificate, the truth was that he would never have lasted a month at sea without his friend Hank.

When Hank married Robbie's mother, he stayed with the sea because it was all he knew. But shortly before his son was born, his ship hit a nasty typhoon just out of Singapore in the China Sea. The fierce winds had dismasted the vessel, and Hank had narrowly missed being thrown into the sea by the falling debris.

The incident shook him. There had, of course, been dangers at sea before; the life of a sailor is a life of constant peril. But with family responsibilities now weighing heavily upon him, Hank realized more than ever how hazardous sea life was.

When Pike heard of Hank Taggart's decision, he turned on his friend in a violent rage. It was thus easier than Hank had anticipated to sever a ten-year friendship than it might otherwise have been. He tried to persuade Pike to leave with him, suggesting that they start a chandlery business together. But Pike was too angry and stubborn to listen. So the friendship came to a rocky end, with regret on Hank's part, and hatred and bitterness on Pike's.

A few months later, Pike's leg was crushed in an accident off Madagascar. Oddly enough, the weather had been perfectly calm at the time, and the falling mast had given way during a routine maintenance operation at mid-voyage. In his demented reasoning, Pike laid the blame on Hank for what had happened.

While he lay recuperating, thinking about how it had been Hank's absence on the ship that had led to the accident, he dreamed of finding Hank and getting even. But by the time he was back on his one good foot, Hank had taken to his landlocked roving life, and the embittered Pike, for whom a wooden leg was a constant reminder of the revenge he sought against his one-time friend, lost track of him. The hatred and insanity continued to eat away at Pike's unsteady mind, until—of all good fortunes he could never have dreamed of!—one day he chanced to stumble upon Hank Taggart's own son!

Robbie would never understand the disease that had possessed Pike's warped mind all those years since then. He would not even try. What mattered now was that Pike lay dying. No longer could Robbie think vengefully toward his father's old friend for the cruelty and pain he had brought him. All feelings of animosity fell away. Robbie ached somehow to reach this man who spent more than two decades trying to exact vengeance on the son of the man who had done nothing but love him more than any other person in the world. If only he could somehow bring peace to his last moments!

"Let me pray for you, Ben," said Robbie, when Pike's struggling voice concluded his twisted version of why he so despised Robbie Taggart.

"Pray for yourself!" replied Pike spitefully. "Ye ain't safe yet—Wang ain't about to give up. He swore he'd see you dead—you an' your whole family! I failed, but he won't. You ain't goin' to be able to sleep nights wonderin' when he's goin' to sneak in an' slit your throat, or that pretty throat of that China doll daughter o' yours!"

"Let go of your hate, Ben. It's killing you inside."

In reply, Pike grabbed Robbie's left arm, holding the stump where the hand had once been. "I'm glad about this, do you understand! *Glad!* Now you'll see what your father put me through all these years! I'll never change! I'll hate you till the day I die!"

"Oh, Ben, you've been so confused. But I won't ever give up praying for you. The Lord loves you, Ben. And I love you too, in Christ's love."

"I hate you!" retorted the old sea captain, his broken voice now breaking into sobs. "You can't love . . . I hate you!" His body shook with deep emotion. "Ye should never 'ave saved me life . . . Robbie . . . I don't deserve—"

"It was the only way I could show you that I forgive you, Ben," replied Robbie through tears, kneeling beside the bed and laying a gentle hand on Pike's forehead.

"Robbie . . . don't leave me . . . Robbie! . . . I don't deserve—"

But Benjamin Pike did not finish what he wanted to say. His arm fell suddenly lifeless to his side, dropping Robbie's maimed arm as he slipped out of this world. He was dead.

With a sigh of grief, Robbie rose, left the hospital, and sent Ying word that there would be another body to tend to that night. The poor young man was receiving an agonizing introduction to his position as the mission's new medical attendant. Within minutes Ying was off to the village once again to seek Chang's help in this most unpleasant assignment.

67

Not My Will, Lord

That night was a sleepless one for Robbie as he tried to put the events of the last days into focus.

How deeply he felt the loss of Isaiah! At least half a dozen times he told himself he'd have to discuss things with the doctor, only to be painfully jolted back time and again to the realization that he would no longer be able to do that in this world.

He felt a weight of responsibility such as he had never experienced before in his life. Not only were there the burdens of his personal questions, there was another element in his thoughts that he had scarcely considered until Ying had come to him two hours ago. The rioting and fires had left several church families homeless, more than could be handled in the village with relatives and friends. The mission-school rooms and hospital were already filled to capacity.

What could the mission do to care for these people?

Suddenly Robbie realized that all of them, including Ying, were looking to *him* for guidance and leadership. The reality of his new role that events had thrust upon him was as jarring as any of the events themselves.

He had to make decisions about the mission and its people. It was now completely up to him to care for Ruth and Shan-fei, and to a lesser extent, Miss Trumbull and Ying. They would all be looking to him for their needs, their guidance, and their protection.

Protection . . . that could well be his primary concern at the moment, with Wang still on the loose. Was it possible that after all that had happened, he would *still* come after Robbie, or his family, again? Perhaps Pike was wrong. Maybe after two defeats, with his followers scattered and apparently deserted to his lieutenant, the old warlord would give up his futile thirst for revenge.

But could Robbie take that chance? Could he trust to that slim hope? Wang's hatred had already survived more than twenty years. It seemed more likely that these defeats would only intensify his hatred still further.

God's mercy would protect, of course. But now that he had more than himself to consider, he had to think of the possibility of removing Ruth and Shan-fei from the reach of Wang's hand. Might not his responsibility for them dictate that he take them away from Wukiang for a season? Was it best for them, or for the mission, to remain? With Robbie and Ruth and Shan-fei gone, perhaps the hostilities would settle down. Would he only bring further needless suffering on the local Christian population by remaining as an ongoing target of anti-British sentiment?

"Dear God, what would you have me do?" he prayed when his mind was so full of thoughts that nothing made sense. "I know you can protect us. But how is it your will to do so? Direct me, Lord, to know your will."

Committing his concerns to God, and feeling drowsy at last, Robbie turned over and fell asleep. When he awoke before dawn, after only some three hours of sleep, he felt a peculiar sense of expectancy. He rose, dressed in haste as best he could, and went out.

The morning was quiet and still. Making use of Pike's crutch, which was far too short but at least kept him from falling, he hobbled toward the river, then upstream toward the wooded area.

Grief-stricken with the morning's remembrance of the past night's terrible events, Robbie yet felt God's presence all around him. Slowly he walked along, his spirit quiet, feeling a peaceful oneness with the gently flowing river beside him.

"Lord," he breathed, "you have something to say to me. I can feel it, but I can't yet perceive the words, Lord."

On he walked for some time, turning back toward the mission at last just as the sun broke over the eastern horizon. Slowly gathering strength from his prayerful solitude, he felt God gradually stirring him up toward . . . toward something! A change was coming! He could sense that the Lord was pointing, directing his steps. But toward what . . . where?

When he arrived back in time for a somber breakfast with his daughter and mother-in-law, prepared in the hospital by a number of the village women who had brought provisions for the ravaged mission, he still had no definite direction. But the sense of expectancy pervaded his spirit throughout the day. After breakfast, at the urging of the women, he lay back down in his bed, dozing off once or twice.

By noon he could remain in bed no longer. His leg was painful, and he would probably limp for weeks, if not months. But the bullet had gone clean through, bleeding had been minimal, and one of the men from the village came to pack it with some medicinal herbs. Against the protests of the women, he got up again, and with Ying's help made a few alterations to Pike's old crutch so that it was transformed into a satisfactory cane for the larger man.

Isaiah Wallace and Pike were laid to their final rest that afternoon. Robbie conducted the simple service. And despite the tense conditions that made many of the local church members nervous to associate themselves with the mission, there was a huge turnout, though no formal announcement of the event had been made. The greatest testimony to Wallace's unique ministry was that a great number of those coming to pay their last respects to him were not associated with the church at all, but rather unbelievers who now realized how deeply they had been touched over the years, in ways they had never been fully aware of, by his godly service and charity to them.

Pike received more of a send-off than he could ever have hoped for. But Robbie grieved that out of the scores of folk who passed by the graves, he was the only one who knew anything or cared about the old seaman.

Later that afternoon, Robbie walked out to the old camphor tree, sat down for a few minutes quiet reflection. Ruth brought him a cold drink, but after a brief conversation left him to help her grandmother in the hospital.

Quietly sipping his herbal drink, again the feeling of expectancy surged through him.

"What is it, Lord?" he prayed.

Robbie closed his eyes and leaned his head back against the trunk of the tree. He wondered how he could feel so peaceful in the midst of such heartache and turmoil. Yet was not that the true mystery of God's peace? He considered all that remained unresolved around him—the housing needs, the medical requirements of the mission now that Wallace was gone, the continued unrest in the district, the church services—and tomorrow was Sunday. And still the threat of Wang and the violence spreading throughout the land hovered over the future.

The mission's home office would of course send replacements, would help them rebuild, would advise in the appropriate course of action. Yet Robbie realized that Wang and the violence in the area were not just his own personal problems to consider. Though Wang's vengeance was directed at him and Shan-fei, the cruel warlord cared not what innocents were caught in the circle of his designs. Robbie's daughter was in danger, but so also was the very work of the mission itself. It was a critical time in the mission's history. Persecution usually did one of two things—destroyed, or fanned the flames of the Spirit still brighter. The riots, Wallace's death, the fire—these circumstances, though destructive on the surface, could indeed be the catalyst ingredients toward a new phase of effective ministry to the Chinese. Robbie recalled the profound quote Wallace had spoken to him many times. The application had always before been personal. Yet now Robbie realized it spoke of the future of the mission as well: "The present circumstance, if surrendered to Jesus, is the best-shaped tool in the Master's hand to chisel you for eternity. Trust Him then; do not push away the instrument, lest you spoil the work."

Yes, God was in control. The mission was *His* work, and would continue to be throughout all eternity. God's work here in Wukiang was not done. If Robbie was to remain here, despite the dangers to his family and the mission itself, they would be under the covering of God's protective care. Yet might not their absence, even if only for a season, be in the best interests of the long-term work?

The thought of leaving struck Robbie with a twinge of sadness. He loved this place. This was the only settled existence he had known in his life. He loved the simple Chinese people, and he loved the work God had called him to. His family was here, his friends. Could it be that he was now being called to leave all this behind? Was the work he had considered his life's calling now at an end? What about the solemn trust Wallace had placed in him to carry the work forward? Why was he feeling the growing sense that he was to leave, when there was so much *here* to be done? What would Wallace say? Would it seem to the local congregation that he was abandoning the work?

"Oh, Lord," he prayed, "remove my own motives, and show me *your* decision. Not my will, Father, but yours be done."

As he uttered that prayer spoken by the Lord on the eve of His own death, Robbie heard a quiet voice deep within his spirit:

"Home."

The moment the single word came, he had no doubt that it had come from God, and, moreover, that it spoke the Lord's direction for him, not toward this distant country that had become his home, but rather to the homeland of his birth—Scotland!

He knew also that this simple yet unexpected word of guidance from above had been the reason for the expectancy he had sensed all day. God was directing him to take his family where they would be safe from the evil designs of Wang, and return to Scotland. No doubt, in His eternal plan, the move would somehow prove best for the mission as well. Whether he could immediately understand all the implications did not matter. Robbie's course was set—he must obey the voice of the Lord exactly as Moses had when God told him to go into the wilderness.

All at once Robbie thought of Jamie. Since his own mother and father were now dead, it was natural that when his mind strayed to Scotland, he would think of Jamie—now Lady Graystone. They had kept in close touch through the years, and about five years ago he had learned that Derek Graystone had been killed in an Egyptian uprising. The family estate and title had thus passed to Edward.

A smile crept across Robbie's lips. Jamie was now a lady in every sense of the term, as she had always dreamed of being. And he was now a man, though in a spiritual way he had *never* dreamed of. Each of their destinies had, in a sense, been fulfilled along paths neither would have been able to anticipate.

What a thrill it would be for him to take Ruth to meet Jamie. That alone would be fulfillment enough in God's leading him back to his homeland. Shan-fei and Miss Trumbull were wonderful influences for his daughter. Yet he realized now, without having thought of it before, that he longed for Ruth to also experience a portion at least of his own Highland heritage, a heritage she could not help but experience in Jamie's presence. What a thrill, too, it would be to see little Andrew again, and Aberdeen, and the mountains!

Suddenly excited, Robbie jumped up from his resting place, wincing when his leg reminded him of his limitations. He then strode as quickly as he was able to the hospital to share with his family the news of their prospects.

The next afternoon Robbie again walked along beside the slowly moving river toward a small grassy knoll where he could spend some quiet moments of prayer. Today as he made his way, however, he was not alone. Four Chinese men were with him: two young, two old.

When they had reached their destination, Robbie asked his friends to sit beside him.

"I have asked each of you to come share these moments with me because in a special way each of you is bound up in all this mission means to me, and all it stands for. And also because I know that Isaiah, were he here, would choose the four of you for me to share my deepest thoughts with. I need to talk with you, then pray with you, about the future of the mission."

Robbie paused, drew in a deep breath, then continued.

"As you know, times are not pleasant for missionaries throughout China. Much of the unrest is directed at the foreign influence. Making that situation all the more dangerous here is the continued threat of Wang, who might attack Wukiang again just to get at me.

"As we learned from the missionary efforts of Paul, for a new church to thrive, it must ultimately be led by its local members. Thus, in God's economy, these recent trials may in fact prove to be our greatest opportunity both to solidify the work of the mission and to reach out into the surrounding villages. I sense that because of Dr. Wallace's death the local villagers might be more receptive than ever to hear the gospel. Especially if that gospel comes to them from the lips of their own people—from men such as yourselves. I believe the Lord has shown me that for a time the mission will thrive if it becomes a mission run by Chinese, for Chinese. I believe my absence will not only strengthen your leadership, but also multiply the opportunities for ministry.

"It is for these reasons, I believe, that the Lord is telling me to return to Scotland."

At the unsettling news, each of Robbie's friends and co-workers began to protest.

"Please," said Robbie, "hear what I have to say. I feel I must get my daughter and mother-in-law to safety. Protecting them must be my first responsibility in God. And in the Lord's wisdom, removing them from this tumultuous situation will at the same time further Christ's work here. You, Nien, have been fully capable of administrating the affairs of the mission for some time. You will preach and conduct services and coordinate the overall work."

Robbie took Ying Nien's hand and gave it a firm squeeze. "God will be with you, my friend," he said. "This is His calling upon you."

"Chang," Robbie continued, "you have been a faithful servant and friend of the mission and of Dr. Wallace and myself for more years than I have even been here. We are deeply indebted to you. You truly are a scriptural elder in the work here. Nien will need your support and prayer and help now more than ever. The younger men will look to you for wisdom and guidance."

In like manner, Robbie reached across from where he sat and placed a firm hand on Chang's shoulder. "Thank you for all you have been to this work."

"Li," said Robbie, turning now to his left, "you are not even yet a believer. But you have been a true friend. Dr. Wallace owed you a great deal, as I do myself—even more than you know. For your early hostilities with the doctor played a significant role in the Lord's work in my own heart. And in recent days you have proved yourself a true man whose character we have all learned to depend upon. I know all these other men will look to the wisdom of your years to help sustain them while I am gone. And I will not cease praying that the Lord will open your heart fully to Him, as you have to His people."

Robbie turned his face toward the old man and bowed his head respectfully.

"And you, my dear friend Kuo-hwa," said Robbie at last, "there are no words to express my love for you and my gratitude for accepting me as you have, though I was a stranger to your culture. I will be praying for a special measure of God's grace to fill you that you may help the others carry on in my absence. I know God will use you mightily to minister His love and goodness to your fellow countrymen."

Robbie extended his right hand. Kuo-hwa did likewise, and the two shook hands meaningfully.

"Now, my friends, let me leave you with these thoughts. I do not leave out of fear—Isaiah taught me better than that! Nor does a part of my heart want to leave at all, for this *is* my home. Had I no one but myself to consider, I do not know how the Lord might lead. But we are told not to tempt the Lord by placing ourselves unnecessarily in danger. Thus, I must obey that injunction in doing my part to protect my daughter and mother-in-law.

"It is my intention to return, as soon as the Lord wills it. Pray for me as I will for each of you. I will contact the home office of Christ's China Mission, but I am certain they will agree with my recommendation that you coordinate the work here until my return. I will also contact Dr. Taylor at the Inland Mission. I will ask him or Thomas to check upon you periodically and to offer their encouragement. But the Lord will be with you and will bless your work!

"Ruth, Shan-fei, Miss Trumbull, and I will be on our way back to England as soon as I can arrange it. Miss Trumbull has relatives to visit, but I am certain she will return with me, too. Hopefully you will see us all again as soon as the Lord directs and it is safe.

"Now, I would be honored if you would join with me in prayer, not only for each of the five of us that we can faithfully live out these new directions of God's call upon us, but also for His blessing on the work of His Spirit here in Wukiang."

The five men reached around to one another, making a circle of spiritual unity, closed their eyes, and lifted their hearts and voices to the God in whose service they were knit together.

68

Reunions

Of all the familiar places Robbie had touched since leaving China a month and a half ago on the steamer *Prince of Wales*, Aberdeen struck by far the richest memories.

Here was the home he had always returned to in his travels. Here was the port he had dreamed of sailing into during his lonely moments in China. Therefore, it was only fitting that the docks of the mouth of the River Dee should offer his feet their first steps onto Scottish soil after this, his longest sojourn away from the land of his birth.

Robbie was anxious to reach Aviemere. But he knew he must delay this last leg of his journey a day or two more so he could renew some very special old acquaintances. Taking Ruth with him, while Shan-fei remained behind to rest in the hotel, Robbie struck out up Union Street. They would walk past the train station, then turn down Market Street and to the dock area where they had landed yesterday. As they left the hotel Robbie could not help but think of his mother-in-law remaining behind in her room. He was still sorry to have wrenched her from her home. To be torn from her country amid her grief over the loss of her husband had been heart-rending indeed, and the inward pain revealed itself on her gracefully aging face. Yet she trusted Robbie's judgment, and wanted only to accompany her son-in-law and granddaughter, whom she loved more than any nation.

As Robbie glanced at Ruth walking at his side, he was reminded again how strange this must be to the two of them. Her eyes were wide with awe, and her tiny hand clutched tightly at his arm. This might be home to Robbie, but to Ruth everything that greeted her eyes was foreign; though half the blood that pulsed through her veins was Scottish, she was truly a foreigner in a strange land. Robbie had not fully considered this aspect of their move until now when he noted the curious glances from passers-by at the peculiar pair—Robbie in his brown broadcloth suit, Ruth dressed in Oriental style with a long linen skirt and jacket embroidered by Shan-fei for their travels. On the ship, even Shan-fei had not been an oddity in her customary, full-length Chinese dress, for world travelers on such an international vessel were well-accustomed to such things. But walking down the plank into Aberdeen instantly changed all that. Suddenly they were the object of every eye on the street.

"Ruth, look . . . over there," he said, pointing to their left. "There are the shipyards again. Let's see what they're about today."

They had spent the morning visiting the Gilchrists in Aberdeen's west side, and were now walking along the Inches toward their next destination. It was a clear summer afternoon, but a fog hung on the horizon and would reach the Aberdeen coastline with its thick moisture by the following morning. *There's nothing like an early-dawn Aberdeen fog,* thought Robbie. And if he had smelled salty, pungent sea air in dozens of other ports, none contained quite the pleasant satisfaction of what surrounded them just now.

"Where are we going, Papa?" asked Ruth, becoming infused with her father's excitement.

"A place I haven't been to in twelve years!" answered Robbie with mounting anticipation.

The Golden Doubloon hadn't changed much, except for perhaps being a bit more worn about the edges. The same sign, displaying the same treasure chest, stood above the door. Though he no longer recognized the faces of the men walking along the street, they were the same sailing types as always kept to this part of town, just as he once had.

Robbie paused before entering. Suddenly his mind was acutely conscious of all the changes that had been wrought within himself in the time since he had last been here. Back then he had been a jolly, carefree *boy*.

Now he was a man. His eyes still shone with merriment, and the mission staff—including Wallace himself—had come to count on his ready laughter to brighten any situation. But there was a solemnity about him now too, a depth to his character that simply could not have existed in the old Robbie Taggart. There was more to him now that went far beyond the physical manifestations of change—a lost hand, graying temples, a lovely half-Chinese daughter. He was, in truth, a new man. In a very real sense, he was complete now, fully the man intended by his Maker.

Robbie opened the door and stepped across the threshold. Ruth retreated behind him, content for now to let her brave father take the initiative in this newest of adventures.

There were few customers in the tavern at this time of day, but Robbie scarcely took note of the few who were present. For he immediately saw what he had come to see. Behind the rough old counter stood Sadie Malone, making preparations for the evening's business.

Unnoticed, Robbie watched her a moment in silence. The years told on her. The ample, once voluptuous figure was now considerably thickened. Her hair was grayer, and the lines about her eyes and mouth were deeper set. Yet Robbie sensed immediately a contentment about his old friend, as if she had at last accepted her calling as a dockside innkeeper. He recalled, though he had not been as aware of it back then as he should have been, that she had always talked about selling the inn someday and making a respectable living.

He had the chance to scrutinize her only for a moment before her watchful countenance looked up from her work. Her face paled and her mouth fell open, as she obviously struggled with her senses at sight of this ghost from her distant past. A moment more, however, and she colored and grinned, bustling out from behind the counter. Robbie reached her in two strides, threw his arms around her, lifted her off her feet, and whirled her around in the air.

"Sadie, my darlin'!" he said, laughing.

"I thought for a minute you was a figment of my imagination!" she exclaimed as he set her on her feet.

"I'm real enough, dear Sadie."

"Well, you haven't changed a hair!" She stepped back to appraise him, then her eyes fell on his missing hand. She gasped audibly.

"Don't give it a thought, Sadie. I've never been better. I hardly miss it now." Then he added, "I've so much to tell you!"

But even as he spoke, Sadie's eyes next noted his little companion. "Look at this, will ye!" she said. "Here you are with another waif in tow." She would not easily forget the day he had brought the grubby shepherdess Jamie MacLeod into her place.

"This is no waif, Sadie." He took Ruth's hand and brought her out into full view from behind him. "This is my daughter, Ruth," he said proudly.

Sadie clapped her hands to her face. "Oh, Robbie," she said, "I ain't never seen a lovelier little thing. 'Course, I should have known she'd be yours. And do I get the honor of making the acquaintance of Mrs. Taggart, too?"

"I'm afraid not," Robbie replied, a momentary cloud passing over his face. "She died shortly after Ruth was born."

"Robbie, I'm sorry."

Sadie took Ruth's hands tenderly into her rough, workworn ones. "She must have been a special woman—I can see it in the girl. And I know you'd have no less."

Now that the initial greetings were past, the innkeeper in Sadie surfaced and she added, "Let me fix you some tea and a bite to eat. You will bide a wee, won't you, Robbie? I want to hear everything!"

"We have the rest of the day," answered Robbie. "We must be back this evening. We're in a hotel up on Union. Ruth's grandmother is there now."

Sadie scurried off to the kitchen to make preparations for her guests. Robbie turned to find a seat, but the moment his eyes fell across the nearly deserted room, he stopped short. Now it was his turn to stare in disbelief at the apparition before him.

There sat Elliot Drew at one of Sadie's tables, a half-empty glass of ale in one hand, his chin resting philosophically on his other as he observed the scene. Robbie's stunned expression seemed to amuse him. At least the cynical side of him had anticipated such a response. With a wink and a nod, he lifted his glass toward Robbie in salute. The smile he let play upon his lips as he watched Robbie's continued bewilderment showed a genuine warmth, and at length broke the spell. Robbie, still limping on his injured leg, moved toward his table and held out his hand.

"Old friend!" he said, not without a good deal of emotion. A flood of memories, and feelings of both joy and sorrow, tumbled through Robbie's consciousness in the second it took Drew to respond. For it was clear that, despite his many prayers for the man over the years, there had been little change in him since their separation.

"I wasn't certain I'd still be greeted as such," replied the Vicar. "But perhaps time dulls the memory."

"*Time* has nothing to do with it, Elliot. Now, return my handshake and let my daughter and me sit down with you."

A moment more the Vicar paused. Then he rose and said, "Robbie . . . Robbie, you haven't changed!" With tears standing in his sad, worn eyes, he moved around his table and went to Robbie with outstretched hand.

As their hands met, however, both men opened their arms in a poignant embrace. Their friendship had lasted but a few short months, yet the bonds that had formed made them now seem like brothers. Even as they stood back from one another, however, Robbie longed more than ever for a true spiritual brotherhood with his sad and lonely friend. For now that Robbie himself understood what a relationship with God meant, he saw more clearly what Elliot had left behind when he turned his back on the church and his spiritual calling.

"But, Elliot," said Robbie as they sat down, "how do you come to be *here*? Of all the places in Aberdeen—of all the places in the world! How could I run into you like this?"

"Isn't Aberdeen as good a port as any to sail from?"

"Why, yes . . . but—here, in Sadie's!"

"I heard you talk about the place a few times. I suppose when I left, something inside me wanted to keep touch with you. This place was the only link I had to my true friend, Robbie Taggart! You know me, Robbie. Ever motivated by sinister emotions like guilt and self-condemnation!"

"Oh, Elliot!" replied Robbie from his heart. "Are you still torturing yourself that way? It doesn't have to be like that, you know."

The Vicar did not reply for a moment. Then he nodded knowingly, and said, "They got to you, didn't they?"

Robbie smiled in reply, fully understanding the meaning of his words even after so long.

"I could tell," Drew added. "You're a different man. You may be missing a hand, but that's not where the difference is. You're a whole man now. I could see it in you the moment you walked through that door."

"Let me tell you about it," said Robbie, picking up Ruth and placing her on his lap.

"I don't think I want to hear about *that*."

"Are you afraid I might get to *you*?"

"I'm too far gone, Robbie."

"I saved your life once Elliot," said Robbie. "I think you at least owe me a polite audience for my story. I know you think you've heard all about God there is to hear. But I'm not so sure you've ever really heard the whole story. I think all you've heard before in your life are the misrepresented notions of people who don't really know Him at all."

The Vicar smiled. "I knew someday I'd have to pay for your good deed."

He folded his arms, leaned back in his chair, and nodded for Robbie to have his say.

When Elliot Drew left *The Golden Doubloon* that evening, he had heard things about God and about the man Jesus that he had never heard before. This was no gospel he had heard preached or had preached himself. The line from the Acts of the Apostles worked several times through his mind, "Almost persuaded . . ."

How he longed for the peace Robbie had described to him, that inexplicable joy he so clearly saw emanating from Robbie himself! But because his rejection of the good news of God's constant presence with man had been, so many years ago, a form of self-punishment, he could not now allow himself to believe that he deserved what Robbie had. God might be merciful to forgive him all his drinking, and his selfishness, his blasphemies, and all his cowardice, but the Vicar was not in a position to receive it, for he could not forgive himself. So as he walked away, not doubting the truth of the gift of God Robbie offered, but yet choosing to reject it, he quoted Lord Byron as he had on the first day they met aboard the *Sea Tiger*.

"'Such partings break the heart they fondly hope to heal,'" he said. "Goodbye, dear friend."

"I didn't give up on you before, Elliot," answered Robbie, "and I won't now. I will pray for you vigilantly! We will meet again, and I believe it will be as brothers in Christ."

The Vicar sighed, then walked out into the drizzly night. The fog had reached the shore and had settled over the city. He was on his way to meet his ship, bound for Venezuela. As he made his way along the street, something inside compelled him to turn back, to give Robbie's new way of life a try. But he could not do it. He doubted that he would ever see Robbie Taggart again, but he'd never be able to forget him, nor the words he had spoken to him this day. Yet to embrace them—that was just too frightening a step to take.

Robbie watched him go, and soon his friend was swallowed up in the mists. A lingering sadness hung over him. Yet he could not feel despair for his friend. Robbie knew God was jealous for the lost soul of the Vicar, loved him more than he could himself, and would spare no effort to reveal to him the life of blessing and fulfillment awaiting him.

The day had been a long one for Ruth, who dozed against her father's chest as he had poured out his heart to the Vicar. Now he took her back to the hotel, ordered dinner for her and Shan-fei, then returned to *The Golden Doubloon* where he devoted the remainder of the evening to Sadie. She marveled at all Robbie had to tell her, and was even inspired to attend the little church in her neighborhood that Sunday.

It was late when he again walked up the hill toward Union Street. Shan-fei was asleep in the adjoining room, and Ruth slept contentedly on the couch in his. Robbie walked over and gazed at her peaceful face, laying a gentle hand on her shoulder and murmuring a brief prayer of thanksgiving for this greatest of all blessings.

He had certainly tired her out today, he thought! New sights, new places, new people. Well, she would be able to sleep all the next day on the train that would carry them to Aviemere.

69

Homecoming

While the coach was yet a half mile from Aviemere, Robbie began to sense that he wanted to be on his own for this most special reunion. He asked the driver of the hired coach to stop, then got out.

"Wait here," he told the man. "Give me ten minutes. It's beyond that grove of trees, about three more furlongs."

Taking only his cane, Robbie struck out on foot along the long drive lined with birch trees on either side.

The last time he had been this way, Robbie had come to claim the woman he loved. He had departed not with a bride, but with the assurance that he possessed the dearest friend he would ever have. Even as he had walked out of the massive doors with the intimidating words *Aut pax aut bellum* engraved over the lintel, not knowing whether he would ever again return, he knew that Jamie—even as Edward Graystone's wife—would continue to influence his life. As she indeed had. The seeds of faith planted by her in his heart had borne fruit manyfold. Of the three persons God had used to awaken his spirit—including Hsi-chen and Wallace—she was the only one remaining on earth for him to share the depths of his being with. She could never replace Hsi-chen, nor could she replace Wallace. But now at last with Jamie he would be able to share his new nature—the awakening for which she had so diligently prayed.

Despite the joyful, sometimes gregarious, and sometimes poignant reunions he had thus far experienced with people over the years, Robbie sensed more than ever that this was his true homecoming. The estate of Aviemere itself meant little to him; he had only spent two or three days here. But as long as Jamie and Edward were here, he knew it would be a home to him, a haven, and everything dear. He knew their hearts were open wide to him, and now at last his was able to open to them in like fashion.

Slowly he made his way in solitude along the wide dirt road. His leg was much better by now. In another two or three months the effects of the bullet wound would be completely forgotten. But there still remained pain when he put all his weight on the leg, which the cane helped to alleviate.

He passed the last bend in the road and saw the imposing gray mansion in the distance. Time had changed nothing. He might still be the rash young man in his twenties, for all the external appearance of the estate about him, rather than the injured, limping, returning sailor of forty.

Yes, he had changed, despite the unchangeableness of the Scottish landscape. *What will Jamie think?* he wondered. Would she be repulsed by his cane, by the stump on his left arm, by the gradual graying of his hair? Would she react to him as little Ruth had to wretched old Pike when she had first seen him that day in the mission compound?

What kind of a man was he now, for all that he had been through, for all that he had experienced, for all that the Lord had worked in him?

Though Robbie asked the question, inside he knew the answer well enough. He had left Aviemere, and Scotland, as one who thought he held the world by the tail, as one who thought he possessed the might to carve out his own destiny, as one in search of adventure, fulfilled dreams, and romantic illusions.

But instead, through the years that had passed, he had discovered something he had never expected—the true meaning of life, the true significance of what it means to live life as a man.

He had entered into the greatest adventure of all—a life lived in tune with the Creator's design.

So many men, mused Robbie sadly, *seek to fulfill themselves in all the wrong places. Oh, Lord, thank you!* Robbie thought. *Thank you for opening my eyes. For all that I was striving to do and to be, I never realized what I was missing at the core of life. Thank you for making me the man you wanted me to be!*

But there was no more time for Robbie's reflections, and his prayers of thanks had to be suspended temporarily. For the crunch of the carriage wheels was rapidly approaching behind him, and the door of the house was swinging open in front of him.

Jamie Graystone reread the telegram.

Robbie was in Aberdeen! He would arrive at Aviemere this very day!

When she had received his first telegram from London two weeks ago with apologies that he could not have informed her of his plans sooner, she had been overwhelmed with delight. He could have turned up on her doorstep with no warning at all, and she would have welcomed him no less. But her excitement with his anticipated visit went deeper than simply the joy of seeing an old friend.

Troubles had fallen upon Aviemere in recent days. It reminded Jamie of the time she had first arrived at the estate as an untried nurse to young Andrew. It almost seemed as though the strife that had so long been associated with the Graystone family was too deeply ingrained ever to be erased. When they had returned to the estate six years ago, she and Edward had been full of hopeful expectations. Yet now things were so different.

Somehow the news from Robbie came as if in answer to a prayer she had not yet spoken. He had always been a strong force in her life; he had saved her life and set her on the road that had led her to Edward and the Lord. And now that he also shared her faith, she knew he would bring something vitally needed to her troubled spirits.

Jamie sighed. She had not forgotten the words of her grandfather: *I will lift up mine een t' the hills, frae whence comes my help. My help comes frae the Lord, who made haiven an' earth.* But she also knew that many times in her life God had used others to inspire and encourage her. She hoped perhaps, in some way none of them could yet understand, that Robbie's entrance back into their lives after so many years was part of the Lord's design for the future strengthening of the beleaguered Graystone family.

All at once Jamie heard the clamor of horses, wagon wheels, and leather harnesses.

A coach was coming down the drive! But who was that man hobbling toward the house in front of—

Oh, Lord! she cried. *God bless him . . . it's Robbie!*

Jamie turned and flew down the stairs. Cameron had already started toward the door, but Jamie rushed past him, threw it wide, and ran out into the courtyard and into Robbie's arms.

"Jamie!" exclaimed Robbie, sweeping her feet off the ground and lifting her small frame in his exuberant embrace. By the time her feet again touched the ground, their eyes were wet, and glistening streams ran down their cheeks.

"Just look at you!" said Jamie, as Robbie set her down. "You haven't changed at all . . . and yet everything about you is changed!" She had expected the missing hand. But she had been unprepared for the limp, and the two deep scars on his handsome face. "You seem almost like the valiant soldier returning from the wars! As indeed is true—for you are God's warrior now, aren't you, Robbie?"

Robbie smiled. "Oh, Jamie, how can I possibly tell you all that has happened? I can't even think where to begin! I did tell you about my hand? Are you shocked?"

"No, Robbie. It's your badge of honor—for the Lord, a constant reminder of His grace."

"It's been a hard lesson for me to learn. But I think He's finally gotten through to me."

"I can tell! It's in your eyes, Robbie. I can sense the presence of God in you. Oh, Robbie, it is *good* to see you!"

"And you, dear friend! But where is Edward?"

A shadow crossed Jamie's face. "He's been ill. He's upstairs now and can't come down. I'll take you to him later. But who is this beautiful girl?" exclaimed Jamie, looking toward the coach.

Robbie walked over, opened the door where Ruth had been peeking out, and swept his daughter out and to the ground.

"This is my daughter, Jamie. Her name is Ruth."

Fresh tears rose at once to Jamie's eyes as she beheld the lovely Chinese child. Suddenly she was aware of the changes in Robbie she had not perceived at first glance. He was a different man—matured and seasoned. He was a missionary, a father, a widower, and indeed a scarred veteran from the battles of life.

Next he reached his hand into the coach and helped out an elderly Chinese lady, who immediately took his arm when she reached the ground, for even with her cane she had difficulty walking.

"And now, Jamie, I would like you to meet my mother-in-law, Shan-fei Wallace, Hsi-chen's mother."

"I am honored, Mrs. Wallace," said Jamie. "Welcome to our home."

70

Looking Ahead

"How are you, Robbie?"

"Well, Lord Graystone. Very well!" replied Robbie, giving Edward's hand a firm shake where he lay in bed. "As you can see though," he added laughing, "the years have taken their toll!"

"On us all, I'm afraid!" said Edward.

"I'm sorry to hear it's going poorly with you. What is it?"

"My heart, or so the doctor thinks. One never knows. I feel well enough, but Jamie worries. Women, you know."

Robbie laughed again. "Count your blessings, man! At least you have a wife to worry about you!"

"You're right. I'm sorry. Jamie tells me you've had a bit of a rough time of it?"

"All part of the Lord's plan."

"Well, you're welcome here, you and your family, for as long as you need. Stay a year! Once I get up and out of this confounded bed, we'll have a ride up the mountain together. I know Jamie will love having you all. Use Aviemere to get a rest and to get your bearings for the future. We're glad to have you."

"Thank you. I don't know what to say. I'll never be able to repay—"

"Nonsense! If it hadn't been for you, Jamie and I would never have met! We owe you a great deal. This is *our* way of repaying *you!*"

Later that afternoon, after some light refreshments had been served in the parlor and Shan-fei and Ruth had retired to their rooms to settle themselves, Jamie and Robbie took a walk in the rose garden.

"I'm so thankful you've opened your home to us," said Robbie. "Things are tense in China right now. You've probably been reading about the missionary riots. I had to get Ruth and Shan-fei out for a while."

"It's more of a blessing to us than you can imagine. We need some new blood here. Things have not been altogether—"

"What is it, Jamie?" asked Robbie with concern, seeing that Jamie was fighting back tears, this time not of joy but of sadness.

"It has been difficult the past couple of months," Jamie went on at last. "Edward . . . his illness?"

"Oh, yes that too, of course. But . . . well, you must have noticed that Andrew is not here."

"I thought he was away . . . perhaps at school. He's about sixteen now, isn't he?"

"Yes," Jamie sighed sadly. "He's left home, Robbie—"

All at once the tears that had been playing about her emerald eyes spilled out upon her delicate cheek.

"He's been gone three months now, and we have no idea where he is."

Robbie placed his hand on her trembling shoulder. "He seemed content enough. Why would he do such a thing?"

"You remember the little child," said Jamie. "As he got older, something happened, and it only seemed to worsen when we moved back here to the estate. Edward blames himself. I think this is what finally aggravated his condition."

At that moment Cameron the butler appeared to announce supper, and the conversation had to be postponed.

Over the days that followed, however, there were many such conversations, and they were finally able to coax the doctor to allow Edward to join them. It proved a time of restoration and renewal for all, even Shan-fei, who found a quiet comfort in the solitude beneath Donachie, for her loneliness in losing so devoted a husband.

Gradually the days and weeks passed. Summer slowly yielded to autumn, and with it the lovely moors and fellsides of Aviemere were transformed into a vibrant heathery purple. Robbie and Jamie and Ruth, as well as Jamie's two younger children, Gilbert and Julia, trekked all over the rich land, occasionally accompanied by Edward and Shan-fei by carriage. When Edward was finally able, he and Robbie had a ride together, while Jamie led all the children up the heights of Donachie to her old homestead, showing them on the way the spot where a happy-go-lucky sailor lad had rescued a shepherd girl stranded in a blizzard. The afternoon was singularly thrilling for Ruth, who had spent her entire life in a low delta region. Even more significant, however, was the kinship that sprang up between her and Jamie, as if Robbie truly were Jamie's brother, and Ruth her niece. And despite the solemn cloud that hung in the background from the uncertainty over Andrew, Robbie's presence carried with it a spirit of exuberance and energy to counter the gloom. More than once Jamie commented that Robbie's laughter was just what the old house had needed, and God knew just when to send it.

Still nothing had been said about their leaving, or what the future might hold. An idyllic season of rest it truly was. Without speaking it, Edward, Jamie, and Robbie all knew that when the Lord was ready to speak further direction, they would hear Him.

One day as winter began to make its approach felt upon the northern land, Robbie returned to the house from a solitary walk upon the moor. The heather had faded from bloom, the winds blowing down from Donachie bore a premonition of snow, and the birch trees along the drive had one by one begun to drop their yellowed leaves.

For some days Robbie had been in fervent prayer regarding God's direction for his immediate future. On three or four occasions within the past month he had visited several of the parishes in the area to share about God's work in China. He had been not only positively received, but was met with a growing response of interest in missionary work. His purpose had not specifically been to bolster recruits for the mission field, but the enthusiasm he encountered could not help but stimulate his own continuing and renewed vision for the east. A sense of expectancy began to come upon him again, as it had during his last days in China, and he knew God was preparing to speak to Him.

When it came, the direction was as simple as had been the leading to return to Scotland. In the depths of his mind the thought first came, "The season of rest is past; it is time to return."

"Is that your voice speaking, Lord?" he asked.

And the more he submitted the matter to prayer, the clearer the voice became, and the more definitely he knew that it was indeed the Lord calling him back to his daughter's homeland. During a morning in prayer out on the moor, all was confirmed in his mind.

He went first to Jamie and Edward. He was not sure how they would view his proposal.

"Robbie, of course we'd be delighted for Ruth to live with us for a time! She's a dear! But Shan-fei . . . do you think she would agree to remain behind?"

"I don't know," Robbie replied. "This has all got to be extremely difficult for her. Yet I do not believe the situation is yet safe for either of them. I feel I must be there, to offer what leadership I can. Yet until this trouble is past, it would be best for me to be there alone."

"You will go back to Wukiang?" asked Edward.

"Yes. But I still do not clearly know what God wants. If the work there is prospering under Ying, I may travel inland. I would like to again visit Dr. Taylor's work, perhaps do some planting in several of the areas not yet touched by the gospel. There are so many opportunities. I will have to survey the situation, go where God leads me, and eventually, when time and circumstances permit it, work my way back to Wukiang and send for Ruth and Shan-fei."

Everyone was silent a few moments. When Robbie next looked up, he saw that Jamie was quietly weeping.

Still no one spoke. Each of the men knew that she would say what was on her heart when she was ready. At last she composed herself, then gave a laugh in the midst of her tears.

"Robbie . . . Robbie," she laughed. "Don't think me sad about this! I have just been overwhelmed with all the changes that have taken place in you. What a man of God you have become! I don't know what to say, Robbie, except that . . . I'm proud of you! And I pray for God's richest blessings to follow you always!"

"I concur, Taggart," added Edward warmly, extending his hand. "Whatever we can do to help! Perhaps you need money."

"Thank you, Edward," said Robbie graciously. "Your help with Ruth and Shan-fei will be wonderfully adequate. Other than that, I would rather be in a position to depend on the Lord."

"Let me take care of your passage at least."

"I will let you help with my daughter and mother-in-law when that time comes, but for myself, I think I should like to work my way back. It's not only a matter of the money. Perhaps it's the sailor in my blood surfacing again after all these years. You know, the Lord doesn't eliminate the desires of our hearts, He fulfills them. I'm still a sailor, and proud to be the Lord's sailor. To tell you the truth, the voyage from China was arduous for me having to sit and *watch* the other sailors work. I'm sure you can appreciate that, Edward. I think God is allowing me this opportunity for another reason also. I have for years longed to share the gospel on the sea. This may be my only such opportunity. On my last voyage as a sailor, many years ago, I had a mate who one day in a drunken whim delivered a sermon to us. The poor fellow was chided and scoffed at. Since then I've often wondered what his reception might have been had his words come from a sincere heart. I may be in for a disappointment; sailors can be a rowdy lot! But it is something I have to try."

Later that day came what Robbie anticipated as a more difficult task. Happily, it did not turn out so.

He found Ruth in the vast Aviemere library, which she had discovered to be almost as fascinating as Donachie. Robbie smiled as he found her engrossed in Dickens, realizing anew how simple her life at the mission had been. It had been full of the best kind of spiritual influences, but what a place such as this could offer her!

She looked up and smiled. "Papa, we didn't have *Oliver Twist* at home. It's wonderful!"

"I need to intrude upon your reading for a moment, Ruth."

"Yes, Papa," she said, sliding over on the divan where she was seated to make room for him.

He sat down and placed his arm about her. "You know that I have been praying about returning to China."

She nodded in reply.

"I believe God has at last spoken to me on the matter," he went on. "But I feel Him saying that I am to go back alone . . . for now at least."

"Alone? but, Papa!"

"Please, listen to me, dear. I told you when we left of the dangers. An evil man wants to hurt us, especially your grandmother. I must see how the work at the mission is faring, and I must go where the Lord directs me. But I have to see if it is safe before I put either of you in risk. I will send for you. Six months . . . a year, perhaps. I will not know until I get there."

Tears began to fall from the young girl's eyes.

"And what will become of us?" she asked disconsolately.

"I've spoken with Lord and Lady Graystone. They have agreed for you and your grandmother to live here, with them—"

"Here!" exclaimed Ruth, brightening.

"Yes, why?"

"Because I like Aviemere! Next to being with you, I can't think of any place I'd rather be."

"Jamie—that is, Lady Graystone—has a great deal to offer you that I as a man could not. If I did not firmly believe that you would be gaining more from this than anything else, I would never do it. It will not be for a very long time."

"I'll miss you so much, Papa, even though I'm sure I'll be happy."

"And I you, little Chi-Yueh. But you must be strong. Your grandmother will need you more than ever. You are half Scot. Half of the blood that flows through your veins came from these Highlands. But your mother's mother is Chinese all through. She will need an extra measure of God's grace, and your love, to sustain her through this difficult time."

"I love you, Papa! I will pray for you every day! I will always be proud that my father follows the Lord wherever He leads."

The father and daughter embraced tenderly. After Robbie had wiped a fresh supply of tears from his daughter's eyes, Robbie took Ruth's hand and together they left the stately and somber walls of the library, and soon found themselves outside, in the cool, crisp, clear fall afternoon.

Hand in hand they walked, mostly in silence, across the fields, up and down several hillsides spread out below the great mountain, and found the rippling amber burn that had its source high on the slopes of Donachie. Up the stream they walked, then turned away, making their way back to the house under the shadow of the vast silent presence which set a tone of quiet majesty over the valley below.

For the rest of the afternoon they walked together, sharing tears a time or two, of mingled joy and sorrow. Robbie taught Ruth a couple songs in the thick Highland brogue, as well as one of his favorite little poems, Burns's *To a Mouse*.

"It's such a sad little story, Papa!" she exclaimed when he was through the recitation he had learned in childhood.

"Perhaps. But think of all the good that has come to the world from the wee mousie's sacrifice. Things are not always what they appear. God always has deeper purposes."

"Like your leaving and my staying here?"

"Yes, child. We cannot yet see what God's purposes are. But if we are faithful to obey Him, they will be revealed to us in time."

When they returned at length to the grand manor that was to be Ruth's new home for a season, dusk had settled over the land. And she was reassured that no matter how far her father was from her, he and his little Chi-Yueh would ever be together in their hearts.

71

Lead Me Where I'm A-goin'

A blustery January wind blew off the starboard quarter of the old barque-rigged vessel as she made her way past the Lizzard. The captain had been doubtful of departing from Falmouth that morning, but worse weather had already hampered their progress two weeks and this might well be the fairest sea they would have until they reached the lower latitudes.

Robbie clasped his chilled arms about his chest as he watched the old promontory recede into the distance. He recalled that the last time he had viewed the same sight it had been a dozen years before he had again laid eyes on his homeland. How long would it be this time? How long before he again gazed into his daughter's lovely eyes?

Not long he had promised her.

He had spoken the words with assurance. They were both in God's hands, he knew that. Yet he had to pray continually for strength to bear the parting. Even at the same time, however, Robbie could not deny the growing surge of hopeful anticipation. Already on the ship he had found fertile soil for God's message; all the voyage lacked was the presence of the Vicar himself.

Robbie sucked in a great draught of the chill air, then made his way forward to the prow of the ship. He was sailing toward his future, and before night fell he had to gaze out upon the open sea before him, with the whitewater curling up on either side of the great walls of the ship as the bow sliced through the icy water.

The sun was about to set, but even its vibrant rays of light piercing beneath the cover of clouds could not warm the winter sky. They had not encountered fair skies since leaving London, which had made for an arduous voyage thus far. But Robbie could not have minded less. He had feared that his handicap would hinder him. But the captain, an old acquaintance from the past who was willing to make some adjustments in the duty assignments in order to have a man of Robbie's experiences and capabilities aboard, had put him in charge of navigation, with the deck-related activities he could handle. There'd be no climbing aloft. That was hazardous enough with two hands. But Robbie was content that he had been allowed this chance to sail once more, and didn't mind deferring the dangers to younger men.

As he stood looking out over the sea, with the wind whipping his hair about his head, his thoughts turned to Pike, whose injury had caused much hate and bitterness to eat away at his heart. How easily the same thing could have happened to him! Yet the cancerous thirst for revenge that could have obsessed him had been replaced instead by a thankful heart and a grand purpose in living each moment to the full.

"Lord," he murmured into the chilly wind, "thank you for taking over my life, for remaking my heart, and for leading me along your paths!"

He wondered what was in store for him on this new voyage upon which he was bound. What would he find when he returned to China? If Wukiang was in the capable hands of his friends, as he suspected, with a strong core of native believers, what else might the Lord have planned for him? He had spoken to the mission board in London about Hunan—a province that had consistently remained hardened against the gospel. Might God direct him there?

Then he realized he did not need to know the answers to such questions. He was being led by the Lord of life, by the God of the land and the sea. And that was enough. He could trust the wisdom of his Maker, for all his life. He had never failed Robbie Taggart, Highland sailor and missionary.

As night fell, still Robbie stood on the fore-deck gazing into the distance, the timbers of the ship groaning beneath his feet, the rigging creaking behind him, and the familiar flapping of the sails high above him lending a cadence of mystery to the night. As the sea spray blew into his face, he recalled to mind an ancient sailor's chant he had not thought of in years. Suddenly its meaning came clear to him as it never had when he had heard it in the days of his youth. Now he could almost hear the old words resounding out through the night, as if on the voices of a men's choir, charting his course as he sped through the sea toward destinations unknown.

Painter of the evening sky,
Lighter of the heavens;
Won't you color my heart, fill its darkest part,
Make it shine with the love you've given?

Charter of the unknown sea,
Guide my every decision;
For the endless sea in its mystery
Lies not beyond your vision.

Maker of the wind and wave,
Lead me where I'm a-goin';
For a sailin' man when you guide his hand,
Doesn't care where the wind be blowin'.

Hey! hey! praises be
To the One who holds the wind and sea.
Hey! hey! praises be
To our God who dwells in majesty.

Afterword

The mystique of China, the Celestial Kingdom, has played upon the imagination of Westerners for centuries. The mysterious East offered riches untold, and fields of millions of souls to the eternally minded, "whitened and ready to harvest." But it was the merchant, not the missionary, who first penetrated the vast Middle Kingdom. Unfortunately, this pattern continued to haunt the cause of Christianity in China.

The Franciscans came on the heels of the Polos. The Jesuits followed the Portuguese who opened the first European settlement in China, called Macao. Yet these traders and shippers by no means received an open welcome, and never could penetrate inland. Over and over the Chinese demonstrated their distrust of foreigners, nor did they desire their presence in their 5000-year-old empire.

Robert Morrison became the first Protestant missionary to take up residence in China. The year was 1807, and even he had hired himself out to the East India Company as a translator in order to secure a position in China. But his efforts, and those of subsequent Christians, were strictly controlled by the Chinese government and limited only to coastal areas.

It was the pressure of the merchant that finally changed these restrictions, with the infamous Opium Wars—the first beginning in 1839, the second in 1856. The treaties resulting from these conflicts forcefully opened to the Occidentals the stubborn portals of the dragon empire.

At last God's emissaries were given free movement in China, but the stigma of the *method* in which this open-door policy had been obtained—through political and military conflicts—never ceased to follow them. Though the missionary movement prospered tremendously in the 19th century, as missions throughout many regions of China were established, anti-foreignism continued to be a constant threat.

Many came to China as so-called missionaries whose motives were self-serving and largely political. And these made it difficult for the large majority to establish fruitful relations with the wary Chinese peasants and villagers. Yet those who came were for the most part men and women of godly character, faithful to the gospel, and with a sincere desire to spread the love of Christ to the Chinese, for whom they developed a deep affection. Dr. Hudson Taylor of the China Inland Mission, perhaps the most well-known of the Christian missionaries to make China his home, was truly a pioneer in overseas missions work. He arrived in Shanghai in the 1850s and spent the next 45 years there until his death in 1901. He was followed by other courageous, farsighted men and women, such as Jonathan Go forth and the fictional Isaiah Wallace who went to that foreign, sometimes inhospitable land, in order to do their part to fulfill the Great Commission of the Lord.

In 1891, riots did indeed break out in Wuhu, Nanking and various other cities and villages along the Yangtze. These Missionary Riots continued on and off, precursors to the Boxer Rebellion in 1900, a much more violent and widespread attempt to rid China of foreign and Christian influences.

After the Boxer Rebellion was put down, Christianity flourished in 20th-century China under the leadership of nationals such as Watchman Nee. However, the work begun in the 19th century seemed to come to a devastating end with the Communist takeover in 1949, and for years little external evidence remained of the early work of the Jesuits, Robert Morrison, Hudson Taylor, and others.

Yet the seeds of God's planting, wherever they may fall throughout the world, are never sown in vain. In every generation, new Robbie Taggarts are continually being raised up to carry the gospel on the four winds to the corners of the earth. And in God's divine providence, even the great and mysterious land of China remains in His hand, awaiting the right moment for the seeds of His Spirit to again sprout forth into bloom.

About the Authors

Michael Phillips is a bestselling author with more than seventy of his own titles. In addition, he has served as editor/redactor of nearly thirty more books. He is known as the man responsible for the reawakened interest in George MacDonald of the last thirty years. In addition to the MacDonald titles adapted/edited for today's reader, his publishing efforts in bringing back full-length quality facsimile editions also spawned renewed interest in MacDonald's original work. Michael and his wife, Judy, spend time each year in Scotland, but make their home near Sacramento, California. Visit Michael's website at www.macdonaldphillips.com

Judith Pella is a bestselling, award-winning author whose writing career spans more than two decades. Her in-depth historical and geographical research combines with her skillful storytelling to provide readers with dramatic, thought-provoking novels. She and her husband make their home in Scapoose, Oregon.

If you enjoyed this book, you may also like . . .

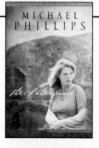

More Historical Fiction

After the man she loves abruptly sails for Italy, Sophie Dupont's future is in jeopardy. Wesley left her in dire straits, and she has nowhere to turn—until Captain Stephen Overtree comes looking for his wayward brother. He offers her a solution, but can it truly be that simple?

The Painter's Daughter by Julie Klassen
julieklassen.com

At Irish Meadows horse farm, two sisters struggle to reconcile their dreams with their father's demanding marriage expectations. Brianna longs to attend college, while Colleen is happy to marry, as long as the man meets *her* standards. Will they find the courage to follow their hearts?

Irish Meadows by Susan Anne Mason
Courage to Dream #1
susanannemason.com

Stella West has quit the art world and moved to Boston to solve the mysterious death of her sister, but she is in need of a well-connected ally. Fortunately, magazine owner Romulus White has been trying to hire her for years. Sparks fly when Stella and Romulus join forces, but will their investigation cost them everything?

From This Moment by Elizabeth Camden
elizabethcamden.com

BETHANYHOUSE